Burning

An Anthology of Short Thrillers

Edited by
Simon Finnie and Peter Oxley

Burning Chair Limited

Trading As Burning Chair Publishing

71-75 Shelton Street, Covent Garden
London WC2H 9JQ

www.burningchairpublishing.com

First published by Burning Chair Publishing, 2018

Cover art by Jennie Rawlings – www.serifim.com

ISBN: 978-1-912946-00-6

CONTENTS

Copyright Acknowledgments

III

VARIOUS AUTHORS

Foreword

Burning (adj)—on fire; very hot or bright; very keenly or deeply felt; intense; of urgent interest or importance; exciting...

Burning (noun)—An Anthology of 14 thrilling stories by 14 outstanding authors.

Back at the dawn of humanity, fire was something mysterious, something worshipped, something to be feared. When we learned to tame this elemental power by rubbing two sticks together in a pile of kindling, the world changed... forever.

Burning evokes many emotions: it represents destruction to some, whilst for others it provides a Phoenix-like new beginning.

And a fresh beginning sums up Burning Chair Publishing. We started the company because we were two indie authors looking for a different way to do things; offering authors a fair and alternative way to get great books out to expectant readers.

One of the questions we are often asked is: "Why Burning Chair? Where did you get that name from?"

There's a long and a short answer to that one. The long answer contains lots of head-scratching, wine, branding theory, more wine, and Pete getting bored during brainstorming sessions involving Simon's endless mood boards...

The short answer, though, is that for us the phrase "Burning Chair" perfectly captured what we were trying to achieve: a fresh, exciting, innovative approach to getting great stories into the hands of eager readers. Stories which are so amazing, so immersive, that you would carry on reading even if your chair was on fire.

So, when we were looking around for a theme for our first anthology, there could be only one answer: *Burning*.

We won't lie to you: there were times when we worried that we'd set the theme too broad. Should we have gone for something more specific, or a more recognizable hook?

But then the stories started coming in, and we realized there had been no need to be concerned. Authors—especially the ones in this collection—really are awesome. Even if we say so ourselves...

Craig Hart's *Loose Ends* thrusts a wise-cracking PI into the center of a deadly—and highly personal—case.

In Fiona Campbell's *From a Flicker to a Flame*, a woman finds herself trapped, a prisoner in a loveless marriage.

In *The Five Votive Candles of Joe Wray* by Simon Bewick, Joe Wray is a husband, a father, a brother and a business owner. They all need his protection. He doesn't have a prayer.

A mysterious man sparks unexplainable fires in Carla Day's *Scintillation*, where a woman's dreams may be the clue to saving the world.

The dark and seedy underbelly of the City of London is

exposed in Will Patching's *Old Flame*: a tale of lust, greed and a decidedly nasty twist.

The repercussions of the Iraq war and memories of WMDs plague the characters of Dana Lyons' *Fire and Brimstone*, with a weapon which could truly be the end of all things.

In *Ava Edison and the Burning Man*, by Marcus Cook, a thief with an unlikely accomplice faces a race against time to get a priceless jewel for a ruthless client.

Tom Goymour's *Circle of Friends* finds a man and his long-forgotten friends being forced to finally confront the mistakes of their youth.

In Peter Ellis' *Reprogrammed*, a woman wakes in a strange warehouse with terrifying new abilities, but with no knowledge of how she got there.

The hero of Michael Peirce's *Accidental Operator* unwittingly becomes the key member of a new, highly deadly team of mercenaries.

Valley of the Shadow by Pat Moore is a moving exploration of love and loss, where those left behind suffer more than the ones they mourn.

Lori Lacefield's *The Fire Keeper* follows Frankie Johnson, an FBI Profiler, as she tries to decode a terrifyingly macabre fire ritual, before the killers strike again.

Free will, morality and redemption lie at the heart of Simon Finnie's *Burning*, as a Professor is forced to confront the mistakes of his youth.

And finally, in Peter Oxley's *Burning Greed*, a thief simply has to battle through a burning island to steal the score of his life: what could possibly go wrong?

Ladies and gentlemen, boys and girls, we present to you... *Burning: An Anthology of Short Thrillers*!

Warm Regards,
Simon Finnie and Pete Oxley
Burning Chair Publishing
London, October 2018

Loose Ends
by Craig Hart

(A Simon Wolfe Short Story)

Key West, Florida
Fall, 1937

Nothing ruins the benefit of a good night's sleep like being awakened by the muzzle of a pistol being jammed into one's ear. And I would be lying if I were to say I wasn't at least a little peeved by the situation.

I'd been dreaming of my lady friend, Tiki, in various states of undress, and been on the verge of making my move when I'd noticed the unpleasant grinding sensation to the side of my head. My eyes had flown open, and my first thought had been that I'd grossly overestimated Tiki's fondness for me and been thrust into the role of a modern day Sisera, playing the part of Jael by hammering a nail through my temple.

A moment later, the fog of sleep abated enough to allow

such biblical comparisons to give way to reality. I was lying in my own bed, in my own hotel room on Key West, and a gun was pressed to my ear.

"Not a move, Wolfe," a deep voice growled.

"I wouldn't dream of it," I said, quite truthfully.

"Smart boy. You expecting visitors?"

"Yeah. King Jabin's army. You'd better get out while you have the chance."

"What the hell you talking about?"

"I take it you're not a scholar of ancient texts."

"I got a gun to your ear, Wolfe."

"That hadn't escaped my notice. Would you mind backing off a little? I think you're denting my skull."

"I don't like smart guys," the man said. "They make my trigger finger twitchy."

"Well, I'm sorry," I said, exhibiting an annoyance only slightly manufactured, "but you've really messed things up for me. Here I'd finally followed the directions of my dear old mother for getting a good night's sleep. Work hard all day, she said, eat a light dinner, drink a glass of warm milk before bed, and then turn in early. I did all those things, and it was going along fine. Now you've ruined it by jerking me from a pleasant slumber. This is likely to wreck my whole day."

"If you don't stop with the wisecracks, you'll be lucky to *have* a whole day." The man sounded unrepentant, but the pressure to my earhole lessened a bit. I took this to be a sign we were headed in the right direction. "You co-operate, and you might get out of this alive. Otherwise, I'll turn your brain into mush."

"There are those who would suggest Mother Nature beat you to it."

"Again with the wisecracks," the deep voice growled. "You don't listen well, do you, Wolfe?"

The pressure returned full force.

"Sorry," I said, wincing. "I joke when I'm nervous."

"At least you got sense to be nervous."

"Can I sit up?"

"Are you gonna do something stupid?"

"Wouldn't dream of it."

"Okay. But take it nice and slow. Go for a gun or get a mind to be a hero, and the firecracker in my hand is liable to go off."

The pressure on my ear lifted, and I began moving slowly. My .38 was nestled under my pillow, but I wasn't about to try for it. Not yet. The odds of retrieving the revolver and getting off a shot were hovering just above zero. I don't mind the occasional risk but, if given my druthers, I prefer to play the odds.

I got one arm under me and pushed myself up. I rolled onto my backside, sat upright, and had my first look at the man with the gun. And the sight almost sent me laughing despite the gaping maw of the pistol barrel that now pointed directly between my eyes.

From the sonorous rumble of the voice, I had expected to find a man of impressive size and presence. But what I saw standing before me was one of the most diminutive figures I'd ever seen. His height couldn't have exceeded five feet two inches. He wore wire-rimmed spectacles that gave his eyes a bulging appearance, as if they might pop from their sockets at any moment. A couple of protruding front teeth and a hairline that had long ago waved the white flag combined to create a convincing and memorable impression of a mole-rat. The man didn't look to have a muscle in his entire body, and I was fairly certain I would be able to snap his thin frame by banging it over my knee. His sloping forehead beaded with sweat and I noticed stains under the arms of his shirt. It was warm, as it generally was in Key West, but not that warm.

"Okay," I said, relaxing in the presence of this less-than-intimidating opponent. "What's this all about?"

"I need a favor from you," the man said.

I motioned to the gun. "And this is how you ask a favor?"

"Well, perhaps it's more of a demand."

"You seem awfully nervous for a guy who's holding six deadly sidekicks in his hand. Why not make an appointment to retain my services? That's what the commoners do, anyway."

"You mocking me?"

"No, I—"

"This is exactly why I brought this." The man became visibly more agitated, and he began waving the gun around in a manner that caused me no end of concern.

"Listen, pal, maybe you should—"

"Nobody ever takes me seriously," he said. "Not until I show them I deserve as much respect as any other man. Just because I'm small doesn't mean I don't have guts. Don't think I'll shoot? I'll shoot, all right, and then I'll burn your body so bad your best friend won't recognize you." He steadied the gun at me and, for one very long and anxious moment, I thought he was going to shoot.

I raised both hands, palm out, and spoke softly while taking care not to allow any hint of condescension into my voice.

"Now listen. Shooting is one thing, but let's not talk about tossing me in a fire. Key West is too hot as it is."

"Can the jokes, wise guy!"

"Sorry. Let's both take a breath and start over, huh? I mean no disrespect to you. It's just been a bit of a shock to wake up with a gun to my head. I'm still trying to put the pieces together and figure out what the hell is going on. Perhaps you could help me out by telling me your name?"

He hesitated, and his eyes got shifty. "Wilson. John Wilson."

"Okay," I said. "Now your real name." I held up a hand as he opened his mouth to protest. "And don't even bother telling me that *is* your real name, because we both know it isn't. Now stop wasting my time and start shooting straight with me." I instantly regretted my terminology, but the little guy didn't appear to have noticed. Or, if he had, any plans of actually killing me had been tabled, at least for the time being.

"The name's Archibald Lamb."

"Mind if I call you John Wilson?"

"Don't forget the fire!" The man reddened and his grip on the pistol, which had been slowly loosening, tightened again. Me and my big mouth, I thought.

"I'm just joshing you," I said. "Trying to lighten the mood."

"Keep your day job," the little man growled in his paradoxically deep voice. "You're no Jack Benny."

"No, I guess not. Fine. Mr. Lamb, then. What can I do for you?"

"I need you to find someone for me."

"Ah, well, missing persons happens to be one of my specialties."

"I didn't know private investigators specialized."

"They do, although it's generally more a matter of necessity than anything else."

"Meaning?"

"Meaning those kinds of cases are the easiest to obtain. And you get paid whether you find the subject dead or alive."

"What's your record like, Wolfe?"

"My record?"

"Of finding them dead or alive. You find them mostly dead or mostly alive?"

"I'd say it's about even. The two statistical horses are neck and neck."

"Then you can call a winner."

I frowned. "I don't follow."

"This case," the man said. "It's gonna make the dead column take the lead."

"And how do you know your missing person is dead?"

The little man smiled. "Because I'm the one who killed him."

My heart performed a backflip. I hoped it hadn't shown on my face.

"I guess that explains the gun."

"I couldn't be sure you wouldn't play the conscientious citizen and drag me to the cops."

"I think you'll find I only have a certain amount of conscience," I said. "Certainly not enough to keep a man from telling his side of the story."

"Good to know."

"So, what is it?"

Lamb looked confused.

"Your side of the story," I clarified.

"I just told you. I killed someone."

"Did you burn them too?"

"Not yet," Lamb said ominously.

"Then exactly where do I fit into the picture?"

"I want you to help me dispose of the body."

I rose from the bed and, as the sheets fell away, remembered that I was completely naked. "Mind if I put on some clothes before we continue this conversation?"

"And have you pull a gun from your underwear drawer? I don't think so, Mr. Wolfe."

"Oh, come now."

Lamb growled. "Fine. But no sudden moves."

I retrieved a pair of shorts from a drawer and pulled them on, ever under the watchful gaze of both Lamb and his deadly little pal.

"Now," I said, "how about a drink?"

I walked toward a low table with a set of swinging doors on the front. The gun came up and followed my every move, but I felt certain it wouldn't go off. Not as long as I didn't do something crazy. Like getting too conscientious. I opened the swinging doors to reveal a collection of glass bottles, made impressive only by how many I'd managed to fit into the small cabinet space. I got out two glasses and set them on the table top.

"What's your poison?"

Lamb shrugged. "Whatever you're having."

"Bourbon it is," I said, splashing some into each glass. I set the bottle on the table for easy access and then closed the cabinet doors. I returned to the bed and stood at the foot. Then I handed one of the glasses to Lamb and held mine out for the traditional clinking. "Cheers," I said.

Lamb obliged and muttered, "Cheers," as he brought his glass to his lips.

The oddity of trading such pleasantries while still having a gun pointed in my general direction did not escape me, and I began wondering what I'd have to do in order to get the damn thing stowed away where it wouldn't be of danger to anyone, most of all myself.

Lamb drained the glass and smacked his lips. "You serve a good bourbon," he admitted.

"Now, Mr. Lamb. You said this was a missing persons case. Then you tell me you want me to help you dispose of a body. Which is it?"

"I figured someone skilled in missing persons cases would be the right one to hide one. You know the angles, where the cops would look first, how to foul up their investigation."

I shrugged. "I suppose. Although I must warn you I'm not in the habit of hiding dead bodies from the police. That sort of thing can get a guy into a lot of trouble."

"You ready to hear my story?"

"I couldn't be more ready," I said, finishing off my drink.

"It happened last night. I came home to find my best friend, fellow by the name of Skeeter, in bed with—"

"I'm sorry. You did say 'Skeeter'?"

"Yeah, Skeeter. I never knew his real name. Not sure even he did. Hell, maybe that was his real name. Anyway, who's telling this story?"

"Sorry."

"Anyhow, I came home after a long day of work to find Skeeter in bed with my girl."

"You have a girl?"

"That so surprising?"

"No, no. And what's her name?"

"Sarah."

"How disappointing."

"Look, pal, if you're gonna spend all day making fun of—"

"Sorry," I repeated. "Please continue."

Lamb sighed. "I find Skeeter in bed with Sarah. I say, 'What the hell is going on here?' Skeeter jumps out of bed and comes at me like a bull, stark raving mad."

"And you pull out this little friend of yours and let him have it," I finished. "A clear case of self-defense."

"No. I dodge to one side, see, and he slams into the wall."

"And breaks his neck on a support beam. Incidental homicide, open and closed."

"No. Now would you let me finish? The guy turns around and he's looking even crazier. Got a big cut on his forehead, blood's dripping down into his eyes. He chases me into the kitchen, then looks over at the counter and sees a knife block. He grabs one of the knives and comes at me." Lamb paused, as if waiting to be interrupted by one of my premature theories. When none was forthcoming, he continued. "I run to the bedroom again, because that's where I keep the gun, but before I can get there, he has me by the shirt collar and is twisting it tight around my neck. I flip around and bring up my arms to protect myself and get a nice slash down my forearm for the trouble."

There may be some who would say I have my virtues— I'm not sure who they'd be, but there may be some—but they would not list patience as one of them. While this may be a strange failing for a private investigator, it is simply a cross I must bear. In any case, listening to Lamb's story was giving me a severe case of itchy feet. I wanted him out of my room as early as yesterday, after which I would scrub the entire place down with the strongest cleaning agent known to man. Lamb was just one of those types who give you the creeps right from the beginning, even without a gun. I was pretty sure he was carrying several communicable diseases and, if nothing else, his constant moistness was making my skin crawl. I'd also noticed that his large eyes, magnified horrifically by the glasses, had an odd way of rolling around in their sockets as he spoke, and he'd developed a spot of foamy spittle at each corner of his mouth.

"Listen, Mr. Lamb, I really don't think I can—"

"Oh, but I was just getting to the best part of the story."

"I'm not interested. Can we just skip to the end?"

Lamb scowled. "You're lousing up my dramatic ending. I had this all planned out, you know."

"This isn't dinner theater," I said. "What's the bottom line?"

"I wanna know how to get rid of the body."

"How about burning it? Seems to be a specialty of yours."

"Funny thing about fires," Lamb said. "They kinda draw the wrong sorts of attention. I want to know where to hide a body so it won't be found for a while."

"How long's a while?"

"A couple of weeks."

"This isn't a very big island."

"You're the expert."

"Yes, and this expert has no desire to be caught up as an accessory, whether the homicide was justified or not."

Lamb raised his gun. "You're forgetting my six deadly sidekicks."

I sighed. "You got a boat?"

"No."

"Can you get one?"

"I suppose so."

"Good. Here's what you do: cut the body up and wrap the pieces in butcher's paper. Take the pieces in a boat at night and go out about a mile. Then drop the pieces over the side and let the sharks take over." I half-expected Lamb to wince or recoil during my graphic suggestion, but he didn't twitch a single muscle. On the contrary, his eyes sharpened with interest.

"What about the blood during the cutting?"

"Got a tub? Use that. And take your clothes off before doing the work so you don't have tell-tale bloodstains all over. Oh, and don't get the sides of the boat all bloody during the disposal or you might confuse the sharks into attacking the boat. Just dump the stuff and light a shuck for shore."

Lamb's face broke into a smile. Most people's countenance is enhanced by a smile, but his took on a horrible, ghoulish look. His teeth, several of which were either chipped or missing, were crooked and stained.

"That's good thinking," he said. "That just might work."

"Best of luck to you, then," I said, moving to usher him to the door. "And my apologies to Mr. Skeeter."

Lamb started laughing, a weird and guttural sound I detested immediately. I waited for him to stop, but he kept going. Finally, I'd had enough.

"What's so damn funny, Lamb?"

"There is no Skeeter."

"What?"

"There is no Skeeter. No Sarah. No lover's spat." He rolled up the sleeves of first one arm and then the other. The gun switched hands as he did so, but the muzzle never left me. "And look, no knife wound."

"What kind of game are you playing, Lamb? Are you telling me there's no body that needs disposing?"

"No. At least not yet."

"I don't follow."

"It's you, Wolfe. You're the one I needed help getting rid of. Much obliged for the help."

"You're crazy." It was a stupid response, but the only one I could think of at the moment. He'd caught me flat-footed.

"Like a fox," Lamb said. "Now why don't you show me to your bathroom. Cutting you up is liable to be an all-day affair, and I'd like to get started."

"If you think I'm simply going to let you—"

"And what do you plan to do about it?"

Lamb waved the gun at me, and I watched it, timing the movements, waiting for my chance. But the muzzle never strayed far enough to warrant a move. And Lamb's finger was whitening against the trigger, a sure sign he was applying at least a certain amount of pressure.

I moved sideways around the bed and then began backing toward the bathroom. My mind spun and whirled crazily, trying desperately to formulate some plan, some way out. I could make a move, a sudden lunge. It was a cinch I'd take at least one bullet but as long as it hit nothing vital, I could still take him out and survive. But if it hit a vital organ or an artery...

I kept moving, backing my way toward the bathroom from memory, never taking my eyes from the gun. I only needed a split second.

Bang!

Something hit the door of my hotel room with a sound like a gunshot. Lamb whirled and fired, the bullet thudding into the wooden door. I sprang forward like a bobcat, wrapping one arm around the man's throat and grabbed for the pistol with my other hand. I gripped his wrist and we struggled for control, but he was entirely outmatched in the strength department. I gave his wrist a violent twist. He shrieked in pain as the bones crunched. The pistol dropped to the floor. I bent to pick it up and came up as Lamb grabbed the door handle. I aimed as the door opened and fired as Lamb tumbled out onto the walkway. My bullet caromed off the metal door lock. Before I could fire again, Lamb was on his feet and running. I went after him but stumbled over something in the doorway. It was the morning paper—that was what had hit the door. I'd always found the paper boy's arm strength obnoxious, but now I hoped he was headed to the Majors.

I continued the chase, my bare feet pounding on the packed earth. I still had the pistol raised but it's difficult to fire accurately while running at a full sprint, and I was concerned about stray bullets out here in the street. What's more, I had a lot of questions for my would-be murderer. Not the least of which was why he wanted me dead in the first place. There was a good possibility he wasn't acting alone. If so, killing Lamb would cause as many problems as it solved. Someone else could simply take his place, and I might not be so lucky the next time.

With that in mind I gave up trying to aim, dropped the pistol, and turned my entire attention to running. My longer legs enabled me to overtake Lamb, and I brought him down with a tackle that would have made my old high school football coach proud.

I flipped Lamb over onto his back and sat astride him, my fist cocked should he attempt anything foolish. But he lay still, gasping for air, defeated.

"You win, Wolfe," he said. "I suppose you're going to kill me now. I wouldn't blame you for being angry."

"I'm more confused and curious than angry," I said.

"Then you're not going to kill me?"

"Well," I said, "not here. And not now. If you hadn't noticed, we're beginning to draw quite a crowd. After all, you see a lot of strange things on Key West, but even here it's unusual to see a scantily clad man chasing someone down the street with a gun."

"I guess it is," Lamb said. "If you're not going to kill me, then how about getting off my chest."

I stood up and then offered a hand, which Lamb reluctantly accepted.

"Now what?" he asked.

"First, I'm going to get some clothes on," I said. "And then you're going to tell me what the hell possessed you to stick a gun in the ear of a sleeping man."

I marched him back to my hotel room under the watchful eyes, and more than a few catcalls, of the gaggle of spectators. I picked up the gun I'd dropped along the way and used it to prod Lamb into the room and down into a chair to cool his heels while I threw on some clothes. I ran a hand through my hair a few times and then jerked my head at the door.

"Okay," I said. "Let's go."

"Where are we going?"

"The bar, of course. I need a drink."

*

We walked to the bar, appearing on much friendlier terms. By which I mean I didn't hold a gun to Lamb's back as we made our way to Sloppy Joe's. I was not, however, unarmed. I had put Lamb's pistol into my desk drawer and grabbed mine from under my pillow. The .38 was now in my waistband under a loose-fitting shirt, and Lamb knew I would use it if I needed to. Besides, his wrist was still hurting him, and I suspected I'd cracked a rib or two when I'd brought him down on the street.

Big Al Skinner welcomed us into the bar with a wide smile. "What'll it be, fellas?"

"A whiskey neat for me," I said.

Lamb nodded. "Same."

Skinner moved away to get the drinks. He was back in moments and set the glasses down on the bar. "You two startin' a tab?"

I shrugged. "Why not?"

"Why not indeed," Skinner said. He grabbed a towel and began polishing the bar.

"Okay," I said, once the bartender had moved away. "Let's hear it. And it better be good."

"It wasn't my idea, I swear," Lamb said. "A guy put me up to it."

"Put you up to it?"

Lamb squirmed. "Okay, so he paid me."

"How much?"

"What difference does it make."

"How... much...?"

"Five bucks."

"I ought to kill you just for that. I don't think I'm out of line to say I'm worth a hell of a lot more than that."

"Look, it's not personal. I didn't know who you were, okay?"

"It seems like anyone would be worth more than five bucks, whether you know them or you don't."

"Five bucks can buy a few meals for a guy."

"I suppose. So, you're broke and desperate. Who was the guy who hired you?"

"If I say, he'll kill me."

"If you don't say, I'll kill you."

"You buying these drinks?"

"Sure."

"Then I guess I owe you. Name's Al Sykes."

"Never heard of him. Does he live in Key West?"

"Nah. Miami."

"What does he do there?"

"Hires down-and-outs to kill people."

"You're in no position to be smart with me."

"Look, I don't know, okay? He just said he wanted you dead."

"How'd he find you?"

"A mutual friend."

"You move in some real classy circles, Lamb."

"Well, it ain't high society, but we do okay."

The little man had finished his drink and was gazing sadly into the depths of the glass. I signaled to Skinner, who replenished both our drinks.

"Now here's the question of the hour," I said. "Why does this Al Sykes want me dead? And don't say you don't know."

"I don't know."

"Dammit, I said not to say that!"

"It's the God's honest truth. He never came out and said."

"He had to at least hint at it."

"Nope."

"So he said, 'Hey, Archie, I want you to kill a guy,' and you said, 'Yeah, no problem, Al'?"

"No, he said, 'I want you to kill a guy and I'll pay you five bucks'."

"Ah, right. My mistake. You're a real piece of work, Lamb. Can you at least tell me what this Sykes character looks like? Or did he make you wear a blindfold?"

Lamb scowled, appearing hurt. "Of course he didn't make me wear a blindfold. He was a big guy, bigger than you, with dark hair."

"That really narrows it down," I said. "Any distinguishing characteristics, like a tattoo or a scar? Maybe a missing limb?"

"No, I don't—wait, there was one thing I noticed. He had kind of a limp."

"How do you have 'kind of' a limp?"

"I mean it wasn't real bad. Almost wouldn't have noticed, except every now and then he'd rub his knee and wince, like it was paining him to walk."

"Okay, that's something solid. Anything else?"

Lamb shook his head. "Nope. Just a regular guy, really."

"A regular guy who goes around ordering discount hits on innocent people."

"Oh, he didn't think you were innocent," Lamb said. "He thought you were—" He cut off suddenly.

"And what? Thought I was what?"

"He seemed to think you were to blame for ruining some lucrative business scheme he'd had running awhile back."

I glared at the little man. "I thought Sykes never hinted at a reason for wanting me dead."

Lamb shrugged. "Didn't think that was important. It's not like he came out and said anything."

"That is, by definition, what a hint is," I ground out through clenched teeth. I decided that I'd spent far too much time in the company of Archie Lamb. I finished my drink and then fished two bills from my pocket. I placed one on the counter and handed one to Lamb. "There," I said. "Sykes paid you five to kill me. Here's ten to leave me the hell alone. Deal?"

Lamb looked first at the ten-spot, then back at his drink as if imagining all the whiskeys he could buy with that much money. Then he flashed that horrible smile of his and nodded.

"You got yourself a deal, Wolfe."

"Good," I said. "And one more thing." I placed a heavy hand on the little man's shoulder. "Once you've boozed your way through that tenner, get the hell out of Key West and don't let me see you here ever again."

I left Lamb just as he was waving his newfound wealth to get Skinner's attention. I had a sneaking suspicion the crew at Sloppy Joe's would end up pouring the little guy into a taxi to nowhere by the end of the day. And that was fine by me.

My hotel room was as I'd left it, bullet-ridden door and all. I'd half-expected the hotel manager to be waiting for me, but there was no sign of the pudgy little jerk. This was also fine by me as he wasn't the kind of guy to enjoy a little thing like a gun battle on his property.

I poured myself a drink and sat down on the edge of the bed. As I drank, I ran through a mental list of past acquaintances, anyone I might have come into contact with during the course of working private investigations. It wasn't a long list, since I hadn't been in the racket very long, but still I couldn't come up with anyone named Al or Sykes, or anyone who walked with a limp. Then my brain clicked into gear and I leaned over to grab the phone. After a lengthy go-round with the operator, during which my call was re-routed several times, I got a long-distance call made to Lowell, Massachusetts.

A gravelly voice stabbed through the wire. "Stubbs, here. Who the hell's this?"

"It's Wolfe."

"Wolfe! Haven't heard from you in a month of Sundays."

"Yeah, it's been busy."

"Since when have you ever been busy?"

"You might be surprised. Listen, I hate to rush, but they're charging me a limb per minute."

"It's your nickel."

"You ever hear of a guy named Al Sykes? Big guy. Walks with a limp."

"Sykes? Yeah, I know him. Surprised you don't."

"Why would I?"

"Because you were along during the takedown."

"I have no recollection of it. Mind explaining?"

"In deference to your pocketbook, I'll give you the short version. You were a wide-eyed greenhorn when I took you along on a stakeout. Don't forget, it was supposed to be a routine job."

"Yeah, I remember. Things got dicey when one of the crooks spotted our car and rang the alarm."

"Damn straight. The whole gang was on the verge of scattering to the four winds. We radioed for backup and then went in. Exchanged a few gunshots and then the crew ran for the back exit, but there was a patrol car in the alley waiting for them. We got most of them, but the ringleader—that was Al Sykes—got away with only a leg wound. I heard he was killed in a poker dispute a year later."

"Well, apparently he's still alive and wants me dead. Why would he target me? I didn't even know his name."

"Because you were instrumental in getting the stakeout approved by the brass. It was the reason I agreed to take you along. Figured I owed it to you."

And then I remembered. It had been a freak thing, an overheard conversation in a dark Massachusetts bar that I'd reported to Stubbs, who had taken my word for it and badgered the captain to set up a stakeout on the address. At the time, I'd considered myself lucky. Now I wished I hadn't overheard a damn thing.

"Thanks for the insight, Stubbs," I said.

"Sure. Keep your head down, kid. And sit facing the door from now on."

I hung up and returned to my drink.

Like every sensible person who lived in the subtropical climate of Key West, I decided to spend the sun's zenith by taking a siesta. The consumption of alcohol helped that natural inclination along and, by the time I awoke, the day was well into the late afternoon.

I stretched and sat up and then my eyes, which had previously been drooping from sleep, flew wide open.

Slumped in a chair and snoring his little head off was Archie Lamb. I shot out of bed and grabbed the sleeper by his shoulders.

"Wake up!" I shouted. "Wake the hell up!"

Lamb's eyelids fluttered and then opened. He looked around in confusion, clearly not recognizing his surroundings. "What the—where am—how do I—oh, Wolfe!" The cloud of consternation at least partially cleared from his face, and he pushed up in the chair. "I guess you're a little surprised to see me here."

"Surprised is one way to describe it," I said. "I have a distinct memory of saying I never wanted to see you again."

"Oh, that. Yeah, well, I got a little tight at the bar and when they said I had to leave, I couldn't think of anywhere else to tell them to take me."

"You're a real piece of work, Lamb."

"Maybe you should start locking your door. You're not still sore about that whole killing thing, are you? I thought that was over between us."

I gritted my teeth, although I felt the faintest flicker of amusement deep inside. The guy was obnoxious, grotesque, entirely untrustworthy, and downright bizarre, but I couldn't help but admire his moxie. Either that, or he simply had a complete lack of insight.

"What's the real reason you're here, Lamb? You want something."

Lamb assumed the look of one who's been slandered before the masses. "Look, I'm kinda paying you a compliment by showing up here. They say the first person a drunk asks for is the one he trusts the most."

"Drunks aren't known for making high-quality life decisions."

Lamb sighed. "Okay, okay. So maybe I *do* want something."

"Out with it."

"While I was drinking at the bar, I realized that Sykes is gonna find out I didn't off you. That's liable to make him mad. And we both know what happens when Sykes gets mad."

"He hires someone to kill the subject of his anger."

"Right. And he don't forget, either. From what I remember, he's been mad at you for a good while."

"You know, this onset of memory could have saved me a pretty penny had it occurred a little sooner. I had to make a long-distance phone call due to your convenient spell of amnesia."

"It's the booze," Lamb said. "It does funny things. Sometimes it makes me forget, and sometimes it makes me remember."

"Get to the point."

"I want to hire you. To kill Sykes so he don't kill me."

I couldn't help it. The laugh burst out and forced me to stagger backward onto the bed. Lamb watched me impassively, apparently stumped as to the source of my mirth. At last, wiping tears from my eyes, I managed to regain some semblance of control.

"Don't see what's so funny," Lamb said. "I was planning to pay you for the work." And with that, he reached into his pocket and pulled out a twenty-dollar bill, which he handed over to me. "There. Now that's a good day's wage if I ever seen one."

"Where the hell did you get twenty dollars? I thought you were broke."

"I was. But I won a bet with a guy at the bar who thought he could out-drink me. Folks think I can't hold my liquor, me a small fella, but what they don't know is that I got a hollow leg."

I handed back the money. "Keep it. I'm not a killer for hire. Just tell me where I can find Sykes, and we'll call it even between us."

Lamb's memory stuck around long enough to let me know the Miami bar where he'd made the deal with Sykes. And I stuck around Key West long enough to make sure my door got repaired and Lamb got tossed out on his ear. Then I got in my old Chevy and started for the mainland.

I got to Miami in the early evening of the day following my first interaction with Lamb and drove directly to the bar. It was a ramshackle place, an old wood-frame house that had been converted into a drinking establishment immediately following the repeal of Prohibition. The conversion from dwelling to business had been done quickly and with very little forethought. It felt like I was walking into someone's living room when I entered through the front door and stood looking around in the dim light. Tobacco smoke hung thick in the air. A dozen pairs of curious eyes stared at me as the regulars wondered who this newcomer might be and what kind of trouble I was about to start.

I moved across the rough floor—the carpet had been pulled up and the wooden floor beneath was in desperate need of a sanding job and more than one coat of varnish. A few carpet tacks remained in place, and I felt them clutching at the soles of my shoes as I walked over them; fortunately, none were long enough to pierce through to my feet.

Half of the wall separating the living room from the kitchen had been sawn away and a sheet of wood attached to the lower portion, creating a makeshift counter. On top of this was a torn square of cardboard that had been folded into a tent shape. One side announced, in faint pencil, the available drinks and their prices.

A rough-looking man wearing a stained white t-shirt and an equally stained apron—which I assumed used to be white—stood in the kitchen and watched me approach. As I drew closer he came to the bar and leaned forward with his hands planted flat on the counter top.

"Get you somethin', mister?"

"Just some information, if you don't mind."

The man pointed at the cardboard menu. "You see 'information' on the menu?"

"Can't say that I do."

"Then we don't serve it."

A ripple of laughter ran through the locals.

"I'm not here for trouble," I said. "I'm looking for a man, that's all."

The bartender's eyes sharpened. "What man?"

"Name's Sykes. Al Sykes."

The atmosphere in the room changed immediately. The bartender stepped away from the bar, as if getting out of the range of... something. The hair stood up on the back of my neck and I turned around, very slowly.

As I watched, a large shadow detached from a chair in the corner. A man stepped out into the meager light that sifted through the papered windows.

"I'm Sykes," the man said. "Who the hell are you?"

My .38 weighed heavy in my pocket, but I didn't dare reach for it. Probably most, if not all, of the dozen men in the room were armed. And I only had six bullets.

"Name's Wolfe," I said, deciding to lay all my cards on the table. "Simon Wolfe. The man you hired someone to kill."

Silence reigned for a full thirty seconds. Then Sykes said, "Looks like Archie Lamb turned out to be every bit the bum I thought he was."

"You always hire bums to do your work?"

"It wasn't much of a risk. Gave him a fin, but didn't expect too much. I would have been more surprised had he managed it."

"He almost did," I said. "Came up on me sleeping and shoved a gun in my ear."

"And he still managed to botch the job?"

"When you put it that way, I guess he did do pretty lousy work."

"I suppose you're here to kill me now," Sykes said.

"Only if I have to."

"And who decides if you have to?"

"You do, of course."

"You want to step outside?"

"Definitely."

We went outside and stood in the evening air. The sun was setting over the water, setting the entire horizon on fire. Sykes was surprising me. I hadn't known what to expect, but this wasn't it.

"You know why I wanted you dead?"

"I think so. You seem to think I ruined some sort of operation."

"Ratted to the cops. I had a good thing going in Old Mass."

"It was pure chance that I overheard those two guys talking in the bar. If you want to blame someone, you should talk to those two for running their mouths in a public place. I was only doing what any law-abiding citizen would do—I went to the cops."

"Yeah, but your existing connection with the cops made your story carry a lot more weight than the average Joe's off the street. Your story initiated an entire sting operation."

"There wasn't supposed to be a sting. It was only a stakeout. Your guys panicked."

"That's beside the point. Anyways, there's blame to go all the way around."

"I don't follow you."

"How do you think I know who you are? You weren't on the official police log. You weren't employed by the cops. How would I even know your name?"

It was a good question. One name, and only one, barreled into my consciousness.

"You're not saying that—?"

"Detective Barry Stubbs."

"But why—?"

"I'll tell you why," Sykes said, interrupting me once more. "Detective Stubbs was on the take for years. Made a good bundle off me and my racket. Then he decides he wants to move up in the ranks, but he needs a good score to tout in front of the Commissioner. What does he do? Goes for the easy kill: me."

"It was a set-up?"

"From start to finish. Those two guys? Plants. Your detective buddy knew where you liked to get drinks, so he put two toadies up to a little acting job. And, like the good little citizen Stubbs knew you were, you went running to him with the story. Now he's free and clear to act, without the risk of someone wondering how he came about the information. He had back-up on call, which is why that other patrol car got to the scene so quick and was waiting in the alley just when they were needed. All very convenient. And it worked, too. Stubbs was promoted the next month."

"But what about you? Stubbs thought you were dead."

"No, he didn't. He knew I was alive. But it was embarrassing to have me on the loose. Looked bad. When he decided to go for commissioner, he floated that story about my having been killed in a card game. It wasn't perfect, but at least he could act like justice had won out after all. The long arm of the law, you know."

"And what about me? Why would he want me killed?"

"You're a loose end. Stubbs is set for a run at the governor's mansion. He doesn't want anything to derail that campaign. So he let it slip into the underworld grapevine that you had something to do with my downfall in Old Mass."

"And you took the bait."

"Not exactly. I can't say that I didn't enjoy the idea of tying up my own loose ends."

"Sounds like you might be focusing on the wrong guy," I said.

Sykes and I stood looking at each other. I noticed his hand was hovering near his pocket, just as mine was, and I knew he had a gun at the ready. We stared, waiting, thinking, weighing the odds and options.

"Listen, Wolfe," Sykes said. "We could try to kill each other right now. Maybe I'd get you, maybe you'd get me. Maybe we'd get each other. I don't know about you, but I'm not interested in dying. I'm at the top of the food chain, Wolfe. I don't die; other people die. You get me?"

"Maybe we both just walk away."

"Close. But there's still the little matter of a score to settle."

"Like you said, we might just get each other. What would that solve?"

"Exactly. Here's what I propose. You mentioned that maybe I'm focusing on the wrong guy. Well, I have Stubbs in my sights, as well. He's not getting off scot-free, believe you me."

"I'm not a hired killer."

"You don't have to be," Sykes said. "I let you go in return for you keeping your mouth shut until I've done what I need to do. And that's it."

"And after?"

"Do whatever the hell you want. Say whatever the hell you want. There'll be no proof. And without Stubbs to back up what you say, no one's going to listen to a word."

"And if I don't agree?"

"Then you can go for that gun I know you've got in your pocket and see if you're quick enough to get me before I get you. Just remember this: there are a dozen men inside who'll come running out at the first shot. Even if you get me, you're not walking away from here alive."

I lay on my bed with the phone close by. Several times I had picked up the receiver and held it to my ear. Once I'd even spoken to the operator but had hung up before giving any instructions.

It was dark in the room and, if I listened closely, I could hear the waves crashing on the shore. There was the distant screech of a sea bird, and the smell of salt water hung in the air.

Stubbs wasn't worth saving. He'd been taking money for years, living off graft, lining his pockets with the proceeds of criminal activity. I wasn't a crusader. I didn't hold the law in complete reverence. I'd even been known to skirt the edges of criminality at certain times. But never out of malice or greed. Sykes' operation had been engaged in all manner of underworld activities, including murder. Sometimes these activities involved innocent people, those who had done nothing more than go about their daily lives. And Stubbs had willingly profited from that. Of course, it would be better to target Sykes, but my warning to Stubbs would accomplish nothing. It would save his life, yes, but it wouldn't result in Sykes' demise. All I had to do was nothing and at least part of the problem would be remedied. If I interfered, both men would continue on. And, in addition, I would have a new target on my back.

And yet my conscience nagged at me. Could I simply do nothing and let a man die? Stubbs, it turned out, was not the paragon of virtue I had thought, but he had done much to aid my interest in criminology and investigation. Of course, now there was the distinct possibility that he'd been grooming a fall guy the entire time, a naïve rookie who could be easily manipulated. But I didn't know that to be so. It may have been happenstance. Even as I thought it, I doubted the idea. Stubbs did not seem to be the type to rely on or even take advantage of happenstance. He was a calculating, intelligent man. I'd known this all long but had thought all his energy was dedicated to ending the careers of criminals. Now I knew better.

And the man was running for governor. Given his sterling reputation, he stood a good chance of winning, which would give him unprecedented power and influence. If absolute power corrupted absolutely, it was a cinch Stubbs would fall prey to its siren song. In fact, he already had.

I looked at the telephone one last time and then got out of bed. I slipped on my shoes and headed toward the door, never bothering to flip on a light. I preferred to remain in the dark that night, at least until I reached the welcoming lights of Sloppy Joe's bar.

THE END

ABOUT THE AUTHOR

Craig A. Hart is a writer, publisher, and stay-at-home father of twin boys. When not defending the couch from sea monsters or delivering snacks across seas of molten lava, he enjoys reading a wide range of non-fiction works and in the thriller fiction genre.

A native of Grand Rapids, Michigan, Craig currently lives in Iowa City, Iowa, home of the world-renowned Iowa Writers' Workshop. Craig is the author of several series, including the Shelby Alexander Thriller Series and the Simon Wolfe Mystery Series.

Check out his official website at www.craigahart.com for updates, news, and a full list of books.

To receive the first book in his Shelby Alexander series for a cost of exactly zero pennies, go to:

https://dl.bookfunnel.com/tluzy7p5zs

From a Flicker to a Flame
by Fiona Campbell

Megan gazed at the candle flame flickering on the table between them. Beside it lay a single red rose. She'd never understood why the flower was supposed to be the ultimate romantic gesture. Evil, threatening thorns and red, the colour of blood. The waitress poured them each a glass of Prosecco. Chris raised his glass and gently clinked it against hers.

'Here's to a lovely evening with a beautiful lady.'

Megan smiled, savouring the moment. Chris wasn't

the type who would turn heads, but there was something cute and endearing about him. Blonde hair, blue eyes and extremely kissable lips. She was looking forward to testing that theory.

That Tuesday lunchtime, Megan had popped into Kelly's coffee house for a sugar fix. She certainly needed the energy for another fun-packed afternoon with primary three.

'A deluxe hot chocolate and a cara...'

The whole time she'd been queuing, her eyes had been firmly fixed on the last slice of caramel shortbread. Now it was on a plate, making its way to the tall, blonde guy beside her. He caught her eye and must have sensed her longing.

'Hey, I couldn't help hearing you were about to order this. Sorry, here you go.'

'No, I can't do that, but thanks for the offer.'

'Compromise, we could share it?'

Megan glanced at her watch, then back at him. She could spare fifteen minutes. It was worth it. The cake was amazing and she seemed to instantly click with Chris.

'I need to get back to school.'

'Now I feel like a cradle snatcher.'

'I'm the teacher,' she said, flicking her hair.

'I kinda guessed that. So, are you free on Friday night?'

'I would need to check my diary,' she said, knowing her only plans were with Maisy her ragdoll kitten, and a tub of chocolate ice-cream.

Instead, she found herself sitting in the 'Crystal Moon' at a romantic table for two. Her Chicken Pathia was delicious and just the right amount of spicy, though she instantly regretted wearing a white top and having red curry sauce to contend with. As she reached for the naan bread, Chris stroked her hand. Her whole body tingled at his touch. There was definitely a spark between them. Chris was intelligent and funny. As well as a shared love of Kelly's caramel shortbread, they had lots in common. From favourite foods and movies to an affinity with cats.

He showed her some photos of his two rescue cats, Marlo and Bob.

'You didn't tell me what you do?' Megan said.

'I didn't want to scare you off.'

'You're a serial killer?' she laughed.

'Close,' Chris said, pulling a badge from his pocket.

'D.C. Chris Taylor,' she read. 'Why would that scare me? Who would protect me better than a policeman? A man in uniform sounds good to me.'

'Would it be a deal-breaker if I said I don't usually wear one?'

After dinner they walked to the car park, hands entwined. Pausing for a moment behind the restaurant, he looked into her eyes, brushed the hair away from her face and slowly brought his lips to hers. He was so gentle and tender, until she reciprocated enthusiastically. Soon tongues were exploring mouths and Chris had pushed her towards the wall, letting her feel what she was doing to him. He delivered her safely home to her flat, with a goodnight kiss and the promise of a second date. Elated, Megan threw herself on to her bed and texted her friends.

'Had a great night. We definitely clicked and he wants to see me again!'

The next few months were a whirlwind of dates as they got to know each other. Chris prepared a gourmet picnic to have on a summer's day in the park and Megan cooked him a romantic meal in her flat. They enjoyed bowling and the cinema and they both joined a gym so they could see each other every day after work. Chris took her to meet his parents and he met Megan's mum and dad over Skype, since they lived in the States.

For their first anniversary, Chris treated her to a weekend away in a luxurious hotel. They spent a fabulous day at the zoo, where he knelt down in front of the Meerkat enclosure.

'Megan, I've loved you since the day I met you. Will you marry me, so we can spend the rest of our lives together?'

She felt like a Disney princess as a crowd began to gather

behind them. Megan focused on the little girls, all willing her to say yes to the handsome prince.

'Yes, of course I'll marry you.'

There was a round of applause as Chris placed a platinum engagement ring on her finger.

'Mummy, can we see the meerkats now?' a young boy said.

Megan pulled Chris to the side. 'We'd better move. We've hogged the limelight for long enough.'

Only six months later, they were flying to Florida with Chris's parents and Megan's sister, Jo. Megan's parents kindly agreed to host everyone in their villa in Clearwater. They had organised an intimate wedding ceremony on the beach. The setting couldn't have been more perfect, with the sound of the ocean and the sun beating down on them. The couple stood opposite each other, holding hands, as the ceremony began.

'Today you join yourselves together in life as friends and lovers, husband and wife. As the sea is sometimes calm and sometimes stormy, so also is a marriage.'

Megan hoped their future would be calm and happy and she was certain their love was strong enough to survive the stormy times.

'Now I'd like to ask you both to take a handful of sand from this spot where you are committing yourself to each other.'

They poured it into a heart shaped glass keepsake. A perfect reminder of their special day.

The second week of their honeymoon would be spent sailing the Caribbean onboard the "Princess of the Seas". Megan was in awe of the size of the cruise ship. She was looking forward to exploring the Bahamas. They spent the days at sea, sipping cocktails by the pool on the top deck. At night, they enjoyed the extravagant midnight buffets and the fabulous entertainment. They had both brought a special outfit for the Captain's Dinner. Chris wore a white tuxedo and Megan a stunning, red maxi dress which she coupled with silver heels. After a delicious five course meal, they headed to one of the more contemporary bars. Megan was delighted to see someone singing karaoke in the corner.

'Chris, it's a competition. I can sing much better than her. I'm going to see which songs they have.'

'I'll get us some drinks,' he said, walking towards the bar.

Megan looked directly at her new husband as she sang one of her favourite Whitney Houston songs. The round of applause and wolf-whistles that followed made her blush. She made her way back to their table, expecting a hug or a kiss.

'Come on, we're leaving,' Chris said, grabbing her arm.

'Don't you want to see who wins?'

'We're leaving now!' he said, loudly enough for people to stare.

Back in their cabin, she saw a look in his eyes which terrified her, like a predator about to pounce on unsuspecting prey.

'You shouldn't have done that, Megan. Paraded yourself like a slut, for all those men to fantasize about.'

'But I was singing for you. I'm not interested in anyone else.'

'Yeah, but plenty of people were interested in you.'

There was something unnerving about the way he had reacted, something which sowed a seed of doubt in her mind. How well did she really know him?

Things were hectic when they returned. They had both been renting flats, so were excited to be moving into their first home. It was a lovely two-bedroomed house in the suburbs, where the cats would be able to enjoy the small garden. Megan was worried about how Maisy would react to Chris' cats. She was such a spoilt diva, while they were kind of rough. They spent the first few weeks deciding where to put everything and christening every room. Living together was a learning curve she hadn't anticipated. She was naturally a messy person who would happily leave dishes in the sink and dirty underwear on the bathroom floor. Chris liked everything neat and tidy. He alphabetised his DVDs and ironed his boxers. At night, he liked it dark and silent but she liked to read with her lamp and music on. Love was all about compromise though, wasn't it? He snored. She bought headphones so she could listen to music in bed and drown him out.

Megan was really enjoying her life back in the classroom, but she was exhausted. She decided to run herself a bubble bath before cooking dinner. It was a great novelty, after only having a shower at her flat. When she came downstairs, Chris was holding her mobile phone.

Who's Ross?' Chris demanded.

'Ross Simmons? He teaches primary five and we're working together on the Christmas show.'

'How does that explain why his mobile number is in your phone?'

'We've worked together for a few years now. We're friends, as well as colleagues. But hold on; why were you looking at my texts?'

'I think I have a right to know what you're up to, don't you?'

'I'm not up to anything, Chris. Like I said, Ross is a friend from work, nothing more.'

Chris began deleting the contacts in her phone.

'Stop! What are you doing?' Megan shouted, reaching for her phone, just as his hand met her face.

No-one had ever hit her before, not even her parents. Her cheek throbbed, but this was more than physical pain. Megan knew that, from that day, something was broken. Something which couldn't be fixed.

'Can I see you after school, Mrs. Taylor?' said the headmistress, as she passed Megan with an armful of clipboards.

'Of course. I'll be in your office at three.'

It was hard to sing and tell stories when she was filled with anxiety. She hoped Mrs. Sim hadn't noticed the bruising on her face. She'd done her best to cover it with foundation and concealer and hide it with her hair. What if she had noticed? Megan prepared a plausible explanation in her head. She'd fallen downstairs carrying a heavy laundry basket.

After saying goodbye to her class, Megan knocked tentatively on the office door.

'Come in and have a seat. I just wanted to have a chat about your email. You'll be sorely missed at Oaklane. It's rare to find a teacher who is so enthusiastic about her job.'

Megan was clueless. Which email? Leaving Oaklane? Why would she give up her perfect job?

'We would really appreciate if you could work your month's notice while we find a replacement. I don't suppose there's any chance of you changing your mind? I know if I had a rich husband and didn't need to work, I would be a lady of leisure too. I would spend my days at the gym, getting manicures, shopping… Actually, I'm quite looking forward to my retirement now.'

Megan was confused and upset. There had to be some sort of logical explanation. Deep down, she knew that Chris had to have sent the email, but she didn't want to believe it.

As soon as Megan arrived home, she switched on her laptop. It seemed to take forever to load. She clicked on her email account and there it was in her sent box. The email to Mrs. Sim, which she hadn't written.

'Dear Mrs. Sim. It is with great regret that I write to resign from my teaching post at Oak Lane Primary School. As you know, my circumstances have recently changed and this will allow me to have a sabbatical from work and to think about starting a family. I have thoroughly enjoyed my time at the school and wish you all the best for the future. Kind Regards, Mrs. Megan Taylor.'

Why would Chris do this to her? She grabbed a cushion and screamed into it, before throwing a framed wedding photo across the room. Shattered glass lay across the floor. Life suddenly felt surreal. This was not the man she married and not the future she had envisioned. Tears trickled down her cheeks. Maybe she should just pack up and leave, and tomorrow she could explain to Mrs. Sim exactly what had happened. It was all a misunderstanding and she would continue her year with primary three and put on a fabulous Christmas show. Yes, that was the only viable solution. Chris obviously had a different side to him that she hadn't seen before accepting his ring.

Megan grabbed some black bin liners and began frantically filling them with her things. She paused to leave her wedding ring on the kitchen worktop. Suddenly, she heard his car pull into the driveway, the slam of the car door and the turning of his key in the lock. Megan closed her eyes and held her breath, fully aware that neither of these gestures would help her current situation.

'Spring cleaning in autumn?' said Chris with an evil laugh. 'Or let me guess, you're going somewhere?'

'The email, Chris. I don't understand. You know how much I love my job.'

'And you know how much I love you, Megan. I need you to be exclusively mine. There can't be any distractions like Ross or any other guy who happens to take your fancy.'

'But I need a life, too. I can be your wife and a teacher to my kids.'

'I think we've established that's not going to be possible. Now get this mess cleaned up, then you can cook me something nice for dinner.'

She obediently took the bags back upstairs. Chris lay on the bed with his hands behind his head, watching her return each item to its hanger or drawer.

'That's better,' he said, kneeling in front of her. 'Now give me your hand and I'll put your ring back where it belongs.'

Megan caught sight of her reflection in the mirror. The tears had resulted in a hideous mascara malfunction and her bruised cheek had turned a lovely shade of purple. She made her way downstairs to prepare some food, deciding to cook her favourite meal: 'Hunters Chicken.' Wrapping the chicken breasts in bacon, she covered them with grated mozzarella and a rich BBQ sauce. The smell was delicious. Megan arranged the chicken beautifully on the plate with some potato wedges, baby corn and mangetout.

'Dinner's ready,' she called upstairs as she sat at the table.

Chris picked up the plate in front of her and emptied it into the bin.

'Hmm, I don't think you'll be eating for a while. Megan. You'll need to be punished of course, for even thinking about leaving. Do you have any idea how embarrassing that would be for me? Besides, you could do with losing a few pounds.'

Chris made her sit and watch him eat, purposely savouring every mouthful.

'Mmm. This is so tasty. I'm so lucky to have my own resident chef.'

Megan was thankful that she had to work her notice. It would give her a month to either change his mind or get away. She went to pick up her car keys, but Chris held his hand up as he spoke into the phone.

'Hello, can I leave a message for Mrs. Sim please? I'm Megan Taylor's husband. I have some bad news, I'm afraid. She had a fall last night and the doctor said she won't be able to work for a few weeks. She's asked me to pass on her apologies.'

Megan froze, looking at her husband with disdain.

'That's just the way it has to be, Megan, and don't think about trying to leave again. You never know what might happen to your precious cat or, even better, your sister.'

She sat on the stairs, as Chris left, locking the door behind him. Beckoning Maisy to come and sit on her lap, she took comfort in cuddling her and stroking her silky coat. Maisy purred in solidarity. This wasn't a marital tiff. This was far more serious. Had he really just threatened to harm her sister? Jo was her closest friend and they texted or called each other every day. Megan picked up the phone handset and began to dial her number, but quickly realised that there was no dial tone.

How could her life have changed so dramatically in one day?

She busied herself with cleaning the house and preparing a meal. Trying to impress him, she supposed. If she could let Chris see that she was wholly devoted to him, maybe things could go back to normal.

'Megan, I'm home,' he called. Finding her and kissing her deeply, as though nothing had happened.

'How was your day?' she asked, pretending to be interested.

'Busy! I think I'll go for a shower before dinner.'

Fifteen minutes later, he appeared wearing only black boxers and bearing an enticing smell of musky aftershave. Small droplets glistened on his dark chest hair. Despite everything that was going on, she couldn't help feeling aroused.

'Can dinner wait, Megan? I couldn't stop thinking about you while I was in the shower.'

He walked towards her, kissed her neck and placed her hand on his shorts. There was no denying that he wanted her badly, but did she want him? Inside, she was hurting, but she still felt a flicker of love and desire. They made love in the kitchen. Afterwards, she lay with her head on his chest in the most divine post-coital embrace. Their breath and heartbeats combining in a symphony of their own.

'Wow. That was really something. Thank you,' said Chris, getting up from the hard floor.

Megan dressed quickly, suddenly feeling very exposed. They ate together. She was so glad that she was allowed to eat with him again.

'I love you, Megan. You know that. I'm not going to keep you here like a prisoner.'

'Good. I think people might start to miss me if I disappear altogether. Especially Jo: I'm surprised she hasn't turned up at the door already.'

'Valid point. Here's your mobile. Send a text saying you've got a bad cold. That'll fob her off for a few days anyway.'

It would have been so easy to send a cry for help, but she couldn't risk Chris acting on his threat. The ironic thing was that she had never had any inclination to cheat on Chris. He made her happy and she'd been looking forward to their future together and hopefully starting a family. Why did he have to ruin everything?

Chris confiscated her keys, her bank-cards and her mobile. He disconnected the landline and changed the password on her laptop. The first week wasn't so bad. As long as she had the house tidy and prepared a tasty meal, then the rest of the day was her own. She relaxed in a bubble bath and lay on the sofa, catching up with her favourite TV programs. Most people would love that life, but reality soon hit her. She was trapped there against her will. She wanted to be teaching and going out with her friends. Megan curled up in bed and sobbed. For a moment, she felt like a little girl again, longing for her mum to hug her and tell her everything was going to be all right.

The aroma of the curry wafted through the kitchen. Friday night was always Indian night. A reminder of their first date. Megan was busy stirring the Chicken Korma when she heard Chris's key in the lock.

'Hi, how was your day?' he called.

How the hell did he think her day had gone? It was another lonely day with only the cats for company.

'Good thanks,' she said. 'You?'

'It was great actually. Mike's talking about giving me a promotion, so I thought we could celebrate,' he said, holding up a bottle of white wine. 'I've got another surprise too. Close your eyes.'

Megan turned down the heat on the hob and did as he asked. He fastened a necklace around her neck, pausing to kiss her gently. She shivered at his kiss, not knowing whether it was fear or desire. Opening her eyes, she looked down at the pendant, a silver key. Was it some kind of sick joke? Giving her a constant reminder that he now held the key to her life.

'Thanks, it's beautiful,' she said.

They enjoyed a couple of glasses of wine with dinner. Afterwards, she nestled in his arms as they watched a film together. Megan sensed he was tipsy enough to ask him for a little freedom.

'I love you, Chris. Thanks for the necklace. I really like it.'

'My pleasure,' he said, kissing her forehead.

She took his hand and gently stroked it with her thumb. 'We'll need to get some more food if you want me to cook. We could go shopping together this weekend.'

'You know I hate shopping.'

'I don't mind going,' she said.

'Yeah, I guess I could drop you off and pick you up when you're finished.'

'And maybe I could meet up with Jo, like once a week or something? Otherwise she'll know something isn't right.'

'Okay, we can sort something out,' he said, but his attention was focused on the screen.

Megan hoped he would remember that conversation in the morning.

Coffee with her sister, Jo, became one of Megan's permitted activities and he gave her three pounds to cover it, plus the money for a return ticket for the bus. Glancing at her watch, she realised that she still had fifteen minutes until they were due to meet. A few minutes of window shopping would be lovely. On the opposite side of the High Street there was a new shop with an enticing purple façade.

Megan inhaled deeply as she opened the door. The scent of incense was exciting and mysterious. The shop was quaint and bohemian, exactly the type of place she loved. She had hoped to have an inconspicuous browse, but the woman behind the desk had other ideas. She was a larger lady, with a blonde, eighties-style perm, large hoop earrings and a jade stud in her nose.

'Hey there, just take your time looking around and holler if you're curious about anything,' she said in a Canadian accent.

The woman sounded so cheerful. Megan wished she could be such a bubbly and vivacious person as well: the complete opposite of the sensitive recluse she had now become. The shop walls displayed colourful scarves and tie-dyed wall hangings. The shelves held a vast array of crystals, glistening in the light. Their names sounded as beautiful as they looked, lapis lazuli, obsidian and rainbow quartz.

'Do you feel drawn to any?' said the woman walking towards her. 'I'm Rayah, by the way.'

'I like the rainbow quartz, but I'm meant to be window-shopping. I didn't take any extra money out with me today.'

'That's cool. Why not take it as a gift? In return, you can spread the word about the shop.'

'Thanks, that's really kind of you and I'll definitely tell my friends. This shop is just lovely.'

Friends: who was she kidding? Other than Chris and Jo, she hadn't seen another adult for weeks.

Through the bedroom window Megan could see the trees changing. Luscious greens turned to autumn hues of red and gold. Before she knew it, it was December. She was excited to decorate the house for Christmas. It would be the first time they had celebrated together. To her surprise, Chris agreed to take her out to buy a tree and some decorations at the weekend. That evening they enjoyed a Chinese takeaway and snuggled on the sofa, with only fairy lights and candles for illumination. He leaned in and she melted into his kiss. Despite everything, part of her still loved him.

'It's work's Christmas dinner and dance on Friday. I think we should go. It'll give me a chance to convince Mike to give me the promotion,' Chris said as he stroked her arm.

Megan spent all day getting ready. She hated painting her own nails, but there wasn't any chance of Chris letting her out for a manicure. She took her time making sure her make-up was perfect. Applying neutral colours but coupling them with daring mascara to accentuate her eyes and wine lip-gloss. She decided to wear the red maxi dress she had bought for their honeymoon. Pulling her hair into an elegant bun, Megan admired her reflection in the mirror. She looked radiant. Her life had been so pointless lately. Having the opportunity to get dressed up and go out was exciting.

'Wow, you look amazing, Megan. Why don't you wear the necklace I gave you?' Chris said.

Reluctantly, she put it on and they left in a taxi. She had to admit that Chris looked really handsome in the black tuxedo he'd hired. The meal was delicious and the free wine went down very well. After dinner, while Chris talked to Mike, Megan sat at the bar sipping another glass of the bubbly, white wine. She was feeling a bit tipsy, so when a sexy man took the stool beside her, she couldn't help being flirtatious. She crossed her legs, revealing her legs beneath the slit in her dress. He had ditched his bow tie and opened the top buttons on his shirt.

'Which department are you in? I don't remember seeing you before.'

'Oh, I'm just here with my husband,' Megan said, holding up her left hand, so her rings sparkled in the light.

'Well, he's not here now, is he? Drink?'

'Why not? I'll have a Cosmopolitan please.'

Moments later, they were clinking glasses and laughing like old friends, until Chris caught her eye across the room.

'Excuse me, but I'm going to have to whisk my lovely

wife away. Thanks for keeping her company for me,' he said with a wink.

He took Megan's hand and led her towards the door. She felt very light-headed. It had been months since she had that much to drink. In the taxi, Chris was silent, but she could tell by the sinister look in his eyes that he was really angry. Closing the front door of the house, he pushed her against the wall.

'Don't you ever embarrass me like that again! What were you thinking, flirting with Sleazy Ed from forensics? For goodness sake, Megan. He fancies anything in a skirt.'

'I'm sorry, Chris. I'm really sorry. We were just talking. Please don't hurt me.'

'You belong to me. Don't forget that!' Chris said, slamming her head back against the wall. 'I'm not surprised though. You do look really hot tonight.'

Chris ripped her dress and tossed it aside, forcing himself on her.

The following morning, she felt horrendous. The events of the night before were a blur, but the pain told her it hadn't ended well. The back of her head boasted a painful lump, her arms and legs were bruised and it hurt to use the bathroom. Chris arrived home that evening with a large bouquet of flowers.

'I'm sorry. I don't mean to hurt you. You just make me so angry sometimes.'

Lonely, boring days turned into months. Megan curled up on the sofa with the cats and watched the snowdrops and daffodils appear. From the meowing, she could tell they wanted to be free to go outside as much as she did. Without Saturday grocery shopping and Wednesday meetings with Jo, she'd go insane. She missed her classroom and her pupils. She even missed the marking. As long as the house was clean and there was a hot meal on the table, Chris didn't complain. He was spending most evenings at the gym. Since they had only slept together twice in the last couple of months, Megan began to suspect he was seeing someone else. She could smell 'Angel' perfume on his shirt. It was a sickly-sweet scent that she would never wear. Someone's head had been resting on his shoulder. Her body wrapped in his embrace. A quick rummage in his jacket pocket revealed a receipt for a meal for two at the 'Crystal Moon'. How dare he keep her prisoner, while he was out cheating on her, especially in their favourite restaurant! She didn't know whether to scream or cry.

Megan made sure that she had time to visit Rayah that Wednesday. It was amazing to have someone to talk to, especially someone who valued her as herself. She wasn't Chris's wife or anybody's teacher. Rayah was a good listener and such a positive person. When Megan confided that her relationship was difficult, it hadn't come as a surprise. Rayah confessed that she had seen the bruises on her face on the day they met. Megan was relieved that someone else knew her secret.

'It was easier to handle when I thought he loved me and only me, you know?'

'Too right. That's what marriage should be like, but rarely is.'

Rayah liked to dabble in white magic and agreed to try one of her spells to stop Chris's wandering eye.

'Let's go with the Santeria Voodoo spell.'

'Like a voodoo doll, when you stick the pins in? I know exactly where I would stick one,' Megan said with a smile.

'No, it's nothing like that. Did you know that the hummingbird, la chuparosa, mates for life? That's why it's the symbol for love, sex and marriage.'

'I thought that I had mated for life,' Megan said, letting her mind drift back her wedding day.

Rayah wrote Chris and Megan's names on small pieces of paper and placed them under a thick, red candle. Megan gazed at the flame, as Rayah read the spell.

'Divine hummingbird, we ask you to enrich Megan's life

and love, remove all bad luck and misfortune, so that her lover will want only her.'

The following day Megan woke with a queasy feeling and, before she knew it, she was retching over the toilet. Chris had poured her a glass of fresh orange juice that morning. Could he have spiked it with something? Maybe it was something to do with the voodoo spell? Her life seemed to be clouded with suspicion. Whatever had caused it, her stomach was upset for a few days and she began to worry. Chris genuinely seemed concerned too.

'You look terrible,' he said, as he hung up his coat.

'Sorry,' Megan replied. 'I just didn't have the energy for make-up today.'

'I'm not the evil monster you think I am. I meant, do you think you need to see a doctor?'

'If you think I should,' she said, deliberately phrasing it so it seemed like his idea. She had a few bruises on her arms, where he'd grabbed her a little too tightly, but nothing a doctor would be able to pick up on.

'Is there any chance you might be pregnant?'

'Absolutely not,' said Chris, 'she's on the pill.'

'Best to rule that out first, then we can work from there. If you could provide me with a urine sample, Mrs. Taylor?'

Megan was scared that Chris would insist on joining her in the toilet, but he stood outside the door, like a bodyguard. Ironic, since he was the one she needed protecting from. Not only did she have to pee on demand, somehow she had to collect it in the tiny bottle. With the mission accomplished, she opened the door. Surprisingly, Chris offered his hand. He was obviously trying to paint them as the perfect couple.

'Congratulations, Mr. and Mrs. Taylor, the test is positive. As we know, the pill is not a fool proof method of contraception.'

Chris squeezed Megan's hand, as they made their way back to the car. She had no idea how he'd react, but she presumed he would be angry with her. On the contrary, he was smiling.

'This is great, Megan. We're going to be parents and we didn't even need to try. Not that I mind the trying part,' he said, nudging her arm playfully.

He dropped her off at the house with a hug and a kiss. Megan made herself a cup of tea and began contemplating her unexpected news. She wanted children, there was no doubt about that. She just wasn't prepared mentally. She didn't know the first thing about looking after a baby. Besides, it definitely wouldn't be feasible to keep a child locked up in the house.

The twelve-week scan was fascinating. To be honest, Megan struggled to make out a baby shape from the blurred photo of her insides, but she could hear the heartbeat. It was strong and healthy.

'We're looking at a Christmas baby,' the sonographer announced. 'We'll put the due date down as December the sixteenth.'

'I need to tell you something,' Megan said, when she met Jo for coffee a few days later.

'Nothing serious, I hope,' Jo said.

'Jo, I'm pregnant,' Megan said, inadvertently stroking her belly.

Jo got up and embraced her sister, 'Wow, that's amazing news!'

'It is, isn't it? I wanted you to be the first to know. I'll call Mum and Dad later.'

'I'm going to be an aunt. Auntie Jo really has a ring to it. We'd better order some chocolate cake, now you're eating for two.'

Megan made sure she left herself time to visit Rayah's shop before the bus arrived.

'Hey there,' Rayah called. 'Someone's looking full of sunshine today.'

'Kind of. I have good news. I'm pregnant, due in

December. I'm so excited, but I could do without feeling like I'm going to throw up every five minutes.'

'Then you've come to the right place, girl.'

Rayah went through the back to her stockroom and returned with some vials of aromatherapy oils.

'Ginger, lemon and frankincense. It'll be a Christmas baby after all.'

'Thanks, Rayah, that's great. I've never asked. Do you have any children?'

'I can't have kids, but I've got plenty nieces and nephews. That's enough for me.'

'I'd better run or I'll miss the bus. I can't thank you enough.'

'No worries. Off you go, Cinderella. Always rushing away with no time to play.'

Chris was convinced that they were having a boy and talked about how he would carry on the family name and how he would teach him to play football and to stand up for himself.

But what if he was a she? Megan was afraid to find out. With the day of the twenty-week scan looming, she tried to convince him to keep it a surprise. She didn't mind either way: she already loved her baby unconditionally.

'Would you like to know the gender?'

'Yes, please,' Chris said, avidly watching the screen.

'Mrs. Taylor?'

Megan gave a silent nod.

'Well, we can never be certain, but it looks like you're expecting a girl.'

On the car journey home, Chris was silent. As she gazed at the ultrasound picture, Megan was secretly pleased. She would dress her little girl in pink and buy her dolls and ponies. When they reached the house, Chris opened the door for Megan and announced he was going to the pub.

The next morning, it was clear that Chris had slept on the sofa. They didn't talk about the scan. In fact, he didn't mention the baby at all over the next few weeks. On the nights when he didn't go to the pub, he would drink at home. A couple of beers quickly escalated to a couple of bottles of wine.

That Saturday night, his eyes were red and glazed as he staggered into their bedroom.

'Is the kid even mine?'

'Of course, it's yours. How could I have slept with anyone else if I'm only allowed out twice a week?'

'I shouldn't have let you out at all. How long's it been going on, Megan? Who've you been meeting instead of Jo?'

He was standing so close, that she could smell whisky on his breath. Megan put her hands over her bump.

'You disgust me. You're nothing but a filthy whore,' he said, making a fist with his hand.

She ran towards their en-suite bathroom. Chris tried to stop her, but stumbled, so she was able to lock the door before he reached her. Her chest was so tight, it felt impossible to take a proper breath. She sat shivering on the toilet, finding herself contemplating an escape out of the tiny window, no matter how unrealistic that was. When she heard him snoring, she unlocked the door and crept into bed. She cried silent tears. Her little girl kicked inside her, as if to say: *do something, get away while we still can.*

After that night, she began to have terrible nightmares. Chris couldn't cope with the baby crying. He would lift her from the crib and shake her violently until the noise stopped. Sometimes he would leave her in the crib and smother her with a pillow. In one nightmare, he simply tossed her out of the window. Her tiny frame lay in a pool of blood on the patio. It was a risk she couldn't take. She needed to be in a safe place before her little one arrived.

If she was brave enough to tell someone she could easily escape; but she knew Chris would hunt her down and her whole family would be at risk. The man she loved had disappeared, replaced with a narcissistic abuser who was holding her hostage. She had to eradicate him completely.

It could be as simple as keeping a kitchen knife or scissors under her bed and waiting until he was asleep. Then there would be evidence, she would be taken into custody and the baby would be adopted. No happy ending in that scenario. It had to be actioned by someone else.

On Wednesday, she told Jo that she had a doctor's appointment so couldn't meet until the following week. Instead, she used her coffee money in an internet café. It was far too easy. Google led her to the dark web and the website of a mob, where she could post her requirements and various criminals would bid for the job. It was surreal. Megan kept a separate page open, with an advert for pretty pink baby accessories. Whenever she suspected anyone was coming close, she would click on that. She took a moment to set up a new email address under a false name. There was a variety of options including threaten, wound and kill. It was the perfect solution, but her eyes widened when she saw that the price quoted was between five thousand to three hundred thousand dollars. How could she afford that? She was lucky to get her three pounds a week for coffee.

Megan gazed out of her bedroom window at the dazzling display of colour in the sky. She caught sight of her reflection in the mirror behind her. So fat and frumpy that she barely recognised herself. She was exhausted and completely fed up of having to pee every five minutes.

'I love you,' she whispered to her bump.

At that moment, her little girl was safely cocooned inside her and Megan could offer her complete protection. In only a few weeks, though, she would be a separate entity. Megan was running out of time. The fireworks were the catalyst for her master plan. She found herself back in the internet café, ordering Rohypnol from Thailand. A few weeks earlier she had copied the details of Chris's credit card while he was asleep. She loved the notion that he would be paying for his own demise. The package would be delivered to Rayah's shop, although she wouldn't share with her friend what it was or what she had in mind. Everything was falling into place. No-one would suspect an eight-month pregnant lady of any foul play.

Megan lit the candle and poured Chris a glass of red wine. She poured herself a refreshing glass of pineapple juice. He wouldn't even question it, assuming she wasn't drinking because she was pregnant. For starters, she served salami with rocket in a balsamic vinegar dressing. Following the Italian theme, her main course was farfalle pasta in a spicy tomato sauce with garlic bread and dessert would be tiramisu, if they made it that far. In the beginning, there would have been far more erotic reasons for not getting through dinner. Megan closed her eyes and leaned in to kiss her husband for the last time. She watched him intently. Every time he brought his glass to his lips. Each pasta loaded fork seemed to have less chance of reaching its destination.

'Everything okay, Chris? You look a bit off-colour.'

'Just a bit tired,' he replied, slurring his words a little.

Megan enjoyed every mouthful. After that day it wouldn't matter how many pounds she put on. Without warning, Chris slipped off his chair, banging his head on the dresser behind him. It was time. She grabbed the rope from the dresser drawer and quickly bound his arms behind him and his legs together. Megan held a cloth over the head wound. He couldn't die from losing blood. That would be far too easy and painless. She needed to watch him suffer. Covering his body in nail varnish remover and hairspray, she held her breath and lit a match. It only took moments for the flames to take hold. The acrid smell of burning flesh made her gag as she ran to the door.

A very pregnant woman stood beside the red roses which lined the back of her garden. The blue sky, now hidden under a veil of darkness, as the smoke ascended to the sky. Windows shattered and amber flames appeared engulfing every inch of the building. Crackling, followed by an explosion, which forced Megan to back away further.

The intensity of the heat became unbearable. It only took a few minutes for their home to be reduced to a pile of smouldering wood, rubble and ashes. The sound of sirens was her cue to leave. To get away from that prison. To finally be free.

THE END

ABOUT THE AUTHOR

Fiona Campbell is a writer, who is studying for an MA in Creative Writing. She is taking a sabbatical from teaching music to care for her three children. Fiona also enjoys writing poetry and is currently working on her first novel.

Fiona blogs at: fimariecampbell.wordpress.com

The Five Votive Candles of Joe Wray
by Simon Bewick

Joe Wray pushed the heavy bronze door open, swapping the Park Avenue heat out on 51st St for the cool air of the church. He mopped at the sweat on his brow and stepped over to the old woman at the desk. He refused change from the $100 bill he passed over. The woman took the money and handed over the two long-stemmed matchsticks he'd asked for, and Joe walked through to the imposing nave. He hadn't been religious in his forty-seven years but thought that was the term. He'd only been here once before—Christmas eight years ago when the four of them had stopped in spontaneously, or so he'd thought at the time, as they headed back to Grand Central Station.

That had been the night that made him come to St Bart's today.

As he walked down the aisle, his footsteps slapping against the stone, he saw two young men praying. At least what he considered young these days—they were probably somewhere in their mid-twenties. Neither raised their heads as he passed.

Joe walked slowly forward to the small, open-doored vestry left of the altar. He entered the room and sat stiffly. The display in front of him was old and rusted—a five-level table, ten candles in small glass jars spaced across each level. Around three quarters were lit, the smell of burning wax wafting on the air.

The sign above the display read, "Our lighted candles are a sign of the divine splendor of the One who comes to expel the dark shadows of evil and to make the whole universe radiant with the brilliance of His eternal light. Our candles also show how bright our souls should be when we go to meet Christ."

Underneath, a small typed note read, "$1 per candle, please pay at reception."

Joe sat for a moment rereading the words, wondering what right he had to be doing this.

He considered the $100 he had handed over for $2 worth of soul brightening—and thought that he had underpaid. He tossed the church matches into the tray below the display and took the small green book from his trouser pocket. He lit one of the ten or so matches left in it and held it to a candle on the third from bottom row.

"For Bobby," he whispered. Pretty boy Bobby. Three years his junior, a cocky grin and the mile-a-minute mouth.

When the small candle had started to burn, he blew out the match and took another one from the packet, igniting it from the burning flame, and holding it against the wick on the candle next to it.

"For Ellie," he breathed softly. Beautiful, funny Ellie, with the most infectious laugh ever.

As the two candles began to burn in earnest the memories flooded through him. Memories of the good and the bad times they'd had together—of how much he and Judith had loved them.

Judith.

He tried to focus on Judith, instead of the bad times and the trouble Bobby had brought them towards the end. He thought of Judith. Of Jacob. Of Thomas. And, although not a religious man, prayed for their safety.

But mostly he thought about Bobby and Ellie. And their murder.

It had been a cold December morning when the call came through to the small Maywood, New Jersey one room office they'd been in for almost two months, the tiny printing area below them presently silent. Joe had answered, still enjoying the autonomy of being able to announce to any caller that they had reached "Wrays' Print and Design Studio: Providers of Corporate Communications"—an exaggerated description for their offering, but it was what they aspired to. He had talked the caller through their services and agreed to send a range of pdf samples on. It was only when he'd put the phone down and Bobby asked him what the caller had been looking for that Joe realized he hadn't thought to ask.

"I'll write you a script," Bobby had laughed as they shared takeaway pizza at his desk half an hour later, "like I used to for my more retarded new starters back at AT&T." Joe had tossed a pizza crust at him, but when the caller rang back the following day he'd told him to hold while he transferred him to 'Wray and Wray's Head of Sales', passing the phone to Bobby who mouthed *'Sales President'* before taking the phone from him and going into his full-on sales mode. By the time he put the phone down with a final, "Look forward to seeing you then, Mr. Leonard," they had an invite to lunch two days later.

"So, who are they? What do they do?" Joe asked, putting

a mug of coffee down in front of his brother.

"They're called *Marshalls*. They're a joke," Bobby said nonchalantly.

"A... joke?" Joe asked.

"Yeah, they're a Joke Company," Bobby expanded. "Seriously."

"Shit," Joe said.

Bobby laughed. "No. *Seriously*, they're a Joke Company. You know? Itching powder, whoopee cushions, fake noses, masks, outfits, all that shit."

"An honest-to-God Joke Company?" Joe asked. "Do they even exist anymore? Like the old place out by the summer house?"

"Yeah, *Ray's Jokes and Smokes*."

Joe smiled, remembering the vacations they'd taken with their parents; long days of him and Bobby making up adventures and occasionally getting into trouble. "I'm pretty sure we were the only ones who bought the jokes," he said. "It was the smokes that kept that place going..."

Bobby shook his head. "Not according to this guy." He brought his PC back to life and typed briefly. "You know how much the joke industry is worth?"

Joe shrugged, and took a wild guess. "$50 million nationwide?"

Bobby looked up from the screen. "According to this Retail and Trade report, the sales value of gift, novelty and souvenir stores in the US is $15 billion, estimated to rise to 17 by 2008."

"*Billion?*" Joe asked incredulously.

"Billion," Bobby repeated. "See Joe: some people, unlike you, like to have fun."

Joe ignored the jibe. "And these guys are worth how much?"

"*Marshalls* are apparently the fifth biggest players on the East Coast according to the guy on the phone. I have no idea how much that equates to... yet. But it doesn't sound like chicken feed."

"No shit," Joe whispered.

Bobby smiled. "A lot of shit, all of it plastic—like one of those curled up specials we used to put on Dad's chair."

They taxied from Penn Station to the restaurant. Bobby matched the fare with his tip. Joe said nothing, hoping he was getting his 'game face' on and not just being 'flamboyant Bobby'.

Joe was in the dark blue Calvin Klein suit he'd last worn for their recent bank loan interviews. Bobby was in a charcoal Dolce & Gabbana number which Joe suspected he'd bought for the occasion. The taxi dropped them outside the small Italian restaurant in Greenwich Village. They arrived ten minutes early and Bobby nodded to a bar a block down.

Once inside the bar, Bobby ordered two Grey Goose vodkas, handing one to Joe, ignoring his protest.

"Act like we've already got this," Bobby said, and seeing his brother's look, smiled. "Don't worry. Just one for courage... You look as if you need it."

Joe couldn't argue. They downed the drinks in one; Joe shuddered slightly as it went down, Bobby did not. Slamming the empty glass on the table and waving a hand in apology at the barman who looked over at the sudden noise, he stood, and said with a smile, "OK, let's doooo this."

The elderly man working front-of-house guided them through to a table at the back of the restaurant where three men sat laughing. When they saw Joe and Bobby the three stood and offered handshakes.

"Don't worry—no hand buzzers. We take funny seriously. I'm Peter Leonard. This is Jerry, and Terry," the stocky, shiny pated man said, gesturing them to sit. "Another round of Martinis, Larry, and the same for our friends here."

"Terrence," the young black man said to Joe as they shook hands. "But Peter thinks Terry is funnier."

Peter Leonard slapped him on the back. "Don't you go

whining back to HR, *Terry*, I'm one step away from the pink slip, and you know they'll call racism."

The three men from *Marshalls* laughed at whatever this in-joke meant, and Joe guessed the pre-lunch vodkas were not going to be noticed.

Peter Leonard, who it turned out was the man who had called them and was clearly the boss, was not technically bald: he had ginger red hair, long at the back and sides. It could, Joe thought as he finished his Martini, be a clown hair gag.

The food that followed was off-menu. Leonard told them to trust him and they'd enjoy the meal. They did both. Clams followed by homemade pepperonis, carpaccio, and large platters of seafood and steaks. Throughout it, they talked: family, the World Series, and some banter about the recent Heavyweight title fight at the Garden where Leonard had won money and his work colleagues had lost. Peter and Bobby were responsible for about ninety percent of the talk. It wasn't until the biscotti and coffees arrived that the talk finally turned to business.

"We liked what we saw on your website," Leonard said, lighting up a cigar: apparently not a problem despite New York's eating laws as Joe understood them. "You guys do good work."

"We've had no complaints," Bobby smiled, his face slightly flushed from the Barolo. "A lot of satisfied customers."

Leonard smiled back. "You've got three customers, all paying next to nothing. You've probably got a king-sized loan, and you're working out of a little room in the backwoods of New Jersey..."

Bobby coughed slightly. "Well..."

"Relax," Leonard continued. "I'm teasing. You're new in business. We'd be pretty stupid if we didn't do some checking, wouldn't we?"

Bobby wagged a finger at him, his confident smile reappearing. "You got us. We're new. But we're good— Joe here was the most respected printer at *Ottermans'*

Publishing..."

Leonard cut him off. "*Relax*, I said. Don't try to sell yourself to us so much." He gestured to the empty plates. "It's like good food—let it speak for itself."

The waiter brought over glasses of Amaretto: "Compliments of the house."

As he moved off Peter Leonard continued, "We want a business who can give us attention. To ensure we are a... preferred customer."

Bobby nodded. "I can guarantee that our custome—"

Leonard raised his hand a millimeter. "When I say, 'preferred customer', I mean... *favored*, if you will. And of course," he turned his hands over, palms up, "We would provide appropriate recompense to a supplier we worked so closely with..."

Bobby glanced at Joe and then to the other men at the table. "Are we talking exclusivity?"

Leonard looked to Terry / Terrence, who had barely spoken during the meal but now spoke, "No. Not exclusivity. As long as there was no...conflict of interest."

"We'd sign NDAs," Bobby said quickly.

"We'd take *that* as given," Leonard said, "We'd *expect* you to drop everything... should the need arise."

Bobby swallowed and looked at Joe, momentarily stuck for words.

Joe, who had drunk less than Bobby throughout the meal, wiped at his mouth with his napkin. "We appreciate the offer Mr. Leonard, and of course, would very much like to work with you..." As the men around the table nodded, he continued, "...however. The fact is we are, as you say, new in business. Part of the reason we decided to leave our previous roles was because we wanted some independence. The idea of working exclusively for you..." he saw Leonard about to speak, and corrected himself, "*almost* exclusively for you, would run the risk that we end up working for a company the way we always have..."

Leonard considered this, puffing on his cigar. "I

understand. I'll say two things and then you can decide. Firstly, I guarantee that working *with* us will not be like working for your previous employers. And you would be working *with* us, not *for* us. How you come and go? How you work? As long as you can provide us the service we need, we don't care. Now, we're likely to have a lot of work—which is good for you. We won't have unreasonable expectations, but you will be busy. Maybe you won't have time to take on other work...or maybe you will. How you manage that is up to you. We just expect discretion, integrity..." he smiled, "...and everything we want. Fair?"

The men around him laughed at the bon mot and Bobby cut in, "That sounds more than fair Mr. Leonard."

Joe glanced at his brother, and then looked back to Leonard. "And the second thing?"

Peter Leonard nodded and handed an envelope towards Joe. "The second thing is our offer. I suggest you gentlemen review it, and we will get back to you tomorrow."

With that Leonard, followed immediately by the two men at his side, stood from the table and dropped his napkin on his crumb spattered plate.

"Gentlemen, it was a pleasure to meet you..."

"Please," Bobby said, holding out his hand to shake. "Let me take care of the check."

Leonard shook the proffered hand and gave a crooked little smile. "There's no check to take care of." He shook Joe's hand. A firm, dry shake, placing his other hand over Joe's. The two other men from Marshalls didn't shake hands but both smiled, and the three of them left the restaurant. From presenting the envelope to exiting the door took them less than three minutes.

As the two candles burned down, both now a quarter gone, Joe Wray wondered what would have happened if he hadn't spoken up on that day.

Would they have been offered the deal?

Would they have ended up working with Marshalls for a

shade under eight years?

But mostly he wondered if he hadn't spoken up that day would his brother and sister-in-law have been alive to celebrate Labor Day this weekend with them?

Joe and Bobby left the restaurant with the envelope unopened. Snow had started to sprinkle during the two hours they'd been inside. Neither of them had spoken since their lunch guests had departed. Finally, Bobby broke the silence. "What time's the train?"

"Every half hour," Joe replied.

Bobby blew cold air out through pursed lips. "So, we've got time before we need to head to the station."

Joe shrugged. "It would appear so."

"You want to open this now?" Bobby asked.

"And I'm sure you want to find a coffee shop to do it?" Joe asked innocently.

Bobby was already heading back to the pre-restaurant bar.

Joe looked at the two large glasses of whisky on the table in front of him. Bobby shrugged. "We're either celebrating or commiserating. Either way we're halfway in the bag already..."

Joe resisted the urge to protest that he had barely opened any bag yet, instead clinking Bobby's proffered glass. "Who's going to open it?"

"You should," Bobby said. "You're better with numbers."

"You're expecting *that* many zeroes?" Joe laughed, but his hand was shaking as he took the envelope, and it wasn't from the cold. Or the drink.

"It's won't be anything special," Bobby said. "This is theatrics—the old 'take what's in the mystery box' routine..." He paused. "Joe? What does it say?"

Joe continued reading for a moment before he handed it over silently.

Bobby took the letter and looked at it nonchalantly for a

full half second before he muttered, "Jesus Christ."

They didn't get the train home.

Two drinks later they ordered a taxi, or the bar ordered a taxi, or...a taxi arrived somehow. The driver gave them a suspicious look when they told him where they wanted to go, but when Bobby fanned out the money from his wallet (Joe guessed lunch money to avoid possible embarrassment of having their anorexic business card refused), he shrugged acceptance.

As they left Manhattan Bobby phoned Ellie. She asked him exactly how much he'd had to drink as he burst into giggles, but she was giggling too when Joe took the phone from his brother to speak to her. Joe, who had surreptitiously poured his final tumbler of whiskey into the pot plant behind him in the bar, assured Ellie that things were okay, and she should meet them at his and Judith's and they would see them within the hour. She made him promise he'd get her husband home safely and blew a kiss down the line. He hung up and dialed Judy to warn her of Ellie's imminent arrival and their ETA, assuming they didn't need to stop for Bobby to throw up (the driver gave him a dirty look in his rear-view mirror). Judith asked him how it had gone, but he told her she'd have to wait, and that they'd see them soon. She reminded him that she loved him slightly less when he kept things from her, and he laughed, telling her he loved her no matter what. He clicked off as she started to blow a raspberry down the line.

Joe had always been the careful one. So, on the taxi drive back to New Jersey, he asked the question he hadn't wanted to ask because it might bring the whole thing tumbling down.

"Bobby. What *exactly* is it that *Marshalls* want us to do for them?"

"You heard them, bro: business cards, flyers, brochures."

Joe sighed. "You've never called me 'bro' in your life Bobby. You've also never been stupid. You've been 'sometimes right, sometimes wrong, but always certain'... But you've never been stupid, so don't start now."

"Remind me never to put you down as a reference," Bobby said. "What's your point 'oh brother of mine'?"

"Business cards, flyers, brochures...catalogues, point of sale, letter heads, all of that. It still doesn't add up to..." He took the paper from Bobby's hands. "*This*."

"It's just to get started," Bobby said. "To get us on board. Tie us in."

"Bobby—you've got the MBA not me, but don't companies normally start low and reward suppliers once they've proved themselves, not before they've done anything?" He paused. "Remember what Dad used to say?"

"You don't get paid to believe in the power of your dreams?"

"Not that one," Joe said, smiling despite himself.

"He really was a minefield of misery, wasn't he?"

"I was thinking when he used to say: 'If it seems too good to be true, it probably is'."

Bobby grinned. "You know something? I don't think he made that one up... When he wasn't being pessimistic or critical, he was stealing trite lines... Look, can we just live in the moment tonight? Let's assume they've recognized your good workmanship and, I say with no false modesty, my pretty brilliant selling techniques. *That's* what they're ponying up for. Can we have tonight?"

Joe sat silently looking out the window, as the snow fell harder. Finally, he sighed. "Did you really just say *pony up*?"

They'd started the second bottle of champagne before Judith raised the question. Bobby had insisted on stopping at a liquor store to pick up two bottles of Dom Perignon. They made it up the pathway without slipping, and into the house to find Ellie with a gin and tonic and Judith—Joe guessed—a plain tonic, both apparently calming their own nerves.

By the second bottle, Bobby had slipped back to his pre-taxi level of intoxication, and Joe was catching up. Ellie had never needed much to drink to sparkle in all the time Joe and Judith had known her, but with the champagne and G&Ts, she was almost spinning. So it was Judith, patting her swollen belly and refusing yet another offer from Bobby of 'just a taste', who asked the question.

"Is this above board?"

Joe put his hand as far around Judith's waist as he could manage with four months to go. "Marshalls are real enough. This isn't some sort of wise guy set up."

She shook her head bemusedly. "You think you know what a wise guy looks like?"

"Not like a drunken Irish Pirate," Bobby slurred, and Joe burst out laughing at how well his brother had summed up Peter Leonard.

Joe woke late the next morning, with a mouth like a hamster's cage. Judith had cooked him breakfast, but he did little more than push it around the plate.

"Mr. Gekko not hungry after his Wall Street success?" she asked.

Joe shook his head as gently as he could. "Breakfast is for wimps..."

She laughed and brought her cup of coffee to the kitchen table. "So how big a deal is this?"

Joe shrugged. "In the horrible cold light of day, it's not *that* big a deal."

"It seemed a lot last night...."

"Don't get me wrong," Joe said. "It's great for us. But *Ottermans* wouldn't throw a worker's holiday for it..."

"*Ottermans* wouldn't give a worker's holiday if they knew the world was going to end. And they had an annual turnover of how much?"

"$65 million last year," Joe conceded of his old company.

"And your projected turnover for this month before this was?"

He calculated: "The Manheim's' Bar Mitzvah

decorations.... the Lambert corner store catalogue, possibly as much as $250. But that's post-tax."

She sighed. "I really married big time, didn't I?"

He smiled. "If you believe Bobby, we'll be rolling in four-leaf clovers..."

"Not if he keeps buying suits like he was wearing last night," Judith said, her eyebrow raised.

"You noticed that?"

She nodded. "Even rumpled and whisky reeking it was a nice suit."

"You know Bobby..."

"Oh honey, I do indeed."

"Well, it certainly puts us on more solid ground," Joe said, steering away from the well-trodden path of Bobby's flamboyance. "Assuming we can produce to the quality they're expecting."

Judith kissed him on the forehead. "I may have concerns about 'Big Balls' Bobby..."

"*May* have?" Joe asked.

"...But," she continued, "I've never doubted you. You did the right thing getting away from *Ottermans* hun, and you know you've got my full support. All I'm saying is be careful."

"Careful is my middle name," he smiled.

"Yes," she agreed, "but Bobby was christened Robert 'Bullshit' Wray."

The documents were signed without amendments. They'd met at Marshalls' office: a Brownstone building just off Canal Street. Peter Leonard had met and ushered them into an expensive looking room on the first floor. He told them to sit tight as he went to get 'Scott the Lawyer'.

Alone, Bobby looked around the room. "Ease your mind any?"

"What do you mean?" Joe asked.

Bobby smiled. "I've seen you the last few days, bro."

"Again, with the 'bro'," Joe sighed. "It's called being

careful, Bobby. You could try it one day."

An hour later they'd signed. Leonard cracked a joke about invisible ink—not, Joe guessed, for the first time. Signed, sealed and delivered, they stepped cautiously down the gritted steps outside.

Bobby checked his watch. "Two hours before we meet the ladies. Time for a quick celebratory drink? A 'careful', 'sensible' drink? I promise I won't put laxative powder in yours."

It was ten to eight that evening, snow coming down hard on Park Lane when Judith, hanging on to Joe's arm after almost losing her balance three blocks back, stopped them outside the middle doorway of St. Bart's Church.

"Let's go in," she said. "I've walked past here a hundred times, and never been inside."

"The bar's next door, Judy," Bobby laughed behind them, three cocktails in and his own arm around Ellie, resting on her behind rather than for support.

Ellie swatted at him playfully. "We're not all alcoholics, hun."

Judith didn't move. "I'm serious. Let's go in."

Joe looked at her. "Really?"

"Since when did you get so godly, Jude?" Bobby asked.

She turned. "Screw you, Bobby Wray. How's that for godly? I just think it would be...nice."

She dragged Joe's arm and he acquiesced, laughing. Ellie bounced behind them, Bobby trailed behind a little begrudgingly, glaring at Ellie as she waved the Christmas hat a group of drunken businessmen had given her in the last bar. They'd begged her to model it for them as she bought drinks; she'd taken the hat and playfully given them the finger as she returned to their table, giving Bobby a lingering kiss.

Inside, the church was silent save for the faint sound of the organ gently playing carol music—not fully formed; apparently last-minute practice before the Christmas onslaught.

Judith shook her hood off, snow falling around her. Joe said nothing as he watched her, as struck as he was every time he looked at his wife, even after all the years they'd been together. She was no longer the seventeen-year-old he'd plucked up the courage to ask out in his first year at college—the most beautiful girl he'd ever seen, it was true. Now? She was more beautiful—everything they'd done, all the time they'd had together, showed in her and added to her allure. Looking at her, his heart almost hurt, his attention so all-encompassing he barely heard Bobby and Ellie giggling somewhere behind them.

Judith stared up at the enormous bright blue circle of stained glass above the old organ, and as he stared at her, at the light playing about her face, she whispered, "It's beautiful."

"That's what the Nazi in *Raiders* said just before his face melted off," Bobby giggled, appearing from nowhere and making them both jump. "Come on, next door is waiting... and *they* have drinks."

"You go on," Joe said, "We'll be there in a bit."

"Holy shit," Bobby laughed. Ellie slapped him, telling him to remember where he was, and he muttered, *"Jesus, I'm surrounded by religious freaks."*

"We'll see you next door," Ellie said, dragging Bobby firmly by the arm. "You want me to get you guys drinks?"

"Sure, "Joe said, not turning. "A beer for me, soda and lime for m'lady."

When they'd gone, their giggles somehow growing louder the further away they got, Joe touched Judith's shoulder. "You okay, honey?"

She placed her hand on his. "It's so peaceful. This place— it's..." She searched for the words, failed, and repeated, "... so very peaceful."

Joe moved away from her, walking down the aisle to get a closer look at the window. He glanced over to his left, peripherally noticing movement and saw a small room with candles burning dimly; the flickering dancing shadows on the stone wall behind them.

"Judy," he said, his voice carrying easily in the silence. She broke her gaze from the window and went to him, looking into the small vestibule.

"Should we light one?" he asked.

She looked at him, saw he wasn't mocking her. "Are we allowed to?"

"Why not?" Joe asked. "There's enough already lit, and no-one to stop us."

"Isn't it...blasphemous? We're not exactly the most religious couple on the block..."

"Do you need to be religious to make a Christmas wish?" he asked.

She laughed. "I don't think it's referred to as a *'wish'*, honey."

He chuckled and took out the packet of matches he'd snagged from the last bar they'd been in. He lit a match, letting the flame catch and burn for a second before touching it to one of the unlit candles' wick until he felt the heat touching his fingers, waved it out and dropped it in the tray beneath.

"So, if we don't wish... What?" he asked.

"Maybe offer thanks for what we've got?" she suggested. "Say a prayer that this," she gestured to the bump, "and everything else..." He nodded, not needing her to finish the sentence.

She looked at him, and brushed a hair out of his eyes. "I will make one wish, though. Not to..." she jerked her head up, "...him. To you." She took his hands, looked into his eyes, and he had a brief flashback to their last time in church.

"You made vows back then," she said, as though reading his mind, and recited, "*I can promise that I'll willingly be your protector, your advisor, your councilor, your friend, your family, your everything. I promise you.*"

"You...remember all that?" he asked.

She shrugged, "I may have found it online afterwards... 'original vow' my ass..."

"Busted." He smiled.

"But I remembered the important stuff anyway…" she said. "Do you still mean it? Will you always be those things?"

He didn't smile, didn't laugh. He squeezed her hands a little more and looked into her beautiful blue eyes and choked back emotion. "I'll always be those things. And I promise I will *always* make sure you and 'thingy' there are safe."

When he said it, he thought it would be true.

The work from *Marshalls* was steady and if not challenging in design or execution, demanding in volume. *Marshalls* was an unusual business model: providing promotional collateral as well as the materials themselves to their sellers. Work came in and they churned it out. It was Joe who produced the actual work, as Judith occasionally pointed out when he came home late again. On those occasions Joe explained that, while Bobby's design skills didn't stretch beyond sketching vague ideas on lunch napkins, he was the one looking into online and offline opportunities that *Marshalls* had not previously explored. When Judith asked why *Marshalls* didn't have a Marketing Department to do all that, Joe didn't have a ready answer.

Jacob Wray arrived into the world on February 19th. Joe and Bobby had been in the office when the call came from Ellie. Joe had panicked; Judith was only seven months gone, and despite all the reading he'd done his mind went blank as to whether a baby could even survive at that age.

Bobby became an iceman—reassuring him all the way to Maywood hospital where Ellie had driven Judith, not waiting for the medics when her waters had broken as they shopped for nursery designs. By the time the brothers arrived, Judith was already in surgery and about to undergo an emergency C-section because the placenta was separating. As the doctor on duty told Joe, somewhat ominously he thought later, "Babies don't have a lot of blood they can afford to lose."

The following hour and a half were the longest of Joe's life as he sat in the hospital waiting room; Bobby talking nonstop, and Ellie bringing a constant supply of shitty coffee, both of them doing their best to keep his mind from where it kept going:

Had he failed in his promise so soon?

When the impossibly young doctor finally came back and told the three of them mother and baby were doing fine, and he could see them, amongst the hugging and crying and laughing as Bobby and Ella squeezed him, any doubt evaporated, the steeliness his father had always said he had springing into its place: *They're both okay. Now man up and keep your goddamn promises.*

"Where's our baby?" he asked, putting the question somewhere between his wife and the doctor when he saw Judith lying pale, sweaty, and alone.

"Mr. Wray," the doctor said. "Your son has been born prematurely. When that happens we..."

"*Where's our baby?*" he repeated, his words iron-hard.

Judith smiled; tired and without her usual twinkle. "They've had to take him to the NICU Joe, because he was so small..."

"NICU?" Joe asked.

"The Neonatal Intensive Care Unit, Mr. Wray," the doctor said. "It's perfectly normal when a baby is born so early..."

"Normal?" Joe said. "How can..."

"Love of my life?" Judith said, and he turned to her. "Listen to the doctor...and yes, that's a nice way of me saying shut up."

Joe turned numbly to the doctor.

"Mr. Wray, we ran an Apgar test..."

"A..."

"Apgar," the doctor said, without waiting for the question. "Stands for *Appearance, Pulse, Grimace, Activity, and Respiration*. It's an assessment of how a baby is doing at birth. The score can be anywhere from 1 to 10. A score of 7 or above is considered normal. Your son scored a 7 and weighed 3 pounds and 8 ounces. That doesn't sound a lot, but believe me, it's a perfectly reasonable weight under the circumstances."

"You hear that, honey?" Judith asked from her bed, taking his hand. "He's going to be okay."

"He's going to be okay?" Joe asked dully.

"He's going to be okay," Judith confirmed, laughing.

Joe Wray started to cry.

Over an hour later, two orderlies wheeled Judith's bed to the NICU, Joe holding her hand as they trundled down the corridor. The visit was brief—little more than reassurance for them. Another couple of hours, once the catheter was out, they told them, and they'd have her in a wheelchair and they could hold him for as long as they wanted. Joe said he'd stay, and Judith barked a laugh. "You'll not. What you'll do is go home and get my stuff. I'm going to be here a while and I look like crap..."

"You've never looked more beau..."

"Uh-huh, save it honey. I know what I look like. Go get my baby bag. It's in the walk-in. Good job I'm obsessively organized, huh?"

He kissed her: not hard or long, but with passion. "I'll bring flowers..." he said, starting to leave.

"Joe?" she said.

He looked back at her. "Something else you need, hun?"

"Could you pick up a candle...", she paused, a slight blush rising in her pale cheek. "Will you...?"

He nodded. "I will."

After an update and hugs (stiff from Bobby, happy-sobbing from Ellie), Joe left the hospital, picking up a pack of utility candles from the Korean 24-hour store closest to their home. In the house, he searched through the grab bowl on the end of the kitchen table, rummaging through knickknacks until he found the green packet of matches. He found a small metal cake tin, lit the candle and held it at an angle, dripping hot wax onto the tin before blowing out the candle and standing it in the molten mess, holding it in place until it hardened. Then he lit it again; the thin hollow flame dancing before settling into a steady glow.

Joe Wray sat back, his field of vision winnowing in on the flame until the small candle burned out.

Jacob spent a month in the NICU, and Joe was there for much of it. He worried how *Marshalls* would perceive it, right until the bouquet of flowers had arrived for Judith with a simple note that said, '*From your friends at Marshalls*'. He had been relieved and touched, and any lingering doubts Judith held had been snuffed out like a... candle.

If he had been a man more given to poetry, Joe may have drawn an analogy between Jacob's development in the NICU and his brother's growth. Handed a challenge he could not shirk, Bobby appeared to have more than stood up to bat. When Joe returned to work the office looked professional: tidied, squared off and freshly painted. But it was under the surface that Bobby appeared to have spent most of his time—swelling with pride as he showed Joe the detailed minutes and memos he'd made from his meetings with *Marshalls*.

"Jesus, Bobby," Joe laughed. "Have you been camped out in their offices the whole time? It's almost as if...I don't know...they *like* you."

Bobby grinned. "What can I say, bro? I've got the charm to disarm..."

Joe, leafing through upcoming projects murmured on auto-pilot: "Don't call me bro."

He looked at Bobby. "We'd better start making some of this stuff, huh?"

Marshalls' Fiscal Year ended March 31st. The invite for the end-of-year celebration dinner at their offices on May 17th arrived an exact month before. Looking at the gilt-edged invite Bobby whistled. "Ellie and Judith invited too. And they know their names."

Joe nodded, equally impressed—Judith had always been 'Julie' or 'Gillian' to his boss at *Ottermans*. For *Marshalls* to know their suppliers' wives' names was impressive.

Bobby smiled. "*We* could have done a better job on the invite though..."

The evening of the dinner, Bobby arranged a limousine to pick them up. Judith was giving final instructions to her mother, who was in turn shooing her and Joe into the arriving car, reminding them she'd brought up three children of her own without killing any of them. Ellie commented once the door had safely closed that she *had* seemed to have dropped Bobby on his head a few times. Judith laughed... slightly nervously.

"How much did you spend on this thing?" Joe asked, as their champagne glasses clinked in a toast—Joe was not sure whether it was for the business, or the normality of an evening out.

Bobby pulled a face to the women. "My big brother. Mr. Careful. Even when he's celebrating..."

Joe joined the laughter and, Judith's hand on his arm, promised them all he'd enjoy the evening.

Marshalls put on a good show—not overly ostentatious or crowded—Joe counted maybe 90 people in total—30 or 40 staff, most with partners. At their table there was just themselves and two other couples not directly employed by the company: one middle-aged guy from the Delivery Services company with his wife, and an independent lawyer and his husband.

As the meal reached its conclusion, Peter Leonard introduced *Marshalls'* CEO. A thin, elderly man with a dapper bow-tie took to the make-shift stage to genuine applause and proceeded to give a short speech expressing appreciation for everyone in the room. As he concluded he said, "My father told me the joke business is no laughing matter..." There was a light smattering of laughter and Ellie whispered, "How many times do you think that one's been rolled out?"

The old man went on, "...you're all too kind. We made a profit again this year: up 3% on last year. But times *are* tough—we're the fifth biggest supplier on the East Coast. We're some way behind the big three, but you know what? That's fine. We avoid limelight we might not want..."

A smattering of laughter, and a few claps. Joe looked at Bobby enquiringly, and Bobby gave a nod, as if to say: '*I'll tell you later.*'

"...So, thank you all. I'm going to sit back down now—and I swear if Peter's put another whoopee cushion on my seat he's fired..."

He sat down, and the room applauded warmly.

Peter Leonard stood up again. "I haven't actually put a cushion on that chair for five years now...but whatever excuse you need...*Lionel.*" The old man laughed and slapped at him playfully. "...Enjoy the rest of the evening. The band will be starting once dessert is cleared."

"Lionel Leonard?" Joe said to Bobby as the room stood to applaud Peter, his father, and each other. "That's some moniker. And he's Peter's father? So, Peter's second-in-command? Did you know any of that?"

Bobby shrugged. "Sure. I thought you did. I guess it came up when I was here for meetings. I've met the old man a few times...That limelight business? The owner of *Baskeys* got caught up in some hooker ring thing. Didn't make particularly big news with the general public, but I guess it's a bit of an in-joke in this business. Maybe it's best not to be number one, huh?"

The beefy man in the suspenders to the left of Bobby had been listening. "Yeah, the guy was a bit of a clown, if you'll excuse the expression—it all tends to get very punny. You guys must be the Wray brothers? The new blood?"

Joe acknowledged they were.

"Thought so," the man said. "I've seen your names on a few documents. I'm David Hudson: the Independent Legal for Baldwins. For when they don't want their names on things…"

Judith, sitting next to him took the offered brandy from the passing waiter. "So what exactly do you do for the company, Mr. Hudson?"

The lawyer's chins wobbled. "This and that. Is that suitably vague and mysterious? I wish it was. Add a little excitement, huh darling?" he asked his partner, who nodded distractedly, returning to whatever he was doing on his phone.

"It pays for the summer home," the man sighed.

"You have a summer home?" Ellie asked looking up from her Tiramisu, suddenly interested in David Hudson.

"Flirt an invitation with him," Bobby whispered to her, "and I'll be seriously impress…ouch!" as she dug him in the ribs.

"We sure do," Hudson said. "We've had a place in Montauk for a few years now; gets us out of the city once in a while, you know?"

By midnight, Joe and Judith, used to being on 'take sleep when you can get it' time in recent months, were flagging badly. Bobby and Ellie on the other hand were apparently just getting into the swing of things and hadn't been off the dance floor for twenty minutes.

Eventually they managed to drag Bobby and Ellie away by one o'clock and all four of them were asleep in the back of the limousine before they'd got out of Manhattan.

By the end of their first full year working with *Marshalls* (Bobby persisted on correcting Joe when he occasionally made the mistake of saying they worked *for* them), they'd settled into a comfortable if unremarkable routine—both at work and at home.

They spent Christmas together at Bobby and Ellie's,

and the New Year at Joe and Judith's. The same routine as they had for each of the five years since Bobby and Ellie had been together, as Judith pointed out over post-lunch liqueurs, snuggling with Jacob and Joe on their sofa; Bobby massaging Ellie's feet as she struggled to stay awake on the sofa opposite.

Five years since Bobby introduced them to Ellie; the stunning dark-haired girl four years—and six inches—his junior. They had met sitting in a bar, both of them having ditched blind dates. Bobby had called it fate, and while Joe didn't know about *that*, he *did* know Ellie was the best thing to ever happen to his brother—calming his excesses, but with an untamable enthusiasm for everything they did. Bobby had fallen in love with her immediately. It had taken himself and Judith less than a month to do the same despite Judith's initial misgivings; "She's too beautiful to be that nice. There's *got* to be something wrong with her."

"*You're* beautiful and nice," Joe had reasoned.

Judith had laughed. "You've got to say that. Hell hun, you've had to say it for fifteen years..."

And their love seemed to be reciprocated: at their wedding three years ago, Ellie made Judith her maid of honor and Joe was Bobby's best man. The honeymoon fortnight Bobby and Ellie spent in Jamaica was the longest the four had spent apart since.

Jesters filed for bankruptcy in February. Joe read the news in the *NY Times* and passed it over to Bobby as they worked on the Easter push campaign.

Bobby read aloud, "...tough times...online purchases...traditional celebrating dying...blah, blah, blah." He jabbed the paper. "Maybe *you're* just a shitty businessman?"

Joe was more pessimistic. "*Jesters* have been around forever. It doesn't bode well for the rest of the industry..."

Bobby disagreed. "They diversified too much with no strategy—not like us. *Porter's Five Forces*, bro. Business studies 101."

"I understood two bits of that," Joe said. "One was you still calling me bro. The other was you're saying, *'us'* now."

Bobby threw the paper at him, the pages fluttering to the ground. "Your fault. *Bro*. You've got me doing it. But seriously, how much are we earning from the other accounts? If we lost them all, we'd not even notice."

Joe nodded. "That's my point—what happens if we lose *Marshalls*?"

Bobby pshawwed. "We're not going to lose them."

"And if they do a *Jesters*?" Joe asked.

Bobby rolled his eyes. "Jesus. Look, if it'll make you feel better, I'll drop it into the conversation with Pete tonight—see what he thinks, Ok?"

"Tonight?" Joe asked. "I thought we weren't seeing them until the monthly catch up?"

"I, ah, forgot to mention that," Bobby said. "Pete's got tickets for the fight at the Garden and asked me if I wanted one. I didn't think to ask you...you know with Jacob and all..."

"Hey—don't feel guilty." Joe said. "You know me and boxing. Go enjoy it with *Pete*."

Bobby smiled. "What was that emphasis?"

"Emphasis?"

"*Pete*, "Bobby mimicked. "Is baby jealous...?"

"I think I prefer 'Bro' to 'Baby'...enjoy yourself." Joe checked his watch. "You'd better move: traffic will be a bitch..."

"Yeah, I guess," Bobby said, getting up. "Give Judy and Jacob a hug from me."

"Will do." Joe said, adding, "Don't forget to mention *Jesters* over your beers."

After *Jesters* went under, *Brewsters*, *The Gag Shack*, *Pranks Incorporated* and dozens more followed, but *Marshalls* carried on and, at the following year's dinner, their table was a little closer to the podium. At home afterwards, Judith mentioned that most of the greetings from *Marshalls* staff were directed to Bobby, which Joe acknowledged with no bitterness. But that was later, after the limo ride back home. In the limo it had been David Hudson they'd talked about; his passing six months ago honored in Lionel Leonard's traditional speech.

"Can you believe it?" Judith asked in the back of the limo. "That poor man and his husband."

Joe looked at Bobby. "Did *you* know about it?"

Bobby knocked back his drink. "Yeah, Pete told me when it happened. Heart attack they think, when he and his husband were driving up to his retreat. Both of them dead—his husband was pretty much Jayne Mansfielded. I thought I'd mentioned it to you?"

"Jayne Mansfielded?" Ellie asked.

"The actress. They said she was decapitated in a car crash… she wasn't. It's an urban legend." Joe said quietly, and then turned to Bobby. "No. You didn't. I'd have remembered that."

Ellie sighed sadly. "It's a tragedy…" She took a sip of champagne. "I wonder what happened to the house."

As the other three gasped she blushed hard, covering her mouth.

Judith snickered first. Joe tried to cover his own laugh with a bad fake cough. Bobby just stared at his wife before he too succumbed.

The next day, nursing hangovers, they put it down to shock, but wouldn't look each other in the eye for fear of a relapse.

It was March 28th the following year that everything changed.

Marshalls were sponsoring part of the annual Mermaid Parade that June at Coney Island and Bobby and Pete had been meeting frequently to discuss plans. That was the official line, anyway. Bobby always turned up late and bleary-eyed the mornings after. Joe hadn't commented:

he'd been taking personal time at home, fussing over Judith and helping out with Jacob until she would chase him out the house, insisting she was seven months pregnant not an invalid. But Joe remembered the last time she'd been seven months pregnant all too well.

The night of the 28th he'd been in the office, searching through his Mac for some design files when he remembered emailing them through to Bobby earlier that week. He pushed his chair over to Bobby's PC and logged on with his brother's username and password. No secrets between brothers.

He had really believed that until he started searching Bobby's inbox.

There were a lot of emails from Peter Leonard: That didn't surprise him. What did surprise him was how many were prefaced with '*Premises*'.

Premises: possible spots.
Premises: real estate stuff.
Premises: permits and other.

He thought about opening one, his finger twitching on the mouse. Bobby would never know...but *he* would. It was just then he realized he could have searched his sent folder for the files. Too tired, clearly. He logged off both machines, and headed home.

The next day a disheveled-looking Bobby arrived, sunglasses on despite the clouds outside. He collapsed into his chair.

"Late night?" Joe asked.

Bobby threw two Advil into his mouth, swallowing dry.

"You look as if you need some hair of the dog." Joe said, pulling on his jacket. "Let's take an early lunch."

Bobby followed miserably.

"So. *Premises*?" Joe asked, and Bobby choked on his Bloody Mary.

"Premises?" Bobby asked back, unconvincingly.

"I saw the emails," Joe said, sipping his lime and soda. "I

didn't read any. I'd prefer you tell me."

"Shit." Bobby said.

"Shit indeed," Joe agreed.

"I wanted to have the full details before…"

"And now you can't. So spill," Joe said.

And over two more Bloody Marys Bobby outlined the 'premises' thing.

The bottom line, he said, was that *Marshalls* wanted to extend and wanted them involved. "*Really Involved*", Bobby winked. *Marshalls* were happy with their work but concerned they were limited by premises and hardware. Joe pointed out the Lexmark had cost them $15,000 and they were still paying it off. Bobby nodded: that was his point and reminded Joe about Thanksgiving and having to farm work out to 'real' printers. *Marshalls* wanted to *help* them. They didn't want them to *join* the company. Pete said they needed more machinery and space. Pete said they needed new premises.

"We're supposed to be in this equally, Bobby," Joe said. "A *joint venture*. A partnership. *This*. This doesn't sound careful. Not careful at all."

Bobby's face dropped, looking like he was a ten-year-old boy once more being told 'he couldn't'.

"It's just *so* Bobby," Judith said. "So *very* Bobby."

Joe didn't have to ask her what she meant: Bobby. Confident, convinced and self-assured. Or, over-confident, swaggering and cocksure. Take your pick

"If you say no?" Judith asked. "Do you lose the contract?"

Joe shrugged. "Bobby says 'maybe', he doesn't know…"

Judith snorted. "Finally, something Bobby doesn't know."

"I'm going to speak to Peter Leonard myself," Joe said. "I'll have Bobby come too, but I need to hear this with my own ears." He looked at her. "You should be there too."

Judith shook her head. "No. I don't want to be the little wife."

"I didn't mean it like that..."

"And I didn't take it like that. But it's your business. Yours and your shit-head of a brother—sorry; that's just for tonight, you know I love him. It would look amateurish if you brought the whole family..."

"There's an idea," Joe smiled. "Maybe Jacob could throw up on him."

She kissed him on the cheek. "Listen and decide. If you think 'no', then we're out. If you think 'yes' then...we can talk about it."

"You sure?" Joe asked.

She nodded, patting her stomach. "But do it soon, honey."

They met at *Per Se* at Peter Leonard's invite. He was not alone; sitting with his father at the bar. After pleasantries, the old man suggested they move to their table. "I took the liberty of ordering the Salon tasting menu," he said. "At my age I'm afraid the Chef's tasting menu is too much."

Joe had no idea what this meant, so simply nodded his agreement.

The meal was exquisite; but as the talk went on—all business this time, Joe found himself overwhelmed by everything—the food, the wines, the promises, and a subtle undercurrent of something not being said.

As the remnants of dessert were removed, Lionel Leonard dropped his napkin onto his plate. "You've heard everything we have to say Mr. Wray. May we know your thoughts?"

Joe thought a moment. "I know my brother. I know when he's excited and when he believes in something. I know he's ambitious—certainly more than me, and he's probably smarter...."

Bobby smiled self depreciatingly. "'That's my bro."

Joe looked at him, unsmiling. "He knows *me* too; how I hate him calling me 'bro' for example." Bobby's smile dropped. "But I know him better. I *have* to. Because I'm the careful one. In everything."

"You've been thinking a lot during this meal," Leonard Sr. said. "And I think you're...smarter than you say."

Joe nodded, accepting the compliment.

"Do you have a question about our proposal?" the old man asked.

Joe nodded. "I do. My very simple question to you gentlemen is, *what do you want us to do for you?*"

Bobby laughed, too loud. "Joe, they've spent the last two hours telling us..."

Leonard Sr. barely lifted his finger and Bobby silenced instantly. Leonard turned to his son. "It's time for this old man's bed. Have the car come around. You may wish to take these gentlemen somewhere more... private... to talk further." He stood from his chair and nodded to Bobby, "Good to see you again." He turned to Joe. "And nice to meet you for the first time. Not the last, I hope."

"Gentlemen," Peter Leonard said. "Perhaps we could retire to my office. I have a particularly good single malt and some decent cigars."

"Do you know how much profit *Marshalls* made last year?" Peter Leonard asked them when they'd sat.

"The annual report said in the amount of $8 million," Joe said.

Leonard nodded, and worked at lighting his cigar. "It was indeed. A good amount, I'm sure you'll agree."

The Wray brothers acknowledged it was.

"It's enough to look healthy. But we would struggle to pay for the life we have become accustomed to with just that, to do..." he shrugged, "...all the other things we do... or want to do."

Joe nodded. "And for that you need... Alternative sources of revenue?"

"Quite so," Leonard said.

Bobby sat as silent as he had been since they'd left the

restaurant.

Joe considered. "And you need us, or someone like us, to help you with this alternative source."

Leonard gestured for him to carry on.

"Something you need high quality printers for, and a safe place to work. You need a secluded..."

Peter Leonard interrupted. "To be clear. *We* wouldn't set up such an operation. We wouldn't lend money to set up such an operation. That would be..." He looked for the word. "...Noticeable. And we..."

"Don't want to be noticed," Joe finished. "Better it be an unrelated company. Someone with little or no ties to your, dare I say it, 'frivolous' company in more 'serious' eyes?"

A clock ticked somewhere in the background.

Peter Leonard blew out chocolate smelling smoke. "My father was right. You *are* smart."

Joe did not acknowledge the compliment this time. "I'm guessing money? Is that it? *Funny money*? Is that the biggest joke *Marshalls* produces?"

Bobby coughed and gave a tiny shake of his head.

Joe glanced at him. "Bobby, we're a little too far into this conversation to start playing coy." He turned back to Leonard. "*Is* that what we're talking about?"

Peter Leonard gave a small laugh. "Funny money. I like that. No—it's not money, but it's something close enough as damn it."

Joe Wray realized that his next words would probably put them across some invisible line, but in his heart knowing his suspicions, if not any action, had already crossed it, and some time ago. He nodded. "Good. Money is a bastard."

Bobby's jaw dropped as he stared at his older brother, but Leonard nodded. "It is indeed," he said. "The Treasury estimates $70 million counterfeit bills in circulation: that's one naughty in every 10,000 real. It's too easy to get caught, too easy to trace back to the source, and is a pain in the ass to make. It's also very... domestic. We're talking about something easier, less risky and more international." He cupped his mouth. "And it's a *lot* more profitable."

Joe smiled thinly. "I assume you have lawyers who will make that kind of business invisible?"

"*One* lawyer," Leonard said. "He's new, after David's untimely passing, but he's thorough."

"If I may, two more questions?" Joe asked

"Please go ahead," Leonard said, adding, "Depending on the questions, of course."

"How many people in the company are aware of this?"

"It's certainly not discussed at department meetings." Leonard said, smiling thinly. "In this country, seven people, all in the family. Overseas? There are more involved, but none who know who they're dealing with. It all gets very complicated to be honest. It's enough to say this isn't new."

"I'm sure," Joe said. "So... Why us?"

Peter Leonard steepled his fingers. "My father intends to step down next year. Before he does, he wants a domestic presence. Maybe it's late onset patriotism. Without wanting to spook you, we've been watching you for some time." Joe thought back to the first party invite—Judy and Ellie's names...

"If there were an offer. Which of course, there isn't," Leonard said. "You would be the first producers it was ever extended to." He stubbed out the cigar. "Which it wasn't."

Cigar extinguished, Leonard drained his drink. "And now gentlemen, the hour groweth late. A driver is outside. Discuss between yourselves; sleep on it. We need a decision sooner rather than later, and, at the risk of sounding redundant, everything said here must remain here. Regrettably that includes your better halves."

Inside the car Bobby opened the liquor compartment. "I'm assuming you don't..." he started, before Joe reached past, poured a whisky and sat back.

Bobby held his glass up in a toast. "You surprised me tonight, bro. I thought you'd walk when you realized..." He stopped. "When *did* you realize?"

Joe looked at him coldly. "The basics when I saw the emails... the detail around the fourth course. When exactly did you realize?"

"Pete's been hinting a month or two," Bobby said. "But he's a cagey sonofabitch, even for a friend. I swear I didn't know the full detail until tonight," he laughed softly, "and I called you careful. You were like *Don Corleone* back there..."

Joe stared at him. "You don't get it, do you Bobby?"

"Get what?"

"I was *being* careful in there. I doubt we'd be sitting here if I wasn't. He's not your *friend*, and we're not *partners* with them. There's no decision to be made. Don't you *get* that?" He rubbed his eyes. "What the fuck have you done, Bobby?"

The house was quiet, Judith asleep and Jacob's gentle snuffling emanating from the monitor left on in the dining room. Joe reached into the kitchen cupboard for a tumbler for a drink he didn't want but hoped would make him sleep. Looking inside he saw the candles, still only the one he'd burned on Jacob's birthday missing. He took a candle, and the matches next to them, and forgot about the tumbler.

An hour later, as the flame burned out and died, Joe told himself he'd made the right decision in impossible circumstances to protect his family.

Thomas Wray was born 8lbs 7oz., one day overdue in New Jersey Medical Center on May 2nd. Joe was there for the birth as Bobby and Ellie waited outside with Jacob, as happy to snuggle into his Auntie as he'd always been. The photograph of them all huddled around Judith's bed was, Joe thought, the last happy time they'd shared.

The brothers didn't ask who'd done the scouting and sourcing of the building they visited; merely signed the papers placed in front of them. The required monies came and went from their business account off the back of selling their existing premises to an unknown buyer. In less than two months the business was fully functional: everything arranged through an independent 'business consultant'. Joe gave up asking for invoices: it was against his careful nature, but he felt like Canute and eventually gave in, waiting to see if they would sink or swim.

They swam.

In late August that year, Joe and Bobby spent three weeks in Peru to walk the Inca Trail, a childhood dream hitherto unknown to an unimpressed Judith. Ellie had said she'd stay with Judith and the boys, and they'd be fine together. Her eagerness for them to go made Joe wonder aloud to Bobby if he had talked to her about their business as they flew in Business Class.

"I love her so much," Bobby said. "She's smart. Guys see her: and they think just because she's beautiful she must be a bimbo..."

"Ellie? A bimbo...?" Joe asked, amused at the thought.

"Yeah dumb shits, right? But because she is so smart... sometimes I think she's going to see through me. All my bullshit and she'll be gone..."

"*That's* bullshit," Joe sighed. "She loves you so much."

Bobby pointed at his heart. "Here, I know, but here?" He pointed to his head. "Crazy shit in here, bro. I think too much. That she's too good for me."

"Well, *that's* true," Joe smiled, and Bobby smiled back sadly.

"I want to keep her happy. To give her the best I can to..."

"It's not money that'll keep her, Bobby. And she's not going anywhere. For some crazy, unknown reason she loves you. Even though I agree, she is too smart."

Bobby smiled sadly. "I think she knew something was up before I did...with *Marshalls*, I mean." He considered a moment. "You need to talk to Judith about it too."

"Judith doesn't need to know," Joe said, his smile disappearing instantly.

"You don't trust her?" Bobby asked.

Joe looked at him hard. "I haven't hit you since I was fourteen, Bobby, but say that shit again and…"

Bobby held his hands up. "I'm sorry, man."

"It's not about trust," Joe said. "It's about protecting her. *Them*." He flicked open his newspaper, knowing as he did that he'd tell Judith everything.

Later, as he was nodding off, Bobby spoke, "It was when I tried to jump the bridge on that bet from the Nixon brothers wasn't it?"

"You'd have killed yourself if I hadn't stopped you. Idiot," Joe mumbled.

"Always there for me," Bobby said, no sarcasm in his voice.

But Joe was asleep.

They spent two days on the trail—enough to snap some photographs. The rest of the time they spent at an installation in no way connected to *Marshalls*, studying techniques the small group of local workers showed them during the long days. At night they talked—Joe's remaining frostiness toward Bobby had thawed by the second day. They talked childhood, family, the future, and without ever saying it they talked around what it meant not just to be brothers, but best friends.

By the time they left they could repeat the processes flawlessly.

As he opened the front door, Judith threw her arms around his neck and they kissed long and hard. Dropping his bags to the floor, Joe took her in his arms and said gently, "Honey, we need to talk…"

She'd been shocked, and she asked a lot of questions; pressing him on a number of things he told her—some areas he was still not sure of himself, and then she sat in silence for a long time.

"You did all this without telling me," she said, finally.

"I did."

"Not even the slightest hint."

"I trust you more than anything in this world," he said.

She nodded as though this was a given. "Do we need the money that badly to be doing something illegal? And it is illegal isn't it?"

"Yes", he said. "The *'no-body gets hurt because of it'* kind of illegal, I think. The *'screw the government'* sort. But it's not for some noble cause, but it is out of... desperation."

"What desperation, Joe?" she asked.

He sighed. "Bobby. By the time I found out about this he'd...." He drifted into silence.

"Of course it was Bobby." She sighed. "It's always Bobby."

"I didn't have a choice. I had to..."

"Protect him?" she interrupted. "You can't always protect someone like Bobby."

"It's not someone *like* Bobby," Joe said. "It *is* Bobby."

She wiped her wet eyes. "You promised you'd protect me. *Us*. If... if I go along with this, and if things look dangerous, promise me you'll never forget that."

He swallowed. "I promise you on my life."

She looked at him for a long moment. "Let's go to bed."

They produced the first finished set two weeks later. Joe rejected the first three batches because of imperfections Bobby could not see with his naked eye or a magnifying glass. He started to say so, stopping when he saw the look on Joe's face.

The following year they weren't invited to the Gala Dinner.

They were sitting at Joe and Judith's dining room table flicking through holiday brochures, Thomas asleep, Jacob starting to flake in front of cartoons on TV, when the doorbell rang.

The man wearing a chauffer's uniform handed over the large box saying only, "Sir. For you." When they opened the box, they found a hamper marked *Fortnum & Mason*. The label read, *'Sorry you couldn't be with us tonight.'*

"Does it say who it's from?" Ellie asked, and as they stared at her, burst out laughing. "Jesus! Does no one have a sense of humor around here?"

They spent twenty minutes unpacking the hamper; Oscietra caviar, hams, foie gras, smoked salmon, terrines, cheeses, olives and truffles: all before they reached the wines and spirits.

"I suppose," Judith said wistfully, "this means the pasta I spent a whole half an hour preparing is going to go uneaten..."

Their laughter stirred Jacob from his cartoons enough to investigate.

In a '50s movie, calendar pages would drop from the wall, the adjacent scenery outside montaging through seasons, repeated again and again. And for Joe that was how the next four years felt. He worked on creative marketing projects for various small companies received via unknown references. But mostly he refined and produced 'the product'.

Bobby's time in New York decreased, but his time on video conferencing and later overseas travel grew exponentially. None of it could be connected to *Marshalls*. Between travel trips, he and Ellie bought a place; a downtown penthouse condo with a private veranda which Judith spent most of their first visit herding Jacob back from all the while saying how beautiful it was. Ellie whispered to her they may only be there a while... until they needed something more 'family suitable'.

It had been December 28th when the phone call came: three days after they'd Christmas lunched in Bobby and Ellie's condo, and one day after Joe had dropped them at Newark as they embarked on Ellie's dream tour of Europe. Judith was bathing Jacob and Thomas upstairs, the boys engaged in a splashing fight that brought back childhood memories for Joe as he picked up.

"Wray residence."

"Mr. Wray," the voice said. "You need to be in Poughkeepsie tomorrow afternoon. Three o'clock. Use the following Sat-Nav details. Do you have a pen?"

Joe didn't play dumb. There was no point. He used one of Jacob's crayons to write the co-ordinates the man on the phone gave him and, as the phone clicked, he swallowed hard, thinking up his excuses for the following day.

The drive took an hour and a half. The bar's name was lit on a shamrock hanging outside. Joe took a small Guinness and walked through to the back. He sat down silently, placing the glass in front of him.

"Joe," Peter Leonard said, drinking a whisky much cheaper than the one in his office so long ago.

"Mr. Leonard," Joe said. "Peter."

Peter Leonard expelled air. "I've had to leave my family for this. As I'm sure you have. I want to get back to them as soon as I can."

Joe nodded. "Is there a problem with the... publicity?"

Leonard smiled humorlessly. "Nice. No. The *publicity* is exemplary."

"That's good," Joe said.

"The problem," Leonard said, "is more of a 'Personnel' issue."

"Personnel...?" Joe asked.

"Your brother" Leonard said, "has been helping himself to the...*publicity*, setting up his own *'window displays'*." He paused and took a drink. "Part of the reason we're meeting is to see how much you knew of this."

Joe shook his head firmly. "I swear to you, I have absolutely no idea..."

Leonard nodded. "I can see that by your face. I didn't think you did. You're different to your brother. You're a family man... a man of honor, I think?"

"I'd like to think so, yes," Joe said.

"I think so too. Your brother? Not so much. No, don't

bother to defend him. It would be insulting to both of us. I'll make this simple Mr. Wray. A question and two observations."

Joe waited.

"The question. 'Will your brother listen to you?'"

Joe didn't ask about what. "I think so, yes."

"Don't *think*," Peter Leonard said, draining his whisky. "My observation: Bobbys in this world are a dime a dozen. In a *family* situation like this, we expect *you* to fix this."

Leonard stood and pulled his coat on. A large man emerged from the shadows behind them and walked ahead, probably to start a car, Joe thought.

"Mr. Leonard?" Joe said.

Leonard looked down at him. "Hmm?"

"You said two observations."

Leonard nodded. "I already made the other one. You're a family man. Speak to your brother as soon as he returns from Europe, Mr. Wray."

The entire meeting had lasted less than five minutes.

Driving home, Joe stopped three times to be sick. He told Judith he'd had bad shrimp at lunch with the Connelly's discussing their New Year display.

Bobby and Ellie arrived back late on the second Sunday in January. Their flight was on time and Ellie shrieked with joy when she saw the 'Auntie Ellie' sign Jacob was begrudgingly holding. Thomas had one tied around his neck reading *'Uncle Boddy'*. Judith had scrawled the middle letters backwards, promising Joe it would be funny, and he had tried to smile. Bobby, Ellie and Judith talked non-stop in the car all the way back, Jacob chuntered along with them. Joe drove silently.

Unpacking the luggage while Ellie and Judith took the boys upstairs Joe said, "We need to talk, Bobby. Tonight."

Bobby looked at him. "You got the January blues? You seem kind of pissed."

"*Tonight*," Joe repeated. "Make an excuse why we need to

go out for an hour."

"Uh, sure. I'll say... um..."

"Come on Bobby," Joe hissed. "Do you need me to write you a script?"

"Fine," Bobby said. "I got a message from Campbells while we were away, and we need to go through it before tomorrow. Happy?"

"I'm very far from *'happy'*," Joe said, lifting two of the larger cases towards the door.

"Oh Jesus," Bobby said, his face suddenly ghost-white.

"Jesus indeed," Joe said.

"How did they find out? I was careful. I swear."

Joe had said nothing until they'd sat down. He had laid out the bare details of the meeting.

"Careful enough not to tell me what you were doing," Joe agreed. "What the *fuck* were you thinking?"

"I..." Bobby shrugged and rubbed his face. "It started as a mistake—I miscounted on a delivery. Emiliano called me—I think he thought it was a test of some sort. When he found it wasn't he... well, he suggested, we could do some off-the-book business. Nothing much, I swear... but, you know..."

"No." Joe interrupted. "*I don't know*. I don't know Emiliano." He held up a halting hand. "I don't want to know Emiliano, or how many Emilianos there have been before or since. But it stops now. Understand?"

Bobby nodded. "It's over. No more..." He paused. "Should I apologize to Pete? Ring him tomorrow?"

"You shouldn't do anything except what you're supposed to do," Joe said. "Don't ring. Don't message. Him or anyone else. You act like it never happened, and we never talk about this again. Right?"

"I've got it. Clean from here on out. I swear." Bobby's nod turned to a sad shake. "How the fuck did they find out...?"

Joe clasped Bobby's hand, spilling beer from his mug.

"They found out. And they'll find out again. So *don't*." He looked at his watch. "Come on. Let's get back. Go clean yourself up first."

Bobby said nothing, just stood and walked to the restroom. When he came back he'd washed his face and the shaking was less noticeable.

They started to walk back, Joe stopping Bobby walking out into the street as a black sedan sped past.

"You with me, Bobby?" he asked.

Bobby stared back at him, his eyes slightly glassy. "I'm fine, man. I've got you looking out for me like always…"

"What have you taken, Bobby?" Joe asked.

Bobby gave a jittery laugh. "Just a Xanax…"

"Jesus," sighed Joe. "When I think it can't get worse." He steered Bobby across the road. "We get back, you say you're jet lagged, and you go to bed. I'll see you at the shop tomorrow… Lay off the pills Bobby."

"I will, bro," Bobby said, but he was already talking to Joe's back.

Three weeks later, after his first trip into the City since his holiday, Bobby dropped his briefcase on the empty chair opposite Joe's desk.

"How did it go?" Joe asked.

Bobby shrugged. "All good. How's your day gone?"

"It's gone," Joe conceded. "Whisky's over there." He gestured with his pen behind Bobby. "Pour me one as well."

"Wow, big brother drinking on a school night. Wild times in Jersey." Bobby smiled. "Are we celebrating?"

Joe said nothing, taking the glass Bobby passed him.

"I met with Pete lunchtime."

"I know. That's why you were going in there," Joe said.

"Yeah. He seemed okay, you know?"

"Okay?"

"Yeah. He seemed okay. With me I mean," Bobby said. "Same old Pete."

"That's good." Joe said.

"The thing is. Well, he didn't seem pissed off about the whole...you know, misunderstanding."

"Good," Joe said again.

"Do you think maybe you..." Bobby made a see-sawing motion with his head. "Over-reacted in what you thought?"

"No," Joe said. "I don't. I didn't."

"Sure, sure," Bobby said. "I was just wondering. But hey, good news, huh? Things back to normal."

"Things back to normal," Joe agreed, finishing his drink. "Let's go. Judith's got dinner on, Ellie's been helping her with the kitchen decoration today. Make sure you say it looks good."

Joe and Judith took a couple's vacation that May. They drove up to Maine for a week. Bobby and Ellie stayed while they were away, looking after the boys. Ellie laid out an itinerary for the boys as detailed as the one she'd made for Europe. Even Bobby seemed excited.

Joe and Judith returned to homemade banners welcoming them home, and only two plasters on Jacob's knees. They let Ellie put the boys to bed. "One last time," she said a little sadly when she returned downstairs.

They left in Bobby's new Porsche.

Joe and Bobby spent two nights in the City late July attending a trade fair, attending with minimal stand space, and manning it for the shortest time they could: a small company fighting for business in trying times.

They stayed at the *Marlton Hotel*, and on the first evening, searched for somewhere to eat.

"Jesus, will you look at that?" Bobby said.

"Want to see if we can get a table?" Joe asked.

Bobby shrugged. "Why not?"

The restaurant squeezed them in, but without the special treatment they'd had eight years ago.

"Guess we're ordering off the menu this time, huh?" Bobby said, holding his glass in a toast. "Here's to eight years of them. And a lifetime of us."

The food was not as good as those years ago, but the meal was better. They talked about childhood back in Vermont, before university, before work, before much of anything. It was a nice evening.

Bobby insisted on paying, and Joe pretended he didn't see the Black AmEx card in the back of his wallet.

It was a month to the day, he got the call about Bobby and Ellie's murder.

Joe Wray sighed as the candles fizzled out, less than a minute apart.

He left the vestibule and walked up the aisle.

He stopped at a table at the rear where flyers lay, each headed "PLEASE PRAY FOR" with six lines beneath.

Much too late for that, he thought.

Walking out to the reception the old woman glanced up.

"Is the chapel open?" he asked, and she pointed left.

Inside, Joe stood before the small font at the front for a moment before walking back, counting the rows. When he reached the twelfth, he sat down.

Somewhere outside a bell rang.

He remembered Judith's words that Christmas night so long ago—it was still silent here, but he felt no peace.

He leaned forward, his arms almost touching the cushion lying on the floor. Moving it aside he rummaged until he touched the package. He pulled at it: once, twice, and then a third time as it ripped away from the tape holding it. He slid the package into his jacket pocket.

Leaving the old church, the heat hitting him like a furnace, Joe switched his phone back on.

There was one message. From Judith. She and the boys had arrived at her mother's. The three-hour drive had been okay, the pre-Labor weekend traffic not too bad. She finished the message telling him she was sorry she couldn't be there with him and for him to get up there as soon as he could. There were blurting noises as the boys tried to blow kisses, and then the message clicked off.

Joe had barely lowered his phone before it started ringing. The Ramones—'Blitzkrieg Bop'. It was one of only three individual ring tones on his cell: 'It Had to Be You' for calls from Judith, 'Tom Waits growling out 'Heigh Ho!' for Ellie, who had thought it hilarious to download when they'd been out drinking one night, and... The Ramones.

Always his and Bobby's favorite band.

When, after a moment, he answered, the voice on the other end was loud enough for him to move the phone an inch from his ear.

"Yo. Where you at 'bro?"

Joe swallowed hard. "I'm just walking into Grand Central Station."

"What you still doing in the city, man?" Bobby asked, and Joe could hear him shouting to someone in the background, Ellie he presumed. "He's still in the City..."

"I had to pick something up," Joe said, his voice a monotone and his hand feeling the package in his pocket. "I'll make the 14:45 train; don't worry."

"You been picking me up a birthday present?" Bobby hooted. "We said you didn't need to."

"No," Joe said, wondering how long the package had sat in the church. He guessed not long after the order last week. Sitting there since: fully functioning and clean—but not so clean there would be any smell of oil on it. He sighed and spoke into the phone, "I know... but... I had to get this. No choice."

"Sounds intriguing, bro." Bobby laughed, and there was a muffled voice somewhere near him. "Oh yeah, that's true... Ellie says I can't call you 'bro' anymore. She's got an idea for a new name..." And then there was more laughter down the line.

"I'll let it go," Joe said, trying to stop his voice hitching. "Just this last time."

"Hey, got to get this BBQ sorted," Bobby said. "Sorry Judy

can't make it... She got to her Mom's place safe?"

"She did," Joe said, thinking of David Hudson and his husband, and how treacherous he'd discovered driving could be. "They're safe. They're all safe."

"Well," Bobby laughed, "you'll have to give her the news yourself, but if there's a liquor store open there you might want to pick up a bottle of something bubbly...." A pause, and then muffled, his hand over the phone: "I didn't say anything!"

Joe closed his eyes and lowered his hand again to the packet that fitted it so terribly, horribly neatly. "I'll be there soon, Bobby."

He headed for the station, crossing the road carefully.

He was careful by nature.

Careful. Protective. And a man who kept his promises.

For Jacob. For Thomas. And more than anyone, for Judith.

He had promised he would do anything to protect them. And although only on the rarest of occasions a religious man, as he boarded the train Joe Wray thought in doing so he was going to burn as surely as his five candles.

THE END

ABOUT THE AUTHOR

Simon Bewick has worked in a variety of roles in the publishing world for 25 years.

His works have appeared in a wide range of online and print publications including *Digital Catapult, Agony in Black, Blue Murder, The Harrow* and *Strange Horizons*—where he received an honorable mention in Ellen Datlow's annual Best Horror of the Year anthology.

He is the published author of *Basement Tales*—an anthology of dark fiction, *You Could Make a Killing*—a collection of crime and mystery short stories, the forthcoming novel *Air of December*, and the screenplay *The 100% Detective*.

You can find more of Simon Bewick's work, including fiction, reviews and other bits and bobs, by following him at bewbob.com

SCINTILLATION
BY CARLA DAY

For a Friday morning, especially one falling on pay-day, there was no happy *Friday-feeling*, no whacking-great smile while traipsing along sodden, grey streets on the way to my favourite takeaway coffee shop, to pick up my ritual flat-white. My fuel to enable me to get through the dull mornings at the bank.

My umbrella, in tandem with a violent gust of wind, decided to turn inside out on the corner of Mill St. and subsequently was sent on tangled flight through Mill Park, narrowly missing a plucky Jack Russell that was destroying the flowerbeds, its owner looking at me in disgust. Like

I could control the abysmal weather. Needless to say, I didn't look amazing and straightening my hair had been a complete waste of half an hour.

I felt the day started a little awkwardly, but was also sure the strange feeling was going to pass. I always felt this way after one of my usual but ethereal and slightly bonkers dreams. I always thought they would make awesome movies, if I could just remember them when I woke, that is.

Last night's dream had been particularly unpleasant and, well, weird. Not only did I remember it for once, but I'm also convinced it was totally real. For a moment I was sure I'd been on some kind of virtual reality vacation, like the ones in 'Total Recall'. I had even patted my head, once hazily awake, to make sure there weren't any electrodes stuck to my head, piping a computerised dream into my brain.

The dream, apart from it starting with the sky exploding like some kind of apocalyptic nightmare and planets combusting, was really quite surreal and calming. Once that blazing show of utter world-ending chaos had played out in the most dazzling oranges and blues, all that was left was my heart pumping and a very black and starless abyss.

A warm circle of light then appeared: soft, pinky-white and swirling anticlockwise. In the centre of it, as the circle grew, was a small fissure: it looked like teardrop and was without doubt heading towards me. I knew it was coming to take me for a journey through time and space and I began to feel fuzzy, yet unexplainably safe and generally eager to be swallowed up. Just as the hole was quivering and hovering above my head, waiting to syphon me from the Earth, a searing pain shot through my entire body. I closed my eyes and a mass of dull stars appeared as if they were dying. The pain continued and my eyes remained shut. I woke, gasping for air, tangled up in cotton sheets and soaked through. But the dying stars were still imprinted on my retinas and I could see them when I looked at the white wall. It took a few minutes for this image to fade. The whole episode completely freaked me out.

So here I am stood in line, the aroma of coffee bringing an unsure smile to my lips and normality is almost tangible. I catch my reflection as I hand over my cash and laugh because my frizzy hair seems to have acquired a couple of small twigs from the storm that is now raging outside the coffee shop.

In the corner of the shop, sat slovenly in one of the tall-backed, corduroy, armchairs, a leg dangling over the arm, engrossed in a book, is a man in a long black beaten-up leather jacket. His hair is lank and Jesus-like and his skin is pasty and tightly stretched over high cheekbones: a pure, stereo-typical goth. The sight of him makes me, for some reason, shudder. I notice the book he is reading has a navy-blue cover and it looks a bit familiar. On closer inspection there is a pink swirling mass on a night sky with a teardrop fissure in the centre, just like my dream, and the sight of it makes me drop my coffee, burn my feet and distracts the goth-looking man from his book.

He rushes over, grabs a wad of napkins and begins to mop up coffee from my shoes. I feel faint and fall ungraciously into his long, spindly but surprisingly strong, arms.

I wake up several minutes later on the chair opposite his, the scent of petunia oil strong in my nostrils. Dark blue, unusually small eyes are peering at me and there is no smile.

"Someone's not eaten their breakfast this morning." He tuts then his lips curl into a grin revealing very white and straight teeth, quite a lot of them.

"I don't know what happened. I'm really embarrassed. Thank you for catching me." I look at the book that is open and lying flat on the coffee table. He sees me staring at the cover as I catch the title: 'Scintillation'. He turns the book over so only the blurb on the back can be seen.

"The book; what's it about?"

"It's a cheesy sci-fi, nothing to shout about, a gift from a friend. Don't let that concern you Marne, you just drink this, you'll feel better." He hands me a cup of tea.

"How do you know my name?" The tea is very sweet.

He points at a name badge that the bank insists on staff wearing even though, when the manager took my photo, I was doing an absurd half-wink. It's always proven to be a good conversation starter.

"Right, I should get going. I'll be late for work."

"No need: I've called the bank to let them know you'll not be in today." For a second, I think this is a total liberty and I'm about to scold him, but he just laughs and suggests: "You mustn't be angry, I'm doing what's best. You need to get checked out by a doctor: you knocked your head on the way down."

I run my fingertips over a gash above my right eye and the pain comes quick and sharp and makes me wince.

"I'll get you a taxi." He stands and shoves the book into a very deep pocket. He pats it twice after, confirming it's still there and safe.

"There's no need, honestly. I'll be fine. Again, thanks for your help."

"Oh, but that's where you're wrong; there's every need. I need to make sure you're safe."

The weekend passed in a blur of black-and-white movies, takeaways and several bottles of wine. My cat was seriously getting sick of eating pizza crusts and the remnants of old Chow Mein. I'd been too lazy to go out to the shop, into the grey days and the bitter cold. The slightly dizzy feeling I had at the coffee shop that subsequently left me slumped in a stranger's arms, stayed with me.

The long-coated man informed me that his name was Ludovik, and the bizarre episode left me with an anxious, shivery feeling, like he had somehow managed to stay with me. As if his macabre shadow lodged itself in the corner of my apartment, watching over me while I hid from the outside world; it was the strangest feeling.

Of course, the shadow wasn't there but I couldn't shake

the queer sensation I had when I was around him that day, therefore, he remained prominent in my thoughts. The book cover's similarity to the picture in my dreams was very spooky, but I had to consider that maybe it was something I'd seen before and maybe that prompted the dream. Unlikely, but it had to be considered.

Monday morning is cold and wet again and from my bed I can see a plethora of umbrellas floating along the street below. The constant drizzle is becoming the norm. I decide to tie my hair back, as any effort into making it neat would be rendered pointless and not doing it would give me more time to snooze. The alarm clock is still flashing 6.30a.m. Even though it is now 7a.m. My window is open a fraction and the bottom of my white curtains are wet. Water seeping up to leave a grey banner. I swing my legs out, the floor is rough and cold, the wood, white, painted in a rush and not sanded. I pad over and bend to pick up something from the floor, a pink quartz-looking rock about the size of a plumb stone. It's very pretty, but not mine. I've never seen it before, and as I'm on the eighth floor, I doubt it's been thrown up by some kids from the street.

I'm eager to get to the coffee shop, and curious to see if Ludovik is there. I have the pretty stone in my pocket and like the warmth that settles on my skin after holding it for a while. He isn't there and the queue is too long to hang around. I don't want to be late. I take a shortcut, swerving through dark narrow streets towered either side by apartment blocks and industrial, abandoned knitwear factories, leaving the light fractured and displaced in long triangles; it's quite eerie and I quicken my pace.

At the far corner of the last street of the metropolis maze, I think I see the tail end of a long coat flap as someone rushes around the corner. I run to see if it might be Ludovik, but it isn't and I can't see a soul, save the same old woman with the defecating Jack Russell. When I reach the office, after obligatory explanations as to my whereabouts on Friday and catching up on lost gossip, I settle at my swivel chair in my glass booth and begin counting the money in my till.

Not long after, a loud bell shrieks outside and I hear the jangle of fire engine sirens. Not unusual, as the fire station is on the adjacent street. Only, the sound doesn't fade into the distance and a few minutes later we are being evacuated from the building with concerned-looking pedestrians bellowing, "Out! Get out now! The building's on fire!"

We are herded onto the corner of the street opposite and stand open-mouthed, under a large old station clock, as the right side of our building is engulfed in flames looking like it's been flambéed. There seems to be a small orb of light, a blue spark hovering about mid-height of the twenty-storey building. It disappears quickly and moves too fast for my eyes to follow it.

People were drawn out of buildings all around and are gawking up at the inferno as it glows fiercely, littering the ground with ash and bits of the building. We start to shift further along to avoid hot embers.

Shirley, my slight and very nervous colleague is snivelling into a handkerchief and her words are inaudible as she squeaks out random sob sounds. I pat Nervous Shirley reassuringly and, as I turn to retrieve a tissue from my bag to stop her snivelling even more, something dark moves quickly in my periphery. It's a long black coat, flapping as someone hurries around a corner, towards the tube station. I think it's Ludovik. He's in a hurry for sure and I have the urge to follow him.

"Where you going?" snivels Shirley.

"I'll be back in a minute," I shout back as I head for the tube station steps.

At the top of the stairs, I see Ludovik running for a tube, jumping on and turning to face me. He pulls the book out of his pocket as the door slides to and shows me the cover, holding it to the glass. He's laughing and continues to do so as the tube speeds off and disappears into the tunnel, leaving me standing there perplexed and layered in goose bumps. The stone is hot in my pocket and suddenly feels threatening. I toss it into a nearby bin, where it lands with a satisfying clang, and make my way back to the street corner. The building is surrounded by thick, dark smoke and the fire is almost extinguished, but the building is deemed unsafe and so we are sent home for the day.

I swing by an antiquated bookstore and poke around in the sci-fi section, hoping to pick up a copy of 'Scintillation'. The owner has never heard of it. I Google the title and only get offers of word meanings: a flash or spark of light, which is very peculiar, considering the day's events.

On my way home the Jack Russell is there again, this time on the pavement, and the hefty woman whose buoyant, grey curls are restricted under a silk, paisley scarf, scoops up a donut of excrement in a bag then scowls at me, as if it's my fault for being there to witness the fouling. I nod respectfully, toss her a slightly wry smile and continue on my way wondering why Ludovik was acting so weird.

I discover on the news that evening that four buildings in the vicinity were on fire today, and that two burned to the ground leaving many fatalities. The cause of the fires remains a total mystery. Complete chaos had ensued across the entire county. The hospitals are finding it difficult to cope with the sudden influx of casualties. The whole situation made me sit up very straight and fear what's happening.

Finding the realization of these horrors sobering, a cold sensation creeps along my spine and my hair follicles feel tickly and numb. Could this be something to do with Ludovik, could it be something to do with me?

It's good to see the sun high in the sky casting a hazy lemon hue across the street. It's still wintry cold, but fresh and bright. The kids are kicking a football about on the park and I see the hefty woman skirting the fence with her Jack Russell, no doubt waiting for it to empty its bowels.

Not far away from where she is, someone is sat under the shade of a yew tree, lost in the pages of a book. I squint, trying to decipher if it might be Ludovik but decide it can't be because there is no coat and his hair I'm certain was black. This person has blue pigtails and no scruffy leather coat. Only a baggy black t-shirt, although I can't see his face clearly.

I flip the kettle switch, parched and ready for a cuppa. The TV flickers to life and presents scenes of madness. Fires across the west side of town. A helicopter camera shows black smoke swirling up in twister-like ribbons, choking the air. I check again outside at the serene park view and it seems impossible that this could be happening just ten miles from where I am. I stumble, tripping over something small and hard. I bend down to retrieve the pretty pink stone. *But that's impossible.* I distinctly remembered the loud clink as it hit the side of the bin at the tube station.

The stone feels both gritty and smooth as I roll it around my fingers. There are golden flecks on it, caught in sun beams flooding through the window. I sit down and stare at the TV as cameras scan scenes that belong in a war zone. Buildings burning, people screaming, nearby cars exploding. Bodies lined up on the pavement covered over with white sheets, blood blossoming through in patches. A presenter explains they are still clueless as to why this is happening, his face panicked. There are desperate cries of people searching for their loved ones among the carnage, fearing the worst. Just as the camera pans along the street to maximize the view of devastation, that's when I see him. His hair now blue and in pigtails. Wearing a black t-shirt. Ludovik's holding the book up, so the camera catches the cover as it passes by. Ludovik is laughing hard, pinned against a red brick wall. The teardrop-shaped fissure in the centre of the swirling mass is weeping actual tears. I switch off the TV, overwhelmed with fear. A shadow washes over the window, temporarily blocking out the sunlight and I collapse onto the settee as if thrown by a force, not visible. Once I am able to move, my hands tremble as I drink a glass of water. I'm still gripping the stone, tightly.

The pretty stone feels hot, so hot that I drop it and it begins to spin anticlockwise. It spins quickly, giving off a strange milky light, slightly pink. It continues to grow and expand until the whole of my ceiling is swirling as if a hurricane is beginning in my lounge. My cat screeches and climbs the curtains in order to escape through the window and onto the fire escape. I'm pinned to the sofa again, this time gripped by fear of the unknown.

The teardrop fissure appears and slowly opens and a calm feeling washes through me as it did in the dream. I begin to drift, not dizzy but light and dreamy, *perhaps drugged*? I close my eyes and see only darkness. I let myself go there.

I open my eyes. It's morning, the alarm is flashing 6a.m. My head feels like it does after too much cheap wine and throbs at the temple. My mind searches for reality, what day is it? Where am I supposed to be today? I grapple for a few minutes with my memory of yesterday and gravitate toward sanity as I recall the devastation. I switch on the TV. My cat curls into my side, purring. My ceiling is still intact. There is no mention of yesterday's horrors. I flick through the channels. Nothing, nothing at all. Am I losing my mind?

I remember it's Wednesday. I visit my Nan on Wednesdays. She lives in the part of town where fires have been erupting. Panicked, I dress and quickly feed the cat. I pass the hefty woman and her Jack Russell on the street. She smiles at me, maybe because the sun is out and for once the dog isn't shitting. The streets are relatively quiet. There's a missed call on my phone from Nervous Shirley, probably informing me of a date for a meeting to discuss our return to work. I decide to call her later, after making sure my Nan is safe.

I jump off the bus on the corner of my Nan's street where a bunch of hooded, scallywag teenagers are having a crafty fag in the bus stop. They don't seem to notice me at first, then one of the girls says, "Isn't that a bit eighties?"

They all laugh. I presume she's talking about my leather jacket that I'd picked up from a fusty old second-hand shop at a vintage market. I choose to ignore her.

"Oi, I'm talking to you, bitch!" I know I'm going to ignite something if I retaliate, so I keep on walking and fortunately they start quizzing the next passer-by. *Why don't they just grow up?* My heart is racing and the intimidation makes me clench my fist around the stone that has found its way into my pocket again. The heat of it seems to transfer to me and rushes through my insides like I've just had a shot of whisky.

I see none of the relentless chaos screened on the TV yesterday. No buildings on fire and no dead people lining the streets. There's just the usual flow of traffic and pedestrians going about their day. I begin to feel very unsteady and have to sit on a nearby wall. I call Nervous Shirley suddenly wanting to find out about the fire at work.

"Marne, where have you been, we've been worried sick," she asks.

"What do you mean? I was waiting to hear from work, after the fire, to see when we could come back. I've not missed the meeting, have I?"

"What are you talking about? What fire?"

"Are you winding me up?" *This can't be happening.*

"Marne, are you alright? You came into work on Monday with a big gash on your forehead and then you left, screaming: Ludovik. We've been so worried. You could have let us know you're okay." *But I didn't leave screaming. What's going on? I need to find Ludovik.*

"Shirley, I'll call you back later." Before she has a chance to reply, I slip the phone into my pocket and make my way to Nan's house, suddenly craving a cup of sweet tea and the familiar sound of her voice. *It can't all be a dream, surely. It was so clear. My jacket still smells of smoke and Ludovik caught me, held me in his arms and his eyes, they were mysterious and dark.*

*

The door to my Nan's house is ajar, there are no lights on and no Radio 4 playing in the background. I instinctively hug the wall and slip off my shoes, imagining that there is someone in the house. Her disability scooter is in the hallway, so she's not out and her crutches are resting against the kitchen wall but there's no sign of her. The sound of a shuffle upstairs stops me in my tracks and I stop breathing for a second, afraid of making noise. As I reach the bottom of the landing, my Nan jumps out on the upstairs landing.

"Marne, what a wonderful surprise! What are you doing here so early? I wasn't expecting you till tea time, like always. I haven't even started preparing our tea: faggots and peas, alright love?"

I must look stunned because she rushes down the stairs, ushers me into her recliner chair and propels me backwards into a half-lying down position.

"Dearie me, you look so pasty. Are you coming down with something?" My Nan hasn't walked without aid since 1997 after a terrible car accident left her knees and right hip severely damaged. *So, what the fuck is happening here?*

"Nan, you're walking on your own. What's going on?" *Her face looks younger.*

"What is wrong with you? What are you talking about? Of course I'm walking on my own; who would I be walking with? Have you been smoking some of that mari-wotsit?"

Nan thrusts a cup of hot sweet tea into my trembling hand and stares into my eyes, as if she's searching for tell-tale signs of drug abuse and my mind begins to spin.

There's a knock at the door, my Nan rushes to open it and I hear my Nan saying, "Yes, young man, this way. She's through here." I can hear the excitement in her voice.

The sight of Ludovik looking lofty, gaunt, Gothic and strangely beautiful makes me even more giddy, especially in my Nan's house, a woman who seems to have gained mobility overnight. His hair is now flame red and pulled tight in a ponytail off his face, his lips are full and his eyes magically dark.

"Marne, you didn't tell me you had a boyfriend. How nice to meet you, young man, will you join us for a cup of tea?"

Before I have a chance to speak, Ludovik has bent down to kiss my cheek and whispers, "Just go with it, you're not going mad, I'll explain later."

I spy the corners of the book pushing out against the pocket in his long leather coat, as if he's kept it there forever. The smell of petunia oil as his skin brushes mine is overwhelming.

Nan talks non-stop about me as a child, and then me as a teenager, and then me as a lost cause, and then as a creative art student with a wild imagination, and finally as a bank clerk. I listen to them and think how I've gone from adventurous to boring in pretty much one sentence. Ludovik is interested in whatever she has to say and smiles at me as she continues to spill out my life story, about my parents dying when I was fifteen, how she brought me up, how I was always lost in my own thoughts and playing with an imaginary friend as a child that I kept until I was eighteen. For some inexplicable reason, I don't mind him knowing.

"You know, once she even had a dog collar—tried being a punk for a while, didn't you dear?" She explains as we finish the last of our food and slip our coats on to leave, as if him being here was the most ordinary thing in the world and my Nan walking us to the door is totally normal.

We reach the corner of the street and I unleash my built-up outrage.

"What the hell is going on, Ludovik? The fires, my Nan, the world, what's happening to me and who the fuck are you?"

"I've come to take you home Marne. My name's not really Ludovik; it's me, Loki. If you come with me, it will all make sense."

"Take me where? I don't understand. I only met you four days ago, what are you talking about? Get away from me or I'll call the police." *I have to run; run Marne, run.*

"Please trust me. Here, take this and read it. I'll come for you soon. Don't be afraid: I'm not going to hurt you." The book is worn and tattered at the edges. The colours faded, the pages thumbed, the words soft. It's warm from being in his pocket and when I look up to ask him more questions, he's gone.

I catch the bus home and I'm relieved to see that the flat is all in one piece and my cat is delighted to see me and curls his feathery tail around my ankles and mewls near his bowl. For a moment I stare at my flat and take in the normality of it and decide to lock myself in and read the book. Maybe it has the answers I need. I move to the window to pull down the blind and I notice Ludovik—or Loki, or whatever his name is—stood under a lamppost smoking a cigarette and looking up at me, his shadow long and thin like a noir-style movie shadow, under the dim orange light. He doesn't smile, but walks slowly into the darkness of the park until I can no longer see him.

The book looks smaller than I remember and the picture of the swirling sky and teardrop fissure is incredible, as if I had painted it from my dream. I open the first page. It's blank. All of the pages are blank, nothing in it at all and when I close it, I see that the colours begin to seep from the cover and the pictures and words start to disappear. I'm soon left with a black book. A cream empty book. I'm startled and also terrified at what kind of dark magic is at play. Is Ludovik / Loki some kind of demon? Or maybe he's a magician... but what does he want with me? Why is he hounding me and cropping up and playing with my sanity?

I drink copious amounts of red wine and let myself sink drunkenly into bed and hope the softness of it will take me to my old world where everything made sense. I begin to dream, a vivid dream. The stars above are dim and flickering as they die off one by one. A tiny blue spark is busily flying between them, trying to give them life. Behind them larger planets are aflame with fierce explosions, and then they scatter and space turns red and the stars disappear.

The blue spark is trying, trying to give them back life, but the ending world is raging and soon there will be no planets left to save. The blue light comes to my face and stops there and it wants me to help save the remaining smaller planets. It wants me to fly with it. I take off and the blue spark is guiding me toward planet Earth and it's so, so sad and I think I'm the only one left able to save our world. The sensation is powerful, exhilarating and I know I have to be the spark that saves our world. I reach out to touch it but it spirals away out of focus and the sadness is overwhelming and I wake up in a panic only to find my cat purring and nuzzled into my neck. I don't recall my dream. I jump out of bed with such force the glasses tremble on the work surface and books fall off the shelf.

The book has vanished; it's not on my coffee table next to my empty wine glass where I left it. My head is once more throbbing and my recollection of the evening is hazy. I know I dreamt, but I have no idea what the dream was about.

On my way to meet Nervous Shirley, I stop by the coffee shop and order a flat white for my journey. I decide to walk through the backstreets again, hoping to catch sight of Loki. I have so many questions. I reach to get my purse and the blank book is in my bag. I'm hoping to find out what it means. It's been two weeks since I last saw him outside my flat and there have been no more sightings of fires and apocalyptic chaos. I presume it was some kind of trickery and that he is some kind of magician. I have to let that be the last thought about it, or I'll go completely insane.

Nervous Shirley is reading a book—*the* book, 'Scintillation'. She is sat on a park bench, her head bowed as she scans the pages left to right, hurriedly eating up the words.

"Where did you get that book?" I say, a bit sharply.

"A man brought it by the office, said I was to give it to you when I saw you. Sorry... I was just flicking through."

"This man, what did he look like?"

"Very tall, smelled like a hippy. Nice teeth and he was wearing a long black leather coat. He was very handsome, charming, mysterious. Anything you want to share?" She throws me a cheeky smile and I snatch the book from her hands and pull the blank book from my bag so I can compare them. The words drain from her copy too only she doesn't see it.

"I can't see the words. Where have they gone?"

"You're always forgetting your glasses."

"Can you read me the first page, please?"

"Okay, sure. Are you okay? You're acting a bit strange again."

She slides her forefinger down the centre crease, opening the first page.

"It was on a Sunday the world started to whimper and on a Friday the Scintillator was contacted. It was on a Monday the rock was planted and in a dream the chaos began."

The blood must have drained from my face.

"Marne, wake up. Not again! What's with you lately?" I stare up at the bruised sky, feeling very dizzy.

There's an ear-splitting crack, we all look up: myself, Nervous Shirley, who's on the phone to 999, and stops speaking; the hefty woman with the Jack Russell by the roundabout, cocking its leg up. A group of small kids also look up and cling to their mothers' legs while the sky continues to make thunderous noises and seems to be opening to reveal a cavernous, black fissure. It's in the shape of a teardrop, it's my dream and its growing by the second. Dark clouds around it are swirling, fast. Out of the fathomless dark comes a piercing flash of light, then another, spears of fire, and the building behind mine is alight and then more buildings explode and then I see people running in all directions. Nervous Shirley has legged it out of the park. The Jack Russell has keeled over and the hefty woman is screaming, "Noooooo!"

Disaster ensues across the city and the pretty pink stone

in my pocket is doing something, moving. The book's words are back on the pages, but are dancing about rearranging themselves. It's surreal yet familiar and when I move my eyes away from the book the words come away too. They all come off, join together and begin to swirl around me, and then I hear them, the noise of the words is deafening and stranger still, the voice that whispers them to me, is mine. I feel as though I'm in a trance.

I see Loki approaching. He looks different: he's wearing a jester's outfit and he's bigger, stronger, laughing, laughing so hard he can't keep still and he's making the earth beneath our feet tremble.

"See Surt, you've waited millennia for your chance to save the world. Throw your pretty stone into the hole. They chose me to hide you, to protect you, Surt. Can you believe it, me of all the Gods?"

He is dancing now, in the middle of the park as the sky splits and rains bolts of lightning and fires are ablaze. He is merrily dancing and taunting me still.

"What is going on, Loki? What am I?"

As I speak the words I realize I know the answer: I am a Scintillator! The words are seeping into my veins and giving me back my knowledge and sorcery, from a book I wrote, worlds away from now, on parchment, containing, secrets, the magic I once possessed, and the tools I have to save Earth. I am the spark of energy that will be lit by the stone, the one in my pocket. Loki has been the keeper of the stone and the trickster needed to keep me safe. Between us there is enough energy to stop all the fires in the universe and calm all the seas. Together between us Scintillators, we can save the world with our extraordinary power. Every golden fleck on my pretty pink stone, is a particle of dust, one collected from every planet, it contains enough energy to give strength back to the stars and halt their extinction. There are two such stones in existence. One given to Loki, God of Tricks and Mischief, and another to me, Surt, the God of Wisdom and the Ultimate Keeper of Secrets.

As the memory of what I am floods in and the strength returns to my limbs and the muscle builds over bone and my ancient words continue to envelope me, my body becomes that of a God once more. Loki's laughter fades and he strides over to me.

"You remember me now, old friend?"

"Yes, Loki, what took you so long?"

"We have a world to save, old friend."

"What will happen to me once it's done?"

"You'll return to being Marne, a mortal, working in a bank, who will live an ordinary life. When that life's up, you'll live another, of your choice. You can't remember anything, that's for your own safety. You are the Scintillator for Earth. I will return with Surt, if there is a sign of trouble a few more millennia from now. I can turn you into a male if you're sick of being a woman?" His laughter roars through the park.

"No, it's fine. Shall we?"

Rapturous thunder circles overhead and it's difficult to hear one another, we proceed toward the centre of the park. We position ourselves and when I communicate to the stone, it comes to me, a soft orb of pink light, glittering gold and spinning. It's so beautiful. The fissure above us is now beginning to lose its shape, and it's tearing at the sides and stardust is raining from the tiny planets that are imploding. I know there isn't much time and I must ignite the stone. The sensation as blue light rips through me is transcending, ethereal and hot light escapes at my fingertip, crackling. The small sphere hovers near to my face and as the blue light from within me connects with the pink sphere, it catapults up into the hole, leaving a trail of glitter, up into space and each particle finds its way to the relevant planet and within a few minutes the worlds and the universe are restored and there's not a hint of what just happened, save for an oversized jester dancing and laughing in the middle of a kids' park.

We don't say goodbye as he wanders off and out of the

park, not once looking back. I make my way home and feed my cat. My clothes are torn from the growth of my body and my bones ache from the distortion. The feeling of euphoria as I drift off to sleep that night is followed by a sense of calm, then a sweeping darkness, a nothingness. No dreams.

It's a bleak morning, the alarm clock flickers 6a.m. The cat is staring at me from the floor, mewling. There is a meeting at the bank today. Nervous Shirley wants to meet at the coffee shop early, so we can eat breakfast and have a natter before work. She's sat in the corner and next to her is a man in a black leather jacket, he's Gothic looking with very high cheekbones, he's reading a book: 'Scintillation'. It looks like a sci fi book and has a swirling mass of sky on the cover. I've never liked sci fi books. He sees me looking and peers up over his half-moon glasses. He winks at me and I blush. He has lovely teeth.

"Coo-eee! Over here lovely, I've got us a table." Nervous Shirley has the knack of stating the obvious, and the man with the lovely teeth looks at me and smiles.

"Yes, I can see. Two flat-whites and two croissants?"

"Sounds lovely, yes please."

As I'm stood in the queue, the Gothic man comes over to the counter to order another coffee. He stands behind me and the scent of petunia oil fills my nostrils. It's such a familiar smell. I try and think what it reminds me of. He orders a Cortado and a lemon slice.

"Lovely morning, isn't it?" He asks from behind me. I turn and he is uncomfortably close and surprisingly pretty for a man.

"Not really," I reply, gesturing to the rain slashing the windows and the trees bending in the wind.

His laughter is musical, infectious, I instantly laugh with him, although I'm not sure why I'm laughing.

"Well, enjoy your coffee, Surt." Strange he would call me that.

"My name's Marne."

"It works every time!"

"A charmer, I see."

He sits and resumes his book, not even looking up to drink his coffee. After the flirtatious banter at the till, he takes no further interest and I conclude it was my imagination and he was just being friendly. The aroma of oils continues to baffle me. Where do I recognize it from? The hefty woman passes the window but she doesn't have her dog with her. She comes into the shop and sits at the table opposite us. She pulls a package out of her bag, wrapped in brown paper and tied with string. She opens it to reveal a book, taking small sips on her hot chocolate like she's savouring the moment. The children's book is called 'Socks' and has the picture of a Jack Russell on the cover wearing a party hat. She openly weeps and runs her fingers over the dog's face. I feel bad for her, she must have lost her dog. I've never seen her without it.

The man reading the sci-fi book looks at the hefty woman and he smiles at her as she dabs the corners of her eyes with a tissue from her pocket, then he continues to read.

"Why do you reckon she's crying?" Nervous Shirley asks, on the brink of tears herself.

"I think her dog might have died."

"Oh no, that's so sad. How awful. Oh I'm sorry, that's really got to me." Shirley cries louder and harder than the woman who has lost her dog and the Goth looks up and laughs at us all.

"It's alright, I'm sure she'll be fine."

"Isn't it sad about the fire at that high-rise last week? The fire spread so quickly, the fire services weren't able to rescue many people. It's such a bloody tragedy." The word 'fire' makes me shudder and I worry about the state of the building I live in.

The Gothic-looking man gets up to leave, slipping the book into his pocket. He raises an arm to wave as he reaches the door and he flashes me his perfect teeth, then he slips out into the storm and into the throng of people wrestling with umbrellas and coat hoods. I wonder if he comes here often.

Nervous Shirley has made her way over to the hefty woman's table and has an arm around her, comforting her. The woman's book is open on the fifth page and the cartoon dog is running off from its owner with a pink stone in its mouth as she shouts after it.

"It looks funny. What's that in the dog's mouth?" I ask.

"My dog died recently on the playing field at Mill Park. He was such a wonderful dog. My best friend really. On the day he passed away, it's funny, he picked up a pink stone. I've never seen anything like it. It was so unusual, pretty. He ran off with it and wouldn't give it to me. The minute he dropped the stone he got hit by lightning. My poor little socks..."

The woman sobs and I feel very bad for her. She pulls the stone from her pocket and places it on the table. She gets up and walks off, leaving it there. "I don't want it. It reminds me of poor old Socks, dying. You keep it dear," she says to me.

I roll it around in my fingers: it's smooth, completely smooth, and there are tiny dimples as if it was once filled with stones, like a strawberry that's lost its pips.

I slip it in my pocket and it feels warm and nice, like it's supposed to be there.

THE END

ABOUT THE AUTHOR

Carla Day is a writer, avid reader and mountain enthusiast. Carla writes across many genres and has recently released a women's tragicomic memoir. She can be found most days, sitting on a weather-beaten log at the beach, scribbling a novel or on a mountain top contemplating life. She resides in South Wales with her partner, son and Jack Russell. Carla is a passionate hiker and keen animal rights advocate.

Author pages...

Facebook—CarlaDay02

Instagram—CarlaDay61

Old Flame
by Will Patching

It was her red hair that he noticed first. The early evening
sun's golden rays streaming through the pub windows set
her head alight as it bobbed among the thirsty crowd. Her
face was not visible, and her back was to him as she squeezed
through the crowd of drinkers, hand held aloft, her freckled
arm waving a twenty-pound note at the barman to get his
attention.

'Yeah, she's well fit, Tom.'

Clarkson, the irritating turd who'd spoken, had an
uncanny knack of spotting when Tom Creed's totty-radar
went to full alert. They weren't friends, merely colleagues

out for a Friday evening drink with a dozen other lads who worked at the Evason Banking Corporation office, just a three-minute walk from their favourite drinking hole, The Brokers Arms.

Tonight, Tom was buzzing—his best week yet and, as a result, he had a six-figure bonus heading his way at month end. Clarkson, despite his exasperating attitude and pug-ugly face, was largely responsible for this latest 'lucky break' Tom had chalked up. He turned to his unwitting benefactor and forced a grin as he peered down at the smaller man.

'How the fuck can you see what I'm looking at, you poison dwarf?' His accompanying smirk was supposed to take the sting out of the insult. It was just friendly banter, after all.

A flicker of resentment tripped across Clarkson's eyes before he smiled, a sly curving of his lips exposing his crooked teeth. He had Tom's complete attention, revelled in it for a few moments, hugging his secret to himself, clearly happy for this rare opportunity to get one up on his obnoxious senior colleague. Tom huffed and went to turn away, but Clarkson laid a heavy paw on his forearm, and, with a gleam in his eye, pointed at the angled mirrors situated above the expensive liqueurs and spirits on the bar's top shelf.

Tom bent his knees to drop his lanky frame to match Clarkson's height but still had to duck his head before he could see her reflection. He gasped, recognition, confusion, and then relief as he realized it wasn't *her*.

Couldn't be her.

He rested a hand on his colleague's shoulder, dug his fingers deep into the knotted muscles that plagued his stocky companion, and heard a mild yelp in response. Clarkson had told him that early onset ankylosing spondylitis had distorted and fused the bones in his spine, encouraging those he worked with to bestow upon him numerous insulting nicknames. In his current role, he was regularly abused by aggressive young traders, including the one tormenting him now—the one he hated most but tolerated through necessity.

'So, there really are some advantages to experiencing life as a stunted hunchback, then.' Tom tore his eyes away from the reflection of the girl at the bar to throw a fleeting sneer at his underling, adding, voice still laden with sarcasm, 'You're such a bloody freak, aren't you? Dead-end job, in your mid-forties, and probably still a virgin. Hah.'

As the girl drifted back into the crowd, a cocktail in hand, Tom noted it was just the one drink and hoped she was alone. He stood to his full impressive height, trying to spot her again as she made her way through the crush of mostly male bodies. He caught another glimpse of her flaming hair as she slipped through the door to the riverside beer garden.

Time to dump the dwarf.

He tossed a final snide comment at Clarkson whose eyes betrayed his weakness—the hurt he experienced from Tom's cruel observations.

'Oh, don't start whinging on about how un-PC we are. Again. You won't get anywhere in Evason unless you toughen up, sonny Jim. I'm only trying to help. Now go and play with the other junior analysts. I've got some hot fanny waiting for me.' He smoothed his bleached blonde hair, took an appreciative glance at himself using his iPhone camera as a mirror, and murmured to Clarkson, 'Later, pal.'

He winked, patted the unfortunate man's shoulder, picked up the ice bucket containing the remnants of his magnum of champagne, grabbed two clean glasses from the tray on their table, and went on the prowl. An alpha-male in his prime, hunting a mate for the night.

The moment Tom's back was turned, Clarkson's expression lightened. He dumped his untouched champagne on the table—that single unwanted glass of bubbly was his only reward for his efforts in securing Tom's latest triumph, and even that had been delivered with false magnanimity and not a little reluctance.

Tom had a nickname too—Tom-the-Tight-Arsed-Ballbreaker—although it was not one anyone used in his presence. Instead, Clarkson muttered it under his breath as his devious, toothy grin reappeared. He watched Tom swagger his way to the door, murmuring to himself, 'Good luck... *Pal*. You're going to need it this time,' before pushing his way to the bar to get himself a decent pint of beer.

The beer garden was as busy as the pub interior. The setting summer sun sparkled and glittered, reflecting fragments of silver and blue sky off the surface of the River Thames. It was a beautiful spot, crowded with office workers winding down from another intense week of making and breaking fortunes in the City. The average income of the revellers was well into six figures, and some, like Tom, were pulling down seven figures, or even more for the partners in the merchant banks headquartered nearby. Many of the faces were familiar to him, as, at the tender age of thirty-one, he was an old hand at his company. A wheeler-dealer with a reputation for risk-taking and lightning trades, who would soon join the firm's superstars, a partner even, having recently identified and promoted two obscure potential buyouts—opportunities the senior team had missed. These successes had showered good fortune on him and his employers, revitalizing his career after a lengthy hiatus.

As far as Tom was concerned, he should be a partner already. Would be, if not for *her*.

Spotting that redhead had disturbed his celebratory mood, his equanimity, and not just because his balls were aching for release. She'd reminded him of his old flame, the witch who almost brought him down. The femme fatale who'd tried to extinguish his burning ambition and the reason he'd failed to achieve his rightful status within the firm.

'Water under the bridge,' he muttered to himself, idly peering west. There, between the Victorian turrets, the road sections split and lifted skyward as a high-masted yacht prepared to sail beneath London's most iconic river crossing.

Forget her, he thought. I'm finally back on track after nigh-on two bloody years of purgatory.

Thoughts about that single hiccup in his career were not going to ruin his evening. Life was good, and dwelling on the past was not his way. He preferred to make the most of his downtime—and that entailed plenty of action between the sheets.

With a friendly nod to several senior traders employed by his competitors, the ones he liked to keep sweet in case he ever needed to jump ship—either for lack of the partnership position he soon expected to materialise, or if someone exposed his unethical methods—Tom searched the milling throng for that redheaded beauty who reminded him so much of Stella.

Stella Kinsella.

It had been over eighteen months since he'd last given her much thought. Only now, with the appearance of this new female on his turf, did he allow himself to reflect on what had happened to Stella. Unfortunate but, like the dwarf, people had to be tough to survive in his business. Even tougher, if they rubbed Tom Creed up the wrong way.

His lips danced a smile as he made his way to the water's edge, his head switching from side to side, trying to spot the wench.

Ah, there she is.

He stood still for a few seconds, observing her. In profile, as she sat on the low garden wall, staring down at the shimmering surface of the river, the reflected light flickering across her face, Tom felt that twinge of recognition again.

It's uncanny, he thought. She's so like her.

A slightly bigger nose, more pronounced cheekbones, different coloured eyes, and a wider, more voluptuous mouth. A shade taller, with bigger tits too.

Absolutely gorgeous.

A clumsy oaf barged into Tom's champagne bucket, spoiling the moment, slopping freezing water and some chunks of ice down the front of his immaculate Italian suit. He turned to snarl at the man but immediately let his mouth curl into a grin as the senior partner from Goldman Sachs laughed at his misfortune, semi-apologetically, his words mildly slurred.

'So, so s-sorry, Tommy! Bit worse for wear, tonight. We're celebrating. And when are you coming to join us instead of spinning your wheels with that crappy outfit you're with?'

'Well, when you offer me a full partnership and a decent golden hullo, Harry.' Tom winked, his face creasing into a wolfish smile. 'Call me when you can afford me!'

He clicked his tongue and spun back in time to see his objective placing her empty glass on the wall, hoisting her handbag to her shoulder before turning towards him. For a moment, they made eye contact, and he felt a shiver of electricity surge through his nerves, a tingle of anticipation, and that unsettling sensation of déjà vu as they stared at each other.

Dammit!

He saw her eyes drop, drawn to the dark damp patch extending from his crotch to his knees.

Tom Creed didn't do embarrassment. No, he was way too confident for that. And if there's one thing he knew women found attractive, it was a man who oozed confidence and was totally at ease with himself. Especially one as handsome as him. A rugby star at school and university, his features unaffected by the brutal game—one he'd not played in almost a decade—he stood head and shoulders above most of those around him, carrying the muscular body of a man in his prime, his crystal blue eyes like beacons drawing the fairer sex onto his rocks.

'No, I did *not* piss myself, if that's what you're thinking.'

It wasn't his best opening line but, given the circumstances, the mild challenge in his voice would have to do.

She glanced behind her as if he was addressing someone there, hovering over the Thames perhaps.

Silly.

She turned back, scowling at him. Playing hard to get.

'Do I know you?' Her voice, slightly accented, pitched low, thrummed with sexual promise.

Or maybe that was just Tom's overactive imagination.

'Not yet. But you will soon enough. I'm Tom.' He held up the two glasses, rattled the ice bucket, arms held wide and open. 'I see you've finished your drink. Fancy some Bollie?' He gave her his warmest smile, unthreatening, his eyes crinkling with amusement. 'I'm celebrating. Why not join me?'

She stared at him, a few beats longer than was normal. Her dark, piercing eyes made him uncomfortable. That was a new one. What was it about her that made him feel this way?

Stella's ghost, perhaps.

Not that Tom suffered from superstition or any other such illogical nonsense. No, Stella was dead, and although she looked like her, this woman was definitely someone else.

Some*thing* else entirely.

Stella had been a pushover. Easy pickings. This wench was feisty. And probably a right vixen in bed, he decided.

'I don't drink with strangers. Or colleagues.' She glanced over his shoulder, her look suggesting there was someone far more interesting behind him. Then let her molten hazel eyes linger on his as she continued addressing him, her withering tone clawing at his ego. 'And especially not arrogant, self-centred traders who think they're God's gift to the female species.'

She pushed past him, eyes no longer on him, dismissing him as a mere irritant.

Well, that went well, he thought.

He watched her sashay her way to the exit, torn between following her or playing it cool himself. A hefty slap on his back made the decision for him. With a grunt, he peered over his shoulder to see the bloody poison dwarf leering up at him, a fleck of spittle on his lower lip, and a wicked glint in his eyes.

'Crashed, burned and died, eh, Tom?' A gurgle of laughter accompanied Clarkson's summation as he added, 'That's not like you, mate.'

'I'm not your mate. Why don't you just fuck off and die, Clarkson?' He snapped the words out, head jerking downward as he spun round, almost butting his colleague, forcing him to recoil. The defective little creep had his uses, though. Tom's tone softened. 'Do you know who she is? Where she works?'

'Nope.' Clarkson sank the last of his pint, burped outrageously, turning heads all around in response to the disgusting noise, the hubbub dying away for a few beats before recovering. 'But keep me fuelled up with these all night and I'll find out for you.' The empty beer mug joggled in his hand, waving under Tom's nose, his other hand gesturing towards the pub entrance. 'The bar's that way.'

'Monday. First thing. Or there'll be trouble.'

'Done... The micro-brewery's craft ale. And a tequila chaser. I'm very thirsty tonight.' He held the glass out to Tom, waiting, smug self-satisfaction crawling across his features. 'Now would be good... *Boss.*'

Tom wanted to slap the grinning dickhead, tell him not be so lairy, to piss off to the bar to get his own drinks, while stuffing a twenty into his grubby mitts to seal the deal. With iron-willed self-control, he kept his cool, his mind on the flame-haired beauty and the knowledge that Clarkson would be as good as his word, would have the skinny on her by Monday morning, even if he had to act like Sam Spade all weekend.

It was a bargain, for less than the price of a bottle of bubbly.

Idiot.

'Personal telephone number, too. Not just her office extension.'

Clarkson's eyes sparkled, and his head wobbled up and down in agreement, his mouth quivering a smile as he rocked from side to side, shifting his weight using the balls of his feet.

The nerdy analyst seemed to find joy and excitement in the most mundane things. Getting his superior to do his bidding being one of them. Tom sighed, shook his head, placed his champagne and the two flutes on the wall where she'd been sitting and made his way to the bar.

Clarkson's eyes followed his progress, his quivering lips morphing into a wicked grin of anticipation as he tugged out his phone, selected messaging and tapped a flurry of letters before hitting: 'Send'.

With a furtive glance around him, checking no one was observing him—they weren't—he slipped the phone back inside his jacket before shifting his attention to the oversized bottle of champagne.

On Monday mornings, Tom Creed liked to be the first in the office, raring to get back in the hot seat, to check on the Asian markets, now well underway by 5a.m. London time. Getting an edge on his colleagues was one of the reasons he was a big swinging dick in the City. Or liked to think he was.

This morning, he was well under par. Friday night had disappeared into a blurry black hole not long after the redhead had left, the champagne mixed with tequila slammers getting the better of him. Or maybe the dozen raw oysters he'd guzzled down had been sat on the plate too long, warmed by the evening sun. He'd puked and passed out in the beer garden. He remembered that much, and Clarkson helping him home. Fortunately, his bachelor pad was only a ten-minute walk from the pub—well, twenty, with him staggering and leaning on Quasimodo for support.

Saturday had seen him nursing a mother of a hangover, one that lasted well into Sunday. Even now, he was far from recovered, but he sat in his chair and booted up his screens ready to go into battle for his employers.

Two coffees and a few snorts later, his colleagues began to dribble in, and by 7am, the place was humming. Tom felt much better for the caffeine and cocaine coursing through his veins, sharpening his senses, his awful weekend forgotten. The sight of a jubilant Clarkson, beaming at him, holding a scrap of paper out to him, gave him an added boost.

While Tom had been engulfed in a forty-eight-hour alcoholic fugue, the luscious vision of the girl in the bar—the Stella lookalike—tumbled through his consciousness, her body naked, his imagination repeatedly ramming his manhood into her every orifice, much as he had with his ex.

'Here you go, boss.' Tom snatched the proffered paper from his hand as Clarkson shared his knowledge, fishing for a pat on the head. 'Italian bint, I gather. Was working in Goldman's Rome office. Just been seconded here.'

Her name looked foreign too: Trulli Luce.

'Truly loose, eh? I like the sound of that!' Tom smoothed out the tatty scrap, two numbers scrawled in Clarkson's appalling handwriting next to the words *Mobile* and *Home*. 'No office number? No extension?' Tom tried to sound peeved but was struggling. He couldn't disguise his pleasure at having her details in his hand. His weekend dreams would soon be reality, of that he was certain. 'I said not *just* her office phone, you moron.'

'It's not *loose*. Her surname's pronounced *loo-chay*. And she's in training.' Clarkson sniffed, his waggy-tailed dog impression replaced by a sour expression, his lips tightening, flabby cheeks twitching before he added, 'Not been with them long. She's got no extension yet. And there's no point calling the switchboard—they won't interrupt their training sessions, especially not for you sniffing around one of theirs.' Clarkson took his handkerchief and mopped his red-rimmed eyes, removing the crusty residue that regularly formed there. It looked to Tom like he was crying, although he knew this was just another consequence of Clarkson's ailment and the side-effects of the medication he took to relieve the constant pain of his crippled joints. 'Those numbers are all you need.' He slouched away, back to his tiny cubicle buried among the plebs on the floor below.

Tom barely noticed his departure, his mind spinning through the options of when best to approach her. Goldman's training sessions often went on late into the evening, so he would wait until 9p.m. to call her. He rubbed his hands together, excited at the prospect, certain she wouldn't be able to resist his obvious charms. They never could.

The day dragged by for Tom, his performance lacking the lustre and thrust of his usual aggressive approach, but he held his own and managed to end up with a small trading profit while many of his colleagues suffered losses.

Not too shabby, he thought. He considered joining them for a drink but decided instead to badger Clarkson for some inside information regarding a potential hostile takeover he'd identified—one he planned to trade in advance. Doing so would guarantee him enormous profits, thereby ensuring his place among the partners. And it had the added bonus of killing some time before he would make the call.

He trudged down to Clarkson's cubicle, the analyst oblivious to his approach, working after hours, the only one still at his desk. A loner, seemingly with no life or friends outside of his job.

No wonder he's latched on to my coat tails, Tom thought.

For a second, he felt a sliver of guilt—not a common emotion for him, and one he always squelched the moment it surfaced. The latest deal the analyst had assisted him in securing had earned Tom a small fortune. Clarkson was a grafter yet paid a pittance by comparison.

His junior colleague had taken risks too, all to Tom's benefit, with rarely a murmur of complaint that he was not being properly rewarded. The fool didn't realize he would be the scapegoat if Tom was ever in danger of being exposed for bending the rules.

Too bad, he thought, shrugging away the tiny twinge of remorse he felt. Tom's was a dog-eat-dog world and he always sought out the naïve to manipulate them to his own advantage. Clarkson had pitched up a few months ago and was friendless, shunned by his colleagues, his interpersonal skills non-existent. The hunchback was happy enough, basking in the reflected glory, content with the occasional compliments and rare words of approval Tom offered when he felt obliged.

Clarkson, startled at Tom's approach, having been engrossed in a telephone conversation while tapping away at his keyboard, eyes fixed on the screen as green digits tumbled before him, dropped the phone into its cradle, apparently mid-sentence. Tom sensed something was amiss, the flash in Clarkson's eyes betraying concern.

Is he worried I overheard something? And if so, what and why?

Tom's mind hit overdrive, his natural suspicion revving into the fast lane.

There were plenty of colleagues who would happily see Tom-the-Tight-Arsed-Ballbreaker get his comeuppance, and he was acutely aware that the only weak link who could make that happen was sitting down here.

Alone.

Talking about God knows what. To God knows who...

With a rapid calculation, Tom mentally assessed how exposed he was. Not very, and the naïve analyst had no idea what Tom had prepared for such an eventuality. After tonight, properly stitching up Clarkson would become a priority.

Just as it had for his predecessor.

Stella.

She'd been a major asset for Tom. With her help, he'd punctured the Chinese walls the firm had erected to prevent Tom's team from trading on inside information— the illusory walls that supposedly protected and insulated all the confidential data the commercial divisions held on their clients. Tom had been careful with her too, had wooed her and bedded her, told her she was *the one* and turned her into his spy, his source of valuable information. Over the ensuing months, he'd come dangerously close to falling for her, too.

Then she went and ruined it all.

Everything went tits up when he'd laughed at her proposal. A traditionalist, she'd waited until February 29th during the last leap year. His response had shocked her— she clearly believed he'd agree to marry her. By way of reply, he told her he'd regularly shagged other women during the year they'd been together and assumed she'd known, had understood that a man like him had 'needs'. Apparently not. She'd been tearful, embarrassed. Devastated. Then angry.

A woman scorned.

As with Clarkson, Tom had made sure he'd set things up to shift the blame so that any potential inquiry would point the finger at her, not him. When she threatened to expose what they'd been doing, he told her so. She still blew the whistle.

Stupid, stupid woman.

A messy month of lengthy hostile interviews for them both, ploughing through masses of paperwork, the forensic department going through everything with a magnifying glass, had Stella screaming her innocence, that she'd been manipulated and abused by her senior colleague.

Tom had managed to shrug off most of the shite with only a minor reprimand. Teflon Tom, she'd called him. While packing her personal belongings, flanked by two security guards ready to escort her from the premises, she spat at him, and vowed the truth would come out—she'd see to that, even if it took her the rest of her life. She had no idea, when she yelled those words, just how short a time that would prove to be.

She'd been a great lay, a fantastic diversion, but Tom didn't take her threats lightly. After she left, Stella kept on spreading her 'lies' throughout the City. That sealed her fate. He could not, would not let her continue trying to sully his reputation and spoil his glittering career.

No. That was not going to happen.

And that was when he uploaded the video.

'Are you all right, boss?' Clarkson was watching Tom with curious eyes, trying to read his expression.

Fat chance.

With his poker face intact, he patted Clarkson's hump with forced bonhomie.

'I'm good. Let's talk Zeitmann's. I've got an hour or two to kill, and you and I have plenty more to discover about that failing outfit.' Tom pulled up a chair from the adjacent cubicle and watched as Clarkson tapped away, head down, doing as he was bid.

Clarkson persuaded Tom to buy him a couple of pints at the Brokers' Arms after they'd finished their illicit dissection of Zeitmann Corporations' preliminary, unaudited accounts. His hangover had long since receded, so Tom acquiesced, counting down the minutes to 9p.m., his mind full of thoughts about Trulli—and the glorious year he'd experienced with Stella.

Bloody nympho.

She'd been exhausting in bed, and he licked his lips, hoping her doppelganger was up to the same athletic standards.

Redheads were his weakness, his favourite female flavour, as they always seemed the most eager to please. Probably from years of being teased at school, always the underdog, the carrot-topped loners, speckled with brown freckles that made them different, set them apart. The spotted skin stains that he found endearing.

Sexy.

And Stella had been abandoned by a single mother and spent her formative years in a convent somewhere in deepest Ireland. That probably helped, he thought.

The bar clock ticked past 9p.m. and Tom, having tuned out Clarkson's incessant wittering for much of the previous twenty minutes, excused himself and went to the beer garden to make the call. There were few drinkers in tonight—Monday was always quiet, with the crowds gradually building during the week until they peaked on Friday—but it was even quieter by the river. Outside, the summer sun hung low in the sky, bathing everything in a red-tinted golden glow that made him feel warm inside. It was either that or the anticipation of talking to Trulli.

He made the call, a grin on his face, totally confident he could woo her, tempt her out tonight.

'Bollocks!'

Voicemail. He considered hanging up as her recorded voice encouraged him to leave a message, decided to go for it anyway.

'Hi, Trulli. It's Tom Creed. We met briefly on Friday—I was the one with the champagne. You blew me off as you didn't know me then, but since we've officially met,' he chuckled, 'I hope we can have that drink together. Call me when you get this message and we can meet later tonight if you fancy.'

He hit the end button and stood there, uncertain, gazing at the view for several minutes, wondering whether to call on a substitute from his list of willing lovelies, but shook his head, too disappointed to bother, and made his way back inside, pocketing his phone as he went. Then he saw Clarkson, his idiotic grin splitting his face in two as he jerked his thumb over his shoulder towards the bar.

Tom glanced in that direction and felt his heart lurch and miss a beat. She had her back to him as she ordered a drink, her hair lustrous, her curvy figure swathed in a short black dress, clinging to her as she leaned against the bar, one high-heeled foot curled against the back of a shapely calf, stretching herself taller, her right foot on tiptoe.

Sexy, much?

Woah!

He felt the urge to charge at her, like a rutting bull, and take her right there in front of the handful of other drinkers. Resisting the impulse, he played it cool and strolled to the bar as her drink arrived.

'Can I get that for you, Trulli?' He held a fifty-pound note out to the barman, his eyes smouldering as she gazed up at him, no surprise on her face as she heard him use her name. She cocked her head to the side, inspecting him, no smile—but no scowl either. She was a cool one. 'I did offer on Friday. Funnily enough, I just left you a message on your voicemail. Inviting you for a drink.'

Her eyes darkened, unsure now. The barman waited for her to agree before he took Tom's money, and she kept them both standing like that, frozen in time. She had an aura, unsettling but attractive, and the men remained patient as she made her decision.

A nod at the bartender, and a hint of a smile for Tom.

'How do you know my name, and where did you get my number?'

She sipped her cocktail, eyeing him over the rim of the glass as he received his change. Was she peeved or complimented by his unexpected knowledge? Difficult to tell, but Tom plumped for the latter.

'Very little happens around here without my knowledge, Trulli.' He gave her a playful smile, tapped a finger to the side of his nose, tipped his glass at her and took a sip. 'With such an attractive woman arriving on my patch...? Well, what do you expect me to do? Of course, I want to get to know you.'

'Get to know me?' The words spun a silky web in his mind—a stocking-shaped one, with him stripping it from her thigh with his teeth. She simply oozed sensuality. 'I've been warned about you, Tom Creed. You don't have a great reputation, according to the ladies I've met.'

'Oh dear. Jealousy and rumours. Nothing more than that. A cross I have to bear, I'm afraid.' He spread his arms, palms upwards, his body language saying—*Just look at me and you'll understand why*—as he chuckled, grateful to see her smile widen in response. 'Give me a chance and you'll get to discover the real Tom Creed.'

As if that would ever happen, but the line had worked

before, so he wheeled it out again, infusing it with as much fake sincerity as he was able to muster.

'Mmm. We'll see.' She held out a graceful hand for him to shake, her expression now coquettish, bewitching, her voice low and sexy again. 'Pleased to meet you, Mr. Creed.'

He took her slender fingers in his palm and dipped his head to kiss the back of her hand, keeping his eyes on hers as his lips caressed her skin. Her scent made him dizzy, his groin reacting, throbbing in response and anticipation of the night to come.

'My pleasure, Miss Luce.'

'A whole bloody week!'

Tom muttered to himself, head shaking as he sat at his desk, morose on Monday morning, thinking of how much time he'd wasted trying to bed *Truly-the-ice-maiden*.

'One sodding kiss!'

Admittedly a passionate one, late on Saturday night, moments before she jumped into her Uber and vanished into the night—just as she had after their previous four 'dates' on successive evenings last week. His balls had almost erupted in his pants when her tongue lingered on his, the silky soft warmth driving him to distraction. He had crushed her to him, knew she could feel his erection pressing into her belly, but she dipped and twisted out of his arms, laughing at him as her taxi arrived.

Tom Creed had never known a woman like her. Every other female he'd planned to screw had either been blown off by him after the first brief spell of getting to know each other—never more than an evening or two over dinner or drinks—or arrived in his bed by the third night at the latest.

What was it about her that had delved so deeply into his psyche, driving her hooks into his very core? Last week, his days had been regularly interrupted by daydreams of athletic nights spent exploring her body—much to the detriment of his personal targets.

Love wasn't on his radar, that he could dismiss. It was

the challenge, he decided, and he was sure it had much to do with her similarity to Stella. Both sexy as hell, similar in looks and standards of beauty, but his old flame had been easy to bed.

Until she snuffed her own life.

Because of him.

The videos of *their* lovemaking had graced his screen during his lonely nights since meeting Trulli, his brain projecting the new lust of his life onto the screen while his sweaty fingers did their best to relieve the pressure in his loins.

Poor Stella.

She had no idea he'd installed top-of-the-range pinhole video cameras, secreted in his apartment behind the mirrors and in the ceiling, aimed at the bed, capturing her luscious naked flesh from all angles as she 'prostituted' and 'slutted' herself, willingly performing for him. The sound of her gobbling his dick, groaning with pleasure, gasping for air after deep-throating him, had echoed around his apartment last night as he grunted in response while pleasuring himself over her antics.

'She was like a bloody horny Hoover.' He found himself muttering again as the images twirled in his mind, her face no longer her own. 'I'll bet Trulli's even more of a nympho.'

All he had to do was breach the dam.

Tonight.

It had to happen tonight, or he was certain he would simply explode.

Before leaving him standing forlorn and frustrated on the pavement on Saturday, she'd fobbed him off, yakking on about having regular Sunday lunch and dinner with her parents—a commitment she was adamant she wouldn't change for him. At his insistence, she'd agreed to meet him again tonight, after work, her eyes sparkling with promise.

'Prick. Tease.'

He gave himself a rueful smile and tried to concentrate on his screens, but the minutes dragged by with agonizing sluggishness and he had to force himself to do the job he usually loved. Eventually, he gave up and trotted down the stairs to Clarkson's section. Unlike the open plan floor where he spent his days of labour—a place buzzing with testosterone and energy—the Morgue, as he liked to call this place, was crammed full of cubicles, the atmosphere more akin to a graveyard than an office despite accommodating three times as many workers.

'Hey, Quasi.'

Clarkson spun his entire body around, the swivel chair allowing him to do so with ease despite his rigid neck and back. He squinted up at Tom, eyebrows lifting, forehead furrowed, clearly wondering what had prompted this official visit from the hallowed hall above. Normally, Tom only ever appeared down here late in the evening, when few others were around, to undertake his illicit research with his willing helper. Officially, Clarkson was the flunky who came to his master's desk when required to deliver legitimate data requested through formal channels.

'So, the mountain comes to Mohammed.' Clarkson folded his arms across his chest, narrowed his red-rimmed eyes at Tom. 'What can I do for you, sir?'

'Walk with me to the coffee shop.' Tom didn't wait for an answer, just headed for the door, certain Clarkson would follow. Like a puppy.

They arrived at the nearby café and Tom paid for their lattes and the carrot cake the sweet-toothed analyst loved to scoff. With his mouth full, Clarkson asked, the words muffled as flecks of masticated brown dough showered the table between them, 'What's up then, Tom?'

He wasn't sure himself, but during his lonely Sunday, mooching around his apartment, he'd realized that during the time he'd spent with Trulli, she'd skilfully avoided giving up much about herself, turning the conversation around each time he probed, diverting him to chat about a subject he loved more than anything else.

Himself.

He needed to know more about her and was impatient to find out. Knowledge was power, and he desperately wanted something that would make him feel less dependent on her whims. Her full story, even the dirt—especially the dirt—if it could be dug. The man in front of him, mouth flapping wide, his tongue and teeth churning over sickly, sticky confection, was just the person to wield the spade.

'Someone's been making enquiries about me.' She hoisted an immaculate eyebrow as she quizzed him with her eyes. 'I wonder who would do such a thing, don't you?' Her accent thickened, bringing to mind the mafia films Tom had enjoyed in his youth. 'Whoever it is ought to realize they're playing with fire... I think you know how dangerous that can be.'

Something in the way she looked at him sent a frosty finger scraping down his spine. It wasn't just *The Godfather* impression she carried off with such ease but the memory her words spurred, saturating his brain with unwanted images.

Stella.

Crying, sitting on her bed, her nightgown soaking wet, viewed from the camera set up to transmit the video, live online.

Tom coughed into his fist, swiped his other palm over his hair, trying to cover his reaction, to shunt the movie from his mind. Stella touched his bicep, eyes still hard, but her voice softer now, solicitous.

'Are you alright? You look very pale...' She frowned and asked, 'Is it something I said?'

'No. No. No.' A laugh caught in the back of his throat as he tried to shrug off the dreadful memories. 'Something I ate earlier, I think. Excuse me for a moment.'

He left her standing at the bar, could feel her eyes following him as he stumbled to the bathroom.

'For Chrissakes.'

He breathed in, deep into his lungs, blew out slowly to

calm himself. Another rare moment of guilt had tweaked his conscience. Perhaps this new woman in his life, this minx who he'd yet to bed, wasn't good for him. The similarities with Stella were dredging up memories he'd buried deep.

With a shudder, he splashed cold water on his face, then stared at himself in the mirror. A haunted reflection gawked back at him.

'I won't let this ruin my night.'

He patted his cheeks to regain some colour in the flesh, dragged a comb through his blonde locks and used his forefinger to smooth his sculpted eyebrows to remind himself of his perfection. With no one else in the bathroom and so few drinkers in the bar likely to interrupt him, he fondled his grandfather's gold snuffbox.

'This'll perk me up.'

With his black Amex card, he hurriedly tapped out a line of white powder on the edge of the sink before snorting it through a rolled up twenty. He pinched his nose with finger and thumb, his nerves steadier from the rush, took another deep breath and made his way back to the bar.

She'd gone.

'What the hell...?'

The barman glanced over his shoulder, his fingers busy with the till, and said, 'The lady had to leave, sir. She sends her apologies and said she'll meet you tomorrow, same time, but something urgent had come up.'

Tom, unsure whether to be pissed off or relieved, sipped his gin with a trembling hand and wondered what had dragged her away so soon. Barely ten minutes had gone by since she'd arrived. He sighed.

'A woman of mystery and intrigue.'

The barman must have heard the words Tom whispered to himself. 'That she is, sir,' he chuckled as he wiped the bar and cleared her glass away.

The gin soothed him, the cocaine numbing his senses, his confidence returning, but Tom wondered if he would suffer nightmares tonight thanks to her words.

*

Tuesday morning saw Tom arrive late at the office. Earlier, when he saw himself in the mirror as he shaved, his fingers unsteady, inadvertently teasing blood from his skin with the blade, his eyes reminded him of Clarkson's.

'What a bloody night.'

He slid behind his desk, waving away the questions from his colleagues, gloating at how he'd missed the early morning rally and the resultant surge in share prices. He stared at his screens, the figures a blur, his mind elsewhere, and this time, not with Trulli.

Stella had spent the night tormenting him and he could barely think straight this morning. He dropped his head into his hands, squeezed his eyes tight shut, pushed the heels of his palms into them, trying to erase the images scalding his brain. It didn't help.

The sickening lurch in his stomach sent him scurrying to the toilets, his mind awash with another vision of Stella, the lighter in her hand, tears on her cheeks as she told the camera how much she'd loved him, how he had tricked her into destroying her career while helping him boost his. Worse still, he'd gone on to wreck what was left of her life, her voice rising hysterically as she proclaimed that there was no point living a day longer. He'd shamed her, had shared their private passions with millions online, uploading the video he'd entitled *Old Flame* for every pervert on the planet to see.

'To wank over,' she'd howled. 'I loved you and you did this to me. Your old flame! I should've known I was playing with fire!'

It was only when she flipped the lighter that he realized why her hair and nightgown were soaked, what she'd poured over herself. His laughter had turned to ash in his mouth as the flare of ignition dazzled the camera, her agonized high-pitched squeal piercing his very marrow. The camera refocused immediately after that brief blinding flash to show her flaming body thrashing around, the duvet blazing too, before she stood in a frenzy and flew at the camera, wailing like a demented banshee, the flesh on her face melting as she loomed in close, her blistered bloody mouth stretched wide, eyes bubbling to her cheeks.

Thankfully, she knocked the recording device to the floor, severing the connection before he was forced to view her final death throes.

The Skype call had surprised him, given that they'd had no contact for two months, and he'd assumed she was calling to apologize for spreading the dirt on him, to ask him to take the video down. To call a truce. Instead, she'd not only seared her terrifying final actions into his brain but simultaneously uploaded the video to Facebook.

After the connection broke, Tom had sat staring at the blank screen, mouth open, tears of his own leaking from the corners of his eyes, unable to comprehend how anyone could do that to themselves.

And she'd blamed him.

Although Facebook took her video down within twenty minutes, she'd made certain that his colleagues saw the film of her painful departure by simultaneously sending them a link to the recording by email.

The worst weeks of his life had followed as the entire investigation into his trades was reopened, thanks to her. Tom survived but had been given an unofficial warning by his superiors: *Keep your nose clean or you're out. We'll be keeping a very close eye on you, Creed.* The early partnership position he'd been promised went up in smoke with Stella. Some of the senior partners still eyed him with barely disguised disgust. Thankfully, he'd been too valuable to dismiss but it had taken him eighteen months to recover to where he was today, and that was largely thanks to the arrival of the poison dwarf.

Yes, Stella had cost him, alright.

'Water under the bridge.'

Tom kept telling himself that as he excused himself from

his workplace and headed home for the afternoon.

The rat-a-tat-tat on his door dragged him from his stupor. He'd been drowsing on the sofa, finally expunging the images from his mind with a potent cocktail of coke and alcohol. The first thing he did on arriving back at his apartment was dig out the *Old Flame* video, the highlights of their acrobatic sex life, and he'd watched it on repeat, snorting powder and swilling gin until he finally managed to regain his sense of humour. He'd laughed himself stupid watching her antics—his own identity having been carefully edited out—then, exhausted, he'd flopped into a semi-conscious state, unaware of the passage of time.

The clock above his TV registered 9:45 and the orange sky blazing through his windows to the west told him it was still Tuesday night, not Wednesday morning. He'd planned to meet Trulli, but she wasn't on his agenda tonight. He'd call her—tell her *something had come up*. A gurgle of laughter accompanied that ironic thought.

The knock on the door again.

It was unusual for someone to gain entry to the building without buzzing his security camera and intercom. The main entrance, four flights below, had no concierge on duty but sometimes residents let people in as they left.

He considered ignoring it, but the tapping became insistent, louder, irritating, so he staggered to the door, automatically tucking in his shirt and preening his hair. He pressed his eye to the peephole and saw Stella staring back at him.

'Jesus!'

With his heart jolting, he recoiled, then pressed a palm to the wall to support himself, shook his head to clear his mind.

Impossible.

A few deep breaths and that tapping came again, more urgent this time, and her voice, muffled but clearly accented.

'Tom. Are you okay?'

Trulli.

Thank God.

Confident his mind wasn't coming unhinged from reality, he opened the door and did his best to smile at her.

'Hi. I'm sorry about tonight.' It occurred to him that she must've been researching him too, since he'd not given her his address. The thought boosted his ego, helping him recover, his brain kicking into gear. 'I've just woken up. I'm feeling better now but was sick all night and earlier today.'

'I heard.' She pushed past him, her breasts pressing against his elbow as she squeezed by. Tom felt a tremor in his lower belly, her perfume invading his nostrils, sending him dizzy. 'Aren't you going to offer me a drink, then?' she cooed, slipping off her jacket and tossing it on the sofa.

Maybe his day wasn't going to be a complete write-off, after all. He just hoped he could perform despite the hefty quantity of chemicals he'd ingested.

'Sure.' Tom needed to freshen up. His mouth tasted like a badger had shat in it and he was sure his breath matched Clarkson's, whose halitosis was another by-product of the medication he was obliged to take. 'There's spirits in the cabinet in the corner, mixers in the fridge, a couple of bottles of Moet in there too if you fancy. Ice bucket's under the sink. Help yourself while I use the bathroom.'

Ten minutes later, dressed in a change of clothes and with another toot of coke fresh in his nostrils, Tom was feeling more like his old self, delighted at his unexpected guest's arrival. He lounged on the sofa beside Trulli as she sipped her champagne. She'd handed him a glass the moment he sat and pecked his lips before settling back into the cushions, stretching her legs out and kicking off her heels.

This time, he would play it cool, although he wanted to throw her on the rug and roger her right there and then. No. He'd take the time to savour his conquest. There was a whole night ahead of him. He knocked back his drink and tipped more into both their glasses.

The remote control for his music system lived in a pocket dangling from the sofa and he flicked on some smooth sounds to set the mood. Old Motown tracks usually worked to get things going—Stevie Wonder crooned a love song in the background.

'Are you trying to seduce me with sexy music, Mr. Creed?' She wrinkled her nose with amusement, knowing exactly where tonight was going. 'I prefer classical to this. Some Vivaldi has a more... lively beat, I find.' Her eyebrows lifted suggestively.

'I'm sure I've got *something* you'd like.' He flirted, clinked glasses with her, took another sip. His head wasn't completely clear of his earlier consumption and he needed to slow down if he was to last the night. Words were forming in his mind when she leaned over, took his earlobe between her teeth and bit down, her breath hot on his cheek and eardrum.

'Ow!'

He went to pull away, but her hand snaked around his neck and held his head close as she whispered to him, telling him exactly what she wanted, how he had to behave, and the roleplaying she had in mind for tonight. Her sultry voice was almost inaudible, but her intentions and desires were absolutely clear to Tom, sending the hairs on his arms erect—along with another rather more important part of his anatomy.

Thank Christ for that, he thought.

She stood, asked if she could use his en-suite bathroom to freshen up, then followed the direction he pointed as he sat and watched her disappear, revelling in his good fortune.

'Well, this is a first,' he chuckled to himself. New experiences were the spice of life.

Tom's eyes monitored the clock as the second-hand slowly ticked, his head feeling lighter than normal but his balls heavy and raring to go—and that's what mattered.

Time's up, ready or not, he thought. He stood, tore off his shirt, swayed a little, then made his way to the bedroom.

*

When Tom woke to his alarm at 4am, he groaned at the bedroom lights still blazing as he slammed a hand on the button to turn off the offending din. With one arm thrown over his eyes to block out the crippling light, his head still thumped and he felt dizzy. He couldn't remember setting the alarm and decided it was a much better idea to take another day off and rest. Then he realized he was alone in the bed, his mind fuzzy and confused. Last night felt like a dream and he began to wonder if Trulli really had appeared at his door.

He glanced around the room to check the evidence. Nothing. He thrust his nose against the sheets and was relieved to smell her perfume. Spotted a clump of long red hair on the silk sheet and sniggered to himself.

But what had happened and why couldn't he remember?

He stood, unsteady on his feet, and inspected himself in the mirror.

'What the hell?'

His trousers were still on, but the flies open, and his naked neck and chest were raked raw, streaked where her nails had stripped the skin from his body.

'Rough sex,' he murmured to himself, unable to remember much about the night before—other than that was what she'd wanted.

He'd had plenty of sparky birds, but he'd never come off as badly wounded by any female as he was this morning, and certainly, he should remember her flaying him alive like this. And no matter how drunk he was, he usually recalled having intercourse, even if just staccato glimpses of his performance in flashback. Last night was a black hole, a mystery.

Mind you, he'd had quite a mixture in his system when she'd arrived.

Time to check the recording.

He padded to the kitchen for a cup of fresh coffee—

automatically dispensed from his thousand-pound machine, wirelessly synchronized to his alarm clock—and settled into his lounge to savour the latest notch on his bedpost. Not for the first time, he was relieved his hidden surveillance system created artificial back-ups for his faulty memory. With a smug grin, he flicked on the TV. A second remote control sent the video feed from his hidden cameras to his screen. There was no delay—they were motion sensitive and, after Trulli had magically appeared at his door, he'd primed them so that the moment anyone entered the bedroom his latest amateur porno movie would start recording.

'I just need some popcorn!' He sipped his latte and giggled, feeling himself harden as he watched her cross the room and disappear into his bathroom. A few seconds passed as he heard the water running, then the cameras faded until she reappeared, the recording kicking off again a few seconds before he entered from the lounge.

Trulli backed away as he approached, face fearful as she shouted at him, 'I said I want to leave now, Tom. We have nothing more to discuss.'

Roleplaying. Even her voice had lost its Latin accent. This wasn't really his thing, but how could he refuse such a beauty?

Onscreen-Tom chuckled and then gave a menacing frown, crossed the room, grabbed her by the throat and tossed her onto the bed.

'You slut. You're desperate for it. I know you want it.' The sexy growl in his voice sounded pretty awesome to his ears.

He watched the recording with his tongue tickling his lips in anticipation. Onscreen-Tom unzipped himself. She tried to rise from the bed, but he slapped her face, knocking her flat on her back. The crack sounded loud on playback, but he vaguely remembered trying to be gentle, not wanting to bruise her face, just as she'd specified. Trulli screamed, cursing him for being a 'Fucking pig!' before springing from the bed and shoving him back, almost knocking him to the floor.

'I said: don't you touch me! I'm leaving.'

He grabbed her hair and pulled her back, but she clapped her hands over his, clamping them down, and spun to face him, bending from the waist, the swift action twisting his arm awkwardly as he tried to let go. She straightened before releasing him, wrenching his arm upwards, the joint making an audible popping noise. Tom heard himself screech with pain, and now, watching the playback, rubbed his sore elbow, thinking how seriously they'd been trying to make her fantasy seem real.

Strange woman...

The video showed him recover and rugby tackle her to the bed as she tried to scamper from the room.

'Haha!' He laughed as he admired his athletic skill. 'Haven't played like that for years!'

Onscreen-Tom clutched at her blouse as he threw her back on the bed, wrenching her collar, stretching the material, the buttons pinging open, her lace bra exposed, his mind now reliving the words she'd whispered, half-remembered from last night.

'Don't hurt me but you need to make me feel it's real.'

It certainly looked real enough to him.

His alter ego on screen rolled her over, one hand pawing at her boobs, wrenching her bra down, exposing her breasts, his other hand trying to rip her skirt off. In response, she dragged her talons down his neck and chest as she screamed at him, furiously slapping at him, the violent flurry forcing him upright. For a fraction of a second, he could see the confusion in his eyes before her knee crashed into his groin.

'For fucksake!' He sat upright on the sofa, staring in disbelief. 'What is this?'

She'd told him—he could even recall her sexy voice purring in his ear—'I want you to fulfil my rape fantasy', but this was unreal. The video showed his face screwed up with pain, jaw sagging open as he went to protest that her blow had been too realistic, had hit the mark—which also explained why his balls ached so much this morning.

Before any recognisable words left his stunned mouth, her arm arced in a blur, her fist connecting with his jaw with a sickening thud.

Gob-smacked, he watched as wannabe rapist-Tom slumped on the bed.

Unconscious.

His hand went to his chin, felt the tenderness there.

'The bloody bitch. She's barking mad!'

With his mind whirring, trying to rationalise what he was witnessing, Tom sat open-mouthed as the video showed her adjusting her bra and tying the front of her shirt, desperate to cover herself, crying and sniffling as she stumbled to his en-suite.

The cameras died after several seconds as there was no movement in the room—he was out cold while she was doing whatever in his bathroom. He had no idea how long she was in there, would need to check the timings on the recording, but the film jumped forward to the moment she reappeared with her handbag, skirting the bed, still tearful, sobbing loudly.

'This is just too fucking weird,' he whispered.

Then she shouted at his inert body, her Italian accent gone, a slight Irish lilt accompanying her words—sending a white-hot poker through his guts.

'I'm not my fucking sister, you evil rapist bastard!'

He doubled over, hugging himself as he watched her run from the room. Astonished, he heard his front door slam, then the cameras dimmed again. The next image was him waking up to the alarm before inspecting the scratches in the mirror, grinning gormlessly at his reflection.

'Oh shit...'

Tom swallowed, wondering what he'd just watched, unable to think clearly, his mind still not fully recovered from his excesses of the previous day. Then he noticed the champagne bottle, still in its bucket where he'd left it, but their glasses had gone from the coffee table.

When had that happened?

With unsteady legs, he stood and glanced across his open plan lounge to the kitchen area. The glasses had been washed and were gleaming on the draining board.

'I didn't clean them, did I?' And Trulli had gone immediately after her weird playacting session.

For a few seconds, his brain struggled, then hit overdrive, his paranoia back with a vengeance.

With lead in his veins, Tom collapsed back on the sofa. He suddenly knew who she was and what she'd done to him.

Attempted rape.

The cunning little fox.

Her sister, she'd said, her accent so like Stella's.

Yet Stella had been dumped at a convent by her teenage mother as a babe in arms. She'd told him she'd never managed to trace her family.

Could she have had a sister and not told him?

Or not even known?

'Oh, God...'

Tom's befuddled mind suddenly cleared.

Stella's image had been all over the internet. A missing sibling might have found her, thanks to the millions of views he'd achieved with his porno movie, *Old Flame*.

Or worse, perhaps Trulli—if that really was her name— had been told by a friend that she had a lookalike, a double, who'd killed herself, live, on camera, only to realize who that was.

It made sense. Had the woman he'd called Trulli tracked him down to punish him?

The recording.

It was incriminating evidence of his 'rape' attempt. If she reported him and the police found that...

'It's all lies!'

The bellowed words echoed around his apartment as he sprang up, head thumping as he stomped to the bedroom to erase the video, then stopped mid-stride, a thunderbolt hitting him.

What if 'Trulli' had downloaded a copy...?

She could've easily accessed his walk-in wardrobe from his en-suite, found the control panel behind his display of watches. God knows how long she'd been in there, off-camera while he was zonked out on the bed.

He let out a desperate moan and slapped a hand to his forehead, staring at the kitchen sink again, wondering about the glasses. Had she slammed the front door merely for the audio to pick up, knowing the cameras would record the sound for several seconds after she left his bedroom?

The memory of her smouldering with sexual promise, handing him a glass of champagne as she sat on the sofa, flashed behind his eyes.

Tom rubbed at his head, fingers of both hands now scrabbling at his scalp, certain she'd remained inside the apartment. Washed the glasses, removing the traces of the drug he was convinced she'd used to spike his drink, guaranteeing she could fight him off during their 'roleplay'.

The clever cow.

There was no doubt her performance was entirely for the benefit of the recording—the cameras she obviously knew were hidden in his bedroom. Cameras that had recorded her sister, slut-shaming her, driving her to commit suicide in a most gruesome fashion.

For once in his life, Tom's confidence deserted him, his mind frantic, floundering as he tried to fathom what to do.

After viewing the video, knowing she had his skin under her nails, he really didn't fancy his chances in a court of law. Even if he'd had cameras recording sight and sound in his lounge, her whisper in his ear would've been inaudible, insufficient proof of anything exculpatory.

'I'm buggered. I need to talk to my lawyer.'

At least the police hadn't arrived.

Yet...

Why not?

Blackmail? Was that it? Was this her idea of revenge?

'I bloody hope so.'

Money he could do. Prison, well, that was something else.

Tom jumped at the noise, felt his heart slump in his chest then rebound, thundering against his sternum as his intercom buzzed.

Reluctantly, he pulled on his discarded shirt as his feet dragged him to the videophone, certain he would see a cluster of uniformed officers ready to arrest him.

'Clarkson?'

Relief flooded his system as he released the security door to let the poison dwarf enter the foyer. Why his underling would arrive at his home at this time of the morning was a mystery, but in his current state, Tom didn't much care. The naïve analyst wouldn't be leading him away in handcuffs.

Then it hit him.

'Dirt!'

Tom laughed aloud, clapped his hands with joy. He'd told the analyst to bring him anything he found on the woman as soon as he could, especially if it was compromising in any way. It must be massive for Clarkson to be on his doorstep at this ungodly hour—might he have found something Tom could use to counter the mad woman's accusations, to stop her going public with her lies?

That thought, and several deep breaths, brought him back to a semblance of normality—his desperate mood lifting as he pulled open the front door.

'Jim! Come on in.' Genuine delight coloured his tone as he held the door wide and stood aside. The little man seemed taller, was standing straighter, confident, unlike before.

'I'm not staying, Creed.' Tom, taken aback by the unusual rudeness automatically took the envelope Clarkson held out to him. 'This is your termination letter from the company. They've been made aware of your illegal actions.'

'What on earth are you—?'

'Yesterday, I gave them copies of all the recordings of

our discussions over the last few months. You're finished, Creed.'

'I... I...' For once, Tom was lost for words, his brain overwhelmed by the twin revelations that had ripped him from his moorings in the last twenty minutes or so, threatening to devastate him.

'Here, take this too.' Clarkson slid a plain white business card into Tom's palm, the emblem of Scotland Yard's Financial Crimes Division printed over a Detective Sergeant's name he didn't recognise. 'There'll be a team of officers on their way to arrest you soon enough, but I wanted to deliver this message personally... You treat people like shit and deserve everything that's coming to you.' The undercover policeman's crooked grin displayed no joy as he added, 'There's a lovely redhead at the local police station right now, being interviewed in the rape suite.' His eyes focused on the raw wounds on Tom's neck. 'They've already taken samples of the rapist's DNA from under her fingernails.'

'I didn't try to rape her!' Tom's hand subconsciously went to his throat, trying to cover the evidence. 'She wanted it rough!'

'Haha! They all say that...' His lips curled in disgust. 'Her name really is Trulli Luce, although her mother's maiden name's one you'll recognise... Kinsella. She's the woman who inspired my investigation into your long list of financial crimes, Creed, prompting me to approach your employers with the aim of bringing you to justice.'

'You knew her all along... The fucking slag—'

'Oh, yeah, she's the one who told me what happened to her elder sister, Stella. A sister she was searching for, came this close to finding,' he held up his finger and thumb, almost touching, 'but never had the chance to meet. Trulli told me what her sister had done for you at Evason. Which is why I've been digging, found out how you covered your arse while hanging hers out to dry... And how you *killed* her.'

'I did not!'

'You honestly believe that, don't you?' The policeman stepped in close, eyes daggers as he peered up at Tom, then shook his head. 'Convinced yourself... You really are a piece of work, aren't you?'

He stepped back, and Tom tried to slam the door on him, but a hefty boot propped it open as four rigid fingers punched into his solar plexus, winding him, bringing their eyes level as pain doubled him over again.

'She asked me to give you enough time to do the right thing.'

'What the hell's that supposed to mean?' Tom gasped.

'Trulli said to tell you, you should leave the building in the way most suited to how you see yourself. A *high-flyer.*'

Tom's brow creased in confusion as he stood upright, sucking in air, glaring down at his nemesis.

'What are you on about?'

'She said I should give you time to head upstairs and step off the roof, but she doesn't believe you've got the balls. Neither do I. So, let me be clear... If you try sneaking away, I'll be waiting downstairs and I'll take great satisfaction in nicking you. If it helps you make your mind up, I can tell you, I've got plenty of contacts in Her Majesty's Prison Service—'

'Prison? Oh no, no, I can't—'

'Seven years for attempted rape, similar for insider trading and fraud, and I'm not sure what the Drug Squad's got in mind for the hundred grams of cocaine they found in your desk after I called 'em an hour ago. You really are a wheeler-*dealer*, Tom, eh?' His voice dropped to a hoarse whisper. 'Your arsehole's going to be ripped red raw every day you're inside. I'll see to that.' With a final nod and a snarling grunt, he headed for the lift, his gait no longer unsteady, his back straight, his final words echoing in Tom's ears. 'Do us all a favour. Just fuck off and die, Creed.'

Tom, standing frozen in the doorway, his career in tatters, his reputation as a ladies' man shattered, his entire life shredded, knew with absolute clarity—prison was not an option. He glanced at the stairs to the roof, his face a mask of fear, unable to move, literally petrified. Seconds ticked by with him clutching his grandfather's snuffbox, fingers trembling, hot tears of shame and self-pity burning his cheeks. Finally, he let out a deep sigh of resignation and his feet began to move.

THE END

ABOUT THE AUTHOR

Although none of the characters in *Old Flame* make an appearance in Will's novels, there are similarities between Creed and another obnoxious, coke-snorting City hotshot who features in the first thriller in *The Remorseless Trilogy*. If you would like a complimentary copy of *Remorseless*, this award-winning Brit grit roller-coaster ride, please head to the author's website WillPatchingAuthor.com for more information.

Will writes thought-provoking crime thrillers, usually with a psychological twist, often putting the reader inside the minds of the worst kinds of psychopaths—the type none of us would want to meet in real life. With testimonials and recommendations from professional law enforcement officers, Will's writing will not only thrill, entertain and occasionally scare you, it will give you insights into some seriously disturbing characters. If you like cosy crime, you should look elsewhere!

Fire and Brimstone
by Dana Lyons

Dedicated to Joanne

"Fire and Brimstone: Let not the two meet in the presence of Air, for Fire is the beginning, and Brimstone is the end."
~ Translated from the Alchemist's Bible, 1684, at a monastery in the French Alps.

Baghdad, March 2003

"Hasan, wake up."
Hearing the words in his sleep, Hasan al-Jamil

tumbled from his dream. He blinked, shading his eyes from a thin beam of light. "Uncle?"

"Yes, and talk softly," Uncle Zaid whispered from the doorway.

"What is it?" Hasan asked. He rubbed his eyes and pulled himself awake. "Why are we whispering?"

Zaid crept in cautiously, looking from one shadowed corner to another, a briefcase clutched in his hands. By the time he sat on the edge of the bed, Hasan's nerves were wide awake and screaming. "What time is it?" He glanced at the clock. "Why are you here in the middle of the night? What's happened?"

Those were troubled times in Iraq, what with the American demands and the Republican Guard arrests. Bad things happened in daylight; worse happened in the dark of night. A knock at the door in the early hours struck fear in Iraqi souls.

"They are coming for me," Zaid hissed.

Hasan frowned. "Who? The Guard? Or the Americans?"

"The Guard, so hopefully the Americans are not far behind."

Zaid pressed the briefcase into his nephew's lap. A freezing premonition seized Hasan's insides. "What is this Uncle? What awful thing are you pushing off on me; for what else can it be in the middle of the night? Why me?" He recoiled from the briefcase.

"Hasan, you're the only one I can trust. The Americans are right, Saddam is insane. I liberated this information from the laboratory." He shook the briefcase. "You have to get this to the Americans. If the Guard catches me with it..."

His uncle's voice drifted off, leaving a silence filled with imaginary horrors. Hasan stared at the briefcase wanted by the Guard and knew his life was about to make a critical turn.

Nothing good comes from a knock in the middle of the night.

He desperately wanted to know what the briefcase held,

so he could reject it. But a shiver at the base of his tailbone told him there was no going back once he knew. He drew a sharp breath. "What is it?"

Zaid held a finger to his lips. The gesture came suddenly as he cocked his head, listening to the dark.

The silence was thick; Hasan's guts tightened and gooseflesh shot across his shoulders. Zaid, his eyes still darting from corner to corner, pulled him in to whisper in his ear. "The worst possible WMD. A weapon to destroy the world."

Hasan's goosebumps turned into a shiver and slid down his spine. He shook his head, immediately shutting down whatever Zaid had in mind. "No, no, no." He pushed away. "No, I want nothing to do with anything."

"You have to get this to the Americans."

If Zaid spoke the truth, whoever possessed this liberated information held the power to end all life. He was not qualified to even touch the case. He declared, "Then you must destroy it. But don't give it to me."

"This is too important to destroy." Zaid thrust a paper at Hasan. "Special Ops teams are entering the city even now. Here's the address and the man to speak with." He pinched Hasan's shoulders in a painful grip. "Deliver it, Hasan. Hopefully I'll live long enough for the Americans to rescue me. Your mother and sisters will meet you at this address at 4a.m."

Hasan tried to refuse the paper but Zaid pressed the address into his palm and rolled his fingers around it. "They are waiting. Tell them what happened to me. Give them the briefcase. Collect your mother and sisters and, Allah willing, escape to America. That's all you have to do."

Hasan's mouth sagged open.

That's all I have to do?

Evade the Guard in its death throes, dodge the advancing column of Americans, collect his family and escape. Sweat broke out on his brow.

"Get up, Hasan. You must go now," Zaid commanded.

Hasan set the case aside and climbed out of bed. Zaid hunkered by the window while Hasan dressed. In moments, Hasan picked up the briefcase. Tingles shot up his arm; apprehension dusted his tongue. "What is it? You didn't say exactly what the weapon is."

"Fire and Brimstone. A chemical combustion that can't be extinguished. If activated, it'll burn up the entire planet, unstoppable."

"That is in this case?" Hasan's eyes bugged.

"No, just the formula. Thank Allah, Fire and Brimstone has not yet been made."

Hasan exhaled with ragged relief and wiped a running bead of sweat from his face. Having the formula was bad enough. To actually have the chemicals would have terrified him. "Good luck, Uncle," he mumbled. While he examined the address, his uncle melted into the night.

He crouched in the doorway and scanned the dark shadows, his eyes furtive like his uncle's; the case now a dead weight in his hands. His hackles rose and he cursed the night before slipping out the door in the opposite direction.

It was barely 1:30a.m. and no one stirred, as if the city awaited liberation... and death. The eerie silence unsettled his already inflamed nerves; as he passed from one neighborhood to the next, his heart pounding a painful beat against his ribs.

Fire and Brimstone. What an awful weapon in anyone's hands.

He couldn't wait to get rid of it.

The address was another hundred yards up the hill. He checked his watch, still two hours until his mother and sisters would come and join him. Just as he inhaled with a sigh of relief, missiles shot overhead. Their whine of death split the silence as first one, two, and then three Hellfire missiles shot into the city.

Disbelieving, he watched as the missiles landed near his mother and sister's house. He opened his mouth to cry out, "No!" But his outburst was silenced with shock. Explosion after explosion brightened the night with flames. Screams from the survivors came few and far between.

He crouched back into the shadows, his hand over his mouth, his stomach threatening to empty into the street. Tears filled his eyes. "No," he whispered, shaking his head. "No." But his eyes told him they were gone. The missiles had taken out several blocks, the entire neighborhood was engulfed in flames. Black smoke poured, obscuring the horizon.

"Trust the Americans," he mumbled.

Perhaps mother is alive. Maybe Ziba and Gulbahar got out.

Utter destruction filled his vision; he knew he was a fool to think they could have survived. "I should go see if they live," he said with waning hope. The briefcase suddenly became heavier, a responsibility he didn't ask for, a responsibility he didn't want.

Tears clouded his eyes and a foul taste rose in his mouth. He spat. The tears obscured his vision and he blinked them away as he dropped the paper with the address onto the floor. It landed on his spittle, where he turned on his heel and ground it into the dirt.

With the briefcase tight against his chest he slipped away, turning his back on the rapid sound of gunfire, more explosions, and a night filled with screams.

New York City

Jenna stayed light on her feet, circling her opponent on the padded mat. He outweighed her by seventy-five pounds, but that muscle wasn't going to do him any good.

He stepped in, going for a frontal assault. She dropped to the ground and swept her legs across his feet, bringing him down to the floor. She jumped on his back, pulled his head back by the hair and drew her rubber knife across his throat.

A round of applause broke out; she and her sparring partner always attracted a crowd. Dave jumped up from the mat and clapped her on the back. "Ripley, how do you do it?"

She grinned and wiped the sweat from her eyes. "All those years of dance, big man."

"Ha," he laughed. "And a third-degree black belt in Jujitsu."

"That helps."

"Untouchable," one of the other deputies called out. "She holds the title."

"I know," Dave answered. "But a guy's gotta' try. She's whipped everyone's ass in the division." He waved at Jenna. "See you tomorrow."

She ducked into the women's showers. Since she'd been in New York, she had earned the respect of the other deputies and coworkers in her division in spite of being beautiful. She'd invested a lot of sweat, long hours and hard work to convince them she possessed more than just beauty, and more than just brains. She was also deadly in more ways than she could count.

All attributes she used to keen advantage.

She left the gym where division employees worked out and headed for home. All she wanted was a black-and-blue grilled steak and a bottle of red wine. Her friends and co-workers had learned that her good looks accompanied good taste.

Her apartment was small but she liked the proximity to work and the gym. Everything else in the world could be found outside her doorstep: New York City. She poured the red and lit the charcoal on her small hibachi grill, thinking about her next career move.

Could be time for a change.

She had worked the Southern District of New York for four years. To get there, she had dedicated tremendous time and energy toward work, leaving little for off-hours activities.

"Maybe I need to settle down," she muttered. That spurred a shiver to tumble down her backside. "No. Not that." She propped her chin on her hand, leaning her elbow on the small breakfast bar.

What you need isn't here.

"Humph," she grunted to herself. "How would you know?" But she couldn't help but squirm over the piercing assessment. She feared her inner voice spoke the truth.

I'm restless. I want something, and it's not here.

The steak touched the hot grill with a satisfying hiss. "Maybe I just need fresh horizons and opportunities." Flames popped and smoke poured from the sizzling steak. The smell of charred meat made her mouth water.

New horizons and opportunities aren't what you need.

She flipped the steak, dodging the flare-ups. While the steak cooked, she sipped her wine and nodded to the inner assessment.

There's no challenge here. I'm not tested. And there's no one here for me to test in return.

"Oh," she murmured. "You asking for a social partner?"

Maybe. Sorta.

"Where do you suggest I find a relationship that will tolerate my work schedule? Getting involved with a co-worker is out of the question."

That taboo had dogged her in past assignments and, so far, she'd managed to avoid succumbing to the temptations. Unfortunately, temptation and opportunity lurked in every assignment. When you worked with other hot bodies in hot situations, hot activity surely followed. There was something about being shot at or nearly blown-up that encouraged the primal animal to reproduce.

The timer beeped and she pulled her steak onto a plate. The meat was perfectly charred on the outside, and the juice on the plate declared it rare inside. "Now if I could just find a man to satisfy me as much as this piece of meat."

She poured the wine, grabbed half of a French baguette and sat at the counter. The wine paired nicely with the steak. The bread sopped up the juices, and the evening left her with a good vibe. She sipped from her glass, willing herself to relax and enjoy the moment in spite of a persistent, troubling thought.

Why do I feel like something is missing?

After she had thoroughly examined the question, no answer readily came. Not comfortable with problems she couldn't solve, her mind hung on to the question when she crawled into bed, making sleep elusive.

The next morning she dressed and anchored the Marshal badge on her belt in front of her pistol, still feeling pride at the accomplishment. Getting the badge had been a steep acquisition, even for her.

She checked her image. She had pulled her hair back into a tight French braid, her fingers twisting her blonde strands into the intricate design. With her hair scraped back like that, no one could accuse her of vanity. She'd been told she looked like Paris Jackson or some supermodel. "Huh. Maybe they look like me."

Her looks were striking, an appropriate term, for people often were speechless when they first came face-to-face with her. More than once she had played that stunned pause to her benefit. "Every resource," she said with pride, "is a tool."

Hasan al-Jamil opened the door to his small rented room in Brooklyn. Exhausted, he trudged in and set his hat on the table before fixing his evening meal. He'd been eating sparsely of late, seeing no reason to feed a body that would soon be dead.

He put water in a pan and lit the gas fire. Two eggs went into the water, then he opened a can of tuna. While the eggs cooked, he parceled out sweet gherkin pickles, Swiss cheese, and hot mustard.

This was a meal he would have enjoyed with his mother and sisters. Even after all those years, memories of them remained, touching his life in moments when he least expected it.

A dark head and a flash of blue eyes in the crowd reminded him of Gulbahar. Or, when passing a restaurant, certain delectable smells brought his mother's face to mind. Their deaths that night in Baghdad had been as he had suspected. But the surprise had come when the Americans apologized. Friendly fire, they claimed.

How can a human being's death by missile be forgiven as a mistake? How can the murder of loved ones be exonerated with words as deficient as, "Well, we didn't mean to."

He had lost everything dear to him that night. At first, his goal had been simply to survive the night. Then to survive the following day, keeping the briefcase full of notes safe and secret. He remembered chanting the words, "Find shelter, live one more day. Find shelter, live one more day."

After that night when all he had had to do was escape Baghdad, Europe had beckoned where America had not. Without any clear intent at the time, deciphering the Fire and Brimstone formula had become his primary focus. But the complex notations had required a career in chemistry, which he had eagerly established in the best labs Europe had to offer.

He couldn't say when his thirst to survive turned to a bitter anger because he had survived. In the early years in Germany, where he lived small and studied hard while taking advantage of 'diversity' policies, the relief at having escaped and survived slowly turned stagnant. He soon learned the horror of being a survivor; what was the point of having a life when he had no one to share it with?

His few forays into the local Arabic culture always brought him back to that night in Baghdad. Every burst of color, every nuance of accent, every scent with the power to transport him merely took him to that night and the horror of war.

He often stayed up late reading about war and the philosophies advocating conflict. After countless volumes, he decided the stupidity of war defeated all reasons for it. Not for religion, not for state politics, and not because of the fervor and excitement. Not for any of those ideas.

And yet war continued. First one place, then another. All because one person did not agree with the next. "Humanity," he spat with disgust. "We are a contentious rabble."

Finally, many years later, after working at laboratories in Germany, the Netherlands, and France, he had succeeded in creating Fire and Brimstone. He kept the two incendiary chemicals packaged in a special hermetically-sealed glass thermos that kept oxygen from Fire, and Brimstone from Fire.

"On the day they are combined in the presence of oxygen, the world can say good-bye." The words left the taste of vengeance in his mouth even though he honestly couldn't say what would happen. There was no way to test Fire and Brimstone, but the science behind the formula supported the claim. Now that he had his weapon, his plan to create the ultimate destruction of the human race needed an appropriate stage.

Grief had taken him down a road fraught with bitterness. In his heart he abandoned Allah, as Allah had abandoned him in his life. Bereft of spiritual comfort he had even gone to his knees with prayers to the Christian God. But, as with Allah, he received no answers. It seemed that, even to the gods, his losses were a mistake of no consequence.

Adrift and alone in his life and his soul, he sought his own answers. Deciding where to deliver his retribution had required as much time and finesse as the creation of Fire and Brimstone.

He contemplated one of the great mosques, or St. Peter's Basilica. The seat of Catholic power, he thought, offered a keenly appropriate altar for Fire and Brimstone.

The White House attracted him and, for a time, he considered the Lockheed Martin facility that produced Hellfire missiles. For years he wanted to bring the heat of Fire and Brimstone to the front door of the general in command that night in Baghdad.

"All were fitting places, each in their time."

But the years passed and his thinking shifted as he came to understand war. War no longer occupied the halls of national honor. Modern, senseless mass murder in the name of ideology is not honorable. War, he sadly understood, was merely a recipe for making money.

It didn't matter who died on what side of the conflict. It didn't matter the cost in human lives. All that counted was the millions made while the war machine carried on.

With this illumination, a new target evolved and he smiled, for he deemed it perfect. He would bring Fire and Brimstone to the war machine's stronghold of wealth. The golden treasure chest that fed the monster of war would become a doorway to hell. In the end, before they killed him, he would say, "Oh, what a mistake! I didn't mean to."

Jenna walked into her office, arriving before the crowd. She liked to ease into the workplace—there were a lot of alpha personalities to deal with in the Security Protection Program. She picked up a cup of coffee and studied the assignment board.

Behind her, the door opened. She inhaled.

Eric Majors.

He was the youngest and newest member of the team. He also used distinctive bath products. "Morning, Eric."

"Hey, Jenna. What's the board got to say?"

"Raphael and Anna are working the Vasquez relocation and settlement. That means you're stuck with me today." He stood next to her with his hand resting on his sidearm, a position he assumed when wanting to assert himself. She smiled. He did that a lot around her.

"Morning Eric, Jenna." Their boss, Deputy Marshal Terrence Morehouse, a tall Irishman, came out of his office and passed a file to Jenna. "I want you and Eric to go over these interviews and evidence, identify the case issues and work up an investigation plan."

When Morehouse returned to his office, she eyed Eric, seeing how his hand edged back up onto the butt of his weapon. Otherwise, his wrinkled nose indicated a less than enthused attitude. "Come on," she coaxed. "We don't get to save the world every day. Some days, we do paper work."

Hasan took the subway across Brooklyn to Flatbush. While a meal in his cramped quarters held little appeal, his sweet tooth longed for a particular cafe that served Maamoul, an Arabic sweet made with dates, spices and honey.

He made his purchase and sat at a small table by the window with his pink bag of sweets and a small cup of black Turkish coffee. The window gave him a view of the frantic sidewalk traffic and the rush of humanity. He came with hope that some inspiration would stop him from destroying the human race.

Every day for a week and so far: nothing.

His coffee was bitter and the treat he nibbled sweet. As he wiped his mouth, a familiar face passed in front of the window. He shot to his feet, watching the figure walk by. Before he could lose sight, he grabbed his bag of sweets and hurried out the door.

Uncle Zaid!

The man walked several blocks before cutting west and moving into a smart neighborhood.

What is he doing here?

He followed, his heart rattling his ribcage. Zaid went through a gate and walked behind a large residence. Hasan hung back at the corner, pretending to look for a bus. When Zaid walked out of sight, Hasan pushed through the gate and ran. He peeked round the corner of the building, watching as Zaid opened a private door to a small garage.

Hasan pressed his back to the building, his rapid heartbeat raising a sweat. He had thought Zaid long dead, along with the rest of his family.

How did he survive?

He peeked again. The garage was small but looked recently updated and the windows sparkled in the afternoon sun. Shaking, he pressed himself against the building, trying to make himself as small as possible. To find Zaid when he was on the threshold of delivering Fire and Brimstone was fate.

Or was it?

Zaid had been enamored with the Americans the night he had foisted the horrendous formula on Hasan, the night everything Hasan loved had met Hellfire destruction. He wondered whether Zaid remained so inclined, even after learning of their family's murder by American missiles that night? What was Zaid doing in America?

He couldn't remain there plastered to the side of a building. Sweat rolled down his forehead and he wiped his face on his sleeve. When he glanced around the corner again, Zaid's outside evening light was turned on. In a rush of uncertainty, he strode to the door and knocked.

Before the door opened he smiled, hesitant, even though his insides quaked. He didn't know if Zaid was family... or enemy. He heard "Coming!" from inside. And then his only living relative opened the door.

Zaid's initially blank face burst into a smile. "Hasan? Is this really you?" He grabbed Hasan's sleeve and pulled him in the door. "I thought you died that night." He opened his arms and stepped forward.

Hasan went rigid for a moment, but the call of family overrode his reticence. A small cry burst from his lips and he wrapped his arms around his uncle. They sobbed into each other's shoulders, uncle and nephew, all that remained in a family robbed of its women.

"Come, sit with me," Zaid ordered. He pulled out a chair for Hasan, and quickly moved to put a pot of water on the stove. "I'll make coffee, and you can tell me what happened... since that night."

"You look well," Hasan said, noting his uncle's healthy appearance. "America has been good to you?" He smiled, even though the words thickened his throat with anger.

"America saved me from the Guard." Zaid spread his right hand out—three of his fingers had been cut off at the knuckles. "I defected and applied for amnesty. After I testified against Saddam, I was placed in protective relocation." He shrugged one shoulder and waved his other hand, indicating his neighborhood. "Where better to hide an old Iraqi but in the heart of Jewish New York."

The missing fingers were a shock. A pucker of revulsion ran down Hasan's backside; he did not relish anyone's torture. Except for intending to destroy the human race, he was quite the pacifist. War and all its collateral damage repulsed him.

"What happened to you that night?" Zaid asked. He set out two small cups of dark coffee and pointed to the bag Hasan still clutched. "Do I smell Maamoul from the Arab café on Lexington?"

The bag was handed over and the sweets carefully placed on a plate with a paper doily. Zaid sat across from Hasan, his lips lifted with happy expectation as he blew on the hot coffee.

Hasan had not been with family, not known this familial connection, in fifteen years. The abject loneliness, the isolation, the entrapment with his anger and loss, seeped from his soul. He grabbed Zaid's intact hand. "I've been so alone, Uncle. Such a life is as much hell as a Guard prison cell." For a moment, Hasan wondered what this impromptu discovery of family meant to his plans.

Is Zaid's appearance a sign for me to stop?

He coughed, not sure where to start.

"Tell me what happened, Hasan?" Zaid asked. "By the time I got out of the hospital, all they would say was they were sorry, that missiles were fired into the wrong neighborhood." Tears filled his eyes and spilled down his face.

Hasan pulled his hand free to wipe his own tears. The whine of the missiles, the loud explosions tearing at the quiet darkness, the smell of fire, the screams from that night came rushing through his mind. His stomach cramped, just as it had on that fated dark morning in Baghdad. Bile rose in his throat and threatened to spew into his mouth.

In reminding him of the horror of that night, Hasan realized that finding his uncle had been fate after all, and as such affirmed his commitment. "I went to Europe, to Germany where diversity programs fed and schooled me," he confessed.

The shift in his tone was palpable and Zaid reached for his hand. "The acts of war which were fatal to our family can just as easily be blamed on Saddam." Zaid nodded, sagely agreeing with his own wisdom. But when Hasan didn't readily concur, he narrowed his eyes and peered into Hasan's face. "What did you do with it?"

"Do not reproach me, Uncle, or deliver a lecture about the whims of war," Hasan retorted. He drew back, filling his chest with the ire of long years of loneliness and grief. "I see America has been good to you. And I see you have forgotten who died at whose hands."

Zaid pulled back, his face stiffening in fear. "What have you done, Hasan? What did you do with Fire and Brimstone?"

"I kept the briefcase, Uncle. I went to school for many years to be able to decipher the formulas inside. I then spent more years going from laboratory to laboratory to create Fire. And even more years to create Brimstone. Now, I am here in New York to bring condemnation down on humanity."

He stood and placed his fists on the small table as he leaned over Zaid. "I am here to end the world and the human race."

That night after work, Jenna sat next to a single candle in her darkened apartment. Her words to Eric today, "We don't get to save the world every day," had bounced through her mind all afternoon. They were words her friend Marcie used to say. The full quote was, "We don't get to put on our heels and save the world every day."

Jenna smiled. If anyone could put on heels and save the

world, it was Marcie Paulson. The muscular brunette had had more fire and gumption than three men on steroids. She had loved the excitement of strapping on her vest and preparing for a high-risk assignment. Her mouth would tighten up with serious concentration, but her eyes always gave away her thrill. She had always bragged, "I could do this with heels on."

She missed Marcie. It had been four years since Marcie died, four long years of therapy for Jenna so she could forgive herself. Four years to recognize Marcie's death had not been her fault. Four years to convince the world she believed the psycho-babble. But the truth was hers to live with, no matter what anyone else said.

I know why Marcie died. She died because I hesitated.

She tucked her chin to her chest and squeezed her eyes tight, but a tear got through and rolled down her cheek.

A fugitive had grabbed Marcie as a hostage. With all her gear on, he ripped off her helmet and stuck his gun to her head. It was classic suicide by cop, so senseless Jenna that was caught off-guard. In the instant between tightening her finger on the trigger and pulling it, he shot Marcie.

"Daddy, I'm just glad you weren't alive to see that day." She sniffed and grabbed a tissue. These candlelight conversations with her father had been frequent when she was troubled. He was her rock in the world until he died when she was twelve. "Know I will never make that mistake again."

Never again.

Hasan stared down at Zaid. The shock on his uncle's face told him everything.

"You cannot mean what you say!" Zaid cried.

Now Hasan allowed his disgust to ripple through his face. He shook his head and peered down at the man who gave him the end of the world, a man hiding amongst the Jews, a man who walked away from the death of his family. "I told you not to give me the briefcase. I told you to destroy it, but you insisted I take it. You do remember, don't you?"

His anger came full circle, from those who killed his family to the only family he had left. "Why? Why did you push Fire and Brimstone on me? Why didn't you throw the case in a fire? With that one act, you could have saved the world."

The words rushed out in a hiss loaded with the venom of his anger. "I didn't want to destroy the world. I wanted a wife and family, a happy life. But you and the Americans and the Hellfire missiles destroyed any life I could have had. You gave me Fire and Brimstone," he shrieked, "and I'm going to deliver it."

Zaid's face paled as he stood. "Kill me, Hasan if you want. I will give my life. But don't do this. You are mad with grief."

Zaid's reproach in the face of Hasan's soul-crushing grief ignited a rage, a rage not of guilt, but of condemnation and blame. He picked up the metal coffee pot and brought it down across Zaid's temple. Zaid yelped and sagged to the floor.

After the raised voices, the sudden silence hung painfully in the small room. Hasan held his breath and stared at his uncle. A puddle of blood seeped from a gash in the man's temple.

He glanced around the small apartment; a quick check of the window showed no witnesses. "Uncle, if you had just destroyed the briefcase..." His words faded and he shrugged one shoulder. After wiping down any surfaces touched, he slipped out the door.

He slinked away, hunched over like that night in Baghdad, no more than a formless shadow, this time in the afternoon sunlight.

The next morning, Jenna read the text from Morehouse: *Trouble. Come in ASAP.*

"That can't be good." She rushed through her morning routine and arrived before Eric. "What's the emergency?" she asked Morehouse.

The large monitor displayed one of their protection cases. "Zaid al-Jamil," he said. "A defector to the US in Operation Iraqi Freedom. He supplied a wealth of testimony against Saddam and the Republican Guard."

"And the bad news is?" Jenna asked.

"Mr. al-Jamil's neighbor noticed he didn't turn off his outside nightlight this morning, and called it in. I got the body discovery notice from NYPD and called up our CSI unit. They're already on their way."

The door opened and Eric came in, his face flushed. "Morning. Got here as fast as I could."

"You're with Jenna going to a crime scene," Morehouse said. "Mr. al-Jamil has been quiet and trouble-free for over a decade. Let's figure out what happened."

Jenna logged the address in her phone and told Eric, "I'll drive. On the way, read the file to me."

At the scene, emergency vehicles filled a long driveway to a small converted garage in the back. They were greeted by the lead investigator. Jenna said, "I'm Ripley, this is Majors. What do we have here?"

They stopped at the entrance to the garage apartment. "A simple case of rage," he said. "This gentleman took a fatal shiner in the temple." He pointed to a metal coffee pot on the floor beside the victim. "That appears to be the weapon. They told me you were coming so I let your CSI team in." He gave a soft salute and left them.

They watched through the window while CSI took photos of the body and dusted surfaces for prints. When they came out, the chief called her over. "It's pretty clean for prints. We have a hair, and there's a scribble beneath the body. Our victim tried to leave a message in blood."

"Thanks, Chief," she said. They put on paper booties and gloves before entering. She walked around and let her eyes wander across the crime scene. Clearly, al-Jamil knew his killer, knew him or her well enough to fix them coffee.

She squatted beside the body to examine it closer and noticed the blood on the end of al-Jamil's right pointer finger, which was missing the end digit.

"What were you writing, Mr. al-Jamil?" She gently rolled the body onto its back. Underneath was a scribble in blood.

Eric came to stand by her. She asked, "What does that look like to you?"

He inspected the letters from every angle before proclaiming, "F-i-v with a squiggle on the end?"

"Maybe not a 'v'." She lay on the floor positioned like the victim, and imitated the writing. "Maybe it's an 'r'. That gives us fir with a squiggle. First?" She gave Eric a sharp look. "Fire?"

"The killer's name?" he offered.

"Maybe. Let's see what Mr. al-Jamil's file has to say."

At the office, Jenna and Eric took a seat at her desk and opened al-Jamil's case file. In seconds, they had a cluster of files marked protection package details, trial transcripts, and personal history from Iraq. She printed up his personal history file for herself and told Eric, "Pick one and start reading."

The afternoon passed as they examined hundreds of pages from each file. Jenna read about al-Jamil's torture by the Republican Guard, noted the missing fingers on his right hand, and his wild-eyed photo taken when Coalition Forces rescued him.

He looked like he'd been tortured. His pain-filled eyes screamed silent desperation, his hair stood out, his face red and swollen from crying and the beatings. "An Iraqi chemist from Saddam's horror laboratories. What evil things has this man helped create?"

She dug into the transcripts until she found the initial interview from just after his rescue. The typed pages were filled with blanks notated with 'incoherent' in parentheses. "Not good enough." She went over to Morehouse's office and waited until he motioned her in.

He finished typing and then turned to her. "Yes?"

Jenna liked Morehouse. He was a no-bullshit guy who delegated with high expectations. When he handed you a case, he provided all you needed, but he expected you to provide results in return. "I need the audio transcripts of al-Jamil's initial interview when Coalition Forces rescued him from the Guard torture center. The paper transcripts are full of holes."

He jacked up one eyebrow. "What are you looking for?"

She shrugged. "Won't know until I hear it."

"Give me an hour," he said.

As she expected, he brought her an audio file marked Baghdad 03.03/al-Jamil. She returned to her desk and, seeing Eric still chest-deep with his file, put on her headphones. She closed her eyes and tuned in to every nuance, every sound, every half-uttered word of Arabic.

She identified al-Jamil's voice from the interviewer. When he spoke his words were riddled with fear, his voice sometimes shrill, other times a whisper she strained to hear. He stuttered, he whimpered, his voice trembled. Near the end of the recording, she hunched over and pressed her fingertips to her headphones. Again, and again, she played the final words from al-Jamil before the original recording shut off, leaving a white hiss to fill her ears.

What she heard made no sense.

As far as I know...

She shot to her feet and headed for the door. "Eric, I'm going out." She took the subway down to the East Village and rushed over to East 9th. Tribal Trends! She could always smell the oils and incense and candles from fifty feet away. The bell on the door jingled as she entered and looked around for her friend, Joanne.

"Welcome," a voice called. Joanne came out from the back room, long hair flowing down her back and a smile on her face. She was a wealth of intuition, spirituality, arcane knowledge, and love. By Jenna's lofty standards, Joanne was genuine. She was also an expert in lore not found on the internet.

"Oh, it's you!" Joanne squealed and rushed forward, her arms open with a hug. Jenna wrapped her arms around her, inhaling the exotic scent of essential oil.

"I never see you anymore," Joanne exclaimed. "Don't tell me Marshal business brings you to Tribal Trends?" She drew Jenna behind the counter to sit. "Now, tell me what you've been up to, and why are you here?"

"We're alone?" Jenna glanced toward the rear of the shop.

Alarm lit Joanne's eyes as she pulled back. "Well, yes. But that expression on your face doesn't look good."

"I can't have anyone overhearing this conversation, that's all."

Joanne whispered, "What are you here about? Are you in trouble?"

"No, nothing like that. But do you have any pre-biblical references about fire and brimstone? I mean ancient, like Druid, or in ancient alchemy texts of some kind."

"Oh, you are serious, aren't you? What's this about?"

Jenna smiled to ease her next words. "It has to do with a case, so I can't tell you."

"All righty, then," Joanne answered, and winked. "Probably something I don't want to know about anyhow. Let's look in the back. The bell will let me know if anyone comes in."

The back room displayed a wall of shelves filled with a vast collection of crystals from around the world, herbs and oils, and a library of ancient lore gathered from Tibet to China, from South and Central America to Europe and Africa. Jenna sat in a big leather chair in the corner while Joanne rummaged through the shelves.

Jenna's Arabic was fluent, as was her French. In al-Jamil's erratic interview, he had repeatedly mentioned fire and brimstone, but out of context. The interviewer's note had translated the ramblings to mean, "The fire and brimstone delivered by Coalition Forces upon the head of Saddam Hussein."

She disagreed. The guttural nuances in his pronunciation spoke of something far more fearful than even Hellfire missiles. He had said, "Save the world," not "Save Iraq."

So he had feared something that could destroy the world.

She shifted in her seat, finding no comfort in the favorite leather chair. Joanne came over with an armful of books and sat down. "For fire and brimstone, we have well-known references in Biblical texts. They have become a standard metaphor for the wrath of God." She set several of the books in a stack off to the side.

In her lap, she kept one large tome with an aged leather cover and markings in a strange language. "The Druids speak frequently of the power achieved from combining Air and Fire, both elements. There is no mention of brimstone in Druid lore, however there is 'brimrock'."

Even though the bell on the door hadn't jingled and they were alone, Joanne's slanted glance gave Jenna a chill down her back.

"The Druids forbade the creation of 'brimrock' upon pain of death."

"Does it say why brimrock is so forbidden? I thought Druids pursued natural power in all its forms."

"Brimrock was forbidden because the conflagration would literally consume Mother Earth. The words were, *'Rock will burn and tree will follow, oceans next, until man burns last'.*"

Jenna frowned and eased back, trying to envision a fire that would consume a planet. "A nuclear fire? What other fire could do that?"

Joanne tapped the tome in her lap. "This is a translation of ancient Persian texts done in the late 1600s by monks in the French Alps."

The hackles rose on the back of Jenna's neck. She licked her lips and nodded for Joanne to proceed.

"This is the only other mention I could find of fire and brimstone. Are you ready?"

Jenna braced herself. The worst news came when you weren't expecting it, just like a punch in the gut. She exhaled and sucked in her gut, as though the punch had already landed, and nodded for Joanne to continue.

"Prior to the Islamization of Persia, the Zoroastrians were dedicated alchemists. This is the single reference they make for fire and brimstone." She cleared her throat, and read. *"Fire and Brimstone: Let not the two meet in the presence of Air, for Fire is the beginning, and Brimstone is the end."*

"That still doesn't tell me what Fire and Brimstone is," Jenna complained.

"We know that it's considered the wrath of God in modern times, and the ancients thought it would burn until there is no Earth left," Joanne said. She closed the tome and delivered a piercing look. "Did I answer your questions?"

Zaid's frenzied ramblings now made a world of sense to Jenna. He said, *'Find Fire and Brimstone, humanity wouldn't survive the flames.'*

She glanced up and saw her friend quietly waiting. She blurted, "Oh, this is all the ramblings of an old man." She stood, and Joanne rose with her.

"All right, honey," Joanne said. "I guess if I needed to know, you'd tell me." She opened her arms again, and Jenna buried her face in the smell of incense and candles.

"Give Ralph my love," she whispered, "and don't worry. It's just an old story with missing pieces."

"Sounds like a scary story to me," Joanne answered.

Jenna left Tribal Trends with a chill resting on her shoulder. She texted Eric: *Chasing a lead, notify me when hair samples are done.* Then she texted Morehouse: *I need the name and location of who was in charge of Saddam's laboratories when we took over.*

While she waited to hear back from Morehouse, she recalled the Zoroastrian warning. *'Let not the two meet in the presence of Air, for Fire is the beginning, and Brimstone is the end.'* Her phone beeped, delivering a name and address. She hailed a cab.

It was a long drive out to the 'burbs. Images of a fire that couldn't be extinguished danced through her imagination as she tried to wrap her head around such a calamity. "Rocks will burn," she mumbled. She envisioned a fire burning everything it touched, getting bigger and bigger. "Oceans next, until man burns last." She saw the last outcrop of humanity adrift on a dwindling sea surrounded by flames coming ever closer—

"We're here, miss."

They were in front of a home in track housing: small, comfortable, a place to spend the rest of your life.

Maybe, if there's a life to have.

She told the driver, "Wait for me, I don't think I'll be long. I'm on Federal business; after this we're going to west 38th."

The walk was short, the lawn tidy, with a light already on over the door. She knocked.

"Yes?"

A man opened the door. She made sure he saw her gun and badge. "Sir, I'd like to ask you some questions. It's critical we speak."

"Please, call me Jerry," he said, and motioned her in.

Jerry epitomized ex-military: fit and solid, square in the jaw, and still sporting a buzz haircut. "What brings a Marshal all the way out here?" he asked. He motioned to seating nearby.

"I'm here about what you didn't find in Saddam's war laboratories in March of '03," she said. She watched his face closely.

He snorted a dry laugh but glanced away a little too quickly. "You mean the weapons of mass destruction?"

She let his dry chuckle fade before saying, "No. Bigger. I mean a weapon to destroy the planet."

His face stiffened appropriately, his expression shouting, *'What do you mean?'* But his body spoke of fear and secrets. "What's bigger than a WMD?" he joked.

"Fire and Brimstone. Tell me what you know about Fire and Brimstone."

He shrugged. "There were rumors about such a thing. Supposedly the Fire chemical was extremely combustible, but Brimstone had to be combined with it to create the

WMD. Zaid, oh, what was his name—?"

"Zaid al-Jamil," she supplied.

"Yes, al-Jamil. He arranged his defection and asylum based on what turned out to be rumors. Operation Iraqi Freedom was largely based on his intel. We went to Iraq for Fire and Brimstone, but called it Weapons of Mass Destruction."

"What did you know about these chemicals, other than you didn't find them?"

"The rumor, according to al-Jamil, was that these two chemicals when combined created a fire... a fire that can never be put out."

"And what happened to the rumor?"

"The rumor was a briefcase of notes—the formula for Fire and Brimstone."

"And this briefcase was never found?"

"Correct. After the Guard worked al-Jamil over, he kept repeating, 'I gave it to Hussein', but we never found it." He glanced over his shoulder at the clock. "Say, why don't you ask al-Jamil all this? He'll tell you."

"He's dead." She rose, and he followed. "Thank you for your help," she added, and stopped at the door. "What do you think happened to the briefcase?"

He took his time to answer. She saw furrows pop up in his brow, and guessed he'd spent considerable time pondering that question. "I think someone found it."

She stepped out. He held the door open. "Did they?" he whispered. "Did someone find Fire and Brimstone?"

The pieces were falling together in a pattern she didn't like. "It's just a story so far."

His face twisted with skepticism.

She turned her back before he could ask any more questions. As she walked to the cab, she remembered Joanne's words. "Yep," she muttered. "A damn scary story."

In the cab, she gave the address for her office and texted Eric: *Coming in.* He returned with: *Good. Got news.*

She walked in, fatigued from being on the run all day and

not eating. As soon as she came in the door, an excited Eric rushed up. He surprised her by asking, "Have you eaten?"

"Uh, no, I haven't."

"Well, I have, so you eat, because I have a lot to tell you." He set her down in a chair and disappeared into the break room, returning with a beef gyro, one of her favorites, from a small restaurant down the street. She gratefully took it and sat, listening to his evidence trail.

"Maamoul, the sweets that were on the table, are a delicacy made at only a couple shops in New York. A bag in the trash at al-Jamil's came from a bakery in East Flatbush. I collected their security video while you were gone, and have isolated who I believe bought the sweets. Our killer."

On one monitor was a still-shot of an Arabic man pointing to the sweets on the shelf. As her eyes swept the image, Eric added, "We also have the DNA results on the hair CSI found."

She remembered from the family notes in al-Jamil's file that he lost all of his family that night in March of '03. His sister, her two daughters, and the girls' brother, al-Jamil's nephew—

"Hasan," she said. "The hair is from his nephew, Hasan al-Jamil." Now she understood. Zaid didn't say he gave Fire and Brimstone to Hussein, he gave it to his nephew.

A man whose family had just died under Hellfire attack.

Hasan al-Jamil had his last supper in his quiet room. Having little appetite since killing his uncle, he nibbled on flatbread and olives.

The rage and grief that had risen in him from Zaid's condemnation surprised him. That he had picked up the coffee pot and killed his only surviving family member had shocked him. The next day his world had reeled, and until only his deepest commitment had become his anchor.

Deliver Fire and Brimstone.

Let all the suffering cease, he thought. The suffering between nations, between economies, between families, even the suffering between strangers can all come to an end. He sobbed and wiped his tears, reconfirming his purpose over the past fifteen years.

To make it stop. Make all of it stop.

He had already reserved a ticket for his tour of the Federal Reserve. Tomorrow, he would release Fire and Brimstone on top of the hallowed vaults of gold.

"The gold will burn first," he whispered, and that gave him satisfaction.

Jenna now had a name and a face to go with the history of Fire and Brimstone: Hasan al-Jamil. Eric's supporting evidence filled in the holes; she now had a report. With Eric, she rapped on Morehouse's door. "Sir, we have a situation."

"Come in," he called. "Close the door."

He listened quietly as they filled in all the pieces, only once jacking an eyebrow when Jenna mentioned a fire that can't be put out. "Can we find the nephew?" he asked.

"I put in a facial search of all city cams; it'll take a while," Eric said.

"We know he likes a sweet made over in Flatbush—they're only open from 6a.m. till 2p.m. We can set up a truck near there and see if he shows."

"All right. I'll call in men and equipment. It'll be there by 4a.m., so go home and get some rest. If what you suspect is true, the fate of the world could be in our hands tomorrow. Let's not let it end badly."

At home, a hot shower and a glass of wine helped Jenna relax. She lay in bed, seeing the day's events when Marcie died, and whispered her vow, "Never again, never again."

The next morning, she met Eric at an undercover surveillance truck parked across the street from the bakery. Inside the truck, SWAT had cameras sending in feed from every angle up and down the block.

A passport photo of Hasan al-Jamil filled a big screen. "Did you see the intel that came from Europe on Hasan?" Eric asked.

She nodded. Hasan had spent a career at every high-end chemical facility in Europe. "Making Fire and Brimstone, sounds like to me," she added. In her mind, a vision opened of flames, oddly giving her chill bumps. "What's the plan?" she asked Morehouse.

He sat at one of the monitors. "We have a perimeter of surveillance; everyone understands he must be taken alive. Let's see if we can figure out where and what he's up to before he does it. Hopefully, he has a sweet tooth along with a death wish."

Lights and activity stirred in the café as employees arrived to begin baking. At 6a.m. the open sign flickered on. Jenna focused on the feed from the front door, the image from Hasan's photo burned in her mind. She stared at the screen until her eyes watered.

"There he is," Eric said.

As with the other day, Hasan pointed to the sweets, paid, and collected the pink bag. He walked out and looked up and down the street. Jenna felt her hackles rise as it seemed he looked straight at them. But he was only checking traffic, and crossed the street to wait for a bus.

"Team 2, you're up," Morehouse said. A man dressed as a student and sitting at the bus stop touched his face in reply.

The bus came and Hasan left with his little pink bag and the undercover deputy. Jenna exited the truck and headed for the shop. She pointed at the same sweets and ordered 6. As the clerk bagged them up, she asked, "The man who just bought these—?"

"Oh, he's come in every day for the last week," she answered with a smile.

"Did he say anything today?" Jenna paid, holding her breath.

"He doesn't talk much usually," the girl said. "But today he was quite chatty. Said he was going on a tour, something he seemed very excited about."

"What tour? Did he happen to mention?"

"He was excited to go see the gold at the Federal Reserve."

Back in the truck, Jenna told Morehouse, "He's going on a tour at the Fed today." She sat at a keyboard and pulled up the Federal Reserve tour schedule. "Let me get on the tour undercover," she said. "He'll never see me, not as a cop."

Morehouse gave her a brief study before saying, "All right. If he reserved a space, find out when and be there first. Eric and I will go undercover with you."

She got a ride home from a uniformed officer. "I'll only be a few minutes," she said, and rushed in her door. She took a deep breath, wondering what to wear, what cover to develop for this situation. "Something with as many unseen weapons as I can pack." She chose her black leather pants and tucked her favorite lightweight knives into special pockets hidden in the pant legs, then slipped her feet into steel shanked high heels. "He'll never see this girl coming."

By the time she got back, an undercover SWAT truck parked halfway down the block from the Federal Reserve front door. When Jenna entered, a silence filled the truck as the officers gazed over her version of undercover. Eric had changed into tourist clothes, anonymous and unnoticeable. He nudged her in the ribs. "How do you walk in those shoes?"

"All those years of dance."

Morehouse said, "There's a space reserved on the 2p.m. tour in the name of Hasan al-Jamil. Our suspect is at this time returned to a small room in Brooklyn. We have a team in place. Once he leaves for the Fed, we'll sweep his room."

Jenna sat and studied a floor plan of the Federal Reserve building. Morehouse joined her. "What are you thinking?"

"I think he wants to set the gold on fire. And according to these floor plans, anywhere within the building is over the vault."

"So, he could start the fire in the toilet and just walk out of the building," Morehouse mused.

She tightened her lips and shook her head. "If his actions are based on rage from the events of '03, he's not going to walk out and leave his fire behind.

"And I don't think we have to worry about a toilet fire because the bathrooms are the only areas not on camera. He's going to make a statement to define his actions, he wants to be on camera. And I don't think he's interested in the tour; he's already waited fifteen years for this."

At 12:30p.m., the team following Hasan reported he had left. "Bomb squad will search his place once he crosses the river."

"He's got it on him," Jenna replied. "He's coming in to do this."

Morehouse looked her over. "I didn't get a chance to ask: who are you?"

"I'm Jenna Ripley, from Paris, recently widowed, and here to see the sights of New York." She spoke with an authentic French accent.

He asked softly, "You got this, Ripley?"

She knew he was thinking about Marcie. She never blinked. "Got it."

"In those shoes?"

"In these shoes." She lifted one heel for him to inspect. The heel point, sharp enough to penetrate any shoe, looked appropriately wicked.

"In those shoes it is," he said. He had changed into jeans, sweatshirt, sneakers, and a NYC ball cap. "We don't know the process or what he intends to do, but Jenna thinks he's coming in to do harm. We can't risk injury to him in case he has something rigged in an unknown location. Is this clear?" Everyone in the truck nodded, and those on microphone affirmed the order.

Morehouse abruptly held his hand up and turned aside with his free hand touching his earbud. He walked off a couple steps and looked down at his feet, not speaking.

"That can't be good," Jenna mumbled. People always look at their feet when they're told something they don't want to hear.

Morehouse turned around and announced, "We have a new directive from the Department of Defense. Hasan al-

Jamil is to be taken alive at all costs."

Jenna closed her eyes. She understood the danger of Hasan rigging something somewhere else in the city, but her knowledge of human nature said this was his moment. This sudden directive from the Defense Department made her skin crawl.

Just when you thought you were going to make the world safe, someone has to ruin it.

She approached Morehouse and hissed under her breath. "Let me guess; they found no briefcase, no notebooks, no computer or thumb drive, and no key to some mystery storage. So the formula for Fire and Brimstone is in his head, and they want it."

He wouldn't look at her straight on; he agreed with her. "Yeah, it stinks, but it's not my call, Jenna, and it's not yours, either. You will follow these orders, Deputy."

She stepped aside, muzzling her disgust. "Yes, sir."

A SWAT team set up base in a room where they couldn't be seen; the air reeked with the tension from hackles standing on end. After a brief security check, she took a position near the front. They waited, the seconds going by like hours.

"Come on," she mumbled. She spotted Hasan as he walked through the front door.

He passed through his security screening and walked through the check point. Along with Morehouse and Eric, he waited in the lobby, looking at the plaques on the wall. She wandered over to stand next to him. "Such a spectacular accomplishment, to have all this gold in one place, is it not?" she asked. She beamed her best smile, practiced and honed to draw in and engage. "I'm Jenna, *monsieur*, visiting this great city, *et vous*?" She held out her hand.

Hasan wore cargo pants and a corduroy jacket. She raked her eyes over him, seeing the slight bulge of inside pockets as well as side pockets covered with flaps. She kept her smile open and her eyes on his face. He stared wide-eyed, his mind occupied elsewhere.

She thought, *stunned by my beauty? Or repulsed?* He seemed neither, when suddenly he blinked as though seeing her for the first time. His hand came out slowly. "Pardon me, your eyes reminded me of someone long ago." His strained smile faded and his eyes crinkled with sadness.

A deputy in a Federal Reserve tour guide uniform came out and announced, "The rest of this group has been delayed, so, keeping to schedule, please follow me."

Morehouse and Eric, in their roles as tourists, fell into line behind the undercover deputy.

Jenna lingered with Hasan. "*Monsieur?*"

Quickly, he stepped off to the side and pulled something from his right jacket pocket. "Stay back, I have a bomb!" he shouted. In the next instant, he threw something at the floor.

Jenna's breath caught in her chest; she had no opportunity to stop him. A tube shattered on contact with the marble. Blue flame shot out like spilled milk.

"Don't anyone move," he said. He held up his left hand, brandishing another tube, threatening, "If I drop this, we're all going to die. Now stay back." He glanced about the lobby. "Are they on? The cameras, are they on?"

Morehouse, the other deputy, and Eric had closed in, but were still several feet away. She was the only one within reach of Hasan.

"Yes, the cameras are on," Morehouse said. "No one else has to die, Hasan. What do you want?"

"You were expecting me," Hasan said. "I'm sorry Zaid had to die, but he was a fool of an old man."

The blue flame consumed the marble, eating away at it like acid. *If this is Fire,* Jenna wondered, *what the hell would happen when Brimstone was added?* She eyed the second tube and weighed her options.

All I have to do is keep it out of the flames.

But the fire was spreading. The longer she waited, the thinner her options.

Not again.

With her hip cocked slightly, she showgirl-kicked. Her long leg reached out and the toe of her shoe knocked Hasan's hand to the left. The tube of Brimstone went flying away from the blue flames.

There came a flurry of footsteps running in different directions. Someone shouted and sprinted to catch the Brimstone; Morehouse ran up with handcuffs for a weeping Hasan, who sobbed with tears running down his face as he confronted her. "Why? Why did you stop me?"

I stopped him today. Who will stop Fire and Brimstone tomorrow?

There were enough modern threats to the world without adding ancient methods of destruction to the lineup. She wanted to kill Hasan. He and this horror threat from the labs of Saddam Hussein needed to die.

But the call came from above her paygrade. She grimaced with disappointment and stepped aside.

A rush of personnel attacked the flames; she turned her back on the panic, cursing under her breath as her own anger caught fire. A quick glance at Morehouse showed his lips compressed with white lines around the edges; he agreed with her. Fire and Brimstone needed to die.

Instead, Hasan was being led away for a life in federal custody and forced indenture in a laboratory cooking up more horrors. She jutted her chin and leaned in to whisper in Morehouse's ear. "Screw this. I quit."

Her heels came off and she picked them up. Like Marcie used to say, some days you get to put on your heels and save the world.

And some days you don't.

THE END

ABOUT THE AUTHOR

Dana Lyons was voted one of 50 Great Writers You Should Be Reading in 2015 and 2016. She is multi-published with full length novels and novellas in eBook and print in paranormal romance and adventure, shape shifter crime mystery, and suspense thriller. Her website is:

www.paranormalromancebookauthor.com/books/

twitter.com/Danalyons111

facebook.com/author.paranormal.romance

Want more from Dana Lyons?

Dana writes in many genres—paranormal romance and adventure, reincarnation, time travel—some are steamy and others not so steamy. The *Dreya Love Series* is paranormal crime mystery with a dash of reverse harem and shape shifters.

Transformation, Book 1 in the Dreya Love Series is free on all platforms—www.books2read.com/u/mVBjPp

Transformation offers a link for a free copy of episode 1 in *The Time Traveler Series, Celeste and Paladin.* Celeste is a Seer, and Paladin a Time Traveler, forbidden by Solaran law to be together. Where does the law stand in the face of love?

Follow Celeste and Paladin as they ride the Winds of Time, fugitives from the Sorcerer, Brachus. Each month a new episode in the Time Traveler Series, along with free books and other offers, is delivered to your inbox if you sign up to the series.

Ava Edison and the Burning Man
by Marcus Cook

The definition of irony is an event that seems deliberately contrary to what one expects and is often amusing as a result. For example, a fire station catching fire, or the gas company being evacuated due to a gas leak. I watched them evacuate the building while eating my lunch from the café across the street. It seemed somebody reported the smell of gas. It was me; I needed the jewelry store next to it vacated. The proprietors couldn't set their alarm due to emergency personnel possibly having to enter in search of the leak, meaning I was easily able to walk in and rob it. I was there only for the rare coins and gold that were not in the display case. Hopefully, they wouldn't check those until tomorrow, giving me an easier time to get them to my buyer.

I started to bag the coins when I heard, "Ava Macey Edison! Have I not taught you anything?"

The ghost of Mary Firth, a 17th century thief, materialized in front of me.

"Not now!" I replied as I bagged the last grams of gold.

"Why? Because I'm dead and you feel you don't have to deal with me?" Mary bellowed.

"Yes! Why do you haunt me? I'm not related, nor have I done you any harm, yet there you are," I responded with much built-up frustration.

"Do you even want to know what you are doing wrong?" Mary questioned.

"Fine. Out with it. What am I doing wrong?" I asked, knowing whatever it was wouldn't have been helpful.

"Why aren't you in an emergency service uniform?" Mary asked.

I went to argue, only to realize it would have been brilliant if I had dressed as a firefighter or a cop. I wouldn't have had to worry about people asking me what I was doing.

"Okay, that was useful advice," I said to her. "Anyhow, I'm done and out the door."

Mary dematerialized as I exited through the back door and into the alley, only to be met by three overweight Italian men dressed as firemen. *How am I the only one who didn't think of wearing a costume?* I recognized the man in the middle as Don Pasuta, to whom I owed money. Money I had originally stolen from him and, after having been caught by his men, had then arranged a time to pay him back. I must have been followed, as here he was.

"Ava Edison, let's go back inside," Don Pasuta's gritty voice said as his two associates escorted me back into the jewelry store.

"Why are we going back to the scene of the crime?" I

questioned as they sat me down.

"Boss said if we suffocate you, then create a gas leak, that may or may not explode, foul play wouldn't be at the forefront of explanation," one of the henchmen responded.

Whatever happened to the bad guys being stupid and the good guys having all the answers?

Out of curiosity, I asked, "And how did you know I was here and what I planned on doing?"

"We tapped your phone and followed you by GPS map," the other henchman answered.

Another point for the bad guys.

The Don walked in and leaned against the counter facing me.

"Hey Don Pasuta, I was just on my way to pay you when I got a little side tracked. It's not my fault." I couldn't believe I just quoted Han Solo.

"Good, I'll take it now." The Don chuckled, until he wheezed and coughed.

"That cough doesn't sound good," I said, trying to change the subject.

"For seventy-years, George Burns smoked 10 to 15 cigars a day and lived to see 100. I smoke three packs a week and the doctors give me another year." The Don looked at his men and they all shook their heads in disbelief before he refocused the conversation back to me. "Enough about my health, you were about to give me my money."

"I don't have the money on me. I have to get this stuff to my buyers and then they'll give me the money, so I can pay you on time," I answered.

The Don appeared agitated. "You stole a precious piece of artwork from me. My guys found you after you fenced it. You told me you could pay me back and, seeing you were a single mom and a widower, I took pity on you. You just robbed this establishment and yet you don't have anything for me?"

I wasn't listening to him as I watched my ghost partner behind them, pointing to a jewelry case. She quickly swung her arm and the case shattered. The incident startled my three captives and they turned their attention to it. This gave me the distraction I needed as I stomped my right foot. A large blade snapped out at the toe; I stood up and kicked Don Pasuta straight in the gut. As his goons went to react, I held up my arms toward them, activating the spring-loaded apparatuses which released a pistol into each hand. With my guns pointed at the goons and my foot firmly attached to The Don, I gently wiggled my foot out of the boot.

Standing in front of them wearing one boot, I smiled and said, "Don, my agenda here is not to kill you. The knife is not too deep, yet deep enough to cause problems. If you leave for medical attention now, you should be able to get the blade out without any further damage. If you wait or pull it out yourself, you'll surely be sleeping with the fishes." I shuddered at the unpleasant thought of dealing with him in the afterlife. "I will have your money next week as we originally discussed. Now gentlemen, take your boss and get out of my face."

The two glared at me, until The Don coughed up some blood. Then they gently picked him up and carried him off, holding the boot in place.

"They called the all-clear," Mary's voice whispered in my ear.

"Do me a favor and erase the video feed. Somebody's going to notice the smashed case," I said as I gathered my gear and loot, then headed out the back door once more.

I was exhausted by the time I arrived home. *Shit, do I have enough money to pay the sitter?* As I got out of the car and paid my Uber, I felt that something was off. It could have been me coming off an adrenaline rush, yet the house seemed cold.

I decided to enter my house through the garage entrance. I stopped at the workbench, reached underneath and pulled out my Glock. I tucked it behind my back and entered the house.

As I walked in, I called out, "Elyse, Roma, I'm home."

Immediately, my eyes focused on my eight-year old daughter sitting terrified in the middle of the kitchen floor. I felt a heavy object slam against the back of my head. *Should have looked around,* I thought, before everything went black.

The next thing I remember was being doused with ice cold water against my face. I tried to wipe my face only to discover my hand and legs were bound. As I opened my eyes, I saw my daughter unconscious and tied to the kitchen island in front of me. Three men dressed in black cloaks stood around the kitchen. One by the stove, one by the back door and the third stood between me and Elyse.

I felt disoriented as I mustered up some words. "I just left Don Pasuta. We worked out a payment plan."

"*Zdraustvuyte, G-zha Edison,*" a Russian accent said under the hood.

Russian. Great, so not a part of my previous encounter. Why are they here? I never stole from them. Did the Don sell my debt and not tell me? They better not hurt my daughter.

"Just in case you do not speak Russian, I said, 'Hello, Ms. Edison'." The cloaked man said in English as he pulled off his hood. He had a rat-shaped face with a short, red mohawk. The rest of his head was covered in tattoos.

"Hello to you," I answered politely. "Now, who the fuck are you and why are you in my kitchen?"

"Forgive me." He bowed. "I am known as Szhiganiye and I have been hired to retrieve something of great value."

I racked my brain to think what I may have stolen and from whom I'd stolen from. Nothing came to mind that should have brought the creep show to my kitchen.

"You don't have what I'm looking for." He answered my thoughts.

Shit, can he read minds?

"Yes, I can," he answered with a grin.

"What do you want and why do you need me?" I said out loud as I looked around for Mary.

"I can't help you," her voice whispered in my ear.

"That is correct. I've warded off your spiritual partner," he said as he pulled up his sleeve to reveal the Star of David tattoo he had on his forearm.

How does he know I have a ghost? Does everyone know I have a ghost?

"No. Nobody else knows. I am very thorough in my background checks." He once again answered my thoughts. This was beyond creepy.

"Okay. I'm going to ask for a third…"

"I need you steal the item for me," he interrupted.

"And you couldn't ask me without the sideshow act?"

He started to walk behind the island and ran his hand across my daughter's face. "So innocent. Do you regret bringing her into this world, with what you do for a living?"

"Not at all," I replied keeping any further thoughts out of my head.

"It amazes me what motivates people to do things they do not want to do."

"Hold on!" I started to panic. "You haven't even told me what you want me to steal or anything. I am the sort of person who really doesn't need motivation when offered a job."

"Ah, that's the word. Job. A job suggests there is payment involved. I do not pay, instead I give you what you want, when I get what I want."

"I'm getting really tired of saying it, but what do you want?" I asked as one of the hooded goons walked up to me and held out a folder. He pulled out a picture of a ceramic egg.

"That is a Fabergé egg commemorating the coronation of Alexander the Third. It was one of four given to his mother fifteen years after his death. This one was lost and recently rumors of its location have arisen," my Russian captive explained.

"Okay and why do you need me?" I asked as the second goon walked over from the stove holding a hot poker. I watched as he handed it to Red Mohawk.

"You have a high motivation factor," Mohawk guy answered as he held the poker inches from my unconscious daughter's face. I started to get pissed as I struggled to get free of my restraints.

"See." He pulled away the poker and I calmed down.

"Where is this fancy Easter egg?" I asked in a calm voice.

"Good question. All the information is in the folder," he responded as he untied my daughter. "We'll be taking your daughter and you will have seventy-two hours to retrieve my egg. In exchange, you will get your daughter back unharmed. Every hour past seventy-two hours and I will have to unfortunately burn one of her fingers. Which only gives you an extra ten hours. Are we clear?"

"Asshole!" I scream.

"Good. Oh, one more tiny thing," he said as one goon grabbed my arm. "No spiritual help." The second goon jabbed a sizzling branding iron into my arm. I smelt the flesh burn as I screamed only to be quickly silenced by a fist to the face. Then once again: darkness.

I wasn't sure how long I was unconscious. When I awoke, I was alone on the kitchen floor. My wrist still burned as I saw the Star of David blistering on my skin.

"Mary!" I called out, but she too was gone. The folder lay spilled across the tiled floor. I slowly lifted myself up, gathered the papers, walked to a cabinet and pulled out a bottle of Malbec and a glass. I felt like just downing the bottle, but time was ticking away. I grabbed one of my larger wine glasses, poured myself a drink and sat at the island. I stared at a picture of Elyse and thought that maybe the asshole had a point. Her father was killed two years prior in a home invasion thanks to me. Elyse was taken hostage also during that situation. My daughter was my Achilles heel. I could have quit my line of work or given her away to a normal, safer family. But she was all that I had in the world. I decided: *I'll get this stupid egg, give it to this Russian douche bag and then, when Elyse is safe, shoot the fucker in the head.*

I pulled out the information in the folder. The first was a

picture of an older, sophisticated looking man.

His information was written on the back: his name was Vincent Espenn and he was a Dutch real-estate mogul. He would be attending the Burning Man Festival the next day.

So I packed a bag for the desert, and within twenty-four hours I was sitting in a Cessna Skyline called The Sandgrouse. My pilot was in his late twenties, with blue mohawk and piercings and tattoos galore.

"So, what brings you to Burning Man?" the pilot made small talk.

"I'm a huge fan of 12 Moons, The Awakening changed my life," I replied, well-rehearsed.

"Well, if you feel like a little moshing, my pit is always open," the pilot stated as he wiggled his tongue.

I almost threw up in my mouth, but I held it together and placed my hand upon his knee. "You couldn't afford me."

"Oh, you're a hooker. Nice," he replied with a smile. "Better buckle up. We're about to land."

I looked out the side window and only saw the Arizona desert. "I don't see an airport."

"Well, nobody said The Burning Man Municipal Airport was fancy," he answered as the plane made a sudden drop in altitude. I realized that throwing up might just happen.

Within ten minutes, we were safely on the ground as I deplaned onto a sand-covered strip. I saw a hand-painted sign reading: 'Burning Man Municipal Airport'. There were several canopies with information tables underneath. Further down, I saw a line of golf carts and ATV's lined-up like taxis at an airport.

A woman standing next to what appeared to be a jeep-golf-cart-hybrid held up a sign that caught my eye: 'Ava Edison.' Surprised, I walked right up to her and introduced myself.

"Ms. Edison, I've been hired to take you to your destination," an Americanized Russian accent explained.

With only forty-eight hours left, I appreciated the fact

that my 'employer' was giving a helping hand.

I jumped into the passenger seat as the driver started the engine. A press of the gas, and we were off.

The Burning Man landscape was amazing and breathtaking: it was as if the movie Road Warrior had come to life in front of me. Thousands of people in scantily outfits and body paint danced around bonfires dotted throughout the desert. I also noticed huge pieces of unusual artwork weaved throughout.

"So, there is a Dutch Billionaire among this," I commented.

"Yeah, I'm taking you to him now. You have to do the rest," the driver replied. "I also brought you more appropriate attire." She handed me a bag.

I frowned. *I'm in khaki shorts and a sleeveless t-shirt. What does she want me to wear?* I opened the bag and saw what appeared to be two pieces of black string, a net, a gas mask and a dossier.

"*Really?*"

"You want to be believable." She stopped the vehicle and pulled down shades to make the car more private. "You have two minutes," she said as she hopped out of the cart.

Now I understood why he needed something to motivate me. I was not sure if any amount of money could have gotten me to put this outfit on. As I finished changing, the girl got back into the driver's side and continued to drive me to my destination. I had just finished reading the dossier as she stopped the cart and motioned for me to get out.

I bravely stepped out wearing a black bikini with a net top, a gas mask around my neck and my own hiking boots on my feet. My hair was tied up in a red bandana and my makeup made me look like I was playing football. Ahead of me stood a cabana, and in front of that a large wired sculpture. I walked towards the cabana to get a better look. There stood two eight-foot wire figures of adults sitting away from each other, as two glowing children stood inside them facing each other.

"It's entitled: 'Love'," a Dutch accent said from behind me.

I slowly turned on my heel to see a very tanned, shirtless, blonde male wearing camouflage shorts with a Caribbean-style straw hat and sunglasses, staring up at me from a lounge chair. I tried hard not to focus on his very smooth and chiseled abs.

"I'm very familiar with Milov's work," I responded, mentally thanking the woman for the cheat sheet.

The Dutchman stood up from his chair and strolled over to me. "Are you just a Milov admirer or do you like Russian art in general?"

"Russian artwork gets my juices flowing," I replied, almost gagging on the words I was spewing out.

"Really? Well, I'll make sure I get your number and invite you over to my place sometime," he replied, slowly touching my skin.

"What's stopping you from inviting me now?" I questioned, hoping he would take the bait.

"First of all, my house is in Cuba," he stated.

Son of a bitch! I'm just over thirty hours to get the egg and get back. Now, I must get him to take me to Cuba and figure out how to get back to the States with a stolen Fabergé egg.

"Second, I don't even know your name," my mark pointed out.

"It's Addison," I blurted out.

How would I get out of Cuba? Do I need a passport? Does he have his own plane? I have no idea how to fly a plane. Think Ava think.

"I would give anything for a big, thick, meaty, Cuban sandwich with a Pineapple Mojito on a beautiful beach right now," I said in my sexiest voice, trying to bait him in.

"That is what is wrong with the desert: there are no beaches. Sand for miles, no water." He giggled as he began to massage my shoulders.

"Your hands are so good at that." My body moved with the flow of his hands.

It felt so good that my body tingled with delight almost begging for more, but I had to stay focused for my daughter's sake.

"How about you come into my cabana and I give you a full body massage," he gently whispered in my ear.

Crazy Russian will burn your daughter's fingers off if you are late. Good looking, smells great, beyond-wealthy, Dutch man wants to nail you in his Cabana.

No time for love, Dr. Jones, I thought to myself. *I must do something drastic.*

I turned to face him and held out my hand. "It's been nice meeting you."

The expression on his face was worth the trip. "You are leaving?"

"Yeah, this is Burning Man. I'm only staying today, so there is a lot to do and see. Enjoy your cabana."

I turned and started to walk away. I could feel his eyes watching me like a dog waiting for his master to return.

"Can I at least offer you a drink?" he called out.

I stopped and faced him once again. "I'm sorry, I don't even know your name."

"You don't know my name?" he responded with his second-best shocked face.

"Just that you're a good-looking guy with a house in Cuba who enjoys art," I lied through my teeth perfectly.

"I'm Vince Espenn." He replied as if I would jump up and down in excitement at his name.

He is nipping at my line, though. I should start reeling him in, I told myself as I walked back towards him. As I got up to him, I once again stuck my hand out and said, "Nice to meet you, Vinny."

He took my hand gently and leaned over to softly kiss it. "My dear Addison, would you please stay for a drink?"

One drink, Ava! Be charming and make him want to take you to his place.

"Sure, one drink would be nice," I agreed as I stepped into his charming cabana and took a seat on the plushest chair. I watched him head over to the bar and pull out two glasses and a bottle of red wine.

"Cheval Blanc, 1947," Vincent announced as he popped the cork.

"It's red, I'm happy," I said as I watched him pour it into the glasses.

"Care to join me here at the bar?" Vincent requested.

"Sure," I replied as I stood up and casually strolled over to join him. I sat on the stool across from him, he handed me a glass and I went for a sip.

"Hold on," Vincent said as he placed his hand over my glass. "You want that to breathe."

"Of course," I replied as if I knew what I was doing.

"You don't drink expensive wine, do you?"

"Of course, I do. In fact, yesterday I had wine and cheese with the Queen of England," I giggled.

I noticed as I laughed at myself that Vincent was just staring at me.

Did I have a bat in the cave? Crust in the crack of my eye? How bad was my hair?

"Is there a reason you are just staring at me?" I asked as I felt myself blush.

"Why are you here?" Vincent asked with a blank expression.

I smiled. "You offered me a drink."

"I mean, why are you here at Burning Man? You don't look like its stereotypical attendee," Vincent retorted. "So, I'll ask you again. Why are you here and who are you, really?"

Fuck! Think Ava think.

"I'm Cinderella!" I blurted out.

"Oh, really? You're a slave to your step-mother and you have a pumpkin carriage in the back? Are those boots made of glass?" Vincent sarcastically replied.

"First, Cinderella's shoes were made of fur in the fairy tale. Disney made them glass," I said in a firm voice. Immediately his cheesy smile disappeared. "Second, you honestly want to know who I am? Because our night may just come to a complete halt once you find out!”

My dander was now up.

“Please. Tell me,” Vincent asked in a sincere voice.

I took a deep breath, collected my thoughts and began. “I’m a mid-western soccer mom, whose husband was murdered in front of me and my little girl over a year ago. Once that happened my daughter became the center of my universe. A friend of mine saw how much time I put into raising her, to the point she felt I was losing myself. Yesterday she offered to watch my daughter for three days; in return I would go out and just love life. So, I came here.”

“You are an amazing woman, Addison. I’m sorry about your loss and even sorrier that I was an ass about that Cinderella reference. You truly are a Cinderella and I’d be happy to be your Prince Charming. I would also like to invite you to a Cuban diner.”

“In Cuba?” I verified.

“Yes, in Cuba,” Vincent laughed.

Oh, thank the Gods.

“Well then yes, I would love to join you,” I replied as I gave him a hug.

Vincent then looked at his watch. “My jet can be fueled and ready to go within the hour.”

Another hour wasted, but I got him to ask me. Guess I still got it. Now I need to figure out how to get back home.

“Well, I guess I’ll meet you in an hour,” I said as I stood up and started to head out.

“Meet me?” Vincent replied with now his third-best shocked face.

“I still want to check out Burning Man and I also need to collect my belongings. What plane should I look for?”

“The Little Dike,” he answered.

I smirked and gave him a friendly hug good-bye. “How long is the flight?”

“Five hours on a good weather day.”

“I’ll see you in an hour.” I waved as I stepped out of the cabana and strolled back to where the hybrid was still standing, the girl checking the oil.

"That was short," she said as she closed the hood and walked over to open my door.

"I'm on a time crunch," I responded, hopping into the passenger seat. I watched her close my door and walk over and hop into her seat. "I need to get back to the airport," I instructed as she started the cart and drove off.

"So, you are leaving already?" she questioned.

"I hopefully found what I was looking for. Now I just got to get to it."

"Where are you heading next?" she asked as I sat and stared at her.

I watched her facial expressions, listening to the tone of her voice and her breathing pattern while she spoke. She had a Russian accent but nothing about her seemed shady or threatening. I then remembered one detail that I hadn't caught until that moment.

"Where do the pilots hang out?" I asked.

She pulled up by the airstrip and pointed to a large circus tent.

"Would you like me to wait for you?" she asked.

"No, I'm afraid I'll be leaving within the hour. Make sure you add a big tip to your bill. You've been awesome." I jumped out, gave her a little wave good-bye, and started to walk off as she pulled away.

The sun started to drop and so did the temperature, but the music got louder as I hustled closer to the tent. I stopped by the entrance flap, took a deep breath and then stepped inside.

Two bartenders were working from a circular bar in the center of the tent. It seemed to be a male dominated patronage. I could feel all eyes on me as I approached my target. I stepped up to the bar and seductively whispered into his ear, "*Ty khochesh' mne poyekhat'?*"

"*Da, cherrt voz'mi,*" the blue mohawk pilot responded in a heavy Russian accent along with a wink and a smile.

I quickly grabbed him by the back of his mohawk and

slammed his face into the bar.

The room became awkwardly silent as I looked around and saw all eyes staring back at me.

"Gentlemen, go back to your private entertainment. I'll take this outside," I announced as I grabbed him once again by his mohawk and yanked him through the bar and out of the tent.

Once I stepped outside, I tossed his body hard to the ground. He attempted to come at me but I revealed that I had taken the gun which had been strapped to his back.

"What the fuck, lady?" he yelled in an American accent. "I think you broke my fucking nose!" I noticed blood roll out of his nostrils.

"Shut your whiny trap, bitch boy and listen up!" I commanded pointing the gun at his head.

He settled down and motioned for me to proceed,

"First, I need you to get ahold of your boss. Tell him I am heading to Cuba to retrieve his package. I'm aware I only have fifteen hours left to retrieve the egg and get back."

"You broke my nose to tell me that?" the pilot replied.

"No, I broke your nose because you were not up front as to who you are."

Also, to let you know who's in charge.

"Let your boss know that once I get the package, you are going to be giving me a ride from Cuba straight to him," I said, laying out the plan.

"Hell no!" he responded as he spat blood onto the ground.

"Excuse me?" I twisted the barrel of the gun into the top of his head.

He looked me dead in the eye and said, "I don't work for you and it's not my responsibility to help you deliver the package." He then gave me a cheesy grin and ended with saying, "I'm also okay with your daughter getting some of her digits burned."

I took the gun by the handle and cracked it squarely across his chin. He fell back in pain, but I immediately yanked him back up.

"Fuck!" he screamed.

I put the barrel of the gun on the bridge of his nose and said, "Don't you ever disrespect my daughter again! Now hear me again: you will pick me up in Cuba and take me to your boss. If you tell me 'no' again, I will pull the trigger and just figure out how to get back myself." I then cocked the gun.

"Fine! You win."

I pulled away the gun and held out my hand. He grabbed it and pulled himself off the ground.

"You are one crazy-ass bitch," he told me as he wiped the sand off his pants.

"I know." I smiled as I pulled out a piece of paper and handed it to him. "This is my number. Text me when you hit Cuban air space."

He took the paper and nodded in agreement.

As I turned away, he asked, "Would you have really shot me in the head?"

I quickly spun around, pointed the gun at him and pulled the trigger. "Click."

I swear he just soiled himself.

"See you in Cuba." I winked and then returned to the bar.

Within the hour I was on a beautiful private jet wearing my previous outfit of a tank top and cargo shorts. Once I had finished this job I would be burning my Burning Man outfit.

Vincent had been pouring a glass of wine as I emerged from the restroom. He handed me the glass and offered me some cheese. I wished that it was smeared across a hamburger, but food is food.

"This outfit appears to be more you," Vincent complimented, motioning me to sit down.

"What, you don't think I look natural in the apocalypse fashion?" I giggled.

"I think you make a paper bag fashionable. But natural? No. You seemed to be the epitome of a fish out of water."

"So why Cuba?" I changed the subject.

"I love the architecture. Not to mention real estate is dirt cheap. Add in the beautiful beaches, food, and culture and it's why not Cuba," he explained.

"Its government. Its own citizens defecting by the minute," I countered.

"I try not to get involved in the politics. I'm a 'you leave me alone and I look the other way' kind of guy."

"So, you're an ostrich."

"If it keeps people from snooping into my affairs, I'm okay with that. I feel I can be honest with you and say not all my business ventures are on the up and up."

"You got to live your life as you want," I answered finishing my glass. "Just be aware you have to answer for it at some point."

"Are you getting religious on me?" Vincent asked, refilling my glass.

"No. Rule number twelve of my first date list of 'Do's and Don'ts' is: No political or religious discussion."

Vincent leaned closer. "And what does this list say about sex on the first date?"

"Rule number one: No. Though I think I can amend that, seeing I've never been a member of the Mile-High Club," I whispered.

This is some good wine.

"Really? Well, I'm head of the board and think I can get you a full membership," he answered as he softly kissed me on my lips.

Don't fall for this guy Ava. He is a mark and your daughter needs you.

The next couple of hours were a blur of alcohol and adult fun. I must have fallen asleep because the next thing I heard was: "Addison."

I opened my eyes and felt totally disoriented. I had no idea where I was, until my eyes focused on a smiling Vincent Espenn. He was standing over me, still on the jet.

I gathered up a smile and said, "Hi. Are we there yet?"

"Yes, we've landed. I have some business to take care of

right now. My staff is preparing dinner as we speak." He added as he turned to exit, "Oh, and you may want to put some clothes on before you leave."

I looked down to see I was covered by a blanket. I lifted it up to find myself naked as a jay bird.

I disembarked once I had found my clothes and got dressed. A full moon brightened the sky, letting me survey the area. I noticed the jet was on a private strip and could see ahead of me a massive, well-lit mansion. As I descended the stairs a golf cart waited for me.

"*Buenos Tardes*, Senorita Addison. Señor Espenn is waiting for you on the beach," the driver announced.

I got into the cart and checked my cell as he drove away. No texts. Where was he?

The cart drove along a paved path. Exotic plants and flowers outlined the edges. When we arrived at the beach, there was a large deck near the water, a beautiful candle-lit table upon it. Vincent stood to greet me.

I knew it had only been a half an hour since I saw him last, but it felt like forever.

Don't get caught in the fairy-tale. You just need to play the game.

I walked over and gave him a small kiss upon his lips. He pulled out my chair. I sat and, like a true gentleman, he pushed my chair in before sitting down across from me. A man came over with two silver platters. Pulling off the lids, he revealed a large, fat, juicy meat-filled sandwich and chips. I was so hungry I forgot my manners and took a huge bite. As I chewed I looked over for shocked-face number four.

I swallowed, took the napkin and wiped my mouth, and then said, "I might be a little hungry."

Vincent laughed. "A little? I guess a cheese plate isn't too filling. Please enjoy."

Suddenly my phone vibrated on my leg. Time was up: I needed to get that egg.

"You know, Vincent, I would love to see your house," I said with a subtle wink.

Vincent gave a nod as he stood up and then pulled my chair back out. "Shall we?" He wrapped his arm around me and we strolled up another path leading to the side door of the house. He opened the door and we entered his amazing home. The décor was Cuban drug lord with over-sized plants and large paintings in gaudy gold frames. A massive fountain stood in front of a spiral staircase.

"Wow! I bet your bedroom is satin and leather," I joked.

"Guess there is only one way to find out," he replied as he scooped me off my feet and carried me up the staircase.

Stay focused, Ava.

He carried me all the way up and into a huge bedroom. In the middle of the room was a four-poster king-size bed. A huge window took up the back wall with heavy curtains tied back to keep them open.

It even had a fake bearskin rug laying in front of a huge dresser.

"Wow, this is bigger than my first apartment," I said as he put me down on the bed then started to kiss my neck.

Damn he is good at this. Maybe a quickie. No. It's 'go' time, Ava Edison.

I gently pushed him off my neck and tossed him down to the bed.

"Oh, you can be aggressive," Vincent chuckled.

"Are you into kinky?" I asked as I pulled off my top, exposing my breasts.

"I lived in Amsterdam for six years," he replied as he started to unbutton his pants.

"Good. Then lay down on the bed, arms and legs spread," I instructed as I walked over to the window. I watched as he pulled off his pants and removed his shirt. I untied the ropes from the curtains, letting the drapes unravel and cover the view. Vincent smiled as he got into position. I tied the one side of one rope to a post and the other to an adjoining appendage. Once I had secured both arms and legs to the bed, I crawled on top of him and started to kiss his body from the chest down, stopping before his happy little dike.

"Do you have a lighter?" I asked in a seductive voice.

"Oh, you looking to burn me?" he said with intense joy. "Last drawer on the right." I got off him and walked over, opened the drawer and pulled out a Zippo. Perfect.

I grabbed a glass jar candle and lit it, walking over to an overly-excited Vincent. I slowly poured melted wax on him, enough to make a small puddle on his chest, and then placed the jar on top of it.

"This is different," he commented.

I kept quiet and walked over to the curtain, thinking about my daughter. I took a deep breath and said, "Vincent, I lied to you."

His expression of joy quickly turned to confusion. "Excuse me?"

"My name is not Addison, it's Ava. I didn't go to Burning Man to find myself; I went to find you."

I could tell he wanted to get up off the bed, but I know my knots.

"The truth is that a man named Szhiganiye has my daughter and has given me 72 hours to bring him a Fabergé egg that you have in your possession," I explained.

"You are working with The Burning? He told you I have the Alexander the Third egg? I don't." Vincent responded. "So, how about you untie me and get out before I have you shot."

I looked at him closely, flicked the Zippo and held out the flame. "You must suck at poker, Vinny. I'm calling your bluff." I turned and set the curtain on fire.

"What the fuck, you crazy bitch!" he screamed in panic as he tried to get loose, the jar swinging right-to-left on his chest.

"I'd stop before you dump that candle and light the mattress on fire," I pointed out to him. He quickly stopped.

"Listen, Ava, don't do this. That man is crazy," Vincent said in a calming voice.

"Well, I'm not. I'm desperate," I replied while I lit a second curtain. "Now tell me where the egg is, and I'll stop before you and your house burn down. "

"Killing me isn't going to get your daughter back," he pointed out, the desperation in his voice telling me he was not going to give it up.

I walked over to the front of the bed and stood on the carpet. "True. But he will see that I tried." I stepped off the rug and dropped the Zippo, igniting the rug. The flames rose fast.

"There's a fake bottom in the middle drawer: it's in there!" Vincent screamed.

I turned to the dresser as the heat of the flames started to grow. I pulled out the drawer and removed the bottom. There it was, and it was beautiful. I wrapped it up in one of his shirts and walked to the bed.

"Please untie me," Vincent pleaded.

I grabbed him by the head and gave him a deep, loving kiss and then slammed his head hard into the back board, knocking him unconscious. I removed the candle from his chest, untied him from his restraints, and carried him in a fireman's lift out of the burning room. I could hear voices coming down the hall, so I laid him down and ran in the opposite direction. I found my way out of the house just as the emergency vehicles pulled up into the drive. I sprinted away from them, towards the landing strip, and there was the blue-haired mohawk glaring at me.

"You got it?" he asked.

I held it up. "You are giving me a ride?"

"Get in," he replied as he turned and got into the pilot's seat. I jumped into the back as he turned on the engines and pulled away. We were in the air in minutes.

"So, you burned down his house, huh?" he chuckled.

"A girl's gotta do what a girl's gotta do," I responded.

I took another deep breath and leaned back into my seat. I knew that this adventure was coming to an intense finale and I needed to be prepared.

"Where are we going?" I asked.

"I have been instructed to take you to a hotel near where

you live," he replied.

"Any chance you could take me home first to change?" I requested rubbing his shoulders.

"Sure," he answered, "You better get some rest, it's going to be a while."

"What's your name?" I asked seeing as how I'd been referring him as blue-haired mohawk.

"Geroy," he responded.

"Thank you, Geroy," I answered as I closed my eyes.

After we landed, Geroy was true to his word and took me home first.

With half an hour to spare Geroy opened my car door and helped me out of the rental car. I was showered and dressed for business. I looked at the fancy hotel and just wanted to sprint in and get it all over with as quickly and easily as possible. Yet, I knew in my line of work that easy wasn't in the job description.

Geroy escorted me to the elevator and up to the penthouse. As the elevator doors opened I saw my daughter sitting on the couch, eating a bowl of popcorn and watching television. Szhiganiye was sat next to her. He looked up as I walked in.

"*Dorogoy* Ava, you made it," he said as he stood up and walked over to me.

I pulled the egg out of my purse and held it up to show him. "I've kept my side of the bargain."

"Your daughter is unharmed as I promised," he pointed out, as two burley men stepped into the room, each holding a hand gun. "But I cannot let you live."

"What?" Geroy spoke out. "She got what you asked for. She has proven she can be trusted to do a job."

"When provoked," he countered. "I'm sure right now she is aiming to kill me."

I'm going to jam this knife right through your gut and split your weasel belly in half, I thought as I stomped my foot, releasing the blade. I quickly swung my leg straight at him and he caught it.

"You forgot I read minds?" he chuckled.

"Nope." I pointed my hand straight at his head. The gun sprang out and I pulled the trigger. Immediately the bullet flew into his skull, blowing his brain out the back. I kicked him off my boot and he dropped to the ground, dead. Geroy pulled out his own gun and shot the gunman on the right as I took out the one on the left. I looked over to see the best shocked face of all in the last 72 hours: my daughter's.

"Mommy!" Elyse called to me as she leapt from the couch and ran into my welcoming arms. I hugged her so tight and looked up at Geroy. "Thank you."

He nodded.

I picked her up and handed him the egg, "Can I trust you to return this to a Russian museum?"

"*Da,*" he answered, taking the egg from me. "You better go. I'll clean this all up."

I nodded and then returned to the elevator, my daughter held tightly in my grip.

"By the way, how did you know I was working for him?" Geroy asked.

I smiled and pointed to my wrist, letting him know I saw the Star of David tattoo. He laughed and waved as the elevator door closed.

A week later, I lay on my bed reading a trashy novel. My wrist was firmly bandaged where I had had the Star of David burn skin-grafted over.

"Ava Edison, you did a great job," a familiar spiritual voice said.

I looked up from my book to see Mary standing by the window and smiling at me.

"Thank you, and I'm glad you're back," I answered.

"Is there a job?" she questioned.

"Not yet, but this past week has taught me that I am a wanted woman. I am easily found and easily manipulated," I explained.

"How do you change that? Quit? Go into hiding?" Mary

questioned.

"No, I just need to be more aware. My daughter is all I have. I know she gives me strength, yet at the same time she is my greatest weakness" I answered.

"So, do you let her go?" Mary asked.

"No. I make her more aware of the world we live in. There is great evil and I need to make her strong enough to face it: with or without me. Whatever comes next, we will be prepared."

"So, what is next?"

My cell phone chirped. I picked it up and read the text, "We'll soon find out," I smiled.

THE END

ABOUT THE AUTHOR

Marcus Cook lives in Cleveland, Ohio with his wife Kathy, the love of his life, and their cat, Freckles. He loves to read sci-fi and thrillers and loves to write whatever hits his imagination. He started out as a playwright with two produced plays and a published award-winning play. He tries to write every day and hopes fans will continue to enjoy his work.

You can follow Marcus on his Facebook page—www.facebook.com/READ-Marcus-Cook-310210383127852/—and can email him at mailto:readmarcuscook@gmail.com.

Circle of Friends
by Tom Goymour

I must have refreshed my phone screen at least three times. Not because the message is in any way complex—just the opposite, it couldn't be clearer. It's a surprise that's all—well, more of a shock really. Some mornings you wake up and get on with your day without giving much thought to anything, nothing grabs your attention or causes you to change your plans; you get dressed, grab a bite to eat, say goodbye to the family and drive off to work—it's called life. But there are other times when something hits you smack in the face and your whole day takes on a new shape. This is one of those days.

I feel like the stuffing has just been knocked out of me, it's as if someone has just picked me up and thrown me across the room hard against the wall to make sure I take some damn notice.

I contemplate whether or not to respond. I haven't heard from her for twenty years, since that day—the day she obviously remembers as well as most likely all the rest of us do. And what about Rupe, the other guy still involved? Has she been in contact with him too?

We decided after that day that the best way forward was to stick to our story, wipe the slate as clean as we could and restart our lives. We all agreed never to meet up again; at seventeen that was a hard decision. It was actually her idea; most things were back then. As far as I know, through all the years that have passed since, we've all stuck to it. We decided there must be no opportunity for us to be tied in with anything that happened that night. But now, here it is right in front of me, an unwelcome reminder in black and white that what we went through that night and everything we did was real.

I need to know, so I decide the only thing I can do is to check her and Rupe out on social media. I don't have phone numbers from that long ago, none of us will have. Rupe should be easy to find though with a name like *Rupert Rodgers*. But then something hits me; how did *she* get my mobile number?

Rupe was always a bit of a smoothy. He didn't seem too bothered about any of it. In fact, he'd seemed the least shocked of all of us about the whole thing. Nothing fazed him; we'd go out into the fields in the evening and just mess around, it was what we did—how we killed our time. It was kind of exciting and it gave us a kick; it always turned into a bit of a covert operation because farm workers were often around. We had to constantly be on our guard so as not to be seen, but Rupe... he didn't much care about hiding from anyone. He would stand upright in the field like a scarecrow—all six and a half foot of him, and then he'd just grin down at the rest of us crouching to hide and call us scaredy-cats. I'm sure we got seen because of him on several occasions... but not on the night that mattered. He had the front to play it cool every time, but on that night, when the moment came he ran off as fast as he could, scared like the rest of us.

My fingers scroll through the results after I've typed his name in the search bar. I find a profile that fits him and so I click.

My God, he hasn't changed much, I think as his picture comes up. I pause for a minute, but the urge is too great, I can't mull this over any more. I have to ask him, so without any more thought I start to type:

'Hey mate, it's Chris Sanderson. You remember me? It's been a long while and I know we were never going to do this getting in touch with each other bit again, but I need to know something. Have you been contacted by Sally-Anne Benteen recently... because I have, and that's the reason for this message. Can you let me know?'

So, I've done it. I press send, and by contacting him I've broken the *Oath of Allegiance*—our agreement never to contact each other again. I had to do it; I have to know if this is genuine, and Rupe is the only guy in the world who can tell me. I stand gazing at the message I've just sent wondering if and when he will reply.

Loyalty mattered to all of us back then, or at least it should have done. We called it the *Oath of Allegiance*, we had our rules, our code of conduct. It was our circle of friends and we all had to agree on what took place inside it. I remember how angry Sally-Anne got when one of us suggested bringing someone else in—Karl that was—Karl Holdsworth, the other guy in all this.

'We do this together' she used to say, every time there was a decision to be made. I reckoned she was a tiny bit jealous because she liked being the only girl in the clan, and she

didn't want Karl, or anyone else inviting another female. I think of Karl and I get that uncomfortable tingle that hangs around just before you start to break sweat. I've had this a number of times over the years, it's never really cleared from my mind.

Will he reply?

People can be funny, I have friends on social media who won't reply as a matter of course if they don't fancy it. Why should he? It's easier to just ignore sometimes.

I want to think about something else, but my phone won't leave my hand.

This is silly. He's going to need processing time, and I have things I could be doing.

We did agree to never make contact again, and right now, he could be anywhere doing just about anything.

What if he has already seen this and it has really thrown him—and made him angry?

My mind is scrambled with all the possibilities. I force myself to take a walk, but I don't get far.

My phone pings and I jump. It's Rupe, he's replied. A round avatar displays on my screen, so I click it.

'Hi, it's Rupe. How you doing? And yes mate, I got a message too. I think we should meet?'

I read it several times. I'm in a daze and struggling to take in the words. At last this is confirmation that someone else from all that time ago is having the same experience as me. Stuff will surely be going through his mind as well. It's a bit like that moment when someone tells you they've been having the same weird dream as you, or they have the same strange habit, just like the one you never wanted to admit you had. Suddenly, you're not alone.

I scroll back to the text message from Sally-Anne and read it again:

'Chris. Been a long time... this is very important. I don't know where you are or what you're doing with your life right now, but we need to meet up. The police are on to it. You'll know what I mean. There's stuff we need to go over. Same

place, same time as the old days. Thursday.

Don't let anyone see this. ONLY reply if you CAN'T make it. No need to look for me, I will find you. S.A.B.'

Now I find I can analyse the words a bit more objectively. I won't reply because if Rupe is up for this I will go—I have to. Thursday is five days away, so there's enough time to meet up with Rupe first. She's made sure there are no details of timings or geographical position that would mean anything to anyone else, and, it sounds like her talking. Right now, I feel a weight lift slightly from me.

The next day Rupe messages me his number and we talk over the phone. He says not to let anyone overhear our conversation. I ask him where he is and it turns out he lives forty-five minutes away; he's married now with two kids. He's heard that I stayed in the area. We don't say much; I suppose neither of us want to open up because I guess we are just not sure we trust each other completely yet. Funny how things turn out really... the whole *friends in a circle* thing was built on trust in the first place, but right now, none of us are sure.

Rupe still has that annoying way he uses his voice to make it sound like he's so sure of everything. Right now, that's a quality I'm happy he has. I'm not feeling so confident about going ahead with this.

My mind drifts back to twenty years previously.

Sally-Anne... What a girl she was. More a leader than Karl, Rupe or I ever were I'd say. It all started out as just a bit of fun when we found *The Shack*—at least, that's what we called it. It was this old shed at the edge of the field surrounded by bushes before the woodland area started for real about twenty meters behind. Sally-Anne was the first to point out how cool it would be if we made that our meeting place—our secret hideaway, as clearly the farmer didn't use it any more. It got even cooler when we found someone had started a crop circle right opposite, about seventy meters into the corn. Crop circles were the thing back then—it was all a bit of a craze. We became fascinated by them, mainly because nobody really knew how they got there. There were lots of theories floating around, but nobody really knew—that was the beauty of it. It was a mystery and we always hoped we'd find one, then we could take it over and make it our own. We would become the innovators.

It was when we were playing this game one evening with this rubber flying bomb toy we had, when we came across it. One of us would throw it into the field and we'd take it in turns to time each other to go and retrieve it and get back without being seen. We saw a light flash low in the sky, I said it was just the reflection from a bit of tape on the bottom of the rubber toy but the others weren't buying it. Karl said it was a sign of something—like a star above guiding us to a special place.

Sally-Anne insisted we go and investigate.

"Come on, let's all go and see." We hesitated at first. "We do this together." She was determined, and so we all had to follow. When we got there, in spite of us all having seen it, we found no light at all, just this flattened circle. It wasn't much, but someone or something had made a perfect circle in the corn, and this attracted our immediate attention.

It became *our* circle, no one else would be allowed in, and we wouldn't tell anyone about it. It's kind of stupid when I think back, but I suppose it was only the sort of thing kids our age did back then. It didn't look finished, we had most likely taken over someone else's creation and it didn't look like they were coming back to claim it any time soon. Mainly, we used the shack as our store and the circle as our meet up place. We messed about—took stuff with us... you know... a few smokes, nothing heavy, but Sally-Anne... she turned up with four cans of beer one night. Boy, how I remember that evening when we notched things up to a new high, just a day or two after we'd first made the discovery.

The sun was low and there was a chill in the air. It must

have been fairly early in the summer, the crop hadn't turned, it was still green, and it smelt sweet and fresh. The three of us had made it up the south path to the field without being seen, then we'd crept through the swaying swathes of corn as they were blown around by the evening breeze. We sat there in the flattened centre of the circle wondering, as we always did, how the shape had been made and planning how we might make it better. It was so neat and regular, yet when we found it a week or two before there had been no obvious way in to it. Now, it looked like there were lots of ways in—we'd certainly left a much stronger mark than its original creator. We were sitting there waiting on that early summer evening when Sally-Anne suddenly appeared.

"Beat me to it guys?" She said, clutching a four-pack of lager. "I had more important matters to attend to." She looked down and pulled the plastic rings from the top of the pack and threw us each a can, grinning as she did so. Myself and Rupe, we were pleasantly surprised, but Karl was ecstatic. How did she wangle this one? Pretty plucky for a sixteen-year-old I say. We didn't ask, and we didn't really care, she had earned our respect, and from that moment on we let her take the lead, not because she was a pretty girl and we fancied her or anything like, but because of the way she always behaved with us. She was a real leader.

So, even after all this time, if it is Sally-Anne who is trying to get in touch, and it's not some sick joke by someone who has somehow found out about what happened, then surely, we have to respond?

Rupe agrees, but I'm concerned when he suggests we don't meet until the evening itself... says it's too risky and we don't really know what this is all about. I say we do know most likely; he pauses, then acknowledges that much, but he doesn't say any more. I take the point he makes about making our way there separately and we agree that we will make sure we enter the circle together—safety in numbers.

*

The days between pass slowly, but Thursday finally comes. I go on foot, it's only about a mile and a half from where I am—where I've been for a good many of my thirty-seven years. I cross the last road before the track that leads up to the side of the woods. From there it's about half a mile round to the edge of the field where the Shack once stood. I realise I've never been back to this spot. I've walked through these woods several times, but recalling the past has never consciously flickered through my mind, no memories have ever been triggered. But I am aware of something—I think I always have been since that day. I feel I know there is something beyond where I am heading—like there's a big cloud that has always hovered overhead; I've never wanted to look up into it in case I caused it to burst and its contents were to pour out and immerse me.

As I walk on, my mind goes back to that first time we saw the light, when good old Sally-Anne rocked up with the cans of beer for us all—and that was just the start. The Shack was just a dilapidated shed with a leaky roof and full of smelly old broken rusty farm equipment but we made it ours. It was a strange construction, it looked as if it had been built on the site of something once far more substantial; it had solid brick foundations—quite a bit of overkill for such a simple, thrown-together old shack I thought. The best bit was the gap by the doorway as you entered. It looked as if there was once an undercroft, or something resembling a tiny cellar. The space was limited but it was okay for stashing away our valuables, and it had the added attraction of forming a sort of trap if someone else was to enter. Most of the other stuff left in there didn't really interest us, but there was this big roller thing in the corner. On one occasion we hauled it out and took it to the circle to help flatten the corn and make a new pathway. We only did that once, as it was far more effort than it was worth. The Shack also had a shelf on which stood a few plastic bottles full of some chemicals or other. They would be in big trouble leaving stuff like that lying around today, but nobody much cared back then. We never found out what was in them, but we did wonder afterwards if they had played their part that night.

The Shack was our heaven. Alcohol was brought in and stored, then snacks were left in a tin that Rupe brought down. Fires were even lit now and again, but we had to be careful not to be seen. I reckon we did get seen because on at least one occasion the Shack got raided, four cans went down to two one night and Rupe's treasure chest was considerably lighter than on our previous visit, but we never did come across anyone else around. We saw no one at all in the six weeks of that summer when we lived out our dream. Sally-Anne even managed to nick some of her dad's spirits, and no small amount either. We tipped it into a bigger bottle and kept adding to it, by mid-summer we had a good supply of brandy.

Ah, the brandy! Without the brandy it would never have happened.

I check myself as my foot slips. For a moment the memories overwhelm me. I find myself glancing nervously around in every direction: I'm starting to feel it. In the distance I can just about make out where we are meant to be heading. We only have a rough idea, everything has grown up all around, but Sally-Anne said she'll be looking out. I step forward and I feel my heartbeat wobble. Deep within the pit of my stomach something stirs; I don't want to do this, I don't want to even be here. I feel like turning my back and running, but I can't.

What's that? Darn it. She said they were on to it.

A problem. I see the unmistakable markings of a police car parked on the verge about a hundred yards up in front. I gasp. I have to change tack, so I find myself moving along into the edge of the field itself in order to get some cover should I need it. If a copper appears I can just fall back into the swathes of corn and I'll be hidden from view.

I breathe in the air and smell that dry freshness that emanates from the crop, and the second I do so my mind is jerked back once more; the corn smelt so ripe and crisp but there were other flavours too that night—alcohol and exhaled cigarette smoke. I've always loved that smell: I think it stems from early childhood when my grandma would come over to babysit me every Tuesday afternoon. She would walk into the living room, take a deep drag before placing her cigarette in the ash tray, then exhale forcefully and say:

"Now then Christopher, what shall we do this afternoon?"

The question was always the same and I would reply pretending I had no idea of an answer just so as to keep her talking. I loved the sound of her voice, it warmed me. Sometimes I almost felt myself purring like a cat, but most of my pleasure came from the smells associated with her cigarette; I would just sit there and watch it burn... slowly at first, but then the deep orange embers would take hold, and it would all burn away to ashes.

I look up and glimpse someone over by the woods. The figure shoots back out of sight almost immediately. I crouch, my eyes fixed on the spot about eighty metres in front. The figure shows again.

Is that him? He's seen the police car. And I see a plume of smoke rising from his face.

That's him; that's Rupe. He hasn't seen me, so I work my way a little faster through the corn to try and catch him up. He's put on some weight and he shuffles along in a way that doesn't flatter his state of fitness, but he's still as tall as a goal post. *That's what a sedentary life and smoking does for you,* I think smugly, feeling fairly sure of the picture I have in my mind of the sort of life Rupe has led since. I remind myself how I don't drink or smoke and how I keep myself in shape with running and five-a-side football every Monday night. I was always the sporty, fit one of the gang: I could climb trees, run a mean cross-country race, beat anyone over obstacle courses, but on that night I couldn't even—

"Down!" I shout as quietly as I can, interrupting my own thoughts. Rupe has seen me and raises a hand. I gesture towards him with my arm at the same moment, he gets the hint and immediately adopts a completely different posture, his lanky legs almost buckling under him as he tries to creep along by the trees. I laugh to myself as I think of how visible he actually is and how unlike any form of a camouflaged disguise any of his movements actually are. I'm level with the police car now and there's no sign of any coppers, at least that's something. My hands and arms shake a little as I emerge from the corn, now nearly within talking distance of Rupe. I beckon him across the track to come and join me. He moves like a drunken crane fly looking around anxiously as he goes.

"Safer over here." I say to him keeping my voice low. "We've got the cover of the field crop."

"Yeah," he gasps, totally out of breath. "How you doing? Been a long time."

We shake hands briefly.

"What the hell is this about?" I ask him. "It's got to be her surely?"

He nods.

"I reckon. Police are on to it like she says." He points back to the police car, quite a way behind us now. "It was a terrible thing that night. Something's come up and we are probably all going to get pulled in. We've got to get our stories straight—can't all be saying different stuff."

I stop and stare at him hard. I hadn't really thought it through. Saliva builds in my mouth and I try to swallow. I gulp and rub my arms as suddenly I'm cold all over.

"You think?" I answer shakily.

"Stands to reason. Why else?" He pauses and looks at me and we both know there is something else that is going to come into it if the police talk to us. Rupe says nothing more before moving on through the corn.

"Come on, it's not far. Unless you reckon any different, I think where we need to be is over there." He points to a spot in the cornfield that somehow looks horribly familiar, and instinctively I know he is right. My legs go numb, I lose the ability to control them. I feel the perspiration trickling over me, seeping through as if it's eating away at my very core. Now I'm scared. It becomes all too much as my mind relives that night.

It wasn't my fault. We were all there, we were all to blame, but now I know what the black cloud that has been hovering over me for years really holds... it's that overpowering feeling of guilt... and that cloud is about to burst.

We didn't know Karl was going to be such a prat. We'd all had a can or two, but he and Sally-Anne had been on the brandy; he'd brought the whole bottle out of the Shack to the circle. He started boasting about this girlfriend of his and how he'd invited her down and she might turn up any time soon. I didn't take to Karl, he was older than the rest of us but not mature, I always felt he was a bit of an outsider trying to get his own way once he became one of us. Letting outside forces you don't trust into the circle just leads to something bad happening. Now he was talking about bringing in someone else, although I got the impression it was just to wind Sally-Anne up. Suddenly, the heat was raised, there were a few curse words between the two of them, then Sally-Anne slapped him round the face... and that's when it started. The disastrous chain of events quickly followed.

"Psst!" My thoughts are interrupted as Rupe beckons me to catch him up. I scramble, now on all fours as if I am being hauled in slowly against my will.

Doesn't he feel any of this? He must remember it too. Do they really blame me? Is this whole thing a set up? I'm paranoid... but none of it was my fault. I was the nearest to him, but that doesn't mean much, sometimes. When the moment comes, you're just helpless.

Karl rolled around on the floor, his hands covering his face. He was mocking being hurt, we all knew he wasn't. Sally-Anne ignored him and swigged some more brandy, Rupe stood up in disgust, pulled the half-smoked cigarette from his lips, and told Karl to stop mucking about. Then, as he twisted his position to face Rupe, Karl's leg knocked over the brandy, and the whole lot spilled over the dry fresh stems upon which we sat. Sally-Anne jumped up and yelled furiously as Rupe went to grab Karl from the floor. I swear all he intended was to drum some sense into him, but there was a struggle. As I backed away I saw it drop from Rupe's hand, but their bodies blocked my line of vision to where it fell. It happened so quickly; Sally-Anne noticed it first.

"It's alight!" she yelled, taking a step towards the flame in an effort to try and stamp it out, but the alcoholic fuel had allowed the flames to flare almost instantly. Then, orange flickers leapt high from the brandy-soaked corn. It was burning, but Karl didn't move, he was still arguing with Sally-Anne about whose fault the waste of brandy was. It took just seconds for our whole circle to become a blazing orange inferno.

"Get out of here," Sally-Anne howled, I sensed the panic in her voice, but I froze with fear, I couldn't move right away. Karl was now yelling because the flames were licking at his feet. Rupe tried to drag him clear but in doing so fell backwards and twisted his ankle. Sally-Anne grabbed Rupe and pulled him to his feet.

"Move!" she shrieked.

I made an effort to pull Karl clear—of course I did—but he was too heavy. Rupe and Sally-Anne moved away fast and screamed back at us as the huge orange inferno now surrounded us. The heat was searing and the dry corn crackled as it burned itself black. Smoke pierced my eyes. At last Karl seemed to come to his senses. I tugged at him again, but he still didn't get to his feet.

"My foot's on fire. Aargh. Help me man," he yelled. I begged him to help himself, I couldn't do any more. I couldn't stay there any longer, my jacket was now alight, I ripped it from my back and then I ran. I didn't look back, not once.

After that I remember the three of us just huddled together, crying, over by the Shack looking back at the inferno before we ran off into the woods.

Rupe digs me in the ribs.
"Okay?"
"Okay," I reply.
He points. There is another police car a few yards beyond the far edge of the field where we are heading, and there are a couple of coppers milling around too.
I say that we just keep low and creep to the spot and wait for Sally-Anne to show. She's bound to, it's her call, she will be around somewhere. Rupe agrees. Then, for the first time, he asks me something directly.
"This has got to be about the body hasn't it?"
I hesitate before nodding in agreement.
The body. There was nothing else we could have done. Anyone else would have done the same if they had thought of it. We were smart... at least, that's what we thought at the time. I remember the fire like it was yesterday, raging its way across the field consuming everything in its path—and so furiously fast! I feel the vivid reality of that night burn through my veins every day that passes, and the reaction of almost disbelief which the devastation was greeted with the next day hangs over me like a cloud. But, that night we worked it out and we acted quickly. Shocked and grieving for our perished friend, I don't know how we managed it, but we decided there and then that we couldn't take the blame for it. Our lives would be totally messed up, and that wasn't fair.
We watched from our woodland retreat as the fire engulfed everything in its path—the entire field area between the circle and the Shack and then all the heathland in front. As it took the Shack the whole place ignited with a bang.
By the time the fire brigade arrived minutes later the centre of the inferno was way beyond where the shack had stood. They doused the field and the area in front of the woods and put most of it out quite quickly, so it wasn't

long before all of the fire crew and emergency services turned their attention to the woods. There were houses the other side and the raging inferno was being blown that way at an incredible pace. That was the moment we decided we had to do it. Sally-Anne was the calmest and it was her mind that worked the fastest in the time of crisis. It was completely dark other than the light of the fire itself and the emergency vehicles. She said we must use the dark as our cover to hide our dead friend's body. We had to act fast, nobody would be looking for anyone out there... yet. It seemed a crazy suggestion, but we didn't argue with her. We crept back towards the spot where the devastation had begun. We knew all the firemen were concerned with was getting the main fire under control, if we moved fast we wouldn't be seen.

I don't know how we did it, I just remember moaning and crying all the time, unable to comprehend what had happened. But Sally-Anne remained calm and determined; she told us what to do.

Everywhere was black and charred, the stench of burning was overwhelmingly powerful and pierced every molecule of the cool night air.

We came across the remains, still warm. We had no light so had to feel our way. I immediately vomited when I touched the body. Sally-Anne grabbed an arm and Rupe another, they told me to get a grip—metaphorically and literally. With my limited help we lifted what remained of our friend's charred, burnt body towards the only light we could see—the distant fire beyond where the Shack had stood.

"That way," Sally-Anne said, pointing. "He was in the Shack and we hadn't arrived yet." We knew what she meant—that was going to be the story; Karl had started it by accident and he burned to death in the Shack. If we got the body in there *before* anyone was looking for survivors, we had a chance of making it look authentic. We hauled the body over to the burnt remains and Rupe kicked some of the debris to one side. It was still hot. Sally-Anne told us that she would go and distract the police and firemen by telling them we were going to meet a friend in the woods and he must be in there somewhere. We would attempt to bury the body under the Shack. The perfect cover story; we were all nearby, we panicked because we thought our friend was in the woods, nobody had to make anything up, we just missed bits out.

Sally-Anne went off to do this and we worked fast. The gap under its reconstructed base... some of the Shack's floor had crumbled away, but there was still enough space to push the body through and let it roll right underneath. We kicked a few bricks and bits of debris over the front and then got ourselves back to the edge of the woods fast to meet up with Sally-Anne on return from her mission.

My mind is swiftly jolted back to the present as Rupe gives me a nudge. I look around and reckon we are about there. This is obviously where the circle once was. Growth is strained here, nothing flourishes quite as well as in other parts. I point this out to Rupe and he scans the false perimeter as he swivels on his haunches. His eyes meet mine and he nods, slowly. I swallow hard, feeling a slight discomfort in my throat. Then I nod back.

"Reckon you're right," he says. "I can see still just about see where the edge reached to."

We can't move about or make ourselves visible as there are police everywhere and we would be seen. We must just wait. Then I hear scuffling, someone is making their way towards us through the corn. We both stay crouched, unsure of whether it will be her or not. I try to control my erratic breathing as the sound in front of us grows progressively louder. We look up and see a formidable recognisable figure standing over us. She smiles down at us. I observe she wears her hair far more ornately than she did as a teenager, and the long beige coat makes her look taller than I remember, but it's the same self-assured smile she delivers that gives her a real presence of authority.

"Hello boys. It's been a long time."

We rise slowly to our feet and greet her cautiously. She speaks without lowering her voice in the slightest. This surprises me.

"I expect you're wondering what this is all about."

"Sally-Anne Benteen. After all this time we meet again and presumably through necessity?" Rupe says. I suggest that maybe we want to do this a little more discreetly, as in case she hadn't noticed the place is swarming with police.

Then she turns to me, the smile disappears from her face and she delivers the reply that is about as far from what either of us want or expect to hear as it could possibly be.

"I *am* the police," she says, holding up a warrant card as two plain-clothed guys appear out from the shadows and stand about twenty yards behind her.

"And it's DCI Benteen, for future reference."

From that moment everything changed. All Rupe and I could do was just stare at each other in disbelief. She took charge, just like she always had done, only this time we were really in trouble. The first thing she did was indicate to her sergeants to back off for a minute to give her some space. Then she confronted us with the reports she'd had of a body being covered up after the night of the fire and she said that the family deserve some closure.

"Well, yes," I said. "Duh!"

"Chris." Rupe interjected, grabbing my arm, and I immediately regretted my remark.

"You know boys, it would be far better if you just co-operate. You're both here, I've found you at the scene and you know that I know the body was hastily buried that night... by you two."

"Yes, but that's not fair, you can't—"

"Who's in charge here?" she howled, cutting me off. "Do you think I can let this one go?"

Silence then prevailed as the two of us stood there like

naughty schoolboys that had just been caught red-handed at something and had run out of lame excuses.

"Now, you are going to lead me to the spot where you think it is and my team are going to dig up that body."

"Perhaps she's just got promotion and wants to impress her seniors by reopening the case or something" I whisper to Rupe as she points in the general direction, knowing full well that's where the body must still lie.

"Perhaps she's just grown up to be a vicious cow," Rupe replies.

She beckons her sergeants over to assist with the proceedings as we head towards the spot where the Shack once stood.

"Think very carefully both of you. We don't want to get this wrong. The consequences could be huge." She stares at me long and hard. Her words burn away at my soul; just like a couple of decades previously, she had that same control over both of us.

Rupe looks across at me. We don't need words to know what the other is thinking. There is no advantage in trying any further deception. We are going to get double-done for this and she is going to get off.

It was pretty easy really; when you looked at the ground closely there were remnants of the stone marks where the foundations had been so the police team she'd brought with her set to work. DCI Benteen called an officer over and asked him to take us to the nearby police van. We weren't to leave until they'd got a result.

"There are some flasks of hot drink in the front. See that they're comfortable can you, Sergeant."

As we walk towards her she clocks our looks of sheer loathing. She touches my arm as I pass and says, "Hey, I will make this as easy for you as I can."

I don't answer.

It had been about 9.00p.m. when we'd met up with her on this early July evening. The light starts to fade as we watch for what seems like an eternity from the police van. All the time DCI Sally-Anne Benteen stands over the proceedings, occasionally answering her phone or making a call, in between glancing across at us. Rupe and I mutter in low tones but generally say little as the guarding police sergeant is in earshot. Neither of us want to make this any worse than it already is.

Why did we do it?

Why the hell didn't we just come clean on the night?

I suppose we panicked, we didn't know what to do, so we did what Sally-Anne told us to.

The pair of tunic-clad officers continue digging under the bright lights erected over a frame and wired to one of the other vehicles. They look like something out of a science fiction movie, but this is all so very real.

An hour or so must have passed but neither of us can take our eyes off the activity. Then, my heart leaps and misses a beat as one of the officers digging calls out and raises a hand.

"Ma'am!" he cries.

We watch silently as she goes over, stoops down and produces a torch to aid the light given from the overheads. She indicates for them to remove more soil and it's not long before something is being brought to the surface. The two Scene of Crime Officers in pale tunics cover the remains of what is found. This takes several minutes and all Rupe and I can do is sit and watch. Eventually she comes back over to us and says we are free to go, but not to leave the area as she will need to interview us properly in the next day or two.

For the next twenty-four hours my mind is scrambled. I don't sleep, my brain is on auto-loop, it's like the past and present have mixed together into one hideous nightmare that I'm just desperate to wake up from. Rupe's gone home to his family—says he will jump when called but he has to think of some excuse first and he can't stay in the village indefinitely.

It's late afternoon and I'm lying on my bed trying to

shut my eyes and blank everything out for an hour or two, but I can't settle. A buzzing sound comes from the window. I look over and see a large bumble bee systematically exploring the perimeter of the glass pane. The window is open wide enough for the bee to escape but it can't find the gap, it's trapped in a cycle of going round and round until something comes along to change its situation. I close my eyes again and I reckon I doze a little as in my mind's eye I see a group of friends calling me over. It's years ago, I'm still a kid and they are huddled close together, beckoning me with raised voices. Other kids are running around like crazy, and as I look up I see there are plastic hoops lying on the floor, each with a couple of kids standing inside calling out. Then I realise, we're all playing that game where you must jump into the hoop before the music stops... but you have to be invited in. If you're not, then that's it, you're out—gone from the game.

As I get nearer, I see Rupe, Karl and Sally-Anne screaming at me to join their circle. They keep jostling for their place, and every now and again someone plants a foot outside the plastic ring before they find their balance and drag it safely back inside. Karl is the clumsiest and has the most trouble staying balanced, he is pushing and shoving the others, but Sally-Anne tries to keep him in while at the same time making room for me. I make it in as Karl loses his footing and falls completely out of the circle.

I join my closed circle of friends from which I can never escape.

Then, with a convulsive shudder for just a second, I find myself fully conscious again staring at the bumble bee on the window. I watch it find a gap and fly free.

If only.

I'm still thinking about the bee as my phone pings. I grab it from the side—it's a message from Rupe. He asks if I've had a visit yet. I ask him what he means; he says the police have just been round and want him to go in later this afternoon and take a fresh statement. But that's not all...

when he asked would DCI Benteen be present the officer told him that DCI Benteen had been taken off the case altogether. I tell him to drive over, we must talk.

We sit in the beer garden of the *Horse and Groom*. Rupe has been given a time—5.30p.m. to be at the police station. No one has approached me yet.

"They must know about her part in it, that's got to be why," I tell him.

"Well, serves her right. She wasn't about to do us any favours yesterday was she."

I know he's right, but at the same time I know he's wrong.

What is going on with her? Why would she risk getting us there to try and push the blame our way when we could just open our big mouths and drop her right in it as soon a she's out of the picture?

"It doesn't make sense to me," I say. "We can't really tell our story without including her in it anyway."

"Listen." He leans forward. "We say exactly what we told the police that next day all those years ago, and we stick to it, just like we have done ever since. She was interviewed as well remember—it will be on record somewhere. Surely it would have come up when she joined the force?"

I try to imagine being the police interviewing her back then. She was away talking to one of the firemen, asking if they'd seen our friend. We had already split with her by that point. Nothing in her story would have implicated her, so why was she there last night getting the body dug up and trying to blame us?

"Anyway," Rupe continues, lifting his beer glass to his lips as he looks at his watch, "It's time I wasn't here. I'm expected elsewhere in thirty minutes."

He stands up and pulls his green jacket over his shoulders.

"Just stick to the story mate. It makes our case stronger—shows we haven't colluded to try and change the facts over the years. It will be your turn soon when they catch up with you."

Rupe throws me a smile and I nod.

I stay in the beer garden alone with my thoughts for a while then, about fifteen minutes after Rupe has left, I see two smartly dressed chaps heading over towards me.

"Mr. Sanderson." One of them addresses me and holds up a card. "We'd like a word if you don't mind."

An hour later I find myself sitting in the small interview room going over it all again: same place, same story, just different people. An officer with a jacket on back of his chair and rolled-up shirt sleeves sits opposite me. His hair's smoothed back, slightly greying at the edges. He asks me where I was that night, who I was with, and what time I left my house. I realise this is not going to be easy.

Come on, think. What time did I tell them twenty years ago? Was it right? I can't remember.

The other person in the room is much younger. His eyes constantly dart from me to the other officer whenever there is an exchange of dialogue between us. I try and sound convincing, but I dry up when he asks me about her.

He knows all about it then.

While I answer his questions, he rolls a pencil between the fingertips of both hands, then he stops, and automatically I hesitate.

With his elbows firmly rested on the desk pad in front of him (on which I notice he never writes a thing), he asks me again:

"You were with DCI Benteen that night, we know that, but what I want to know, Mr. Sanderson, is what time did you leave your house that evening to go and meet up with her, Rupert Rodgers and Karl Holdsworth?"

The other copper is getting on my nerves with his darting eyes... he might as well be watching a tennis match! I reply.

"It was about... 7.00p.m.... I think, maybe 7.15p.m."

I wonder how Rupe is doing? He's here somewhere.

"For the purpose of the recording, Mr. Sanderson is nodding his head." The darting-eyed officer delivers this remark in tones that I am beginning to find annoyingly youthful.

"No, I'm *not*," I protest. He throws me a vacant frown.

I cover up by changing the subject and asking why DCI Benteen has been taken off the case. The first officer releases what little pressure his fingertips had on his pencil and it falls to his desk. His bottom lip drops slightly, and his steel-grey eyes pierce mine.

"I should have thought that was obvious... even to you Mr. Sanderson. There's been a death and DCI Benteen has admitted to being near the scene at the time. It's not appropriate for her to continue in charge, but that's not really your business, Mr. Sanderson. She has already given us her statement, so now can we get on with yours?" So, I tell them we knew Karl was going to the shack that night and that we had arranged a rendezvous, but he must have got there early. I explained how we could see the fire as we approached from the south side of the field and that it was already out of control by the time we got to the edge of the woods. Rupe and I went off to look for Karl in the hope he was nearby and on his way, Sally-Anne had already left us to go and talk to the emergency services that were there before we arrived.

Surely this is about right? It's what we said all those years ago.

When I finish speaking the DCI says nothing. Slowly, he brings his palms together in the praying position then rests his bottom lip upon them.

"You haven't mentioned the body," he says.

Shit. Has she gone and brought that into it too?

I place my elbows on the desk and clasp my hands and immediately I feel the dampness between my knuckles, and I find I can't keep my fingers still.

"Body?" I say.

"Yes, the body you took us to... last night Mr. Sanderson... remember?"

"Oh... yes... *that* body," I stutter back a reply.

"Well, yes Mr. Sanderson, *that* body indeed. Whatever

body could you possibly think I meant?"

"I... I didn't think we were talking about last night," I reply.

He pauses, and I know I'm about to learn something new.

"There is something we think you might be interested to know, just in case it helps to jog your memory at all."

"Oh?" I reply.

"The body that we exhumed yesterday evening—the one you were able to show DCI Benteen where to find—it was an interesting discovery."

The Detective Chief Inspector rises from the table and starts to stride around the small room.

"Oh... really?" I hear my own voice wobble as I struggle to reply at all.

"Oh yes. You see, it was quite small, far too small to be the burnt-out corpse of a man."

He has completed a circuit of the room and is now looming over me with his face uncomfortably close to mine. I can't respond.

"No, you see, it turns out it was the body of a young woman... and we thought you might like to take a little time to think about that."

A short time later I'm sitting across the room from Rupe. I watch his eyes. You can always tell what someone is really thinking from the look in their eyes. He sits back and folds his arms, thinking about what I've just said to him. We've both had a little time to think things over since we were told that the recovered remains weren't Karl's. I, for one, have not wasted that time. Something I've learned over the years—if you want to get close to understanding why someone might react in a certain way, then you must put yourself in that other person's shoes. Sally-Anne was our friend. The other night it had seemed very much not to be the case, but what must it have been like for her? She trained to become a police officer and clearly has risen through the ranks. There are lots of details we don't know… hell, we haven't been in touch for twenty years, but in spite of that I figure there are really only two possibilities that should matter to us now: that Sally-Anne knows more than we do and is trying to pin everything on us to get herself cleared. Or that she was as surprised as we were the find out that the body exhumed the other night was *not* that of Karl Holdsworth—in which case, like us, she is going to be shocked and stressed out trying to work all this out. I think the latter is far more likely… so this is what I have just put to Rupe.

His arms unfold and move to a semi-relaxed position behind his head.

"Okay, I'm with you on this," he says.

I immediately feel a stone lighter. We're all in this together, we always have been.

"So, what do we do now?" Rupe asks.

"I reply to the text," I tell him. It wasn't the same number that she contacted me on the other day but that's understandable, she has to be careful now. Sally-Anne has asked if we can meet and go over a few things. She said she knows it looks bad but there are some important developments and there was a reason she behaved the way she did when we were discovered the other night.

We agree to meet back there tonight at 9.00p.m. It has to be the same place, there's more work to do if we are ever going to be free of this nightmare. Even though she is officially off the case, we must talk. For once I find myself taking control.

The day has been dull and the light is fading by the time we find ourselves trudging along the path by the same uncut cornfield. Now it is I who leads the way as Rupe hangs behind making very little conversation. I sense his anxiety, so I tell him that this time we will be the ones asking the questions. There's got to be a reason for all this; she must know something.

"Yeah, but what if she doesn't? How are we going to make

the situation any better? The plain facts are we buried our friend's body on the night of the fire, we didn't tell anyone and now, years later another corpse turns up. We're deep in it for covering up, and she's in even deeper trouble for covering up *and* being a cop."

My friend has a point, but I tell him we have to trust her and we need to find out what she knows.

We walk on getting ever closer to the now all-too-familiar spot. No need for secrecy tonight, it's unlikely we'll meet a soul.

I see her first: a solitary figure sitting on an upturned barrel a few yards to the left of the old Shack site. She looks very different tonight. Her legs are outstretched and crossed in front of her and her hair is free and untied. She wears a leather jacket and jeans in contrast to the image of the official figure she portrayed the other night. She greets us but doesn't get up. I return the compliment immediately, Rupe then follows. Her lips turn upwards slightly as her eyes dart first to mine, then to Rupe's, then back to mine. She unfolds her arms after a few seconds of silence.

"Well I guess I'll start then," she says.

I nod. Rupe just gives her a hard look but says nothing. *What does he see?*

Sally-Anne does not at all seem fazed by Rupe's harsh reaction. She looks keen to reveal information she says might help all of us, including herself. As she starts to talk I look into her eyes and see something: they are pleading. They are the eyes of someone who doesn't know the answers but craves to find out—a real detective. I sit down on the grass beside her, Rupe does the same.

"You're taking a hell of a risk coming here and talking to us tonight. We've been interviewed by someone else now, as well you know." She shrugs but says nothing, words aren't needed.

"So, what's this new information then?" I ask.

"Well firstly, you guys know I've been taken off the case?"

She pauses, looking at both of us in turn as if half-expecting an answer before continuing.

I don't think she knew that we know that—she seemed genuinely relieved when we didn't react.

"Well, there is something I need to tell you; I'm not doing this just to clear my name. What I've found out might help us all."

"Yeah?" This time Rupe decides to interrupt her. "I'd like to know why you were so keen to get us to do your dirty work the other night."

"Hold on Rupe, there is a reason for the other night, but there's something else you should both know first. This goes back a bit, so bear with me, guys.

"I always wanted it—to be a copper. Back in the day I never left a stone unturned if I thought there was something to be found on the other side. You guys know that. Well, that never changed, and as soon as I qualified and took up my first post I found myself lifting those stones—asking questions at every opportunity.

"What did change was my job. I got a transfer to this dump, and to be fair, I've done alright for myself... until now. A few weeks ago, I got a call from an old colleague at Blanthian Cross—that was where I was based originally. He told me that the Murphy case was coming our way, all because of one piece of mis-written information in a police report that changed everything. It meant that we would need to reopen investigations here, and from the minute I heard this I knew it would uncover the events of that night."

"The Murphy case?" Rupe asked.

"Sixteen year-old Amy Murphy disappeared—just didn't come home one night. Blanthian Cross had the case, I was never involved; it was long before my time. But I did hear it get talked about and I got interested. Remember... unturned stones fascinate me. Well, a few weeks ago, new evidence came to light that placed the case firmly with us. It left me with little choice but to follow every lead I got... but there was a problem."

I look at Rupe and see he is as gripped as I am. Sally-

Anne's hands rest upon her knees, but she's agitated by the prospect of what she is about to tell us and she can't remain still. I encourage her to continue.

"Well, it was the date she had last been seen. It was written in the witness statement as 08/11/98. When this was picked up much later as being as contradictory to other timings in the report, checks with the parents confirmed that the date should have been 11/08/98. It had been written down incorrectly by the police officer over from the States who forgot he was in the United Kingdom and couldn't break the habit of writing the date in different format."

I let out a gasp, the kind that grows from the pit of the stomach, when I hear that date mentioned.

"Surely you can now see why that placed the case firmly on our patch and why it has put me as well as yourselves in a difficult position."

None of us speak. Sally-Anne takes a deep breath and I sense she feels better for having told us this. The date bears obvious significance for all of us, but I don't see how this makes the problem we already have any greater.

"Okay, but so what? A girl hadn't been seen since that day in August that year. We were miles away, well... here, to be precise. It's coincidence it just happens to be the same day," Rupe says.

Sally-Anne stands up, places her hands against the back of her head with her knuckles interlocked, crushing every strand of her golden-brown hair. She walks in circles around the oil barrel she'd been sitting on. We wait for her answer.

"Don't you see? Think guys. What else happened that night *before* the fire?"

There have been a few times in my life when I remember a particularly huge moment because of something iconic that took place as a back drop. I remember my nan used to tell me about the day President Kennedy was assassinated; she says she was knitting when she flicked the TV on and saw it. Every adult remembers what they were doing at the moment when they first heard that news because it was such a big deal. This moment becomes one of those 'big deal' moments for me right now; I shall never forget being here, back at the place with the same people when Sally-Anne Benteen told us the date Amy Murphy was last seen... on the night of the fire.

"Work it out... Karl went on about inviting a girl he'd been seeing into our circle that night. Don't you recall? She must have been around... because the body the officers dug up the other night was hers."

For me this is the moment it becomes suddenly clear. This is the point when I think I know what has happened to us and I become reconciled with the path this is going to lead me down. But Rupe and Sally-Anne aren't quite there.

Rupe challenges Sally-Anne:

"It's easy for you to use that case as your reason to reinvestigate our one, but why did you put us through it the other night when you know what really happened. We could split on you and drop you right in it, Sally."

The look in Sally-Anne's eyes doesn't change as she tries to answer him honestly.

"I didn't know what to do, Rupe. I was put on the case and I knew there was a body somewhere there. I thought if we retrieved Karl's body, then the case of his disappearance would be reopened, and we could go from there with a chance of explaining our way out of it plausibly. It was complicated with you two being there; I had to think quickly and put you to the task. If I had implicated myself, then the case would have been dropped. We all did wrong by covering it up. I've had nightmares for twenty years over this, but I promise you, I didn't know it was going to be the girl's body we would find."

"And when it was, all of a sudden everything we'd said all those years ago now looks very suspicious." Rupe's gaze was suddenly deep and distant. He doesn't look directly at either off us, but I think he's starting to get the picture now.

"Exactly. So, I get called in and put on leave the next day

while an enquiry into my conduct takes place."

We pause for a moment. Sally-Anne looks eagerly at both of us as if waiting for us to ask her what the next step is. She has that look of being in control again. Clearly, she feels she has explained and we can move on from here.

I get up and stretch my legs. The light is fading now. I take a moment to study our surroundings: the trees sway gently, their tops blurring with the low cloud line, and the expanse of empty field in front of us provides an eerie backdrop to my thoughts. I try and piece it all together in my mind...

So, the body found the other day was that of Amy Murphy, but what about our acquaintance Karl Holdsworth—presumed dead after the night of the fire?

I am about to ask, when Rupe confronts her with something else we both missed.

"Hold it guys." He gestures for me to sit down again, before addressing our friend.

"You just said something that doesn't add up."

Sally-Anne's eyes widen and her hands plunge into her jacket pockets; but somehow, to me this body language says *interested* rather than defensive. Rupe continues.

"Why did you say *it was complicated with us around...* and you had to *think quick and put us to the task?*"

For the first time tonight he raises his voice. Sally-Anne has the face of a frightened rabbit caught in the headlights. My brain crashes—out of working memory. There are too many programs open and right now it can't deal with all the queries they are trying to process.

"You bloody asked us to be there, it was the only reason we met up. You put us through all this shit and now you want us to help you get out of it. Don't trust her, Chris: we're just going to get in deeper trouble every minute we spend talking to her."

"No, Rupe. Listen." Sally-Anne stands up.

"No, *you* listen, Miss DCI Benteen. If it hadn't been for you, we might never have been in this mess."

"Hey mate, that's not fair. Let's cool it." I try and intervene. I've never seen Rupe so angry; back in the old days he was always so relaxed and laid back, but he does have a point. I try and rationalise while playing peacemaker at the same time.

"What do you mean? When it comes down to it you started the frigging fire that night!" Sally-Anne retaliates furiously.

"You brought the blasted brandy in the first place... remember... the stuff that *burns*!"

"Guys... enough. We have all played our part in this farce." I raise my voice. They stop, and I say to let Sally-Anne speak.

Slightly short of breath, Sally-Anne gathers herself and turns to both of us.

"I didn't *ask* you to be there. I was *told* to go there. When I saw it was you two I had to think quick. Remember... I am a police officer."

Now Rupe and I look at each other in astonishment: surely she isn't going to try and lie her way out of this one?

"But Sally, the texts?" I say.

"Yeah? The texts. What about them?"

"Come on Sally, we can show you our phones right now. You set us both up... turn up yourself on the night at the same time and place, and now, at the eleventh hour, you try and make out you don't know anything about it!"

"I didn't say I don't know anything about any texts, I got one too. But I'm telling you now, the only one I sent was to you Chris... about tonight. I never contacted either of you guys before then. It was a total shock to see you there that evening, crouching in that very same spot where our corn circle had been all those years ago."

None of us say anything. We look out towards the site of the circle just seventy meters or so from where we now sit. Everywhere is quiet, just the distant rumble of traffic on the main road three-quarters of a mile away breaks the silence. The light has nearly gone now, a few birds deliver distant tweets as they head off to roost. I hear something crackling in the shrubbery way over to our left, but then Sally-Anne speaks and my attention turns back to her.

"There's something else," she says. Unzipping her jacket, she gets out a notebook containing something inside. As she unfolds it I can see it's a printout of a news item.

"I printed this from the Blanthian news website a couple of weeks ago," she continued.

The item was titled, *Is this the man who cheated death?'*

As Rupe and I look we see that the picture is of Karl—not very clear, his head is down and he is accompanied by two other men, but it is definitely him. I read the first few words of the article:

'Officers from Blanthian Cross Police are looking into the possibility that this man, known to his friends as Alan Canning is really Karl Holdsworth, the teenager that went missing in an extraordinary woodland fire across the other side of the county twenty years ago...'

Rupe throws me a vacant look. I don't know what to say. Sally-Anne fills in the blanks:

"He survived and decided at 18 to start a new life—new name, everything. Ironic really, when it was going to be us that were going to try and start again. His parents were as certain he was dead as the rest of us, there were no further investigations. The thing is, he's spent much of the last twenty years in prison... for murder! Apparently, he set a car on fire with someone inside. He was released from prison just two weeks ago. It was all over the local news and someone must have recognised him."

"My God, so he lives on after we left him for dead. What about his body and the girl's being found in its place?"

Rupe's state of shock has prevented him from working it out clearly.

"We didn't ever bury Karl," I tell him. Sally-Anne nods in agreement. "We must have buried that poor kid. It was pitch black when we got back there remember? We just found a body somewhere nearby and assumed it was Karl's!"

I can't take it in, Rupe can't either: this is crazy. What do we do now? Sally-Anne starts pacing up and down, already searching her brain for an answer to the question I haven't actually asked of her yet.

"Why would Karl ever do that... set a car on fire to do someone over?" asks Rupe.

Sally-Anne stops dead in her tracks and faces him; she has an answer for that one.

"The victim wasn't known to him... but it was his name that was significant—*Rupert Rollings*. He got the wrong person!"

Before Rupe can answer, we are all distracted. I see it first.

"Look," says Sally-Anne, pointing out into the field. We all see a light darting in the sky, not very high but quite deliberate.

"Somebody's out there." Rupe whispers. "What do we do now?"

"We go and take a look," Sally-Anne says. "We do this together."

This is how it started, and this is how it will end. We follow the light that shines for us and discover something that seems so exciting and so perfect, but it leads us to a place of darkness.

So, we creep through the wispy swathes out into the field, and into the darkness. The air is colder now but it carries the smell of corn—so nearly ripe. It takes me right back.

"Listen, over to our left. I thought I saw someone." Rupe's eyes dart around, straining in the dark. I look too, but we see no one.

But there is another smell.

"Can you smell something?" Sally-Anne asks.

"It's like... alcohol..."
"No, not alcohol," I say. "Look!"

I thought I could smell brandy... but that was just a trick of the mind—a memory. This time it's a different smell— much stronger.

We see a figure standing not twenty yards from our circle, and between it and us begins a light... at first just a bright flicker... then a furious fire erupts. Sally-Anne calls out... Rupe runs to the far edge of the circle, where the smell is coming from. I call him back.

"Paraffin!" he shrieks.

"Don't go to the edge," I tell him. "Stay close, we have to stay together."

We look back and see the retreating figure silhouetted by the firelight. It calls out to us.

"Twenty years ago you left me for dead; but instead, she died. Now you all pay the price."

The three of us huddle together, Sally-Anne screams as the flames lick the edge of the circle, and in seconds... all around us is burning.

From this there is to be no escape.

THE END

ABOUT THE AUTHOR

Tom Goymour was born and raised in Cambridgeshire, UK. and has lived in Peterborough for over forty years. He writes mainly in the mystery and suspense genre about what he sees, thinks, and instinctively feels.

Being part of a large family has given him many powerful experiences from which to draw inspiration. He is an exponent of art and design and a composer of piano music, but tries hard not to inflict any of this on others!

Empowered by his many, and sometimes strange experiences, he has found writing to be his voice-piece. He is a meticulous studier of life, and his stories nearly always contain a twist or a strong moral message that hits home hard... designed to make the reader think.

He is the author of the Ghost mystery series *The Spirit of Peterborough* and the dark short story series *Second Chance*. Those books await you over at:
www.tomgoymour.com
where you can start building your library for free.

Reprogrammed
by Peter Ellis

Elena's eyes shot open. There was a mild burning in the back of her mind. She shook her head and rubbed her eyes and it seemed to subside. Elena didn't know where she was. Why was she stood up? Lights bearing down from above made it harder for her to focus. The hazy shapes around her became more refined the more aware she became. They were people too. They were still and silent, and Elena started to realise they were all very, very naked. She looked down at herself and saw with horror that she was too. She felt incredibly exposed, covering herself in vain with her hands and arms. The people around her didn't seem to care, come to think of it, didn't seem to acknowledge her commotion at all.

Rows and rows of people sprawled out either side of her, stretching out far beyond and behind her too. All of these people and not a single one was moving, except for Elena. They all stood equal distances apart, hands down by their sides, all facing in the same direction. She wandered through the lines-upon-lines of men and women, cautiously admiring the variety of them around her. The majority of them seemed to be of a similar physique, but all colours and creeds seemed to be present.

Elena noticed a small, rectangular blue light on the side of a darker-skinned man's head. It didn't flash, it didn't flicker. She got up close to it, almost hypnotized by its glow. She put a finger on it: the light was hot, like it'd been on for a while. It looked like it was connected to a small piece of wiring beneath his skin. The wires concentrated by his temple and then seemed to streak around to the back of his head, and then down his spine.

Elena looked across at another man adjacent to them: he had a light in the exact same place too. The wiring followed the same pattern. This man had several faded scars over his arms and down his back. The woman in front of him was the same. They all had lights on their head. She realised that everyone had scars in *exactly* the same places, just with different levels of visibility. Elena looked down at her own arms: they too were scarred in the same manner. Hers appeared fresher, but there weren't any stitches. She ran her hands hastily over her back; she could feel the scars there too, plus whatever was running under them. Her eyes lost focus, she didn't look at anything else as she slowly glided her fingers up to her left temple. She could feel where the light was. Except it wasn't *on* like the others: it had cooled. Why wasn't it on? Was that why she could move? Did that little light have complete control over every single person in this room?

She looked up at the ceiling and noticed that it was

mirrored. All of the walls were too. Without moving it was hard to tell where the walls *actually* were, so Elena cautiously turned right and walked in a straight line through rows upon rows of silent, naked people until she could see her own reflection. She held out her hand in front of her to touch the mirror, unsure of the young Latina who was looking back at her. It was her, but the scars and the contraption by her temple were all she could see. As she had suspected: the light was off. Elena tried to force a smile at her reflection. She didn't look bad except for the scars.

Clothes. I need clothes, she thought to herself. But she needed a way out first.

Elena followed the mirrored wall: surely soon she'd meet a corner? Or maybe a door?

An alarm sounded. The sudden noise shocked her as it pierced through the air. Security lights flashed aggressively. Elena held her hands to her ears in a failed attempt to quieten it, her face screwed up at the extreme sound. Somewhere in the vast room a door opened, crashing open and hitting the wall.

"Spread out," roared an angry voice over the alarm. "We need to find her before she gets out."

The alarm died but the lights continued flashing. Elsewhere, heavy footsteps thudded against the ground. Elena stood up and perfectly still for a few seconds to try and see if she could spot who else was now in the room. Security guards. A couple of them towered over the crowds of silent, naked people. They wore armour which seemed to be made of onyx and helmets with tinted visors. Each set of muscular arms carried an assault rifle.

Elena kept her footsteps light, moving slowly and surely. The guards had spread themselves out across the room, allowing her to make assured steps towards the opening in the wall they had entered through. She passed more silent, naked people, the lights in their heads shining hypnotically. She used them as natural cover, getting up close to each of them to hide her body as best as possible. None of the people had a smell: no bad body odour, no fresh-out-the-shower fragrance. They smelt of *nothing*. Even with the matching scars over each body, each person was impeccably clean. The room was, too, from what Elena could tell. The flooring was perfectly smooth and unstained: it actually felt quite fine to walk on barefoot.

A smaller guard appeared from between the rows of people. Elena swerved out of eyesight and hid behind a woman close to her. She prayed to her god that they wouldn't look her way. The woman's hair didn't match hers: it was platinum blonde, Elena's hair was pure black and tied in a ponytail. She unwillingly learned that the woman's hair, on her head at least, was dyed. The burning in the back of her mind flashed back, threatening to make her cry out in pain. Elena steeled herself, pushing back against the fires in her mind. The burning died away just as quickly as it had flared up. Daring to peer around the silent, naked woman, Elena got a glimpse of the small guard walking away from her.

She could see the door now. A few more steps and she was there.

She looked back at the room, at the rows-upon-rows of silent, naked people with blue lights on their temple. The guards were all over by the other side: far, far away from her. Double-checking that they weren't heading back any time soon, Elena grabbed a hold of the large, square door. It should have felt heavy but, to Elena's surprise, it was rather light. The edges were rounded off and it must've been six-or-so inches thick. Looking back one more time, she started to heave the door shut behind her.

It let out a loud, metallic groan. Everything stopped. A moment of silence fell on the room again. She could make out the heads of the guards turning to her general direction.

"Vessel escaping!"

Elena pulled with all the strength she had. The door whined and creaked some more as it began its 180-degree turn to shut. It wasn't heavy, but it didn't seem to move particularly quickly. She could hear the guards bearing down on her but she knew she simply couldn't stop. She looked up to see one of the larger guards running straight at her raising his gun and firing two shots. Elena ducked behind the door as the bullets pinged off its mirrored surface. Grabbing hold of the bulky circular wheel that locked the door in place, Elena pulled and pulled and pulled. The footsteps were closer now. Just a little more. The door clicked into place. She couldn't afford to hesitate, she could hear hands clamouring on the other side of the door. She leapt up and twisted the lock. Machinery moved around within the door. With a heavy mechanical clunk, the door was locked.

The hallway ahead of Elena was also impeccably clean. Gone were the mirrors all over the walls, replaced with a pearlescent white paint, spotless and glimmering as if it were brand new. Unlike the warehouse-like room she had woken up in, Elena could see windows and doors equally spaced apart down the hall. She walked timidly forward, away from the heavy hands banging against the warehouse door. Each room she passed was filled with computers, desks and machinery: but no people. No one who could help her figure out where she was and why she was there. She tried each door but none of them opened, so she carried on. The rooms didn't look lived in. Everything was too neat, too tidy, too organised to look like any real person had ever actually worked there.

The double doors at the other end of the hallway were in sight. They were illuminated by a light off to the side of them. Lights. Life. Elena set off quickly down the hall to the source of the light, hoping she'd find somebody who wasn't going to point a gun at her. She peeked into the window. No one home, but the computer inside was on. Mercifully, somehow looking neat even hung up, there was a lab coat on a rack. The door was left ajar, so if anyone had been there, they hadn't been gone long. She slipped into the room and clicked the door shut behind her. The lab coat felt uncomfortable and rough against her bare skin as she wrapped it around her body and buttoned it up, but Elena had no other options.

The computer was only on the home screen so Elena grabbed the mouse to see if she could find anything that could indicate where she was. The computer's home screen bore only the logo of a company named 'Epsilon', with the ancient Greek Sigma replacing the 'E' and the Omega symbol replacing the 'O', for some reason. At least she could put a name to where she was.

"Surprised this isn't locked," she mumbled to herself.

Maybe whoever worked in that particular room wasn't as obsessively neat as everyone else there. Elena had no concept of the time that had passed since she had awoken. The computer told her it was quarter-past four in the afternoon. The date confused her, though. How is it the seventeenth of September 2020? The year was right, but... what was the last thing Elena remembered? What day? What month? Nothing came to mind.

She shrugged it off as she noticed that the person who'd been using the computer previously had been observing some camera footage. There were multiple angles of the warehouse she'd woken up in. Looking down on the room from the camera gave her a better idea of just how large it was. She guessed there were several thousand people in there. All silent, all naked.

Elena closed the camera feed and instantly forgot about it. She was hovering over another folder, one titled "VESSELS". Something about it jumped out to her, besides it being all capitals. Inside it was nothing less than a legion of documents. Each one titled with 'Ve' followed by a number. Again, all in order. She opened up a random one and found a file on a young Asian man. No name was listed, but his height and weight were, as well as his designation number: "Vessel #5309". Elena noticed there was a comment at the bottom of his profile that said, "Updated, ready for distribution."

She scrolled back through thousands of nameless people. Elena thought that they could possibly be some of those who stood idly in the warehouse with her. Faces blurred by, some she recognized from the warehouse, until she scrolled back to the beginning of the folder: the file for "Vessel #0001".

Elena was looking at herself.

Shock overcame her. Questions flooded her mind. What was a Vessel? What did that make her? Elena scrolled to the bottom of her file: "Failed." An arrow appeared next to the text. Feeling compelled to see what else the document could tell her, Elena clicked on it. A number of "catastrophic errors" appeared. Each with subsequent "Updates" and further failures. Just what was going on with her body? It had to be to do with the light and the scars.

"Um, can I help you?"

Elena spun around to see a young man, probably in his early twenties. He appeared to be as shocked to see her as she was to see him. Pinned to his lapel was name badge with the name: Marc. He had dark, defined eyebrows, pasty white skin and dirty blonde hair. His hair didn't shine like hers, but it was rather curly; he had a bit of a rock star look to him. He looked like somebody's assistant, likely an intern. Maybe he could still help.

He looked her temple, at where the light should be. "Oh, you're one of them. I didn't realize we were letting anyone test the prototypes."

"Is this your computer?" she asked bluntly, adjusting the coat so she was completely covered and retained some dignity.

Marc nodded rapidly as he struggled to get words out, still amazed by her presence. His gaze annoyed her.

"You can keep staring or you can use words, I know what I'd prefer," she said.

Marc cautiously swept his hair back and gulped too loudly. "Sorry. It's just I've not seen a Vessel actually working before. Who is it that's operating this unit again?"

"There must be some mistake: I am not a Vessel."

Marc walked up to the computer and noticed that Elena had looked up her own file.

"Very funny," he said. "This is that unit that keeps going wrong."

Marc handed her his tablet as he sat back down at his desk. He hadn't spoken to her like she was a regular person; Elena didn't like that. Marc looked like he hadn't expected her to read the potential information now in Elena's hands. She poured through file after file on the tablet, going through folders she probably wasn't allowed to look at. She found one titled "Vessel Announcement Speech, KW". She tapped on it and the file leapt onto the screen. It read:

'In the past twenty to thirty years, we've made huge progress in technology. Our children's video games now look as good as the world outside our windows, our home appliances are all connected and interact, we can have almost seamless conversations with our mobile phones too.

'Virtual reality is something we are big fans of at Epsilon. But we wanted to take it a step further. What if the reality we played in wasn't *virtual? Our recent advancements in our robotics division led us to the creation of what we call Vessels. These synthetic bodies allow users to connect with them wirelessly and, using our state-of-the-art headset and docking station, control them as if they were the bodies we were born with. Once you've completed the set-up of your Vessel, you won't be able to tell the difference between looking at the world through its eyes or yours—'*

Marc snatched the tablet back, giving her a puzzled look. Elena stood still for a moment, allowing the information to digest. Could what the file had said really be true? Was she a Vessel? Elena knew her body: this was still it. It had to be.

"Those files are wrong. I'm not one of those... things," she said nervously.

"Again, whoever you are controlling this unit," Marc said, appearing to ignore her. "I'm going to need you to stand perfectly still while I desync you and upload some new patches."

"What if I refuse?" Elena asked, as if for a moment she wasn't herself.

"Look, I'm already behind schedule. My boss will literally kill me if I don't get this Vessel sorted out."

Elena hadn't planned on standing still, but she found herself not doing anything else. Marc had fished an odd-looking headset from somewhere and put it on. Why hadn't Elena seen that before? He hadn't opened any drawers or cupboards, so it must have just been lying around.

Marc activated the headset and Elena felt the light at her temple switch on. An eternal moment of nothingness passed and, on the other side of it, Elena was met with the burning sensation again. This time, the pain was unbearable. She screamed as the fire spread through her mind with ferocity. The flames felt like hands, pushing Elena out of her own body. She couldn't move her arms or legs, but she thrashed her head about as the fires burned.

Marc cursed in bemusement. "I thought I desynced you?"

Elena was equally puzzled; those words had come from her mouth too.

"Ah, there we go, that's more like it," they both said in unison again. Elena fought against the flames in her mind, trying to force it back. The light flickered off. She regained some control over herself again. The right side of her body refused to obey her. Marc whipped the headset off and stared at her in disbelief.

"What is going wrong with you? That patch should've sorted things out."

He got up and looked right into her eyes and over the scarring on her skin. Elena grabbed him by the neck.

"I. Am. Not. A. Vessel."

Marc tugged at her ironclad grip, desperate for air.

"I am Elena Avery. I am not some synthetic machine. I am a human being, and you've turned me into a freak."

She let go of Marc's throat, and he gulped in the air as

though he'd never breathed before. Elena didn't realise she'd grabbed him so tightly or lifted him off the ground. She had to prove it to him somehow. She spotted a letter opener on his desk. She had to use the left side of her body to drag the immobile right side along. She picked up the opener and after a brief hesitation, went to cut into her right hand. Marc leapt forward to stop her: he couldn't risk damaging the Vessel.

"Impossible," exclaimed Marc as he'd regained some composure and air in his lungs.

"*Please, help me,*" she begged. She wanted to cry, but tears refused to form or fall.

Marc didn't know what to believe. Could this Vessel, or whatever it was before him, really believe it was human? It walked and talked independently like one. It looked like it was in pain, it wanted to be real, to exist. What if this was some elaborate prank from one of the other programmers or technicians? He just had to act like he was doing his job.

Marc went back to his computer with the Vessel still in distress. He opened up the security footage of the main warehouse and wound it back. He watched as the Vessel, or Elena as it claimed to be called, appeared to wake from a rest mode. If it was someone controlling the unit, then they were being very elaborate for a prank. He watched as the Vessel hid from the security guards that investigated the alarm he'd heard earlier. Surely, they'd have owned up then? Surely, they wouldn't have snuck out of the warehouse; they wouldn't risk damaging millions of pounds worth of company products?

"I need to get security," he said. "If you're who you say you are, then you need to be given a proper examination."

"No, please don't call them," Elena begged quietly. "They tried to hurt me."

"Yes, but you've also locked them in an air-tight room for over half an hour."

Elena tried to remain insistent that he didn't alert them, but Marc was clearly frightened. In time, they finally agreed he'd help her get out, but they had to figure out if she was the only human in their production line. Perhaps he could remove the machinery from her and see if anyone else had suffered the same fate.

Marc led Elena through the various clean corridors of the complex to a changing room. His spare lab coat covered her but she needed to be properly clothed if they were going to try and blend her in as they snuck around. They were relieved that the other employees they came across were busy looking at their paperwork or talking to their peers.

"Try some of the clothes in the lost property room," he suggested. "I'm sure there will be something that'll fit you."

She nodded in agreement and Marc kept watch by the door. Even the lost property room was clean: that was impressive. She came across rows of coat hooks filled with all manner of clothing. Men's, women's, even some children's clothing was hung neatly, organised by those same gendered, aged labels. Everything looked freshly pressed, like none of it had actually been worn before. She found a plain white blouse: no frills or fancy buttons, modest on her frame. Elena felt like the white would fit in well; she didn't want to wear anything that would draw too much attention. There weren't any bras that would fit her, though. She was disappointed but kept looking around for more clothes.

In time she happened across some plain underwear and thick, comfy socks. Then a pair of denim jeans caught her eye. Elena examined them: they were slightly faded and the left knee was ripped. *The left knee was ripped.* Elena grabbed them off the hook by the waist and checked the label on the inside. Sure enough: her initials 'EA' were there in smudged red marker. How had they ended up there? How had she ripped the knee again? She was certain they weren't bought like that: ripped jeans weren't her thing.

She found a cubicle, slipped them on and instantly felt more comfortable. A feeling of familiarity washed over her, something that she knew was *hers*.

The burning returned and the comfort evaporated. It was intense. Elena grabbed at her skull in a desperate attempt to control the searing pain. A cry escaped her mouth. Footsteps followed. They stopped outside the door of her cubicle.

"Everything okay in there?" It was Marc.

"Are you... trying to control me again?" growled Elena in between pulsations of fire through her mind.

"No?" he responded. "I've been keeping watch outside."

"Agh. Well, somebody is."

The pain was horrific as the light on her temple flickered again. It blinked temporarily, then stopped. Elena couldn't move her body. Somebody had connected to her.

"Hello, Elena," the words came from Elena's mouth, but it wasn't her doing the talking. She felt her body carry her to the mirror, unwillingly looking herself up and down. Her hands ran over her body; she desperately tried to stop herself, but her body was out of her control. The burning continued, she could feel it all over now. The light flickered, but Elena couldn't move her body, only her face.

"Who are you?" she asked.

The light turned back on and Elena lost control of herself again. She watched as she smiled at her own reflection and her lips began to move. "I'm someone who's wondering why one of my prized Vessels is running around without anybody controlling it."

"But... but you know I'm not a real Vessel," said Elena to her reflection, "I'm a real person."

She flinched, and the light flickered. "Do I? That's quite the assumption. If that's the case, then no one else in this building knows that."

Marc opened the cubicle door. Elena's eyes met his in the reflection of the mirror with an accusing hostility. The light went on again. She spun to face him. She looked him up and down seductively and placed her hands on his chest. Marc noticed the light on her head and backed away cautiously.

It flickered back off again and she jumped away from him. "I'm so sorry. That wasn't me."

"That's okay. What's happening?" he asked, looking increasingly worried.

The light returned, and Elena felt herself lose control of her body once more. It was frozen in place for a moment until the other voice took over. It made her move on Marc again; he kept backing off until he bumped up against the wall.

"I'm just taking this Vessel for a test drive," the other voice said through Elena's mouth. "It is just delightful, such a thrill!"

Elena could only watch as her hand stroked Marc's cheek. Whoever was controlling her body was enjoying herself. She danced about the room, she tried singing. Neither to a high standard, but this other person didn't care. Marc remained up against the wall the entire time.

"Well, that was a rush! See you soon, sweetheart."

Then, for some reason, they let Elena go. She could feel her arms and legs and body again. She looked at Marc, and without a word slowly walked up to him. He realised it was Elena again and relaxed. She buried her head in his chest and hugged him tightly.

"Help me, please," she whimpered.

"Our best chance is getting you to a lab," he said, "But I don't know how we're gonna try and fix what has been done to you."

Nodding in agreement, Elena followed him towards the door. But, before they could leave, an announcement blared from every speaker in hearing distance.

"Good evening, people of Epsilon!"

The voice was female, a playful middle-class English accent. "Now I hope you're all having a productive day. This weekend we're going to be going live with our new Vessel program!"

There were rounds of applause and cheers from the other rooms around them, but Elena and Marc remained silent.

"It's come to my attention," the woman continued, "that somebody has taken control of one of our precious Vessels and is parading around the facility right now! Crazy, I know. I'm sure you all know what to do: I need every available employee to help me find this Vessel and bring it to me. Do *not* destroy it. That'll be all!"

Herds of footsteps could be heard all around, like the whole world had got up in unison to find Elena. They backed away from the door and towards the cubicles.

"What're we going to do?" Elena asked.

Marc paused for a moment; he'd realised something which had been staring him in the face all the time. He scrambled in a deep pocket for his tablet and opened up the program to analyse Elena.

"I need you to run on the spot quickly," he requested.

"How is that going to help?" she shot a dirty, confused look at him.

"Can you just do it, please?"

Putting what little trust she had left in him, Elena began to jog on the spot. Nothing changed on his tablet.

"Quicker."

Elena broke into short sprints on the spot. The screen on his tablet faltered, but it intermittently would allow him to connect with her.

"Try running up and down this row."

Elena wasn't sure what she was doing, but she did it anyway. She ran up and down the aisle several times. Marc looked back at his tablet: he couldn't connect to her anymore.

"Okay, slow down, but don't stop."

"Why am I doing this?" she asked finally.

Marc handed her the tablet as she passed him again. She looked at the screen.

"I can't connect to you now," he said as she passed him once more. "You're moving too much."

"So if you can't, does that mean no one else can?"

"Hopefully. But you can't stop moving until you get to

the lab."

"No pressure, then."

Elena handed the tablet back to Marc. He downloaded a file from the company's cloud server, pushed a button, and all of a sudden Elena was seeing things: holograms overlaying what her eyes could see.

"What the hell is this?" she asked, trying to swerve out of the way of the digital arrows zooming towards and through her.

"This is a map of the entire facility," Marc explained, highlighting areas on his tablet, which Elena then saw appear in her vision.

"We're down here. The lab you need to get to is on the top floor, all the way over there. I can give you an ideal route to take, but you *cannot* stop."

"Aren't you coming too?"

"I'll meet you there. I can't be seen with you. Ms. Westerfeld must already know, but she never mentioned me. I fear she's playing games: she's like that. Our best hope is that nobody else knows and that I'll be able to walk through most of the complex without getting into trouble. Once we're both there, I'll let us in with my key card."

Elena untied her ponytail, doing her best to cover the little light protruding from her temple. With the clothes she'd found, she should be able to blend in from a distance, but if anyone got up close to her—especially those security guards she hoped were still locked up—she was done for.

Elena didn't hesitate following Marc's directions to the labs and the arrows overlaying the corridors ahead of her. They weaved through the Epsilon complex: through empty, abnormally clean cafeterias, production lines and toilet blocks. But she didn't dare stop moving; she couldn't risk losing control. Her path to the labs had been clear, all she had to do was get as close as she could and then wait for Marc.

She turned into another changing room to analyse her

route, to see if there was a quicker way. Satisfied she was alone, Elena closed the door quietly behind her, moving to the furthest part of the room and sitting down on an impeccably clean bench. Rows of lockers and other doors blocked her view of the entrance, but she'd be able to hear if it was opened.

One thing Elena knew was that her pursuer had a name: Ms. Westerfeld. She could only assume that woman was the one in charge of Epsilon, and most likely the person who'd been trying to take control of her body. There had to be a reason she had been brought to that place, why she'd been turned into... something else.

The more Elena thought about it, the more she could feel foreign objects and materials in her body. She could feel them all latching onto her insides, her muscles, her bones. She was an amalgamation of flesh and circuitry, an unholy marriage of woman and machine. What had been done to her, even if she didn't completely understand what that was, shouldn't have been possible. Elena remembered her file on Marc's computer again. She remembered how she'd been labelled 'Vessel #0001'. Was she really their first? Had all those other people who were in the warehouse with her, who stood still and silent and naked, been through everything that she had been through? Did they have families and friends wondering where they were too?

Families. Friends.

Until that moment, those are two things that Elena hadn't thought of. Though, when she tried, no one immediately came to mind. How could she not remember *anybody* from her life, not even her parents?

Her thoughts were interrupted when the entrance to the changing room was booted open. She could hear a solitary guard not-so-subtly stomp his way into the room.

This is fine, she thought to herself, *I can get by one.*

Thanks to his heavy boots, Elena could tell where the guard was. There was another door at her end of the room. She didn't know what was on the other side, but she couldn't risk opening it as the guard would definitely hear her and then just follow her anyway. No, the best thing to do was to just snake around the room and hope he'd leave.

Her footsteps didn't make a sound. Each step she took was timid: she couldn't risk slipping and kept having to check where she put her feet. Thankfully, the guard insisted on continuing to plod around. She realised he was getting closer to her and she would have to wait until he was in her part of the room to try and sneak out. The doors closed slowly, so once he came in the room, she'd have to move quickly and quietly. She heard him approach the door in between them and cautiously push it open. He stood still, listening for any sign of her presence. There were three rows of lockers between her and the door. She'd have to get past the first two rows as he entered and hope to everything holy that he'd only glance up each row as she reached the door.

The guard finally made a move: he went left, and so did Elena. They silently danced around the lockers in a clockwork fashion. The door was already closing. Elena made it past the first couple of rows of lockers easily without a sound. He was checking down the next row, and Elena could hear the strapping on his gun clatter against his uniform. The gun was raised out in front of him: she heard him lower it and then take a step towards her row. She was at the other end of the lockers to the guard. His helmet popped into view and she darted around and towards the door. Just before it closed completely, Elena managed to hold her hand out to it and slipped through to the other section of the room. That was it. She just had to sneak to the next door and she was out. No point stalling, the sooner she was out, the sooner she could get to the lab. She broke into a short run.

Then her foot slipped and she collided with several lockers, hard. Another moment of uneasy silence passed, then the guard's heavy boots came clambering back through the locker room towards her. Without thinking, Elena got up and ran to the door. She kicked it open but didn't leave.

Instead, she doubled back around and hid in the opposite corner to where she had fallen, hoping the guard would buy her distraction.

Sure enough, he did. He looked at where Elena had fallen, looked up to see the door closing and stormed off in what he thought was a hot pursuit. Elena allowed herself to smile properly, for the first time in what felt like an eternity.

Idiot, she thought to herself.

She headed back to the other door. The arrows directing Elena were telling her that it wouldn't make her journey any quicker, but she was curious to see what was behind the door anyway. The handle was heavy. She yanked it down and a rush of air swirled into the room.

Fresh air?

The desire to run was very tempting. She was running and moving about on the spot as she deliberated the decision. Would she be safe? Where would she even go? What was to stop Epsilon finding her and bringing her back anyway? She'd be back to square one.

Go back inside.

Yes. She had to find Marc. She needed to get rid of what they could of what was inside her. Once that was gone and she couldn't be controlled, then she could get out.

With her mind made up, Elena took one last look at the outside world and pulled the door closed. She turned to see the guard before her, his gun raised and his face looking rather agitated underneath his visor.

"Hands up: now," he snarled through gritted teeth.

Elena didn't argue, cursing herself. How had she not heard him come back? That didn't matter: he was there and she needed a way out. She spotted a ventilation shaft just to the left above his head. That could be her way out, but she needed to deal with him first. Somehow.

"Hey, eyes on me," the guard hissed, noticing her focus wandering above him.

Elena took a step towards him and whatever plan she might have had dissipated as her mind went blank. She swiftly kicked him hard in the groin and he dropped to his knees, howling in pain. Elena tore the gun from his hands and tore it in half, then stared at her hands in awe. She put one foot on the crumpled guard's back to boost herself up to the ventilation. Her hands gained an inexplicably firm grip and her heels dug into the sides of the shaft, pressing the metal inwards and denting it.

How am I doing this? she asked herself, though remained thankful that she was doing it.

She reached out to the latch to try and yank it open. As she got a finger on it the guard was up and trying to grab her legs and pull her down. Elena lashed out with one of her legs to defend herself. She caught the side of the his visor and sent him reeling off-balance. How was she so strong? The man was easily more than double her weight, and yet he felt no heavier against her shoe than a football would.

He banged into some of the lockers, his bulky armour leaving notable dents and buckling a couple of the locker doors. As he was getting back up, Elena again reached for the latch. She fiddled with it briefly, unhooking its lock, as the guard closed in on her as she was still hanging upside down. The door began to drop down and Elena used her palm to push it harder. It swung violently and caught the guard on his visor, once again sending him flying back. The effort to swing knocked Elena off-balance and she pirouetted as she landed almost perfectly on her feet.

She looked back up at the open vent: that was her way out. It looked too high to jump, but she wondered... if she had had the strength to knock that mountainous guard off his feet, surely she could make that leap to safety? Without looking back, Elena tried using the row of lockers to spring herself up to the open vent. Before she could get a firm grip on the edge of the opening the guard ran at her from behind, catching her in mid-air. Gathering her in an his ironclad grip, he didn't stop running until they both crashed into the opposite wall.

The guard's hulking frame threatened to crush Elena,

but she remained abnormally calm. She pushed back with her arms until they were straight, then used her legs to send them both flying backwards. The guard let go of her as he tried to regain his balance and avoid being embarrassed a third time by that tiny woman. Elena had no idea what she was doing or how she was doing it, but she didn't dare let her brain interrupt. She ran at the guard with tenacity, barely allowing him to find his feet, and drove a knee into his stomach. He cursed as he curled over, managing to block most of Elena's follow up punches, kicks and elbows with his arms. He swung for her face several times but her small, athletic form allowed her to easily duck his lunging arms with ease, opting to carry on going low, with lots of short, snappy punches to his abdomen. Growing frustrated, the guard swung a treetrunk-like leg forward and swooped Elena off of her feet. She landed perfectly that time, but the guard was already on her. His hooked punch caught Elena's cheek sweetly and she staggered back from its sheer force. The impact felt like being hit by a tank, but she turned back to look him dead in the eye. The punch hadn't hurt. It hadn't hurt her at all. There wasn't even the feeling of a bruise threatening to form under her skin. She felt like a pocket-sized Terminator.

Okay, she thought. *This isn't so bad.*

The surprise on the guard's face was visible, even through his tinted visor. She smiled wickedly at him, a renewed sense of confidence in her posture. Anger emanated from the guard as he rushed forward for another swing but Elena calmly slid between his legs, twisted round onto her feet and kicked at the back of his knees, knocking him to the ground again. She drove a couple of short jabs into the small of his back and flipped over him to kick him down to the ground.

Now she could make her escape. She bent her knees and leapt up for the vent. She underestimated just how much strength she had and flew into the roof of the vent, headbutting it violently and dropping back towards the ground. A desperate hand grabbed onto the edge, the metal bending and crinkling in her grip. Her other hand came to meet it and she stabilised herself, pulling her body up into the vent. She pulled herself up enough to rest on her elbows as she tried to pull the lower half of her body up.

A pair of vice-like hands clamped around her ankle and yanked down, threatening to pull her back out of the vent. She held her arms out either side of her, keeping down to her waist still in the vent. She kicked down at the hands, but they began to climb up her body. Those powerful hands found their way up Elena's leg. There was no care, no feeling of caressing: the guard's hands dug into her calf and thigh, fighting to gain a hold. Elena lashed out with her free leg again, the connection to the guard's helmet sending him swinging, but he didn't let go. They were now both off the ground. Somehow, Elena was not only keeping herself up but also that frightfully large brute. His hands grabbed around her waist and he heaved himself further up. She could feel his visor brushing against her calves. An idea flashed through her head at such a pace that she found herself doing it before she'd even realized what it was. A knee crunched into the guard's visor, splintering it. He let go and began to fall but Elena caught him up in her legs, wrapping them around his neck and squeezing. She only just managed to process what she had done and what she was doing. She was hanging him with her legs. She was killing him.

The guard didn't let up, a flurry of arms bashing into her legs and her sides, but they weren't affecting her as they should have done. Shock settled in: was she really willing to kill this man just to get away?

"Please, let go," she said quietly. She was still in disbelief that she was even able to hold herself off the ground with that monstrous man holding onto her. He didn't listen; he kept fighting. Elena dared to wrap her legs tighter still. She was hoping he would give in, but he wouldn't. A hand tried pulling her legs away from his throat in a vain attempt for air but it was too late: her legs coiled around his throat tighter like a snake with its prey.

"Please don't make me do this," she pleaded once more.

The guard started to gag and choke. What little air he had was leaving him. He reached down to his belt and pulled out a knife. Its blade was narrow, but it was about seven inches long. The bladed hand swung about violently and caught the outside of her thigh, breaking through her jeans. He reached up as far as he could and slashed at her forearm before slipping and driving it straight into her side. She couldn't feel the pain even as blood began to seep from her wounds. She tightened her grip around his neck once again and twisted his head about before an ugly crack escaped from him and the flailing stopped, his whole body going limp. Elena dropped him unceremoniously and he landed in a silent, unmoving heap. That was it. He was dead.

She hoisted herself into the vent and sat with her legs hanging out of the opening. None of the places where the guard had cut her seemed to hurt: even the flow of blood was slow. She looked down and realised that the guard's knife was still rammed into her side. It was almost hypnotic to look at. It should have done enough damage to kill her, but instead she felt nothing. The knife's purpose to wound her had somehow been blunted by the machinery and wiring within her. She stared at it a while longer before pulling it out without a flinch. It was stained with a black liquid: not blood, then, but definitely from her. She fought the urge to poke around her wounds, as she knew she was just wasting time. The arrows had disappeared from her vision and a little egg timer spun in the corner of her eye. A few moments later, a new route appeared laid out in front of her. Whatever programming was inside her knew she was up in the ventilation system and showed her the way leading right up to the labs and, hopefully, Marc. It wouldn't take her long: just forty minutes of crawling through the pitch black, climbing through dark columns stretching far above and below, all things Elena was fairly sure she hadn't ever wanted to do, nor would enjoy doing.

*

Elena didn't speak to herself once as she eased her way through the seemingly never-ending ventilation system. A gentle cool breeze passed around her, but it didn't bother her. As she thought about it, the dark didn't either: nor did the lack of space. She was convinced she used to be terrified of enclosed spaces, she just could not remember if that was true. Nothing was bothering her. Not the knife wounds, not the dark, nothing. She was just cruising through on autopilot to her final destination at the lab.

She found herself coming to a halt in front of yet another sheer drop. The lab was above her; she just had to climb up five storeys in the darkness and she would be there. Marc would be waiting and they could fix her. Finally, she'd get to be her normal self.

She put one hand out in front of her until she could feel the other side of the ventilation shaft. Pressing against it lightly, she brought out a foot to push into the same side. She pulled herself up and then she was free from the opening. Elena couldn't believe it: she was climbing up through vents without *any* safety harness, and she wasn't even remotely fazed by it. Slowly she shimmied her way up the five stories, trying to move as quietly as she could. The layout in her eyes showed her that where she was, no one would hear her anyway, but Elena wanted to be sure.

The only noises she could hear were the squeak of rubber on metal as her shoes scuffed against the side of the shaft. The climb wasn't tiring her: she felt like she could do it all day. So she increased her pace, confident she would be fine. Sure, she made a bit more noise but she only had half a storey to go and she would be there.

Without warning one of the panels in the shaft slipped out of place and she found herself falling. She drew her limbs in before pushing them out straight to either side. Her feet and hands crashed into the walls of the shaft and bent it out of shape. She squealed to a halt and found she'd only fallen two storeys. That was nothing to her now.

She found her balance again, which was much easier now the shaft was misshapen and she could almost stand up properly. She bounded up towards the vent, no longer caring about keeping quiet. She made one last giant leap for the edge of the opening to the lab and her hand clamped on it so hard that she left an indent in the metal. With a swift pull, she was up and sliding along on her front for a few metres until she reached the vent. The opening was above head height, so she would have to drop down the ground. Satisfied that no one was in the hallway, she smashed the locked vent off its hinges with one punch.

She could not stop being amazed by what she was capable of. That was, until she looked at her hand. The skin was cut up all over her knuckles and fingers. She felt like things were out of place, but it didn't hurt and there was little to no blood... or whatever it actually was. Hopping down to the ground she realized she'd hit the vent so hard that it'd flown across to the wall on the other side of the hall. It was bad to even think it, but Elena was starting to enjoy the strength Epsilon had given her.

A door down the hall creeped open and Marc popped his head out, smiling as he saw her.

"Thank God, you made it," he said, relieved. "Now get in here quick, I've got everything set up."

Elena smiled back and followed him in. The lab was unlike any she had ever seen. Computers and technology littered the walls, technology that shouldn't even have been possible seemed to have been made in that very room, the diagrams and videos running on laptop screens showing her just how much Epsilon was building. There wasn't a sector they weren't manufacturing for: business, communications, emergency services, government contracts, military hardware, everything. Elena was left wondering where she fit into that equation, where *all* of the Vessels fitted into that equation. Every big firm and industry imaginable appeared to have Epsilon making something for them. But who wanted Vessels? What good could they possibly bring?

Marc gestured for her to go over to an operating table, surrounded by surgical equipment and machinery, needles and tiny saws attached to glistening, elongated arms that looked like they belonged to a spindly, metal spider. Elena lay down on the table which, as with everything else she'd seen in the building, was impeccably clean. She lay still for a few moments, thinking back over everything that had happened that day. It seemed impossible, hell, it *was*, but she was safe now.

Marc came back with his tablet. "Everything all right?"

Elena nodded back, looking down her nose at him, "Yup, just want to get all of this out of me now."

"Yeah, about that," Marc began. "It's going to take some time. Not only am I having to remove all these modifications from within your body, but I've also got to disable the programming that's synced up with your brain without accidentally erasing your conscience with it."

"Oh."

"Yeah, no pressure, right?"

"Please tell me this isn't your first time using all of this stuff?"

Marc paused for a second, then looked back at her and smiled again. "Okay, this isn't my first time using all of this stuff."

Elena leaned back and Marc disappeared from view again. She tried to relax, but she couldn't tell if she was or not. Music suddenly started playing from the speakers in the room. It was familiar to Elena: she'd definitely heard it before. She felt like she knew the band. Who was it again? The music was modern, rocky, also quite catchy. How did it go again? She found herself humming along with the tune.

Elena remembered. It was the Arctic Monkeys. The song was *Fluorescent Adolescent*. She *remembered* something. She realised she hadn't remembered anything other than her name and her trousers all day.

Elena felt a memory form in her head. It was blurry at

first, but soon it began to take shape. She was driving with somebody, singing that very song at the top of her lungs. It wasn't her driving, it was someone else. Who was it? Their features slowly came back to her. It was a guy. Six-foot-tall, dark and defined eyebrows, pasty white skin. She smiled as she remembered his shoulder-length curly dirty blonde hair, he always looked like a bit of a rock star. Elena's trail of thought screeched to a stop. It was Marc. She was singing with Marc.

What was he doing here? Why hadn't he said anything? Elena heard the door open. She tried to move, but her body refused to obey. The light on the side of her head was on. She felt metal restraints wrap over her body and click into place. There was no way she could go anywhere now.

"Don't worry, Elena," Marc said. "I managed to rope in some other people to help me out."

The whole table began to move. She was being stood upright. The familiar sound of heavy boots filled her ears. The guards were all there now, a sea of blacked-out armour and helmets all facing her, not moving or uttering a sound. The table stopped turning and Elena's body jolted forward the restraints not quite tight enough for someone of her size.

She wanted to curse at Marc. She wanted to throw the whole operating table at him. But then the sound of high-heels clinking against the ground filled the room. The guards parted and a woman walked straight towards her. Elena wasn't much shorter than her, but this woman's shoulders looked broad in her navy-blue blazer. Her hair was a radiant ginger, bouncing and shining with each step. Elena didn't need to guess: this was Ms. Westerfeld.

She smiled flirtatiously and stroked Elena's cheek. "Aw, sweetheart, why do you look so sad?"

Elena wished she could move; nothing would be better than hitting that woman in her face.

"Oh, how silly of me, I forgot I had Marc play with you," her laugh was unbearably superficial. "Marc, honey, you can let her move now."

"Sure. Apologies, Katherine."

The light on her head went out and Elena could move again. She thought she could break free, but she found herself hurling every expletive under the sun at both Marc and the other infernal woman. *KATHERINE*. Ms. Westerfeld held her hand up and Elena was beyond annoyed that she stopped shouting almost instantly.

"You've been causing me a lot of problems, Elena," Katherine started. "You're one tough young lady! You are incredible."

"What have you done to me?" Elena demanded.

"What have I done? I've done nothing, I simply signed all the necessary bullshit to bring you in. What my *company* has done, however, is something quite extraordinary."

She grabbed the table and turned it to face the giant display of monitors. Elena watched as dozens of videos of her appeared across every screen in her vision. They started off following her in the outside world, then videos of various surgeries in Epsilon. After Elena got through each of those, several videos popped up from earlier that day. At least that's what she thought. They started and ended differently. They were on different days. They were different days and Elena couldn't remember any of them except for today.

"We picked you up just over a month ago," Katherine said, walking around and behind Elena's table.

"You've been troublesome from the very beginning," she continued. "Most of the people we took for the Vessel program were fully formatted within two or three surgeries. Easy enough, not much to worry about. But you, oh, *you*, you have taken damn near twenty."

"I don't understand, why am I so different?"

"We have absolutely no idea. Your boyfriend there was a synch, though."

Marc walked back into view, he put the tablet down and removed his lab coat. His arms were covered in the same scars as Elena's. He pressed into his temple and a flap of skin folded back to reveal a little blue light, shining just like hers had been. Marc had been taken, just like her. Turned into some... freak and he didn't even know.

"We realised that a lot of our Vessels were quite weak-willed people. Losers. Wastes of space, vermin that contributed nothing to our society and would not be missed by anyone. When we found you two, we couldn't resist a challenge. That ended up being more problematic than I would've liked."

Katherine gave another half-assed fake smile.

"Two beautiful human beings with great prospects and loving families, or so you thought."

Katherine showed a video of who Elena assumed was her parents: she still couldn't remember them, but there they were with her. Another clip showed up: they were agreeing to sell their daughter to Epsilon, in exchange for serious money. The next thing that came up was a news article stating they'd been killed in a plane crash. There was so much information to take in, Elena didn't know what to do with it.

"Any good parent would've turned that money down," Katherine whispered in her ear. "But they were practically biting our hands off for it! I know, even I was shocked. Still, we couldn't risk them talking, so we might've accidentally had them killed. Don't worry, we included Marc in the story too, so now neither of you exist! Ta-da!"

"But I'm right here," Elena said. "I'm still me, I'm still a woman."

"Oh, sweetheart," Kathrine said unnervingly. "You're not you at all."

The images changed. She was looking at various X-rays which stretched across multiple screens. Her bones and organs all looked perfectly healthy; she now remembered being a keen runner.

"You see this, Elena? This was you. Young, beautiful, healthy Elena. Wow, I wish I had that kind of physique when I was your age."

The images changed again, and Elena wasn't ready for what she saw. "This is the new you."

Everything was gone.

"I don't get it."

"Elena, you came here to 'fix' yourself. There is *nothing* of the old you left except for your brain and we're currently working on that. We've stripped out everything that makes you human: your intestines, your stomach, your heart, your eyes, even your lungs."

Elena couldn't help but laugh at the sheer insanity of it all. "You really think I'm buying all of this bollocks? That's not possible."

"Really?" dared Katherine. "Did you remember to breathe at all today?"

Elena froze. She couldn't remember at all.

"That doesn't mean anything. Everyone just *breathes*."

"True, we do. But you haven't been, have you? You didn't breathe when you woke, you didn't need to breathe running from my guards, nor closing that giant door, nor did you breathe while hoisting one of these great men off the ground using nothing but your legs to break his neck. He's fine by the way: he's just another Vessel we like using for internal demonstrations or fun. What about climbing through the ventilation? I suppose that was light work too?"

Elena became overwhelmed at the fact Katherine was right. She hadn't taken a single breath all day. She couldn't.

"You were such a strong woman, Elena. My girls would've loved to have met you. But your will is strong too. Every time we've tried to use our programming to boot your conscience to the side, you keep fighting back. You're like a fever we just cannot burn out. You won't give up. I like that. But it became an inconvenience, you've lost my company untold millions just to keep *fixing* you."

"You haven't fixed me, you've taken everything I am away from me."

"We're both right, sweetheart," Katherine smiled again. "Today is the last time we're gonna need to update you.

Once that's done, you're fixed! Isn't that wonderful?"

Elena was furious, too angry to speak.

"You are nothing but a product now, and we *own* you."

Elena wanted to cry, she wanted to sob her eyes out, but she didn't have real eyes. She didn't have tear ducts either. Katherine clicked her fingers and whoever was controlling Marc now stopped: the light on his head went out and his body dropped to the floor and stayed there. As Katherine spun her back around, Elena noticed a jerry can labelled 'flammable liquid' a few feet from her. They took her outside the complex. Back through the beautiful white corridors that were all so clean. The guards brought Elena to a heap of boxes, which Katherine started reading through. A birth certificate, student awards, exam results, a driving license, contracts for phones and internet and car insurance. It was all Elena's. Every little thing that proved she had ever existed, all in one giant pile. She felt the blue light switch on again, the burning sensation in her mind returning with it. She could only watch as her body walked over to the jerry can and picked it up. Her steps were slow and methodical as she made her way over to the pile of her belongings, her history, her *life*. Elena wanted to scream out in protest as her hands chucked the liquid over it all. Nothing went uncovered. One of the guards handed her a box of matches. She took one and lit it. She was screaming in her head but it was no use. Her hand let go of the match and the pile roared as the flames spread instantaneously. She'd just helped erase herself from existence.

"Well done, sweetheart," Katherine put her hand on her shoulder.

Elena stood deathly still. It was like back being in the warehouse again.

The light flickered and she found herself in control again, but she stayed still: no one else had noticed yet. Her memories were searing through. She was remembering who she was. But it was no use. Katherine and Epsilon had won. They owned her. Soon she'd be back on that table and she would never be in control of herself ever again. She spotted a pile of old school books smouldering at the bottom of the flames. She bent down to pick it up and examined it. All of the guards were watching her now, none of them were armed. Elena smiled and threw the books at Katherine, setting the back of her blazer alight. She screamed and several guards rushed to help her get it off, while two others went for Elena. She threw one out the door and broke the other's knee. That one was real. He screamed in agony until she used everything she had to punch straight through his head. She yanked her arm back through and let herself fall into the giant burning pile. It didn't hurt, and that was fine. If she couldn't have her life and her body, then nobody would. She felt her skin burn and bubble and peel. Her hair and her clothes became cinders. Katherine was now screaming for the guards to tend to Elena instead. Elena didn't care. She closed her eyes and drifted away to the beautiful sounds of everything around her burning and Katherine screaming in agony.

Elena stirred slowly, her eyes adjusting to the beams of light shining in her face. Why was she awake? How had she survived?

Katherine walked into view looking unbearably smug. Elena looked down at her body, or she tried to. Every limb was disconnected. She could see her smouldering remains at the back of the room. No. Something new was being built for her. The 'skin' was peeled open on each and every limb, little machines working relentlessly on them. Attaching cables and electronics to a metal skeleton. She couldn't see inside her torso, but it too was split open for everyone to see.

Katherine stroked her cheek. "You really don't make things easy, do you, Elena?"

Elena said nothing; she realised she didn't have a lower jaw to help her speak. She looked up to the mirrored ceiling. This wasn't her anymore, it was a metallic face with no skin, two impeccably white eyes standing out against the gunmetal grey of everything else.

Something was plugged into the back of her head. It was the first time she'd felt any twinge of physical pain in what felt like forever. That wasn't so bad; it wasn't as intense as the burning in her mind had been.

"This has been fun and all," said Katherine. "But I insist we really get rid of you now. We can't have any viruses in the operating system on launch day."

So, that was all Elena was: a virus. She'd been a virus in her own head, but she wasn't even that now. She was barely still holding on. Whatever plugged into her head was feeding information, bringing her memories back. Pain eased into contentment. She knew it was intended to help push her out. That's exactly what it did. Memories of graduating, her first steps as a baby, her first kiss with Marc all bombarded her at once. It was... nice.

Elena was done with fighting, she had nothing left. She felt her memories disappearing back out of her mind so she fell with them: down the digital rabbit hole.

Epilogue

The sun did its best to shine through the overcast grey sky, but Katherine had no plans to let it affect her mood. The press conference to announce the Vessel project to the world was going swimmingly. The stage that had been put together for her was magnificent. A sturdy metal frame held it all together, the platform had a luscious deep blue carpet which was impeccably clean. Even as she walked about on it, her footsteps didn't leave a mark, barely even disturbing the fibres from their natural resting place. The company logo—'ΣPSILΩN'—hung proudly on a sturdy board above the stage. Epsilon wasn't a big name outside the world of technology, but they were about to be.

She had made a rousing speech about the state of technology in the modern world. She was certain that the troublesome girl, Elena, had read some of it. She spoke of how Epsilon had always had a desire to push the boundaries of what was possible with humans and technology. The Vessels were to be their magnum opus, the bleeding edge between virtual and reality. It would allow people to see the world through other eyes and live lives they otherwise couldn't.

The large monitor to her side amplified her words with pictures and diagrams of how the Vessel worked. Users connected to their Vessel through a docking station, much like the one behind Katherine, as some of the reporters had noticed. Katherine didn't try to hide her enjoyment. The Vessels, she said, were all designed to look as realistic as possible, as close to human as machinery could get. Their looks and appearance were predetermined, but their personalities would be up to the users.

The Vessel was docked in a sleek, rounded pod, in which it could update itself automatically. The pod was connected to a virtual reality stand. It featured the lightest, most accurate VR headset money could buy, and it was linked to a mouldable gel-like exoskeleton skin which users wrapped around their limbs to accurately record their movements. They stood on a six-foot by six-foot 360-degree travellator, which allowed for complete freedom of movement without ever leaving that exact spot.

Katherine's smile beamed back at the flashes of cameras as she was met with thunderous applause. She had *nailed* the speech. Chairs screeched out of place as reporters and news outlets lunged forward with microphones, desperate for questions. It bothered her, things being out of place, but didn't let it show. This was a good moment.

Some reporters held back, watching her carefully; she knew they would be the tough crowd to convince. She picked one of the more enthusiastic reporters, his name was Brian.

"First of all, Ms. Westerfeld: wow. What a presentation," he began, stumbling over his words in excitement.

"Aw, thank you so much," she replied with a cheeky smile. "You're too kind."

"I have to ask: what is it that inspired you, and Epsilon, to design these Vessels?"

"A good question. It'd be hard to try and tell you we don't all love our sci-fi here at Epsilon. So, if anyone's wondering, yes, we did look at some of the classics. Blade Runner, Total Recall... you name it, we looked at it. But we wanted to take things further. Why did virtual reality have to be virtual? Why did it have to be in our head, or on our screens? Why couldn't we become something else in the real world?"

Brian smiled like a little schoolchild and sat back down. Up next, she picked a young red-haired woman named Stephanie.

"When are you aiming to release these wonderful machines to the market?"

Katherine smiled again, "Well, as of... right now. We're taking pre-orders! Isn't that great? We're aiming for a general, worldwide release during Q4 of 2023. The Vessels will remain ours until then. Once we've got the designs and software nailed, we'll let them loose on the world!"

Some people in the crowd laughed. *This is going great,* Katherine thought to herself. One of the older, reserved gentlemen now raised his hand and stood forward. His name was Craig. She knew he'd have a tough question, but Katherine felt like a million dollars. She was on fire, in fine form.

"A very dazzling display, Ms. Westerfeld. If I may, while the technology behind these... Vessels, is incredibly impressive, are you aware of the potential military or even criminal applications they can be used for? Do you have anything to prevent everyday people from committing horrific crimes and getting away with it?"

Katherine loved a challenge.

"Yes, I do," she began simply. "Each Vessel has a blue LED light in their left temple, so that is how to tell them apart from us regular folk. The Vessels will record and store data based on everything each user does with them every day. If anyone were to partake in any criminal activity, we'll know straight away and coordinate with the right authorities to track the said person down. As for military applications, I think they could be great on the frontlines. They could prevent lives from being needlessly lost. However, I must say you cannot modify them in any way. They come as they are; any attempt to break the outer skin, and it will shut down and remain in safe mode until one of our engineers either unlocks or destroys it. We've thought of every outcome to this. While they may look and sound like us, they are not human. They are empty, metal shells, devoid of any personality. Unless, of course, you give them one!"

Several reporters clapped again. Each clap invigorated Katherine with more confidence and her stage presence grew. Now, she wanted to pull out all of the stops.

"Shall we have a demonstration?" she asked the crowd. The crowd cheered and whistled in agreement. Katherine insisted Craig come up to join her. Reluctantly, he put his pad and paper down and made his way to the stage. Katherine came down to help him; his frail body could only carry him so fast. She smiled at the crowd as she led him up the stairs to the docking station. An assistant popped up from seemingly nowhere to help Craig sort himself out.

Once he was ready, the assistant gave Katherine the thumbs up. Showtime.

"Ladies and gentleman," she said excitedly, "what you're about to see is the world's first look at a Vessel in action. Please bear in mind, this is a work in progress, so things may not go smoothly the first time!"

The pod began to open, and various hands with cameras leaned further forward to get a glimpse of the Vessel. It looked like a young, Latina woman. Her hair was the deepest black, her features matched it. It was beautiful.

"Today, Craig has become our very first Vessel, number one off the production line! We've called her Elena."

The light on 'Elena's' head switched on and it opened

its eyes. Craig looked around and the Vessel copied him perfectly.

"Good heavens!" they both exclaimed in unison. "I'm a woman!"

The crowd laughed again. This was perfect. Katherine had won them over. She made Craig jog on the spot: Elena copied him. She asked him to do a 'funky' dance: he tried his best, but Elena did exactly the same thing. The crowd oohed and ahh-ed in waves, their cameras splashing up against the front of the stage at Katherine's feet. She asked Craig to touch his toes.

"Blimey, I don't think I've done that in thirty years!" he responded.

More laughter from the crowd; excellent. For some reason, they started chanting for Craig to touch his toes. So he leaned over and tried. Elena did too. The very tips of his fingers brushed his toes, as did Elena, and the crowd cheered once more. Suddenly, Craig lost his balance and stumbled over, landing on his face. Elena did too.

"Everything alright there, Craig?" Katherine asked, her face wrought with worry for the first time that day.

"I'm alright!" he and Elena both replied. "I think I'd better get out of it now. I'm getting old and this headset is giving me a bit of a migraine. A real burn in the back of my head."

"You poor thing, we'll be sure to fix that! Give it up for Craig and Elena, everyone!"

The crowd roared once more. Katherine had them. She noticed Elena's face was scuffed on the cheek. That was fine, she could fix that.

"Give the people a wave," she asked. Craig happily obliged, Elena also waved with him, but their waves weren't in sync anymore.

Katherine clocked it straight away but pretended to ignore it. That could be fixed.

"Now, give us a smile!"

Craig gave a cheesy grin from behind his headset. Elena

didn't. The light on her head flickered. It shut off for a few seconds, Elena stood there, idly waving with an empty expression. Her head dropped slightly. The light returned and then Elena jolted and synced back up with Craig. Her smile matched his: cheesy and broad. But her eyes. Her eyes weren't right. They stared forward into nothingness. Elena was empty. Elena was a Vessel.

THE END

About the Author

I've spent most of my life growing up in the small town of Chippenham in the South West of England. Literacy/ English was one of my favourite subjects from an early age. I love writing stories, I love writing. It's the thing I am the most passionate about.

In 2015 I started writing articles online for other actual people with eyes to read, because I knew I couldn't be happy keeping it to myself. For the most part it's been a success, I've amassed thousands of reads since then and received some great feedback.

In 2018 I embarked on the challenge to write my first novel, after having planned it for nearly eight years and doing nothing with it. It's the scariest and most exciting thing I've ever tried, and hope to have it released some time in 2019.

I post articles regularly on Vocal and my personal WordPress blog. Be sure to follow me if you like what I write and want to keep up to date with me!

Author Links:
Facebook Page: @PEllisOfficial
Twitter: @PM_Ellis1
Instagram: pm_ellis
Vocal Page: vocal.media/authors/peter-ellis
Personal Blog: peterwritesthings.wordpress.com

The Accidental Operator
by Michael Peirce

Billy Hawkins thought he'd been cold before. Having grown up in upstate New York, he figured he had the measure of bad weather. Naturally, he'd been wrong. Afghanistan was a whole new world of cold and misery. He continued to plod up the side of the hill, on slippery rocks with sleet in his face and anger in his heart. He knew damn well he had no business on that mountain, playing soldier in arctic weather.

Being pissed off is not as good as ginger brandy, but it does help keep you warm.

It all started when the National Guard had sent him to that miserable country and he'd been put in with some Rangers who needed a talking head. It certainly wasn't his fault that people started thinking he was Delta when a clerk had confused one Billy Hawkins with another, which would have taken months to sort out. That kicked off all sorts of rumors, and there are no worse gossips than soldiers.

It hadn't helped when, asked about his background by an officer at the air base near Bagram, he had innocently stated that he was a qualified ham radio operator.

The guy must have only heard the word: "Operator," because, no matter what Hawkins told anyone, they refused to believe he was the simple country boy nerd that he appeared to be. There were others who regarded him as a fake, even though he claimed no more than his National Guard status.

Killing those four guys on his first patrol with the Rangers had really screwed him. No one would believe he was who he said he was, and now the Rangers wanted no other translator. Yet he really wasn't all that fluent in Pashto...

For this patrol, Hawkins was on loan to an Afghan intelligence officer. He'd been told to stay up in front with Gerdun the Afghan guide in case a linguist was needed. The subtext was that Major Farooq had heard about his work with the Rangers, and the major's own bells were ringing; he smelled trouble and wanted a radical fighter on point. Hawkins had no idea what it was all about; he was still figuring everything out, and certainly didn't see himself as a 'radical fighter'.

Gerdun was an amiable enough fellow and, although Hawkins liked him, he reckoned him to be as crazy as a shithouse rat. Because of a British identity disk some ancestor of his had passed down over the years, many of the males in his family called themselves 'Gordon', which came out as Gerdun in their thick accent. Tales told around a campfire tend to grow as time passes, and Gerdun had been known to brag that he himself had killed Gordon Pasha and eaten his heart at Khartoum. Wherever that was...

Hawkins took his mind off his frozen feet by focusing on his list of complaints and rehearsing his pending appeal to get out of that dreadful place. He had something of a knack for languages like Spanish and French, but he did not speak much Arabic and was just starting to figure out Pashto. His military career had thus far equipped him with Farsi in expectation of a coming war with Iran. A war that so far hadn't materialized and was looking less likely every day.

Learning the languages had been interesting for him but he hadn't really joined the Guard hoping to go play cowboys and terrorists in some faraway land. Regardless, it had landed him in the mountains of Afghanistan where hard-eyed Mujahedeen peeked at unwary travelers over the sights of Russian-made firearms.

As Hawkins bitched and fussed mentally he was only peripherally aware that he was also swiveling his head, watching and looking for patterns, listening carefully and even sniffing the air around him.

Hawkins was one of those short, scrappy kids who was good with his hands. People who had seen him fight said he had 'instincts'. But life is rarely fair and his tow-headed farm boy appearance meant that other men never hesitated to try him, despite the consequences.

It had made working as a bouncer at the Tap House less than a dream job, but he'd needed something to back up his other, short-order gig at the diner. Supposed to be temporary, the diner job was starting to stretch into the future and the owner was beginning to talk about promotion to management, which was horrifying to think about: like drowning in a seething vat of home-fried potatoes.

Local lawmen back home hadn't loved him much. They were aware he didn't cause trouble, but trouble often found him and that kept him on their radar. Sometimes it seemed the only peace he found was up on the mountain with his deer rifle, alone.

Civilian life wasn't going anywhere fast for Hawkins and he really didn't have any thoughts on how to improve it. He didn't like the academic regimen despite his knack for languages and tech gear, and he wasn't sure he wanted to fool with that anyway. His high school sweetheart, Melissa, had broken up with him when he'd admitted he just didn't want to go to college.

Deputy Judson Magruder was a friend of his dad's and was known to Hawkins as a decent fellow. Magruder suggested he join up, get a grip on his life. So he'd joined the National Guard, hoping to find some direction or at least buy some time. Nothing had worked out as he pictured it. The Guard deployed him and the other unfortunates from the same Farsi language class to Afghanistan for exciting six-month tours as translators. The assumption was that they'd help interrogate prisoners and talk to villagers.

He'd long since decided his life was something of a bad joke and had learned not to be too surprised at how ridiculous things seemed to get for him at times. Like many before him he found it unsurprising that terms like 'SNAFU' and 'FUBAR' originated in the military. Had some clerk simply decided that one of these 'enemy' languages was pretty much the same as another and just clicked a checkbox? Is that how he ended up on this frozen mountain?

Although he knew much better than to daydream in the combat zone Hawkins foolishly allowed his mind to wander from the thought of his life as a 'joke' to 'Marx Brothers' to 'What the hell was the name of that movie...?'

Just as he slid inelegantly on the frozen landscape, it came to him and, without thinking, he said it out loud.

The last word he would ever say out loud: "Coconuts!"

As he fell he instinctively reached out for Gerdun and dragged him to the ground with him just as the whole world seemed to explode in their faces.

Hawkins' finger probably shouldn't have been on the trigger, but it was and he pulled back on it by nervous reflex, emptying his M4 Carbine as he fell. The Muj was hit numerous times, but had already primed his grenade which he dropped in front of him and it exploded in the air. A second insurgent had been struck by one of Hawkins' wild rounds, as was a villager whose arm was splattered a hundred meters up the hilly pathway.

A ricochet from his own weapon trimmed the top of his ear and pieces of grenade shrapnel hit Hawkins in the throat and chest as he seemed to fall in slow motion.

Major Farooq of Afghan Army Intelligence watched this in amazement. Who was this crazy American who'd singlehandedly disrupted the enemy ambush? He began shouting orders to his men.

Hawkins drifted slowly into consciousness. The side of his head stung sharply for some reason and there was such a mess of gauze and bandages around his throat and chest that he felt trapped. He called out for someone to tell him what had happened and his throat seemed to explode in pain.

The next time he awoke, a young medic gently pushed him back down onto the pillow. "It's OK, Sergeant, just chill. You're getting better, but it takes time. Don't try to talk."

Hawkins thought to himself, "Sergeant? Huh?"

An army doctor came in. "So you are the one everybody's talking about? Good work out there son." He bent over and removed the bandages from Hawkins' throat and nodded to the medic, who pushed an injector into the IV. Hawkins felt warmed by the morphine and relaxed just a bit.

Doctor Steinberg looked at him sadly. "Sergeant

Hawkins, you've suffered significant trauma to your vocal chords. I know this sucks, you being a 'translator' and everything... but it's unlikely you'll ever speak again above a whisper."

A rugged-looking American officer strode into the hospital bay, accompanied by a dapper Afghan Major, who Hawkins would later learn was named Farooq. "You Delta types talk a good game but by God son you went and backed it up good and proper..." A brief flash of embarrassment crossed the officer's face as he recognized the nature of Hawkins' injury. Obviously Hawkins wouldn't be talking much anymore. The officer recovered and pinned a Bronze Cross with 'V for valor' on the pillow next to his head. He clutched Hawkins' shoulder briefly and then stepped back.

All Hawkins could think was: "Delta? What the fuck? Who are these people?"

Major Farooq looked at him, very carefully, then said in a vaguely British sort of accent, "I saw what you did. You saved some lives on that damned mountain, maybe even mine. I'm stationed near here for now and if you don't mind, perhaps I can drop by later and visit." Hawkins nodded and the Major pinned an Afghan letter of commendation to the pillow next to his Bronze Star. Both officers saluted briskly and strolled out of the room.

Steinberg finished rebandaging Hawkins' neck, looked at him and sighed. "Kid you must be a special kind of bad ass... we'll get you healed up a bit and then we can send you home. I'm hoping a specialist can do more for you than we can here."

Educated first in the UK, and later in military school in India, Major Farooq was well-off and well-traveled. He'd spent considerable time in the United States before his conscience reminded him of his duty and he returned to Afghanistan to offer his sword to his people. Despite his relative youth—he wasn't yet forty—Farooq was a rather wise fellow, having achieved a maturity some officers never attain.

The major wasn't sure what to make of Hawkins. He knew that Special Ops types sometimes hid behind other titles, even other services, yet he really didn't think Hawkins was an operator. Yet everyone who had seen him fight said he had 'instinct' and was exceptionally fast. Plus he was good with languages, but hadn't even been trained in the local dialects.

Stranger things had happened in the military. He'd laughed with American officers when he'd worked with them on a signals course and they had been kidding about the infamous Lyle Burton.

Lyle Burton had been an American Marine in the Second World War who decided early on that plodding through Japanese-infested jungles was not for him. Ever since, with typical military efficiency, the US Army had organized the Japanese-speaking Nisei into a shock battalion that was then cut to pieces in Italy, translators were in demand out in the Pacific Theater.

Legend had it that Lyle Burton had volunteered as a translator and served almost three years before cracking up and becoming a psychiatric casualty. Burton had gradually constructed his own version of what he thought Japanese must sound like and maintained the pretense, even instructing others in the made-up language. Finally the strain of remembering all the nonsense syllables he'd come up with broke him.

Was Hawkins gaming or had he simply slipped into a situation courtesy of a military bureaucracy so vast that individuals sometimes simply seemed to be absorbed into a sort of 'Borg Collective' and forgotten?

Farooq had better connections than your average major and used them to help Hawkins get it all sorted out administratively. It had been Farooq's idea to promote Hawkins to sergeant. The National Guard had agreed when they saw the commendations, and Hawkins would at least go out higher in rank than he came in. He also got a nice write-up in the 'paper back home.

Hawkins had attended church back in New York and tried to keep up with all that. He was sitting on the side of his bunk with his head bowed and his eyes closed, trying to formulate a prayer, looking for a way to ask his God to explain just what was happening to him. There was a letter from a recruiter on the side of his bunk, offering him a job when he got home and finished treatment. It was from a Private Military Company (PMC) and was not the first one he'd received.

Major Farooq waited respectfully and then approached and sat down across from him, on the bunk opposite. "Has God spoken to you today, Sergeant?"

Hawkins whispered hoarsely, "I'm having trouble forming the right questions to ask Him, sir. I'm very confused..." Major Farooq knew Americans had trouble with names like his and had suggested Hawkins just call him 'Felix'. But it took some getting used to, officers and all that...

"When He is ready, my young friend, He will give you the question along with the answer." Farooq smiled sympathetically. He'd been visiting Hawkins regularly, liked him and was pleased with his progress. He'd brought him a gift once, a silver whistle like the MPs used for traffic control. He sensed that Hawkins was a very special sort of warrior, even if Hawkins refused to believe it himself.

The major knew Hawkins's story well and had connected him with admin types, so he could get back through his own National Guard chain of command. For some reason, despite the help he received freely, it always seemed to come with a wink and a nod. A strange world, he reckoned, where the truth was harder to believe than a lie. Farooq knew Hawkins was no Lyle Burton, yet everyone acted as if he were either a total phony or an undercover Audie Murphy.

"Billy, you will be returning home tomorrow—I've seen the orders. Soon you'll be discharged and your wounds healed, as much as they can ever heal. You've told me of your confusion over this 'hero' business and your distaste for all these offers from companies that refuse to believe who you really are. I want you to think very carefully about that."

"What do you mean Major... erm... Felix? I can only be who I really am, not who some lame-brains think I am. The medals are bogus. I slipped on the fuckin' ice and my gun went off, that's all. I don't know for the life of me how that other Muj got all tangled up on my knife..."

"I saw you slip Billy, with my own eyes. I saw your rifle '*accidently*' home in on those guys and destroy them. I saw something else as well; you slaughtered that other insurgent with your knife so quickly I couldn't be sure exactly what had happened.

"I talked with some Rangers you'd worked with, and they say you killed four Muj on your first patrol. Billy, each of those men was killed with a short burst to the head and it was all over in a flash. It's possible that you may have a gift..."

"Felix, those Rangers were pretty decent guys. They treated me like a brother. I couldn't let those Muj just kill them like they were going to. It was no big deal... and those other things you heard about... well, you know."

Farooq replied, "Right..." He paused. "If you find something to do in Civvy Street that suits you, all well and good, but forgive me for saying this: linguists who can't speak above a whisper are not in demand. So if you don't, there is a company in New York City that I'd like you to talk to. They are known to me. I do some, well, consulting for them on occasion. When you are ready, give them a call. You can be as honest with them as you wish, and be sure to use my name.

"Things are not always as they seem, Billy. We're not always even who *we* think we are, and sometimes there are deeds awaiting only the man who can see them." He handed Hawkins a business card. "My address is on the back of the card. Please let me know how it goes for you..." He saluted, British-style, smiled warmly and walked crisply to the exit.

Hawkins' arm was still raised in salute as he thought, 'I wonder what that is all about?' At any rate, it was nice to have friends.

His name was James Caldwell, and he was satisfied with himself. His West Point ring weighed heavily on his finger. Twenty years of service had included steady promotion, field experience and a lot of 'adjutant' type of responsibilities. He'd retired with honor, if not with distinction.

However, Caldwell was not satisfied with Hawkins, whom he had decided was a phony. Definitely not a serious player, this kid wouldn't look like an adult until he was forty. He reminded Caldwell of Alfred E. Neumann. Except maybe for his eyes...

"I'm keeping these 'so called' commendations to share with the FBI. 'Stolen Valor' is a crime in some places you know. I heard about you claiming to be a Delta Operator; that really makes me laugh."

Hawkins looked at the guy and wondered what the heck had happened.

"So you're a tough guy. I don't know how you ended up here but we take only the best, so hit the door and wait for a visit from the friendly local Feds. Now beat it." It was obvious that Caldwell had done no more than lightly scan Hawkins's documents.

"I don't recall claiming to be anything but what I am. That Delta stuff was just an admin mix up and I've always denied it," Hawkins whispered. Then he stood up and smacked Caldwell twice in the face—backhand, forehand— then rasped in anger, "But you don't get to talk to me that way!"

Caldwell's rage was obvious. He'd been caught off guard, but slipped into a martial arts stance and snarled, "You miserable punk..."

A smartly-dressed executive hurried in through the side door of Caldwell's office. "Stand down, James. You are supposed to stress-test interviewees, but that's quite enough.

This interview was supposed to be a mere formality. What are you doing here anyway? I'd scheduled Claremont for this interview and briefed him fully."

"This guy is a poser and I just proved it!" Caldwell was just starting to get that maybe he'd screwed up.

"You took that way too far. What were you thinking? Perhaps you didn't see the signature on that commendation? *My* signature?"

Major Farooq was attired in a suit like Hawkins had never seen before. He'd always hated what he called 'monkey suits', but damn, Felix hadn't just put on clothes that morning: he'd gotten *dressed*. His cufflinks sparkled and the regimental tie was knotted perfectly.

Standing next to him was a kid wearing a Megadeth T-shirt, blue jeans and trainers. Gerdun smiled broadly and shouted, "Coconuts!"

Caldwell was outraged. "Fuck him. I tell you he's a punk. Look at him! That bastard put his filthy hands on me..."

"Of course. You insulted his manhood and called him a coward. In my country he'd have been justified in killing you and, believe me, he is up to the job.

"As to his exploits, I was there for one of them and witnessed exactly what happened. Billy saved Gerdun and pulled him down, shooting the two insurgents in front of them then butchering a third with his knife. How do you think he got wounded? Who cares if he is not a Hollywood stereotype? Are we a bloody modeling agency here? I don't think so... It would be wise for you to take my words very seriously."

"So, it's OK that he shot down a civilian in cold blood without even blinking...?" Caldwell was trying with some difficulty to discipline his mouth, remembering belatedly that Farooq wasn't just an executive, but an investor.

"Your point? One of his rounds hit a goat as well: shall we inform PETA?" Farooq looked at his friend and smiled warmly. "Relax, Billy, I'm very glad to see you. Everything is fine." He held out his hand. Before Felix could reach him,

Gerdun had poor Hawkins lifted off the ground in a bear hug.

Farooq looked over at Caldwell, "That will be all for now... James."

"I didn't know whether to shit or go blind. I'm serious, this is some National Guard dude and he's gonna be our team leader? He whispers like he's Clint Eastwood or something." Sloan was worried. Usually the Company put together pretty decent teams and he could count on the guys around him.

Silvanus Sloan had tours in Iraq and Afghanistan with elements of the 82nd Airborne Division as an engineer. Blowing shit up, making shit work, and generally making himself useful. He wasn't actually from ancient Rome despite the name but liked to say that Rome was no big deal anyway: New Jersey had better TV reception and plumbing. Or so he claimed...

Charmaine Jackson shook her head, "Maybe we're missin' something? Farooq is no fool." Her role was usually communications, her background Air Force Security Police via a trailer park in Arkansas. Her hair was short and punk, dyed a white trash silvery blond. Her experience: solid.

Edgardo, who referred to himself simply as Gomez, had been an Airborne Ranger and worked on occasion with Special Forces, training indigenous troops. He was very precise with machine guns. It was not his way to jump to conclusions. He said nothing.

The door to the team room opened. Major Farooq entered with Hawkins and Gerdun and looked around the room. He knew them all either personally or by reputation and was satisfied. This four would complete the team that would train the paramilitaries they'd need to complete the assignment in Mexico. They all could find their way around in Spanish, more or less.

Gerdun looked at them and suppressed a sinner's grin that should not have appeared on such a youthful face.

Gerdun knew talent.

Leonard Smith, the Marine, preferred his nickname: 'Consequences'. He was blunt: "Major, is this the time to bring on a new guy? We don't usually have time for handholding. What's with that whispering shit anyway?"

Smith was rough, tough and hard to decipher. He was also colorblind and his sense of fashion reflected that. He was wearing a shirt with green and white horizontal stripes and dark red trousers.

Hawkins stepped deeper into the room, walked up to stand next to Farooq and in front of Consequences. He opened his coat and removed the silk scarf that he wore around his neck to hide the barely-healed scarring. He whispered, "Grenade..."

Consequences looked at him very carefully, and stuck out his hand. "Glad to meet you, brother."

They gathered in the briefing room for coffee and talk. After a refill, everyone including Hawkins and Gerdun had turned and looked closely at Major Farooq who began: "The mission is straightforward. This team will proceed to Mexico and take over security for a businessman and newspaper editor named Emanuel Gonzalez Patel in a town called, inappropriately enough, *Jardín de Dios*."

Everyone, even Farooq himself, had chuckled just a little at the words: 'straightforward'. That would be the day.

Silvanus asked, "What do you know about him?"

The dapper Farooq looked vaguely uncomfortable for just a moment. "His origin is somewhat obscure, which doesn't please me, but he seems to be from a family of Asians who migrated to Mexico a generation ago. He went off to school in Mexico City and later to India for postgraduate work. He came to prominence when his newspaper exposed the local Chief of Police for corruption."

Silvanus said evenly, "So he may actually be the real deal: a principled man who can neither be bought nor intimidated."

Charmaine groaned, "I know the type. They think they're bulletproof and ignore wise advice from bodyguards. They tend to die young."

"Just so," Farooq continued. "That's why you'll be training a team of Peruvians to keep that from happening. We have twenty of those men vetted and heading in-country shortly. Literate, all have at least some military experience and several of them have worked for us before. That said, it's always a crap shoot: so you'll need to keep your eyes open.

"There is one other thing to consider. The police chief was tied into a rather small but extremely violent drug cartel run by a guy that calls himself 'El Bastardo', which some think may be an expression of his parent's lack of connubial formality. It's more likely designed to frighten those who oppose him, and he is known for exceptional cruelty in a competitive space where cruelty is the norm."

Hawkins looked thoughtful for a moment and then whispered, "There's more, isn't there? There are other players in the same game space?"

Major Farooq smiled grimly. "So you can smell your old enemies even this far away, Billy. You are quite right and that should help explain how seriously we're taking this one. There is a Zeta training site where they are making extra cash training Islamic fanatics to use firearms and explosives. It's sort of a worst-of-the-worst-case scenario to have them in the same space as our players but so far there has been no observed interaction. Zeta runs a tight ship.

"Although there are some who would pay well to know just what *is* going on in that Zeta camp. Just in case you were to wander over there and take a look."

Consequences stood up and laughed. "So there it is, boys and girls. Should be a piece of cake; no major threat other than a loosely-defined cartel kill order. Oh, and some crooked cops and Zeta paramilitaries."

Charmaine grinned and twirled a finger in the air. "And a few ISIS head choppers, just to keep it contemporary..."

Gomez who rarely talked, said, "No Apache renegades or Spetsnaz killers? Boring..."

Charmaine nudged Gomez with her elbow and, doing her best Vasquez imitation, said, "Don't spoil it for the rest of us."

Gerdun, who's English wasn't so hot nodded sagely, and said, "Coconuts."

Charmaine looked over at Hawkins and inclined her head toward Gerdun. "Friend of yours?"

"Yeah..." he whispered. "We've played cowboys and Mujahedeen together in the mountains..."

Mr. Patel met them at the airport, and they took two vehicles to his downtown office space. He showed them into a very nice, paneled meeting room filled with a large polished table. Patel was a dignified-looking fellow, pushing forty but slender in his white tropical suit.

He got right to the point. Speaking in English he said, "There has been a change of plans. The Peruvians are going to be my personal security and augment my regular bodyguards sooner than we'd hoped. I just talked to your Major Farooq and he is sending one of his people to work with them. A Mr. Claremont. For now, they're at my hacienda outside of town getting the rundown."

He waited for questions; there were none. "It is all moving too fast. There are too many ways to wind up dead here in God's Garden these days.

"There is a power vacuum that is in danger of being filled by worse people than those originally striving for it. To prevent that we have to do things we'd rather not. In short, I'm brokering an alliance with El Bastardo."

He looked around the table and everyone was wearing their poker face; he couldn't rattle this team. "There is a meeting between him and myself, day after tomorrow. I'll take everyone but you as bodyguards for that meeting. You men will be my 'quiet' people, scouting the location, looking for ambushes, ready to employ as snipers if needed.

And women, of course." He nodded his head politely at Charmaine.

"Have a look around, get some lunch, contact your bosses. Meet in the *Place de Jardín de Dios* tonight around 1a.m. and we'll catch up. Here are the parcels Major Farooq sent ahead for you." He nodded at his assistant, who proceeded to hand them each a canvas bag containing Glock pistols, MP5 Submachine guns, body armor and walkie-talkies.

That evening, Charmaine brokered a satellite phone call between Hawkins and Major Farooq. Speaking for Hawkins, she said, "They're frightened enough to join forces, so there is plenty of reason to proceed with caution. We don't know all the things we need to know such as 'why are they that frightened?' We have to assume it's the other players... yet something else may be going on. This doesn't feel right at all."

Major Farooq replied, "Billy, talk to your team. Scope it out. Make a judgment call. Let me know. I'll keep digging."

Hawkins nodded to Charmaine who said, "Roger, out."

Charmaine winked at Hawkins. "I like strong men who let me do the talkin'." Hawkins was not sure how to reply to that so he grinned at her, stood up, and bowed from the waist. Charmaine smiled broadly, took his arm and they walked slowly to the team room, somehow sharing a brief and wonderful fantasy that they were someone else, somewhere better.

Charmaine laid it out for the team. She already knew what Gerdun's answer would be. Gerdun was part-teenage wasteland and part-homicidal maniac, but a good-natured fellow for all of that. She was pretty sure that if the options were 'danger and a chance to kill some people,' or 'flee' that he'd opt for 'danger and so on' every time.

Consequences and Silvanus Sloan were trying to argue themselves into going ahead with the mission by talking against going ahead with it.

Gomez, as usual, said little. He asked simply, "What is

the 'win' if we complete the mission?"

Consequences ran with that. "Yeah. We get paid regardless. So is there a win in this somewhere, for somebody?"

They agreed inevitably, and voted to let Hawkins decide based upon his communication with Farooq and his knowledge of their collective will. If there was a 'win' for somebody, they wanted to know. If not, they were just hired killers and that was unacceptable. Somehow they failed to notice that they had begun to trust Hawkins.

The hired killer part didn't bother Gerdun even a little, but the rest of the team was more squeamish. Hawkins understood Gerdun and knew how to manage him. There would always be something for men like Gerdun.

Major Farooq was very pleased; he'd thought from the start that Hawkins was more than just a gifted warrior, which was why he had wanted him for team lead, despite his handicap. That was the leadership he knew they'd need when it all went to shit, and it looked like it was all going to shit right out of the gate.

"So Billy, you asked exactly the right question. No killing is justified if there isn't a 'win' somewhere, for righteousness. Tell your team I salute them, and I'll ask them to die before revealing what I'm telling you because that would expose a source that cannot be compromised.

"We learned this morning that the Zeta training camp is looking like it's much more; those people are training the Middle Easterners not for terror attacks in some far off Middle Eastern hell hole, but to help the Zetas carve out an outlaw zone right there in Mexico where they can rule. It's probable that the Daesh types have their own agenda as well, and that would put them right next to door to the USA."

Hawkins grabbed the phone and whispered, "So that's why Mr. Patel agreed to join forces with El Bastardo: to put together enough guns to try and stop that from happening."

Felix answered quietly, "That seems likely. Security being what it isn't... it's also likely Zeta players are already aware of this."

Hawkins said wistfully, his whisper making it sound sadder, "Who are the good guys here?"

Felix replied, "You'll have to sort out the answer to that one, Billy. Make a judgment call and we'll figure out where to go from there."

Hawkins looked over at Charmaine, who smiled an encouraging smile. He made their decision. "We'll continue the assignment at least for now. None of us are too happy about Daesh on our border. Stopping that counts as a 'win'."

Major Farooq replied, "Proceed cautiously, Billy. We just received new information that the Sinaloa Cartel has threatened repercussions against Daesh for interfering with the drug trade in Lebanon. We don't know how that will play into this situation, but I don't need to tell you what worst case looks like."

The team split up for various chores and regrouped later in a quiet park which was usually deserted by that time of night. Consequences and Silvanus looked too out-of-place for undercover so they rented vehicles and became tourists. The locals thought they were gay, which did not amuse them even a little.

Charmaine handled radio watch and Gerdun remained in the hotel as well, since he would attract attention. Gomez went gossiping and Hawkins took a Land Rover borrowed from Mr. Patel to have a look at the likely terrain.

Hawkins cut to the chase. "What did you find out?"

Gomez was not a talker by choice, but he was their most fluent Spanish speaker and he'd learned a lot gossiping in Delgado's with the locals. It was funny how the quiet man attracted the talkers.

He said, "It looks like somebody way up the ladder, outside this game space, wants the Arabs dead. They're leanin' on Zeta to comply. It could get very complicated."

Hawkins nodded to Charmaine, who said, "That adds

up with what Felix told us. ISIS has intercepted some of their drug shipments in Lebanon. El Chapo himself threatened to '...show them what terrorism was all about'."

Senor Patel stepped out of the darkness with two bodyguards trailing. "You're quite right, Miss Jackson. The major cartels have decided that the Arab fighters must be brutally killed and their hearts ripped out of their chests. It is a statement to be made."

He continued, "Zeta agrees but will be losing business so it is decided that Zeta will be gifted a third part in the Patel / El Bastardo alliance. I seem to find myself a partner in a crime cartel. Major Farooq tells me you people are quite clever. Are you clever enough to find me a way out of this?" Whatever Patel's game was it seemed obvious that it had gotten way out of control.

Silvanus Sloan was a military history aficionado. He said, "Napoleon beat the coalitions against him by taking them out one at a time then turning them against each other. If there was a way..." He looked over at Hawkins, who was nodding his head in agreement.

Hawkins grinned approvingly at Silvanus and then turned to Mr. Patel. "What if, just for the sake of argument, somebody was to tip off these Daesh maniacs that Zeta is planning to betray them?"

Patel replied, "Why, they'd massacre their instructors... oh. I see."

Hawkins cursed his lack of a proper voice once again and continued in his whisper. "These Daesh clowns are very volatile, all hopped up on emotion and religion; it's likely they could hurt Zeta pretty badly, maybe even finish this bunch. Not real likely though, more likely that Zeta will kill them all. Disciplined fighters, trained by the best will usually defeat that kind of trash once the surprise wears off. Particularly if they have a contingency plan and I'd bet they do. I would."

Mr. Patel was thoughtful. "So betray Zeta to Daesh in

exchange for intel on Zeta organization, equipment and camp setup. Let them assume it's between us and Zeta. We assume that Zeta will be badly hurt but that ultimately they will crush the ISIS recruits as the teacher raps the student's knuckles for insolence."

Consequences looked at Hawkins. "You are one cold motherfucker! That could work. Mr. Patel and our good friend El Bastardo will need to have every gunman they can scrape up to finish off the loser." He chuckled grimly.

Patel was starting to get it. "Zeta? We'll swear it was done by the ISIS fanatics who were then righteously slaughtered by an outraged El Bastardo to avenge his Mexican brothers. That should appease the Zeta big shots elsewhere.

"I'll go over this very carefully with El Bastardo at our meeting the day after tomorrow. I'll see you at 7a.m. at the hacienda then and we'll leave from there. I have some phone calls to make."

Consequences looked carefully at Hawkins. "It would be a hell of a shame if good ole El Bastardo were to meet an untimely death avenging his Mexican brothers..."

Daesh of course jumped the gun. They accepted that Zeta was planning to betray them and prepared accordingly. But they too had satellite phones and had a long, excited chat with an ISIS intelligence officer who made some rather sinister suggestions. As always with Daesh, the more dead the better.

Using what must have been hacked Zeta intel, they intercepted El Bastardo as he was just arriving for his meeting with Patel. He was crucified on an X-shaped cross, with seven of his gunmen butchered and his daughter, Consuela, kidnapped.

"What was that infidel pig saying as we nailed him up? Who is Saint Death?"

Consuela had been walking with her head down, her hands tied behind her back. She looked up and said, "She is the patron saint of the *narcotrafficantes*. He put the curse of death on you."

Ahmed slapped her, hard, twice. "Women are not permitted to speak in our camp."

He detailed off four of them to take Consuela to their bivouac.

Men with cold eyes had been watching. The four Arabs didn't get too far.

Hawkins killed two Islamic fighters with his knife and Gerdun another. The last one dropped his weapon and tried to flee. Gerdun laughed quietly and threw his dagger... Consuela had no idea who was who at that point but figured that those were some frightening guys. Yet somehow they didn't frighten her as much as the Arabs had.

Gomez had them covered on overwatch with an AK-74 rifle Mr. Patel had supplied for the mission. He'd been more than a little surprised by how quickly and lethally Hawkins and Gerdun had taken the Arabs down. It was like watching choreographed dancers. They had MP5 submachine guns with suppressors but they chose to use knives. He knew then that they were naturals.

Hawkins blew the whistle and they regrouped.

After untying Consuela, Gomez said, "I think those bad men were going to hurt you."

She replied, "Yes, I believe they were..." and burst into tears.

Assuming they still needed El Bastardo's gunmen, Mr. Patel had Hawkins' team escort Consuela back to the cartel under truce while it was all sorted out. It was a wise move but Mr. Patel had no idea how extreme the consequences would be. Consuela didn't just have 'gunmen'. And she was nobody's fool.

The late El Bastardo had a lot of 'friends' and they trusted his daughter Consuela as a worthy successor. Perhaps more worthy than her lamented father, who often went to extremes... but was she tough enough? They would soon find out.

One of those friends happened to command a helicopter gunship battalion in the Mexican military at a base about 100 kilometers from *Jardín de Dios*, and was persuaded to take one of his assault companies on a very realistic training exercise. After all, why shouldn't he accept a small gift for doing a job that his government should have had him doing anyway? One that provided him with some very real personal and professional satisfaction?

Unidentified helicopter gunships hit the Zeta camp, guns free, spraying salvos of rockets, tracers bouncing everywhere and coming down in tight streams from the sky: a light show of havoc. They made a quick turn in perfect formation and unloaded the rest of their ordnance. Those on the ground had no time to even man the anti-air positions. Nor could they, since Daesh fanatics were throwing grenades at the emplacements and the doorways to the attached bunkers.

Many of the Arabs were themselves destroyed in the hail of fire from the gunships; the choppers flew off at high speed and were gone.

Then El Bastardo's enraged minions stormed the Zeta camps with murder in their hearts, slaughtering Zeta and Arab alike. Consuela demanded that Ahmad be taken alive if possible. She noted contemptuously that Mr. Patel held his meager forces back. 'Covering her flank,' he claimed.

Consuela snarled at Ahmad after his capture by El Bastardo's gunmen. "You asked me once: 'Who is Saint Death?' Now you will know." She had him nailed to an X-shaped cross and continued to question him. Late in the day he told her much. When she knew all she cared to know she had her men rip out his heart and put it with the others. They were to be packed in ice and shipped to an address in Iraq. El Chapo's people would be grateful.

Hawkins and Charmaine were in one of the foxholes covering the interval between Consuela's gunman and Mr. Patel's people, including Claremont's Peruvians on his right. They'd seen the choppers go in. It was breathtaking.

Charmaine grabbed the sat phone. "Billy, it's the major." He nodded and she said, "This is Hawkins, sort of actual. Over."

Major Farooq said, "This is Felix. I've gotten some background on our Mr. Patel. His family is indeed Asian, from India specifically. But they were not Hindu. Other members of his extended family have been associated with extremist Muslim fanatics. This could be significant Billy so don't take chances. I'll inform Claremont as well, over."

Hawkins whispered, "Felix, when we got here there were, realistically, four gangs struggling for dominance. I think I see how this is fixin' to play out, and however it does, one gang remains standing: they've beat the hell out of the rest and provide some security for the locals. I'm not seeing any traditional good guys. Does that make any sense? Over."

Felix understood perfectly and replied, "Billy, we're in contact with Consuela now. She might be willing to take on our Peruvians and my friend Claremont as her personal protection force, exclusive of her less savory operations, if something untoward were to happen to our Mr. Patel."

He continued. "From what she is saying it sounds like she has information that lines up with what I told you earlier. It looks like Patel is a sleeper agent for some Jihadist group or the other and it's likely he betrayed El Bastardo to the ISIS killers. Something unpleasant will be coming his way or I miss my guess. Do not interfere. Repeat, do not interfere. This is Felix, out."

"Mr. Patel. Hawkins..." After the slaughter, Consuela and her crew came up the driveway. She had her gunman wait and walked up to where Mr. Patel stood, looking concerned; he hadn't expected her to survive the firefight.

"Consuela, my dear, are you alright?" Patel had ordered Hawkins's team to shoot her when he raised his hand to his mouth. He failed to notice that they were quietly backing away from him.

Consuela did notice. She raised her HK UMP and fired a long burst at Patel. With smoking gun in hand she looked at Hawkins then over at Gomez, paused and asked, "So why am I still alive? You're his bodyguards. You could have taken me down." Their guns were pointed at Patel's two regular shooters.

Gomez smiled. "We resigned. We figured out that our dear Mr. Patel was tied in with the Daesh freaks right from the start. It seemed likely you'd figured that out as well. We don't like being played for fools."

Consuela looked slyly at Hawkins. "But you do like playing? I've seen your handiwork. If you need a job... I'd take you all."

Hawkins looked at her kindly; he really did sort of like her. "Consuela, if we were going to work for any drug cartel in the world it would be yours. But you know that ain't how we roll. We can't do it and still be us, if that makes any sense."

Consuela smiled sadly. "No, I suppose not. But answer me this: how did you know I wouldn't turn that gun around and shoot at you as well?"

Charmaine grinned at her and said, "Gomez told us you were good people. Besides we were wearin' our vests and you are very precise..." She glanced down at Patel's body, at the tight grouping of shots placed where they'd do the most good. She didn't mention that Gerdun had been concealed in the background with a rifle, watching carefully, eagerly.

Consuela looked affectionately at Gomez who blushed slightly. Hawkins reckoned the team might go home short a man after all.

Felix met them at the airport. "That was well done people. Very clean bit of work. I know it's kind of late but we need to head back to the office now for a briefing. Something has come up."

Charmaine grinned at him and said, "Tomorrow will be fine, major. The world won't end. Billy and I are going dancing!"

Hawkins saluted sharply, grinned happily and then Charmaine took his arm and they sashayed right on out the door. The team began to applaud and even Gerdun and Major Farooq joined in and smiled.

THE END

ABOUT THE AUTHOR

Mike Peirce has been a musician and songwriter, as well as a soldier in an African War and private security agent. His "Red Dirt Zombies" trilogy started life as a musical and draws on his experiences in those other areas. The "Red Dirt Zombies" trilogy is available on Amazon in paperback or Kindle.

The TV show "The Walking Dead" shows the consequences of losing the war against the Zs. Peirce's books focus on the consequences of winning: addressing veteran's issues such as PTSD, alienation and the impact of war on romantic relationships.

"The General's Daughter" has recently been released and, while set in the Red Dirt Zombies world, it is crafted as a stand-alone novel.

Later in the year a non-fiction book called "African Days and Hollywood Nights" is in the works as well as several short stories.

Peirce has stories in a number of anthologies with proceeds going to veteran's organizations, primarily PTSD support.

Contact Mike and he will send you a copy of a new prequel to the Red Dirt Zombies series which includes the origin story of the infamous GPU Agent codenamed "Susie

Creamcheese."

Mike hangs around here and there:

Website: MikePeirceAuthor.com

Facebook: Mikepeirceauthor-157704697938574/

GoodReads: www.goodreads.com/author/show/553311. Michael_Peirce

Twitter: @MPeirceAuthor

Valley of the Shadow
by Pat Moore

"Valley Cove!"

The glossy brochure landed on the table with finality. Cyril eyed it with suspicion and let Ted Robinson squirm with guilt. Ted breathed deep as he took a drag. Wisps of smoke escaped from his tight mouth. He swept one hand through his raggedy, thinning hair—as if it could be tidied.

"Yes," he said awkwardly. "I'm thinking about it."

He took another drag, looking down. "I can't be there all the time, you know," he apologised. "I have to work."

A bitter force of air came from the corner of the room. It

was the wrong answer, even if inevitable.

Ted turned and pressed his head against the windowpane. The dampness cooled his brain. The room was too small, too close.

"That's gratitude," came the voice from the corner. "You bring 'em up—and they jail yer."

Ted closed his eyes. A headache was forming. Gratitude? All his life he had cared; had given his life for his family. "Family, family—take care of your family!" It was a rule that was bored into his soul... and he had done it. Fifty, single, living at home. Caring. Caring—but now? Now he worried. Now the ancient flame of independence had lit again, though he had doused the fire for years.

His thin hand shook as he lifted the fag to his lips. "Dad... I..."

"If your mother were here she'd be sick," sneered the voice. "Turned out of my own home! Mine, mind! Not yours! Not yet at any rate. Huh. Gratitude." He grunted.

Betrayer? Yes. He had betrayed his own feelings, denied his dreams, and told himself that duty ranked above all. Ted chewed the bitter tip and inhaled the stale air. He stooped to stub it out with quivering hand.

"I've got to stop," he mumbled.

"What?" rasped the voice from the chair.

"Smoking—it's bad for me. I've got to stop."

Habit of a lifetime—hard to break. He had no fight left. The image became the comfort, became the necessity— became the need. One thing at a time. It was not the stress, but the symptom.

This was the end. The clock chimed the hour. One more hour of life, gone. One more hour of self-denial, opportunities passed. It seemed he was stuck. No way out; no way back. He should be grateful. He should be honouring—but daily, another part of him was torn. Daily, good memories were buried deeper till they were impossible to find in this heavy staleness that engulfed them both.

What to do? Nothing to be done. Time created the

agonising moments to fill. Against his will, he struck another match.

Burning.

The flame drew him—hope or destruction? Hope was so far away he almost didn't believe in it anymore.

A sharp pain brought him back into the world and he shook the flame out hastily, blowing his blackened fingers, wiping the dirt down his coat.

"Tut." Another glare of disapproval. He had to get out.

"I'll fetch a paper, Dad," he announced and did not wait for a reply. He left—though the newsagent was at the end of the street—hardly a long trip.

With Ted out of the way, Cyril's eyes landed again on the picture of the welcoming house. Valley Cove. There it stood: tranquil white with a lawn of perfect green and the happy, caring couple beaming out their love for you. Cyril let out an exasperated gasp of disbelief at this new predicament. He spoke his mind—if only to the walls.

"They jail yer!"

Sixty years. Sixty years in this house and you want to pack me off to a home. Sixty years of memories and you think they can all fit into a box. Her voice is all over this house—every room calls to me. You want me to close the door and lock it on that?

Cupboards I built, walls I plastered. Hard graft went into this place. We weren't made o' money. We just did it up ourselves. You think I can settle for a chair and a bed?

It's me that's being boxed in. Creaky bones, aches and pains. I can't do what I did and that's a fact... but my brain is sharp. I could still teach you a thing of two—if you would listen. I'm not worthless!

I can't leave; I can't cope. What's to come of it all?

He reached for the now cold mug of tea and wet his lips, grimacing at the brown, bland, tepid water. He put the mug down, adding to the collection of tea ring stains on the table and lifted the biscuit tin. With no thought of dunking, he opened the lid and fingered the folded papers inside—letters, always kept near him now.

In the hospital ward, Eve steadied her hand to write. There was no shock there. She didn't need a medical opinion. She had one nonetheless. Sometimes, even Doctors don't know when to stop talking.

'Write now,' she thought. 'Say it now—while I can.'

To feel the urgency of words—and the loss of ability to speak them!

Write—while you can think—while you can process—while there is life.

She began.

My beloved and best friend

They tell me my time runs short. It becomes hard to think. I cannot concentrate. They give me a TV screen as if I want to waste my life away with trivia. Why should I watch the stories when I am in the drama of my own?

I will write every day, my love. Forgive me if the letters grow short.

There are no tubes. There is no help. I am in His hands now. I want to remember the good and be grateful.

Fifty-nine years of walking by your side and no regrets. We had words but all that is forgotten now. You tried to keep it all together while our lives were falling apart. Illness has taken its toll on you and made you angry. I am not angry. I am numb. I feel detached from life—perhaps because I am leaving it.

Is it better—to know?

It is a heaviness I bear, thinking of you, my childhood sweetheart, my companion for life. You kept your promise. You were faithful even when I pushed you away.

I am tired—so, so tired! Sleep overwhelms me. If you come while I sleep, let me rest. Hold my hand and I will know you are there.

Eve.

Donald peddled distractedly with college planning in his

head. Orders were coming down from on high that his planning was not up to scratch. More detail was needed. What exactly was he planning to say? With a deadline of tomorrow, he had only that night to sort it. He used to believe in life after work; now it seemed that work stole his precious time and threatened dismissal if he did not surrender his hours. He would have done it gladly—if it hadn't been so boring.

'The trouble is,' thought Donald, 'no-one wants the lecture. They don't want Art History—not even on the Old Masters. They just want Art! No-one signed up for history.'

How do you get people interested in bygone lives? Life was for living and that was now! Sometimes he felt that planning was pointless. How to engage students in history?

He thought of his Third Age class. They were his living history. All he really needed was to engage them in conversation and let them share their own life stories. For many, painting was a social tool. The meeting was the point! It was time to rewrite his lesson aims: to deepen friendships; to understand each other; to build a supportive team.

He felt radical. People were the point! In fact, people were the lesson! He really should put more effort into a social life. Just one would be a start—just one person to share a beer with. He was too solitary.

A picture of middle-aged fitness, Donald brought the bicycle wheels to a stop. He dismounted, chained it to the beach rail, and remembered.

This was his route home, if an empty house is a home. He had plenty of time, because there was nothing to rush for and no one to rush to.

The sea breeze called him to attention and he watched the water ebb and flow. He should bring his students there—run an evening class at the rocks—paint the ever-changing seascape: golden sunsets fading to deep red lines streaking the sky; heavy clouds and steely grey waves. The sea was moody, changing by the hour. If it was good enough for Turner, it was good enough for him. He should bring students there—face his enemy, bring the sheer size of it down to canvas.

The under-current; few understood the strength of it. There had always been a secret battle. Turner knew the terrible strength of the deep. Tumultuous waves, stormy skies, choppy waters; ships in danger. Holiday-makers saw no danger. The sea was their playground for a week. Unfortunately, it rarely chose to comply with their wishes.

Voices rode in on the waves.

"Dad, I can swim!"

"Don't go too far."

"Watch me!"

"Mind the rocks!"

His girl, she always did like the rocks. She was fascinated by them, exhilarated by the constant war. There, the sea never won. He saw her hand scoop up stones to skim. How far and how high and how deep was the 'plop' they would make.

Having stretched to its limit, the foam rippled back from the shore. Tiny stones rushed to follow, crying, "Take me! Take me with you!" Their playful innocence was blind to the smoothed sand that stretched to the eye's edge. They would be taken—ground down to small, insignificant particles robbed of individuality, and expected to merge with the rest.

It would be useless for the grain to object. "I didn't come here to be all washed up, no more than I agreed to be in a desert!"

There is a hand of fate.

He fingered the creased photo in his pocket, kept there since the accident: Daddy's girl.

He took a stone and threw, then another and another, till they were more like rocks than stone, more able to lob than throw, more a smash than a plop. Anger. The sea should not have her! It was wrong!

Mist gently covered his face. His tongue searched for the

salt on his lips. The sharpness brought him to consciousness.

Home. Lesson plans would not write themselves.

He had been teaching too long. The enthusiasm of youth had gone, taken over by the shock and desperation of having to meet the monthly mortgage. Many of his students were too young to care. First, he was asking them to read—then to write! When would the painting happen? Did he really mean they had to write about that too?

Nowadays, Don preferred the Third Age. No-one wanted essays from them. (They knew there wouldn't be a class—and classes meant funding!) At least there they could slop colour onto canvas.

He looked back at his bike. Was he getting old? Did he look foolish, riding at his age? Was he simply holding on to the past, trying to look "cool" to the youngsters? Did they laugh behind his back? He began to unchain his bike.

He had thought of moving once—getting away to a cosmopolitan city life, but the sea would not release him. Life and joy moved in for the holiday season but misery returned in the autumn. Empty coffee shops, shut-up kiosks, slow-paced streets: life for the locals. Still, if the complaint was of too much space and sharing your chips with gulls, then the alternative—life in the city—was claustrophobic, noisy, fast-paced and pressured. He couldn't see himself cycling through traffic or stop-starting in rush hour queues. He couldn't see himself parted from *her*.

The mantle clock marked time with its deep and solid stroke. The brochure remained untouched. Ted remained absent without leave. Cyril set aside his anger, only to uncover his despair. The clock ticked on. Why was time so short?

He spoke into the space. It came natural somehow to break the monotony, to talk to his wife. How could he stop the habit of a lifetime, just because she was no more? One step at a time—or never.

Is this it, Eve?

Is it time to give it all up?

I can't clear out the attic. It's Ted's stuff. He should clear it.

Listen to me—as if I could get to the attic at all! Pop-up books, building bricks, soldiers, all stored away. What will he do with it?

You thought of grandkids. That's the problem. You wanted little voices clinging to your legs, licking the spoon and having a dip in Granny's baking tin. You would have lived from visit to visit.

You held on to hope.

Eve took time to savour the contents of the vase. One could sip water and dwell on beauty at the same time. Roses—cut off in their prime, released from the bushes to display their delicate petals for an audience of one. They delivered their best for her that moment. She replaced the cup and her wrinkled, bruised hand reached for her pen. She was on a mission—to write, to bless; to give a gift to the living.

The roses are beautiful. Their aroma reaches my bed.

It is sunny today. The rays pour in through the window and the nurses are all smiles. I imagine I am in a garden—our garden with Ted and a paddling pool. He has his own little world and we have ours. We drink in joy and he pours out water. Our words are all laughter.

Ted will help you when I'm gone. Let him do all the practical things for you. Don't take it upon yourself. Don't keep it all in. Ted will be there for you.

I love my flowers, Cyril. It is just so sad that roses always carry thorns. Why is that? Even with the touch of velvet and the red of wine, pain lies in wait and draws blood. I should have known better than to hold the stem.

I just wanted the perfume—one last time.

Ted turned the door handle slowly, quietly, disbelieving his own actions; at his age, he was sneaking into the house.

'It's not possible,' he thought, 'to go off radar, but even a few snatched minutes of peace, of an absence of aggression, would be worth it.'

He practically tip-toed through the room, hearing the sound of dozing from the chair. The house felt cold—cold and damp. Unhealthy—with an empty hearth. 'Time to roll up paper,' he thought. The Evening News was always recycled into fodder for the fire.

The armchair groaned on and he passed through.

Ted went to the bathroom, stripped to his vest and splashed water on his face. He withdrew the box from his pocket, fiddled with the cellophane, breaking in with his teeth and nails. He administered the patch and held it on his arm, soothingly; a bit of self-care—as if he could will it to begin its healing, as if the simple patch could minister to the wound, keep him calm, free him from his whole situation; a miracle patch.

He opened the door to find his father standing, waiting. "You took your time."

Ted brushed past and into the lounge. The scent of the chair controlled the room. The brown and cream flowers spread boldly over the covers, releasing their perfume. He studied the flattened cushion, mind forming the picture of 'empty'.

From the high-backed upholstery opposite came the accusation even for the thought! Her voice was controlling still. This house would be run on her terms. This room would be ruled by her presence.

He stepped back into the plant behind and was entangled by tentacles. He turned to struggle free as the tree dominated, reaching to the ceiling. It stood as a marshal, tall, forbidding and stern. Each large hand carried its own pair of eyes. He was perpetually watched.

The toilet was flushed and the water pipes rattled.

"It'll be company for you, Dad. You won't feel so alone."

"I wouldn't be alone if you didn't run off every chance you get. I hardly see you. You do live here I suppose—and rent-free?"

"I thought I'd look around, you know—see what's on

the market."

"You got a girl?"

'As if,' thought Ted.

"It's about time if you have. Been tellin' yer for years. It's not natural."

'This is not natural,' thought Ted. 'What would I bring her to? For better, for worse!'

"No Dad, I do not have a girl."

"Humph! You should crack on with it. Life's not forever you know."

But what if it were? Not a forever of failure, of fear, of frustration but of peace? Oh, to find peace!

"We were together for fifty-nine years," he moaned. "Fifty-nine! One more year and we'd have had the Queen's card. She was thinking of it. She was planning a little celebration."

He turned to Ted with moist eyes.

"No-one celebrates fifty-nine—but it's a lifetime, lad. I was with her a lifetime!"

The words choked. He sniffed and fixed his blurred vision on the floral cushion claiming the empty chair. Oh, cruel fate! Ted could not do it—could not take a grieving man from his home, from his wife, from his memories— but neither could he cope, could he give his final years, could he give what was left of his health.

Depression was waiting in the wings. The flame surged within him. Independence burned—hot, fervent, defiant— daring to be quenched again. How could he choose a lifetime of embers, of ashes, living to fulfil no purpose of his own?

The clock chimed its warning. Time was moving on.

"How about a holiday?" The words escaped before he knew it—a mini break for space to think, to breathe, to be!

"I'm going nowhere," came the voice.

'I know' was his inner reply, 'but I am!'

"Just a day! Just a day out.... Maybe the beach. I could push you."

"I'm staying put!"

Ted rose. "I'm going, Dad, just for a day."

A day of freedom.

Abandoned once more, Cyril reached for the tin. Reading Day. Best done while Ted was out of the way anyhow. There is a time to be alone.

Feeling cold. It is damp and dismal outside. The rose has wilted. I could not put it back in the vase properly and the stem did not reach the water. It has been without water all night.

These are things that you need for life, Cyril. Don't shut off the things that feed your life. I am writing this down so that you have it when you can read again.

What do you need for life, Cyril? Find what you need.

I am pulling this blanket around me as tight as I can—as tight as tucking Ted in for a bedtime story. He always had the night light on.

Put the light on if you need to, my love. It is not a time to worry about bills. Have the light if you need it... but I have no fear of the darkness.

"Find what you need."

He shut his eyes up tight. "I need hope," he cried. "I need to know that life is not done; that I still have a part to play, that I still have a chance to give."

He sighed from the soul—heavy and searching. Words formed under his breath.

I need faith. It didn't matter for years. I dismissed it when I was young, strong, making my own way in life. Age... changes you... softens you... makes you think about...

Where are you Eve? Is it true?

Keys jangled in the lock and Donald entered via the kitchen. How could he get down to work when his brain needed de-fogging? Famished, he opened the fridge door and searched for food.

The bottom shelf held "Pasta Splodge", four days old

in a serving dish. Dare he raise the lid? Would the smell of mould greet him? The job of washing up was too messy to contemplate. He left it to fester, untouched.

The menu for tea was an easy affair. It comprised of whatever was left; the universal meal. 'Put-it-in-the-Pot', or 'Pot it!' for short.

One egg, one scrawny slice of bacon, one piece of hardened cheddar. Very well, then. Eggy bread spread generously with brown sauce, flavoured with bacon and cheese, followed by copious biscuits.

Inspired to work, he set about his task with strained calf muscles and clay sweated hands. Of course, the rule would be "Wash your hands!" but there was no wife to tell him off, and he found himself too hungry to comply.

Burning Bacon—sizzling, spitting, cooked to crackling. He was in love with the pan. Taste-buds exploded with anticipation—though the one sliver shrivelled to nothing before his eyes; one bite of delight.

Piled on the plate, he took it into the lounge to munch. The room greeted him with silence. The voices had left. Artificial ones would have to fill the void.

His place was an organized mess:

The pile on the table was College work.

The pile on the sofa was "I'll get round to it" notes.

The pile on the floor was Arts work—his most immediate project, close to the fire. (He liked to sit and roast.)

It signified many burnt toast days, when he just *had* to draw. He had to draw her! She was alive on the page; she was a whole album. A golden plait—though here it was black and white in fine pencil strokes, weighted and crossed. Just the back of her head carried the joy—the swaying tail as she chirped with her friends. Though she flashed him a smile, he kept his distance, respecting her independence and encouraging it.

"Thanks Dad," she would say later. "You're my hero."

"A hero for doing nothing," he remarked.

"No—a hero for being there," she replied. He smiled

wistfully. He had always been in the background, but there—an invisible strength to be called upon.

Why did he do this? It welled up again, that gaping ache, the throbbing head, stinging eyes. It had to stop. Noise—that was the cure; noise to fill the house and drown out the soul. He fumbled amidst a sea of paper for the remote control; buried.

It was a tip.

It was a creative tip.

He was no housewife.

The kettle boiled. He poured hot water into his sixth mug and dunked the teabag. The other eight were piled up by the sink—waiting.

Having used up all the food in the house: no milk, no marg, one crust of bread . . . he was unable to put off the trip any longer. Tonight was grocery night.

The nurse turned her back and left the ward. The tray of soft sloppy mush (some form of stew) was left by her side. The flowers were gone. Eve laid back upon her pillows. Writing would take time tonight. Somehow, the gaps were longer between thoughts.

Funny, I don't feel hunger at all. I know I should eat. I know it is a good plan—but I have no inclination to. Nurse is trying to encourage me. I can't be bothered. Maybe later—but the decision is mine. This bit, I can control.

Do you remember our twenty-fifth? We had a good spread and our Ted cleared the lot. He put on some weight that year! All our friends came. Couples. He should have brought a friend. I'm sure he could have. He never brought anyone round. I would have liked to meet a friend.

Donald never liked the shop. He felt awkward with the wire basket. He wasn't made for pottering and lingering. At least shopping was short, if tedious. There was only one mini-mart attempting to survive the season with inflated prices for a captive audience.

Shopping for one was a pain. Packs were set up for families. He would have to eat more to compensate or good food would go out of date, sat in the fridge. Biking would contain the calories—if he ever considered them to be a problem!

He loaded up with pies, mushy peas, bacon and eggs. A staple menu stuffed into his backpack. A full bag was the end of it so that he could cycle home—his only mode of transport. Cars were too expensive to run when he could virtually walk everywhere. Even the bike was just a time factor and no necessity.

His mind wandered to work. Sad really—though he could at least boast that work and his hobby were one. It should be enjoyed, then. Since when had painting become boring? Since it wasn't his! Creativity cried out for freedom. It did not wish to be chained to copying others—even if they were Old Masters! It did not wish to stick rigidly to exercises and techniques. Teaching alone did not satisfy. The Artist Within had to express their uniqueness, or he would be frustrated even in this creative job.

Art for others paid the bills; art for himself expressed the soul.

The artist could not help but dismount and linger, to see dusk descend—to watch the sun die, to feel the changing atmosphere.

This was why he could not leave, he thought. The horizon was a new canvas every day. Many shades of colour blended subtly by a Master-painter. He had taken years of trial and error to develop his style, but Nature got it right every night.

The truth was he needed colour in his life. Once he had thought in terms of black and white, while his girl had danced down paths of colour... but the accident had ripped the palate from his hand and filled his mind with grey. After that, colour was elusive. Vibrancy had gone. Pastel made brief appearances.

Joy had gone.

On the sea-front was the sculpture extravaganza, designed to inject new life into the ancient place: The Arches. A photo opportunity for holiday romance. Three marble arches from small, to medium, to large—and dancing waters that dribbled, rose and curved into arches of any size or direction; soaking fun for children who tried to run through the loops before they shrank and disappeared.

If only he could go through—find the escape and watch the loop close forever behind him. "Time heals," people say. "Time moves on"—but it was not so.

He imagined there to be a path—a one-direction walk to release, healing, wholeness, but he was stuck in a maze! Circles of doors that swivelled and clicked into place by some giant hands of fate. At times—progress. Doors aligned, then suddenly, out of the blue it seemed, a trigger, a sound, a memory and 'click.' The doors swivelled, and he found himself back there even after years:

Back to how things were.

Back to losing again.

Back to the sweet days of colour.

Back to the grey.

He wanted to padlock the rooms—to never return; to keep time in its place—to keep the past in the past!

He needed a goal. That was it! A goal to look to the future, to move forward, to break out! It was hard to have a goal when normality surrounded, when days blurred into days and he found he himself just existing.

There had to be more to life. There had to be another way.

Life was the real mystery.

When you were young it was a thriller. Even danger had that edge of excitement. You felt empowered. You felt energized and just a bit invincible! If you had no driving purpose it was because you were enjoying just being—enjoying the ride so to speak.

It took school to try to put a purpose in you—try to educate you, make you think of possibilities, set off on a career path. He had no major thoughts of destiny—no prize to strive for. He had spent his days gazing out of the window, seeing pictures in drifting clouds, doodling on books (though the doodles had been pretty good and developed into cartoons and caricatures—to the admiration of the other boys). School tutted and gave him extra Math. They had tried to force grades upon him, but he felt that he had graduated in 'Cut and Stick!'

All his friends left. This quiet, out of season, faded town held no future for their aspirations. He had never 'moved on'. Even if his mind journeyed, the sea called him home.

Life was still a mystery—but no thriller. His girl had gone and he carried a huge void that could not be filled. He was walking wounded.

Many of his students were of the Third Age. Retired. Work-life done. Family grown. They were content to live life in the slow lane and though they had carried the interest for years, no time to pursue Art till now.

No time for creativity in their lives.

She was creative, his dancer. From the first golden princess dress, to the plastic sparkle shoes, she delighted in costume, lost herself in the role and was his princess forever from that moment.

She had grace—a fluidity of movement hard to describe but even ordinary things had style with her. She never walked—she glided. She never squeezed through a door— she made an entrance. Life was short—but she made her music.

Now his life was a lament. He created her again and again on canvas but he could not give her the breath of life.

Outside, Ted breathed in freedom. He closed his eyes to savour the moment. Sound was his space. He heard the distance, the height, and the depth.

Ebb and flow. Ebb and flow. Water overlapping, rolling back the shale. He could hear like he'd never heard before. Senses were heightened. Each sound and layer of sound—

distance, direction—all clear. The sea was healing—giving space, giving comfort. Thin water came slowly, caressed gently like the brush of a hand. Sea breeze whipped the spray to his face delicate as dew. Lips tasted the salt in the air.

He could hear children of a far-away family giggle and splash on the wind. It was enough. The child within him rose, jumped the waves; ran from the biggest ones then back down to the water's edge, playing Nature's game of Tag.

Children!

He opened his eyes and shook off the thoughts.

The cliffs ahead, the water below, footsteps approaching and passing, voices marking the territory... He heard the cry of the gull on the wind. "Feed me! Feed me now, now, now!" The gull, however, would not be fed. Here was where the servitude stopped.

'I should get a job,' thought Ted. 'Any job—doesn't matter, as long as it's more than benefits.'

He would have to be reliable. He would have to be available. He would have to fight his drowning anxiety, his aches and pains, his intangible illness—the sorrow of life.

He could get a house—just a small terrace, two up, two down, maybe by the sea—and he would walk often in this spacious place. He could find a wife. It was not too late— and she would understand, for she would have lived life too... And they would talk over coffee, gazing at the gulls in the cloudless sky through the bay window of some out of season café. They could huddle together and stare at the fire—the comforting flame of stability, of light, of warmth, where the embers would only be signalling the end of hours filled with stillness and peace.

Hope burning.

Over the miles came a church bell ringing, summoning Middle England. Images flashed through his mind: weddings, funerals, tradition, quaint cottages and cricket. He was untroubled by its toll.

There is a call in the land—for those who are listening.

He wandered to the newsagents, where one could buy the latest stories of horror, doom and fear—and a bag of sweets. As he made the exit, Donald rode by on his bike, slowed to stop at the junction.

'Trainers—he's wearing trainers,' thought Ted. 'The emblem of Youth; not for maturing men.' Though he envied their comfort and the rebellious freedom to wear them. After all, who made the rule: 'Thou shalt not wear trainers?'

Donald dismounted and walked the bike nearer to the rocks. He stood, staring. The battering waves crashed, fell back, crashed, foamed back.

Ted crossed the road, paper in hand, to see the view. The rocks stood, resilient. They may be slammed, but they would never surrender.

The sky, turning grey and gloomy, cast its shadow on the deep water.

The men stood a meter apart. Each had his own life to live. It did not require the presence of the other.

"Ted," nodded Donald, in acknowledgement.

"Donald," returned Ted.

Two men, staring—neither wishing to go home. Ted made the first effort.

"I've decided. It has to be done. I can't carry on like this anymore. I have to be free."

Silence—as both considered the concept of freedom— no turning back. 'Burning boats', as the phrase went.

"Life, eh...? Well, you survive, don't you? Survive or drown." He laughed, but his eyes were frozen in time. Hands in pockets, he felt for the photo and held it out.

Ted took it and stared.

The proud father; hands casually wrapped around him. Blonde trestles fell, as Hannah was draped around his shoulders: Carrier. Workhorse. Transport arranger. Taxi-on-tap.

"She would be twenty-three... My daughter. I was married at twenty-three; seems young now but not then. It felt just right then. We didn't know how much we didn't know!"

He stared at the image of a child and added maturity.

"I know what she'd be wearing. Fit for a princess—off the shoulder, wide and swishy, with tiny white roses and trestles in her hair."

He filled up and took a moment.

"Wide as the aisle, that dress. Oh, she'd make an entrance. She always did!"

He turned away. It was just imagination—not real—never to be! Her day would not exist. He would not walk her down the aisle. He would give her away to no-one.

Loss—for what would never be. A silent grief: unrecognized, misunderstood, dismissed. Who would pour compassion on a dream when the world was full of tangible tragedy?

They stood in silence, neither pressuring the other to speak.

"I tried," he said, pressing his lips together fiercely. "I tried to be a good father, you know. I tried to be in her life. She left me. She was taken. The sea took her." He looked down at the creased, fingered photograph. "She would be twenty-three, my daughter."

Ted was a good listener—or, put simply, Donald became aware of doing all the talking. Who wanted to hear all that angst?

"Sorry," he mumbled.

Sorry for feeling? Sorry for longing?

"Sorry for your loss Ted. I heard about your mother."

It was Ted's turn to consider the complexities of life. Grief upon grief. Father was barely making it through the day, he knew—but what of the future? There was no winning way here: deny himself or accept bitter rejection by doing what he must. The outlook was bleak. Oh, to be free!

"I could draw her if you like—your mother. Would he like that? A portrait for the wall. All I would need is a picture."

It was a spur-of-the-moment gesture for an old man in

trouble. Don meant it. Although he hardly knew Cyril, it was time to reach out to community. He was fed-up of work making all the demands. Here was the chance to make a difference to the life of one.

A fragile beginning—but accepted by the briefest of nods. It was a support in Ted's dilemma and the tiny seed of friendship.

"If you have time," muttered Ted.

Don scratched his head. "There's only me now; only one in the house. I'm free. Time—I have too much of it. Food—loses its taste on a plate for one. Conversation—is pretty limited. I talk to myself all the time. I fill the air with my voice. Yeah, I'm free all right. Long live freedom!"

Nothing left to be said, they sat on the beach watching the gulls fly. Water lapped and the sea came close enough to eavesdrop.

Silence.

Don sniffed, nodded his head and stood wearily. Ted stared as the wave retracted.

Don cleared his throat. "Yes. All I need is a photograph, see?" He produced his phone and flicked the screen till his portrait of Anna appeared. "I drew that—from that!" He held the pictures side by side. "Only, I added imagination."

Ted looked at the beautiful young woman drafted in charcoal.

"Twenty-three," repeated Ted quietly. He was captured by her eyes. 'She could have been mine,' he thought. 'If only I had tried. If only I had looked around, been less nervous, been more fashionable.'

The years of denial and pain; the years of loneliness and self-doubt welled up inside him. His breath became louder, broke unsteadily, elongated into sighs.

Through the dew of time the blurred image transformed into a young, carefree blonde, hanging on her father's back, arms wound round his neck. The jewel laughter carried on the seagull's wing.

"My Daddy! My Daddy! My Daddy!"

Fingers tightened round the mental photograph and he grieved...

For the loss of his daughter.

The afternoon was moving on. Autumn dusk was nearly upon them and Cyril's thoughts mused towards the fireplace. There should be a fire tonight, if only for the comforting glow. He reached for the Evening News and began rolling the pages, twirling deftly in strong fingers. When enough were assembled, he lowered his bony body to the ground. 'I regret this already,' he thought. 'I'll need Ted to help me up.'

Close to the grate he built his summit of paper, twigs and coal... and struck a match. He closed his eyes to shut out the world and listened.

No fumbling in the kitchen. No sneaking through the house. He was alone. The actions were his own. He had control. He blew the smoking elements and opened up a double page of news. Covering the grate, the updraft built and he could watch the orange flicker grow strong through the thin and flimsy texture in his hand. He removed it at the sound of the roar.

Flames darted up the chimney like a sea of orange sucked up the sides. Red soot glowed above; flames too high; too fierce.

Cyril stared at the sight, face orange in the glow. Flames danced and crackled. Sparks spat out and fizzled into nothingness. Occasionally, a rebel piece would fall onto the hearth. He should put the screen there now—a barrier between himself and the heat. He should be mindful. Accidents happen.

He turned back to the chair, the tin, the table and Valley Cove. Reaching out, he clasped the sticky gloss cover, opened up to the silky-coloured contents and flung the brochure into the fire. The cover melted. Pages curled, brown-edged. Holes appeared. The flame devoured from within. That was not—and never would be—his home.

Using the poker, he stoked the fire. Ash fell beneath the grate. New yellow burst from beneath.

He reached for the tin. (Confounded knees! He could not get up now. When would Ted return?).

One last letter, unfolded. Words, seen through a background glow.

Time is yours my love—but not mine.

I feel weak. Everything is an effort. Keeping my eyes open is an effort. Keeping my thoughts clear is impossible. Even the pen feels heavy in my hand.

I wish you peace, my love. Where there is life, there is purpose. Find your purpose; unfinished business. Keep the memory. Go to the old places. Get out of that chair. Get out of the house. Let Ted carry the weight, my weary warrior.

I think I cannot write more.

I wish you Life; Beauty for Ashes.

He brought the precious words up to his lips and kissed them. "Rest now. Be at peace now. No more talking. You are with me always—but I let you go."

The letter was in the flame, turning to ashes, but the words, for his eyes alone, were written in his soul.

Beauty for Ashes.

Could beauty come from the darkest place? Could ashes still be replaced with life? After so much within him had died, could there be a hope of more tomorrows?

Cyril watched the precious words disappear. Could he do it? Could he let go of the past? Could he clear out the house? Was there any future left for him alone? One final season was upon him. He could still choose life. Stuck on his knees, the urge to utter a prayer came to mind. Perhaps it was position, perhaps it was hopelessness, perhaps it was a new urgency and awareness forced upon him through the punishment of time. He mumbled quickly, embarrassed to be caught.

He could hear the fumbling coming up the path. A key turned in the door.

Ted would be here to help him stand. They could both

choose life together.

He spoke to the flowered cushion of an empty chair.

"My darling Eve—goodnight."

The door opened. Ted stood there and fresh evening draught blew through the flames.

A quiet in his soul; an end to the fight.

Beauty for Ashes.

THE END

ABOUT THE AUTHOR

Trained in Theatre Arts at Bretton Hall College, Pat Moore has three decades of teaching experience. She has written and directed musical plays and sketches supporting sermons, and has served on the Worship Team for thirty years. Co-writer of Salvation belongs to our God (see many YouTube videos).

Visit praisepen.uk for blogs and resources. Budding songwriters, visit praisepen-academy.thinkific.com for a free Writing from Scratch course.

THE FIRE KEEPER
BY LORI LACEFIELD

FBI Special Agent Frankie Johnson and undercover Drug Enforcement Agent Hector Martinez were working a friendly, safe neighborhood in East Charlotte, North Carolina. Occupied by mostly blue collar, hard-working individuals, the area also contained the sprinkle of bad guys running drugs, committing thefts, and participating in a variety of illicit gang activity. That day, a particular gang member with the rank of High, only one step below that of the Godfather, was expected to make an appearance at a large drug transaction at the warehouse they—DEA, U.S. Marshals, FBI—now secretly surrounded.

And the High, real name of Pedro Poblano and street name of Skull, was a man wanted on multiple federal charges, including murder.

"In position," Frankie said into her hidden mic. Posing as Hector's girlfriend, she was stationed in a car parked in a narrow alley one block from the warehouse. She had acted as one of Hector's street girlfriends a few times before, showing up with him to meets or deals. Most of the time she would remain in the background while he took care of business, just visible enough to be seen and recognized as one of his regulars. That day her plan was to remain in the car, but only until the deal was finished; when she, along with an entire army of DEA, FBI agents, and U.S. Marshals would descend.

She heard various rounds of chat and updates in her ear. "Coming in from multiples," an agent said, meaning the parties to the deal were arriving from different directions, either solo or in pairs.

"Protectors front and center," said another. Meaning other gang members were focused on the warehouse as well, observing for police or rival gang activity.

"Dingo has arrived." Dingo was Hector's street name. He'd entered the warehouse.

In the car, Frankie snapped her gum and checked her make-up in the visor mirror, like any girlfriend would do while waiting for her boyfriend to return. She had to keep acting the part, just in case anyone was watching other than her fellow agents.

"You look sexy with that red lipstick and bandana in your hair," Ben Andrews said on the frequency reserved for the FBI agents. "Like Rosie the Riveter."

She did a bicep curl like on the old WWII posters, and added a middle finger. "Bite me, Andrews."

A hint of laughter. Ben had been Frankie's field training supervisor and the two often partnered together. He was the Charlotte field office's lead behavioral profiler and coordinator with the Behavioral Analysis Unit in Quantico;

Frankie was his second, learning most of what she knew from him.

He liked goading her.

Since joining the FBI three years earlier, Frankie had regularly been tapped to work brief undercover assignments, mostly as the wife or girlfriend of an undercover agent. Part of it was because she had acting experience—her mother was an actress living in New York City and Frankie had practically grown up backstage on, and off, Broadway. The other part was because of her mixed heritage. As the product of a French-African mother and Irish-Italian father, she could just as easily pass for Mexican or Venezuelan as she could a mix of African-American and Caucasian. People had never known how to categorize her, even while growing up in Queens, which was just fine with her. She wasn't exactly the kind of woman you could keep in a box anyway.

"Eyes up," Frankie said. "Just saw the mark pass point one. Paw on the upper right arm and a five-point on the other." Those referred to his tattoos, a three-circle pattern in the shape of a dog paw that was actually a burn rather than ink, the other a star.

"All points ready. Wait for the command," the lead DEA agent said. He was the one in charge, heading up the entire joint-task operation.

"In position," Ben said. Then, on their frequency, "Rosie be ready to jump."

Frankie huffed. "Jump? I'll be lucky to get out. The door of this damn car weighs more than I do." It was true. The car was a 1980s Chevrolet Monte Carlo and she'd had to put some muscle into it when she'd opened the door earlier to hop inside.

The silence that followed extended to five minutes, then ten, then twenty. Frankie could only imagine what was taking place inside. She pictured Hector, A.K.A. Dingo, with his large wad of government cash being exchanged for a haul of heroin with a street value of more than one million dollars. For more than five years, Hector had worked to infiltrate this gang and gain their trust and, finally, this would be his day. Everything he'd worked so hard to expose, the network of traffickers across the state and country, the money laundering operations that went along with it, would soon be shut down. At all those locations, outside homes and workplaces, agents and officers were stationed nearby, simply waiting for the call that Skull was in custody. Then the arrests would be made, a domino effect across the country. Trafficking, racketeering, distribution, and yes, murder.

Frankie had to remind herself of the danger they were in; who they were dealing with. Skull was suspected of ordering the murders of four dismembered gang members found in various dumpsters in East Charlotte, and that was just in the past month. This guy, his tats, his markings, told a story, and there was a reason he'd made it to the rank of High.

There was a disturbance among the people on the street across the front of the warehouse. One of the agents stationed on the rooftop described the movement, the drawing of a weapon by one of the protectors outside, when all hell broke loose.

Gunshots. Screams. Panic.

And bodies started exiting the warehouse from all directions.

"What's happening?" Frankie yelled. She grabbed her Glock, shouldered the car door open, slammed it closed and started to run.

"Something's gone wrong," Ben shouted. "They're scattering. Take cover."

Frankie stopped running toward the street. Cover? The only cover was the car. She headed back, opened the heavy door with a grunt, crouched behind it with her weapon poised between the window and side mirror.

"Frankie, can you hear me?" It was Ben. "Skull is headed your way. Alley-bound."

"In position," Frankie said.

"Don't kill him, we need him alive," a DEA agent yelled.

"If he comes at me, I'm not taking a chance," Frankie shouted.

"Frankie, don't shoot," Ben said. "Chances are he's wearing a vest anyway. Get back in the car. Get down, get your head down so he can't see you. Lay in the seat. Prop open the passenger door but keep it closed, get your feet ready. He's going to run by you. He won't be able to make it through, understand? Not unless he runs over the top of the car."

She could tell Ben was on the move, his breaths huffing and puffing. "Get in position," he continued. "I'll tell you when to kick the door open. A team is on the way. Right behind him."

Frankie jumped back in, not believing that this was what Skull's capture would come down to. She lay down in the seat with her feet against the barely cracked-open door, holding her Glock front-and-center pointing toward the passenger side window. If that didn't take him down, then a bullet to the head would. She'd have no choice.

"He's headed toward the car," Ben said. "In ten, nine, eight..."

She positioned her feet hip distance apart, planted her knees at a ninety-degree angle into a half-curl. Her abdominal muscles screamed, lungs burned with short bursts of air. She held the gun, slightly angled up.

"Seven, six, five, four...."

"Now, Frankie, now!"

She kicked the old Monte Carlo car door straight out, heard its heavy edge scrape the brick of the building next to it and jam, felt the thud of a one-hundred sixty-pound running man losing his momentum against the sudden obstacle. The window shattered as he hit and he grunted, his breath leaving his lungs at the singular impact.

Frankie jumped from the car, aimed her Glock at his head through the now-broken window. "Freeze, motherfucker. You move, you die."

Skull lay flat on his back, dazed and confused. His own gun had taken flight during the encounter with the door and now lay on the pavement near the Monte Carlo's front grill.

Ben arrived with a host of others and kicked the gun further away.

Two of the DEA agents moved in quickly to secure Skull, having him handcuffed and back on his feet in record time. Skull swayed from side to side, still unaware of what the hell had happened.

Frankie lowered the gun, took several deep breaths. "Martinez?" she asked.

The head DEA agent nodded. "Okay. He's okay."

Frankie breathed a sigh of relief. Ben, wearing a navy FBI jacket, his thick, black hair blowing in the wind, leaned on the open car door and offered Frankie a fist-bump. "So, Rosie got the bad guy. Such language though. My ears were burning."

"Save it," she said, returning her Glock to her waistband. Her whole body vibrated more than shook now, the late release of a hose-full of adrenaline. "You know how I get."

"Yes, I do," he said, chuckling.

Ben's cell phone rang and he glanced at the number, wrinkled a brow, and then answered. As Frankie removed the bandana from her hair and wiped the lipstick from her face, she could see a disturbance cross his face. "You sure? Human?"

Frankie stilled.

"Let's wrap this up," the DEA agent in charge shouted from afar, circling the air with his fingers and whistling. Frankie started toward him when Ben grabbed her arm.

"Not you. That was the Special Agent in Charge of the Asheville office. They've discovered a disturbing scene, a body in the mountains, and he wants us to meet one of his agents at the site right away."

*

After a brief pit-stop at the office, Ben informed his boss, Assistant Special Agent in Charge—or ASAC—Manny Vicks, of the call received by the Asheville resident office. A fire in the mountains and something about human remains. Vicks took the news like he took most news, with a grunt and a deep V appearing between the bridge of his nose. Still, he told them to go, as the DEA had promised to handle all of the paperwork from the arrest of Skull. An hour later, Ben and Frankie were on the road, headed to the site just outside the little town of Bryson City, gateway to the Smoky Mountains.

With Ben driving and Frankie navigating the directions provided by the Asheville SAC, they took a left off Highway 74 West near Bryson City and traveled up a second road that narrowly wound up a mountain. From that road, two others, which eventually yielded to dirt and rock outcroppings in an area better served for camping and cookouts than a possible murder. There they found a couple of Swain County Sheriff cars as well another belonging to the U.S. Forest Service.

Frankie and Ben stepped from the car and made introductions. First up was FBI Special Agent Dan McCracken with the Asheville office, a tall man with cropped brown hair and hazel eyes. Second was Swain County Sheriff David Cousins, whose gray mustache and southern drawl was exactly what Frankie envisioned of a North Carolina Sheriff. And lastly was Forest Service Criminal Investigator George Riley, who looked shocked to be called in to something other than illegal outfitting or the theft of government property.

Ben explained their role as coordinators with the Behavior Analysis Unit of the National Center for the Analysis of Violent Crime, or NCAVC, and why the Asheville SAC thought their services might be needed. "He said there's some evidence of pattern behavior? A possible repeat?"

The Sheriff huffed. "Well, we didn't think so until a Park Ranger came to speak with us yesterday after hearing the news about this discovery. Seems he happened upon a similar site about a week ago, but he just thought it was the remains of a large group of campers who'd illegally cut some forest and had themselves a pig roast."

Frankie frowned. *A pig roast?* She didn't like the sound of that.

"He took us to the site yesterday," Agent McCracken explained. "It's about twelve miles southwest of here. The NCBI, as well as the Sheriff's detectives, are there now processing the evidence."

Frankie nodded. The North Carolina Bureau of Investigation was the state agency that helped collect, process, and analyze forensic and lab evidence for criminal cases across the state, and was particularly helpful in aiding small communities without resources or manpower.

"They collected everything here yesterday, but I brought photographs so you can see what the scene looked like in its original state," McCracken added. "The NCBI promised to get the other scene collected, labeled, and photographed today."

Sheriff Cousins glanced over the rise. "Well, it's a bit of a hike so we best get going. Come on in and take a look. Hope y'all didn't eat lunch before you came up."

Frankie and Ben exchanged a glance. *What were they about to see?*

"Lead the way," Ben said.

They hiked a good mile through wooded terrain before they came upon the clearing—a particularly flat stretch of land approximately fifty feet wide newly cut clear of trees. In the center was a large circular fire pit made from rocks and four logs, each pointing in a different direction. Six feet or so above the pit was the remainder of a crude bed made from sticks and bark stripped from the cleared trees and mounted on four poles.

"Don't tell me..." Ben said. "You found a body up there? A burned body?"

"What remained of it," Sheriff Cousins muttered.

"What? Like a sacrifice?" Frankie asked. She glanced up, feeling the chill grip her. "What the hell?" she whispered, uncertain if she was asking the others or herself.

"That's what we're hoping you could tell us," Cousins said. "And who the hell could, or would, do such a thing."

"And why," Agent McCracken added.

Careful not to disturb the scene, in case the NCBI needed to return to document any additional details, they walked the perimeter and took notes. About twenty feet out from the sacrificial bed, a large circle had been drawn in the dirt around the site and divided into seven sections. In each of those sections lay a single evidence marker.

McCracken brought out the photographs. "In each section was a tin cup."

"Containing what?" Ben asked, alarmed.

"First glance, a little bit of dark liquid stain, but thankfully it didn't appear to be blood, which was my first thought," Agent McCracken said.

It was Frankie's too. She wished she could've been there to see the evidence first-hand: to have picked up one of the cups, sniffed and taken a look, but that was a rare occurrence for profilers. They usually got called in after the scene had been processed, forced to resort to photographs, autopsies and lab results.

She knelt outside the circle to get a better look at the ground. McCracken knelt with her and handed over additional photographs. "Scattered in the dirt here, both inside and outside the circle, was what appeared to be various animal parts—feathers, fur, and bone—and also a well-worn path of footprints. You can still see them."

Up close, it appeared to Frankie as if the footprints were many, of various sizes, and had been gone over many times. *Walking in a circle? Stomping? Dancing?*

She stood, not liking the beginnings of the profile developing in her head.

"Are we thinking one individual did this, or a group?" she asked. "Footprints are different sizes." She wheeled toward

McCracken. "Did NCBI indicate if the substance was the same in all seven cups? Different DNA?"

He shrugged. "They won't know until the analysis comes back."

"It's a group," Ben said, hands on hips. "I feel certain of it."

Frankie took a deep breath. So, they weren't profiling or searching for one unknown subject, or unsub, but several. Most likely, seven. One for each section of the circle. One for each of the seven cups.

"Do we have any idea of who the victim, or victims, might be?" Ben asked. "Anyone reported missing?

"No," Sheriff Cousins said, with a deep frown. "Which is concerning because the medical examiner said the bones... they looked young. Maybe not a child, but a teen or young adult." He wiped a bear paw of a hand across his mouth, as if the thought made him sick.

"Which reminds me," McCracken said. He reached inside his pocket and removed two vials of ashes. "The M.E. and NCBI were wondering if you might be able to speed up the analysis of the ash content—get a detailed list of the types of plant and animal life contained in these ashes. It appears many substances were added to the fire."

"Sure. We can coordinate with the lab in West Virginia," Ben said. "They have the detailed DNA of everything you could imagine." He signed-off on the chain of custody McCracken provided and put the vials in his pocket. "I'll work with them to get this expedited. They'll understand that what is contained in these ashes could be the clue to finding our unsub or unsubs."

Sheriff Cousins removed his hat and scratched the tufts of white hair remaining on his head. "I think that sounds like a fine idea," he said. "And tell them to make it snappy. We got us two burned bodies in two weeks, and I fear what we might find in the weeks ahead."

Ben nodded. "Unfortunately, I think your fear is well-founded." He turned to Agent Riley, who had remained quiet the entire time. "Does the U.S. Forest Service have an extra patrol they can bring in? Watch for cutting or burning, seven or more men who may be camping or hiking in the area?"

Riley, who continued to appear as if he were trapped in some sort of live nightmare, gave a nod. "Yes, sir, I'll reach out to the other Ranger Districts here. We have three here in the Nantahala Forest. I'll get as many rangers relocated as possible." He immediately stepped aside and reached for his phone, seeming happy that there was something he could finally take charge of and help in the investigation.

Ben turned back to Agent McCracken and the Sheriff. "Let's try to keep this out of the media as long as possible," he said. "I'm concerned that if word gets out, if the perpetrators know we've discovered their sites and are scouring these woods searching for them, they may move their operations elsewhere. If they do intend on performing another ritual or sacrifice... whatever this is, our best chance will be able to locate the site and move in as they gather."

"What makes you think they don't already know?" McCracken asked. "All these techs, law enforcement, and others here?"

"Maybe. Or maybe they're focused on their next site," Ben said.

Sheriff Cousins cringed at Ben's words. "So that's it? You don't think this is over?"

Ben bowed his head and shook it. "No, I don't. You've got two victims—unless there are others out there we haven't found yet, I'd expect five more. The number seven is too evident here. It has a purpose, a meaning, I'm certain of it.

"Speaking of which," he said to the Sheriff, "see what you can find out about any missing persons in the area. Runaways included. Look back as far as a year ago."

With the orders given, they all gathered to return down the ridge. Frankie took one last look at the scene before heading out and saw a torch just outside one of the boundaries of the circle, its flame continuing to flicker, unwilling to die out.

Fire. An essential element to life. But she had a sick feeling that, until that flame was extinguished, this nightmare wasn't about to end.

Frankie and Ben drove back to Charlotte with a promise to try and get some sleep, taking some time to think about what they'd observed before deep-diving into research the following morning. They also hoped to get some preliminary results and analysis from the NCBI or even the FBI lab within the next couple of days; Ben's first act on his return to the office was overnighting the vials of ashes to West Virginia.

The next morning, Frankie stopped to get her morning jolt: a large coffee with three shots of espresso and two sugar donuts. She settled into her office, decorated with the framed posters of various plays her mother had performed in over the years, and waited for Ben. He arrived moments later, fresh from a shower, smelling of aftershave and his hair still damp.

Instead of coffee, Ben brought in his morning regular—a smoothie with a blend of kale and spinach, berries, and protein powders. He was the healthy one.

"Insights and revelations?" she asked Ben between bites of donut.

"You first," he said. This was typical Ben: always the teacher, never influencing her thoughts on profiling one way or the other. He let her form her own views, then offered pro or counter opinions of his own along with detailed explanations as to why he did or didn't agree. She had learned more from him in three years than the previous ten from textbooks.

"Pretty obvious to me it's ritualistic. You've got fire, what looks to be the use of animal feathers and bones, the residue of plants and herbs in the fire, and possibly in the drink as well. Walking or perhaps even dancing in a circle."

Ben was nodding. "Yes, and let's not forget the human sacrifice and seven sections divided within a circle. Seven is a number of great importance in several religions, both ancient and modern."

"Yes, as is human sacrifice," Frankie added. "My initial instinct leaned toward some type of satanic or pagan ritual, but most of what I've studied on satanic ritual involves the numbers five or six. Here, we seem to have four and seven. Four logs of which the primary fire was built on top and, something I noticed only this morning while examining the photographs, they seem to be pointing north, south, east, and west. Plus, the use of seven participants and seven cups. Not sharing one cup, but separate, distinct cups. What's your take on that?"

"I'm not sure yet. Without knowing what was in the cups, it's hard to make a solid determination. A substance, like blood, consumed from one cup and shared among those who partake would seem to symbolically make them one, or whole. Separate cups tells me they each retain their identity, but partake of something in common that helps strengthen each one in some manner."

Frankie finished the last bite of her donut, swept her hands of sugar and grabbed her laptop. "Well, let's get down to it, see what we can find out. Search not just for rituals, but ceremonies and festivals, anything that involves fire and sacrifice."

"Already on it," Ben said.

They both settled in, Frankie with her coffee and Ben with his smoothie, exploring the realms of rituals and ceremonies. Frankie headed to the internet to conduct an advanced search, having gained an understanding of keywords, metatags, and algorithms from a particularly geeky boyfriend during her senior year at Georgetown. Friends in her psychology club had marveled at seeing her skills on display one night as she studied for her senior thesis, finding something hilarious at the regular sight of this woman in a library with a do-rag, dreads, and square reading glasses flying through web pages and search sites like a computer hacker. Looking back, Frankie thought the bad sex with the guy had been worth it, just for the knowledge he'd provided her with. The dreads and do-rags had long gone, but the research skills remained.

She talked through the topics as she read. "The Celts held a sacred fire festival on the first of November to mark their New Year, when they would ceremonially extinguish their hearth fires then relight them from the King's fire," she told Ben between sips, unsure whether he was listening or not. "There is a Taoist celebration that involves walking barefoot across burning embers. For them, fire is believed to overcome impurity and repel evil influences. Walking over fire signifies a man's strength over evil. No sacrificial elements though that I can see with either."

Frankie read the next one, grunted. "Ugh. Here's one where a corpse is cremated and the resulting ashes are mixed with fermented banana before being consumed by the tribespeople. They do this to make sure the spirit of the deceased continues to live among them."

She glanced over at Ben drinking his smoothie and winked. "Hey, you sure that powder you add in the morning is protein?"

"Funny," Ben said, a green mustache lining his lip. "You're funny."

Frankie cackled. A minute later, her laughter faded.

"Listen to this," she said. "The New Fire Dance of the Cherokee. The fire, conducted in the spring, is presided over by seven persons chosen to kindle the new fire, representing rebirth or renewal. Often each individual will sacrifice something of value to the sacred fire, be it food, plant, or herb."

Ben glanced up from the screen of his laptop. "Or a young human?"

"I don't see anything to suggest that, but, who knows?" She tapped a few additional keys and brought up a map of western North Carolina. Bryson City was just minutes outside the Qualla Boundary in the Oconoluftee River Valley, the land the U.S. Government had given the Eastern band of the Cherokee and where many still resided.

"You think it's a coincidence the sacrificial sites are near the Cherokee Reservation and lands?"

Ben tightened his lips. "I'm not sure. I hope it is a coincidence, because I really like those people, especially their Chief: William 'Red Crow' Walker. I've had the occasion to meet with him. He's an honorable man." He read the description of the fire ceremony over Frankie's shoulder. "Damn, I hate to think one or more of their own might be responsible for this, but we'd better go pay him a visit, get his thoughts on the matter."

Ben's cell phone rang and he put the call on speaker. It was the FBI lab.

"Agent Andrews? Analyst Sarah Wilders. How are you? Or is that a stupid question?"

"I've been better. What do you have for me?"

"It's very preliminary. I've just started the analysis, but I can tell you your ashes contain the residue of a variety of animal and plant life. So far, hits on bird, rabbit, and deer, and ginger root, blackberry, sumac, and rose. You get the idea."

"A regular witches' brew," Frankie piped in.

"When will you have a detailed analysis?" Ben asked.

"Give me three days," Sarah said.

Ben thanked her and hung up. Before he could say something else the phone rang again. This time it was a lab tech with the NCBI. "We're going to send you copies of everything we have so far later today, but I wanted to give you a call and let you know—we were able to analyze the residue in three of the cups."

"And?" Ben asked when the tech said nothing further.

A hefty sigh. "And it appears that your unsubs that participated in the sacrifice? They took a blend of the ashes, including the human remains, mixed it with some natural black bark tea, and um... drank it."

Ben hung up and grabbed his suit coat. "Come on. Let's pay a visit to the Chief."

William 'Red Crow' Walker had been Chief of the Eastern Band of the Cherokee for six years. Although short in nature, he was formidable in his own right, a stout man whose weathered skin told of more years spent outside than in, and whose alternating gray and black braids seemed to reveal his growth and wisdom as a man, much like the individual rings in a tree. His walk was as slow and purposeful as the words he spoke and, as soon as she met him, Frankie could immediately sense she was in the presence of a force—a man who exuded a life energy that existed in very few.

Chief Walker told his assistant to hold all calls as they followed him into his office. To describe it as an office was really a misnomer; the moment they entered, Frankie could tell it was more of a museum. Surrounding them on the walls were photographs of chiefs and clans that went back to the mid-1800s, as well as a detailed depiction of the Trail of Tears. A copy of the deed and land trust of the Qualla boundary was displayed, as well as a historic photo of the East and West Chiefs reuniting the once separated bands at Red Clay, Tennessee in 1984.

Frankie marveled at a poster displaying the Cherokee alphabet's 85 letters and the various artifacts housed in glass cases—a peace pipe, a blowgun and assorted hand tools. Although she'd heard and read about the Cherokee, nothing quite equaled reality. Textbooks were one thing, but to be sitting across from an actual chief and viewing the historical documents and artifacts of their people was quite another.

"I see you have some interest in our history," the Chief said to Frankie. "We have a wonderful museum here. My beautiful niece works there. I am certain she would be happy to give you a private tour."

Although she expected him to have an accent, he spoke perfect English and even had a touch of southern twang.

With all the history around her, she had to remind herself this wasn't 1860. "I appreciate the offer, sir. Perhaps another time when we're not working. Unfortunately," she said, taking a seat in a soft leather chair next to Ben's, "the case we're working on is quite urgent."

"Agent Andrews indicated as much on the phone. So, what can I do for you?"

With some caution so as to not offend the Chief in any way, Ben explained the two crime scenes discovered in the Nantahala National Forest outside of Bryson City, followed by a question of whether they could be related to a Native American ritual or ceremony in some way. Ben described the items recovered in detail, including the mix of ingredients in the ashes. As he spoke, the crevices in the chief's heavily lined face deepened.

He sat in silence, frowned. "What you describe is most disturbing. You are certain the remains in the sacrificial bed are human? Of Native American descent?"

"Human, yes, but we're not certain of the ethnicity or identity of the actual victims. The Sheriff and his team are actively seeking out missing persons, as are other agents in our field office. So far, we have no possible matches," Ben explained.

"Are you aware of anyone missing off the reservation?" Frankie asked.

He thought. "No, not that I'm aware. Should I warn them?"

"Maybe later," Ben said. "First, what we really need is to gain an understanding of the individual, or in this case individuals, that we might be searching for. Whether they are Native American or not, if they are mimicking some ritual or ceremony similar to a Native American one, we need to understand what their motive might be in conducting such a ritual so we can find them."

"Let's start with the basics," Frankie said. "What can you tell us of the people here? What is daily life like?"

The Chief shrugged. "To most people's surprise, life

inside the reservation is not much different than life outside, with a few exceptions. We have our own independent government, consisting of a Chief and a Vice Chief, a legislative council of twelve, and our own judicial branch. We pay for schools, fire, water, sewer, and emergency services without assistance from the federal government. Our schools teach the same curriculum as other North Carolina schools, although we now include the Cherokee language. Twenty years ago, we were in great danger of losing our language, as our elders began to pass and our people feared teaching the younger generations Cherokee would isolate them from the mainstream. But we discovered the error of our ways, the value of our language, and now, our schools only teach in Cherokee.

"Otherwise, the people here work, and live, much as the people elsewhere. Many are employed here in the city, selling the creative works of our people, or in tourism, taking the visitors rafting and hiking."

"What about ceremonies and festivals? Any specific ones still practiced?" Ben asked.

"In particular the New Fire ceremony?" Frankie added. "That one, at least from the minimal research I was able to do, seemed closest in description to the scenes we found in the forest. As well as the timing, near the spring equinox."

Chief Walker nodded. "Yes. The New Fire, or the Sacred Fire, as we refer to it, is still practiced. It is presided over by seven persons chosen to kindle the new fire of spring. The fire is to be created using the bark of seven different kinds of trees, selected only from the east side, and must be free and clear of blemish. One man, called the Fire Keeper, is in charge of feeding and tending the fire, to make certain the fire never goes out. It is a significant role. Fire represents the spirit of our Creator, of the sun, the life-giver of the people, and the Cherokee have kept it burning for centuries."

Frankie thought back to the scene on the ridge the day before, that single flame still flickering from the torch at the edge of the clearing. The Fire Keeper. It seemed to fit. The prior day's chill returned to the back of her neck.

"To explain to you how important fire is," the Chief continued, "at Kituwah, the birthplace of our people, where the Creator handed down the laws and gave us the gift of fire, there existed a mound in the middle of the fields where an eternal flame was lit. Members of distant villages would walk hundreds of miles to visit the flame. They would leave dirt or ash from their village on the mound before collecting a part of the flame to take home.

"Even during the Trail of Tears, when our people were forced from our lands to Oklahoma, it is said the fire travelled with them."

He paused for a moment, as if to reflect on that solemn time.

"Fire is also central to the Stomp Dance, held near Labor Day. There are grounds with seven arbors, one for each clan, placed in a circle. Seven medicine men, representing each of the seven clans, conduct the ceremony."

Frankie and Ben regarded each other. She knew they were both thinking the same thing—seven clans, seven cups, seven individuals.

Chief Walker looked uncertain if he wanted to continue the story. He raised himself from his chair and walked across the room to a bookshelf. He removed a book, thumbed through the pages and set it open facing toward Ben and Frankie. He pointed to a photo.

"Four large logs representing each corner of the world are placed as the base of the fire. The Fire Keeper arrives and creates the fire. Each of the medicine men add special roots and herbs of healing power to the fire, to make it stronger. The members make small offerings, a piece of food or herb of their own. In this way, each member gives thanks to the Creator. Then there is the smoking of a pipe. Every member of each tribe will take seven puffs off the pipe before passing it to the next member. They are all partaking of the same fire and its healing properties. Many ceremonial dances are also held. The first dance is by invitation only, followed by a dance representing an important element of Cherokee life—the sun, bear, deer, warpaint, birds, wolf, savannah."

Frankie again glanced at Ben. She could see him absorbing the Chief's words, knew he was analyzing them in conjunction with the evidence collected at the crime scenes and formulating ideas about the profile of the unsubs they sought. She too was generating opinions on the matter.

"What is the significance of the East?" she asked. Her fascination of their heritage was in earnest. Part of it was to build an accurate profile of the unsubs they sought, yes, but the rest was personal. Like her own ancestors, captured off the shore of Africa and taken to Louisiana to be slaves and house servants, these were a hearty people who had survived many tragedies.

"The red light of the sky that immediately precedes sunrise is said to hold miraculous creative powers," Chief Walker explained. "It represents hope, determination, and life. East is where the giver of life rises and is born. West is where it dies, until its renewal."

The sun, the life-giver. The fire, the creator. She wondered why there was no reverence for air or water, as in many other ancient religions.

"Your description of the ceremonies included the description of four logs and seven medicine men," Ben said. "Those numbers, four and seven, they are important to Cherokee culture?"

"Yes. The numbers four and seven are significant, even sacred, to the Cherokee. The number four signifies the four corners of the earth—north, south, east, west—and of wholeness. The number seven is rebirth and renewal, as the Sacred Fire Ceremony itself represents. There are seven clans of the Cherokee, and seven councilors, one representing each clan, who preside over the festivals."

He seemed to hesitate before continuing, but as soon as he did, Frankie understood why. The topic nobody wanted to broach.

"Ceremonies also used to include a larger sacrifice every

seventh day and in older times, a major sacrifice every seven years."

And there it was. Frankie took a deep breath.

"Sacrifice? What type of sacrifices? I thought you just said most Cherokee offerings were a bit of food or herbs?" Ben said, sounding a bit accusatory.

"Yes," Chief Walker said. "It is true. In current times, anything else wouldn't be acceptable. Only items that add power and healing to the fire are approved as offerings. Adding any item of impurity or desecrating the sacred fire in any way is forbidden. Children are taught very early to respect the sacred fire. They are not allowed to even approach it without permission."

Ben cracked his knuckles, a habit he often displayed when his nerves and adrenaline were running on high. "Okay, let's just get it out there. I hate to ask, but what about human or animal sacrifice?" he asked. "Is that, or has it ever, been part of these ceremonies, or others?"

Chief Walker frowned. "Again, it is not part of our ways now," he emphasized. "Life is sacred to the Cherokee. All life. Even an animal's life taken to be consumed is first prayed over, thanks given. But..."

The skin around the Chief's left eye twitched.

"I cannot say for certain that animal or human sacrifice was never in practice. There have been rumors of occasional bands, religious gatherings, where sacrifice was practiced."

Frankie considered those words, thinking that they accurately represented the unsubs they were searching for—a rogue group of seven people whose religious ideology had taken a turn for the older ways.

Ben squirmed in his chair, likely dreading the next part he had to discuss with the chief. "It appears that those who attended may have... consumed the ashes after the sacrifice. Do you know why they might have done that?" he asked.

Chief Walker grunted, clearly disgusted and bothered by Ben's words. "That is also not of Cherokee tradition, although I have heard of it. To offer a sacrifice of a young life with much purity is said to gain their youth, vision, and future life for yourself. In this way, those that sacrifice act much like the role of a night goer, the entity who comes at times of illness to hasten death and take the remaining life of another for themselves."

The hairs on the back of Frankie's neck stood up. The night goer. These were the type of stories she often heard from her Cajun grandmother, who still resided in Louisiana. Acts of sacrifice, voodoo, spells. She assumed such tales resided within all religions.

"I desperately wish to believe than none of our people could be involved in this matter that you describe. It would be..." Chief Walker shook his head. "It would be of utmost disgrace to our community and I fear, would do great harm to the reputation of our people."

He stood. "May we step outside? I need some air."

"Of course," Ben said.

They followed the Chief out and joined him on the boardwalk that ran the length of the little downtown area. Solemnly, he glanced across the street, at the little shops peddling blankets, hats, baskets, and bowls. Visitors window-shopped, children ran and played. "So much could be lost by this," he said.

Frankie followed his gaze and felt empathy for him. "Look, I certainly hope none of your people are involved in these acts, but could you put word out to the community to notify you of anyone missing, or who may have recently left the reservation? We're looking for upwards of nine individuals at this point, two possible victims and seven participants. Even locating one could lead us to the rest."

The Chief nodded reluctantly, and Ben and Frankie thanked him and told him they'd be in touch. As soon as they reached the car, Frankie asked. "What are you thinking?"

"Seven clans, seven sacrifices..." Ben said. "I don't like it."

"One every seven days," she added.

Ben started the engine. "Right. Which means we're

down to just three days before we have our next victim. Not good. Not good at all."

As they headed out of town and into the heavily wooded area where the roads wound and twisted, Ben spoke of the profile and Frankie typed notes on her laptop. "We're looking for seven individuals with at least some knowledge of Native American culture. Even though I'd like to believe otherwise, my inclination is that the unsubs are Native American, specifically Cherokee," he said.

"Agreed," Frankie said. "And I would put their ages in the twenty to thirty range. They're young, male, and they want to bring back the old ways. The question is—why? Do they feel the new ways aren't working? Do they feel powerless? Chief Walker mentioned the sacrifice of someone young could mean they are hoping to gain some part of that individual's future life or wisdom."

She started to type in these thoughts when Ben suddenly slammed the brakes and pitched Frankie forward. The laptop flew from her hands and crashed to the floor. Only the seatbelt kept her from hitting the dash and windshield.

Ben muttered and cursed. "What the hell?"

Her hands had instinctively gone over her head for protection. When she realized she was okay, she slowly returned them to her lap and glanced out the window. In front of the car stood an old man in a plaid shirt and jeans, with black, shoulder-length hair and a walking stick four-feet high. He stared at the car, refusing to move.

Frankie and Ben unfastened their seatbelts and slid from the car. Although Frankie sensed no harm from the old man, she kept the palm of her right hand on the butt of her Glock. In contrast, Ben exposed both hands, showing he was of no threat. "Are you okay?" Ben asked, his voice shaking. "I nearly hit you."

"You're from the FBI? You're the two?" the man asked. His voice carried over the wind whistling high in the treetops. His skin was weathered and naturally scarred, much like the mountains he lived in.

Ben nodded.

"Come," he said. He turned and took off into the woods.

Ben glanced at Frankie and put his hands up in a small questioning gesture. They both shrugged, figuring it couldn't hurt to hear the man out. They left the car parked on the shoulder of the road and started down the path, following the man with plaid shirt and walking stick.

They came to a cabin, where he stopped outside the porch.

"I saw Red Crow's message go out to the people but a minute ago, asking about missing individuals. Just yesterday, I realized I had not seen Wild Bear in many days. I went to his place, here, and discovered some things which made no sense—until just now, after I spoke with Red Crow and he briefed me on your visit."

He motioned to them and opened the door. "Please, come."

Ben ducked through the door jamb and Frankie followed, her heart racing. Inside was a small living area with paneled walls, a tattered brown couch and a coffee table with rings. To the right was a tiny kitchen and a dining room with a round table and four chairs. The entire place was a mess, dirty dishes and food left on the counter and sink, papers all over the table, laundry on the floor.

"Yesterday, I found this." The man with the walking stick grabbed a notebook off the table containing pages and pages of writing, handed it to Ben.

Ben opened it. "This is written in Cherokee. I can't read this. Can you interpret it? Also, who are you and how do you know this Wild Bear? Are you related?" he asked.

The man paused, clearly realizing he had jumped ahead. He motioned to the table and asked them to sit. "My name is Randall Blevins. I am known as Walking Stick. I am a medicine man, a healer and high priest of the Cherokee people.

"Wild Bear was, is, my student. The Cherokee believe

that every individual is granted a gift from the Creator. Each of us knowledgeable in our ways seek children with similar gifts. When I met Wild Bear, I saw a young man with a tremendous spirit and the gift of counsel and influence. I believed him to be a future high priest. I started teaching him the sacred texts, the laws handed down to us at Kituwah.

"He began to grow wise and embrace his role. Learned of medicines that heal, of our religious ceremonies and festivals. I gave him the role of the Fire Keeper last year, and that's when things began to change. He developed an obsession with the sacred fire and Keetoowah."

Frankie thought about the brief profile on the ride here. And now they had a suspect that matched their unsub. Likely the leader of the seven. The Fire Keeper.

"What is Keetoowah?" she asked.

"The Keetoowah are the religious arm of the Cherokee people. When the Keetoowah first formed, they had to hold their meetings in secret as the Europeans related their practices to voodoo or witchcraft—as they tended to do with anything outside their knowledge. The members of the Keetoowah could only recognize other practitioners by the way they gripped their lapel or tilted their hat.

"Wild Bear studied intently the Keetowah, and also the fulfilling of the prophesy made by Cherokee religious leaders following the Trail of Tears—that in the seventh generation following the forced relocation of our people, the Cherokee would return to power."

Frankie churned over all the details in her mind, trying to take it all in. All the history and information being conveyed in such a short time was overwhelming, yet of grave importance. "Let me guess," she said. "These Keetowah, they have seven members?"

Walking Stick nodded.

Frankie sighed. "Any idea who the other members might be?"

"Their names are in the book. I didn't recognize all the

names, but I can tell you each will come from one of the seven clans."

"What else is in the book? What does it say?" Ben asked. He looked eager, ready to bolt, to call in resources and a helicopter and go chase Wild Bear down.

"It is a recording of his beliefs, his own teachings. In it, he says he has heard the voices of our forefathers and of the great Creator. He says the sacred fire speaks to him. He calls for a new Keetowah, and of seven great sacrifices to take place this year and every seven years thereafter. He says it is his responsibility to renew Keetowah, to receive and interpret a new set of rules and, through their implementation, finally fulfill the promise of the Seventh Generation."

"Wait," Frankie interrupted. "I thought I read that most Cherokee believed that the prophesy had already been fulfilled by the reconciliation of eastern and western bands in 1984?"

"Yes, that is true. But Wild Bear, he does not believe this."

Ben stood and whipped out his phone. "We need people up here. We need a warrant to search every piece of this cabin as well as the homes of the other names listed. Walking Stick?" he said, turning to the man. "We need you to interpret every word of this... manifesto. Can you do that?"

"Yes, of course. I will begin right now."

Just then the door of Wild Bear's cabin opened and Chief Walker appeared. He seemed greatly shaken, his legs trembling upon standing. "I have some news... it is not good. My daughter just called. My grandson, Young Rabbit, is missing."

Over the next twelve hours, everything went into hyperdrive. Search warrants were issued and served on multiple homes. Analysts arrived to comb through Wild Bear's laptop and every person, website, and social media service with whom he interacted. That activity turned up the photographs of the seven, including three who were members of the western band of Cherokee in Oklahoma. A conversation between the two Chiefs led to the discovery that not only were those three individuals missing, but two younger members as well: one a seventeen-year-old girl and another a fourteen-year-old boy. The FBI out of the Tulsa RA was on their way to collect DNA from family members.

Extra rangers from the U.S. Forest Service, members of the National Guard, as well as the members of the Cherokee themselves, took to the Nantahala Forest in record numbers, searching for the seven that may have taken Chief Walker's grandson. The anger, outrage, and grief among them was apparent, as women wailed and men spoke in harsh tones. Frankie imagined it was the same so many years ago, when the tribes prepared for battle.

Though his exhaustion was clear, Walking Stick stayed with them, continuing to interpret every document, email, or posting written in their language.

While techs and analysts dusted, collected, and labeled the evidence, Frankie and Ben huddled together in a corner of the room trying to figure out the motive of the seven to take the Chief's son, and where they might set up the next sacrifice.

They knew the clock was ticking: two-and-one-half days and counting now.

They would not sleep, would not rest, until Young Rabbit was found.

"What do we know about the clans, Ben?" Frankie asked, pacing and circling the table as if she was conducting a dance of her own. "I feel like the clans have to play a major part in this. The missing girl and boy are said to be of the Long Hair and Panther clan, as are two of the three western band members taking part in Wild Bear's council. What if each of them is required to select one of their own?"

Ben glanced over the photographs they now had of each of the seven individuals recruited for Wild Bear's new Keetowah. "I think you could be right. Seven sacrifices, one from each tribe, a selected member with... what? Untapped wisdom, youth, or power?"

"But Young Rabbit is also part of the Long Hair clan, isn't he?" Frankie said.

"No," Chief Walker said, overhearing their conversation and joining them. "Clan lineage is through the maternal line. I am Long Hair, but my daughter is Wolf, as is my grandson."

He hovered over the table, examined the photos of those that had betrayed his people. "What you speak of, you are correct. They believe that by sacrificing and taking part of one of future promise, they will inherit their gifts. Including my grandson."

His hands shook as he picked up one of the pictures. "This man, Marcus Fairweather of the western band, is of the a-ni-gi-lo-hi, or Long Hair tribe," Chief Walker said. "My tribe. The Long Hair is a tribe of peace and negotiation. Of welcoming strangers. The young woman missing, one of the presumed victims, is also from this tribe. In the order of ceremony, their arbor is east." He set the photo to the far edge of the table, selected another.

"A-ni-so-ho-ni, the Blue or Panther clan, is the oldest clan. They were known for creating many special medicines for children. In ceremony, they sit to the left of Long Hair." He placed it next to the other photo, tapped a finger on it. "The west Chief says this man, Ableman, is of this clan, as was the missing boy.

"The next clan is the a-ni-wa-ya, the Wolf clan. This is the largest clan of the Cherokee. They are known as the protectors. As the Peace Chief often comes from the Long Hair clan, so the War Chief comes from the Wolf." He turned the photo to show Ben and Frankie. "Brent Coateney is one of ours, the eastern band, and is known as a great fighter. I believe it is he who took my grandson. Young Rabbit wants to be in law enforcement, a great protector of the people."

The Chief's voice broke as he set Coateney's photo to the left of Ableman's.

"If the seven succeed in the sacrifice of my grandson, the next one will be of the a-ni-go-te-ge-wi, the Potato or Savannah clan. This is the clan of Steven Hiawasee, also of our band. They are the gatherers, the keepers of the land. Today's gardeners and farmers," he explained. "They sit to the left of the Wolf.

"Then comes the a-ni-a-wi, the Deer Clan. They are known as fine hunters and runners, but hold great respect for animals. They are in charge of caring for all animals of the Cherokee. This man, Silver they call him, is from the western band.

"A-ni-tsi-s qua, is the Bird clan. Birds are thought to be messengers between earth and Heaven, the people and their Creator. This man, Ross Winter, also of the eastern band, is from this clan."

He picked up the last photo, Wild Bear himself. "The last clan is a-ni-wo-di. Warpaint. Great medicine men come from this clan as well as priests. Walking Stick is also of this tribe. In ceremony, they are left of Bird and right of Long Hair, thus completing the circle."

Frankie and Ben examined the circle. Ben fidgeted, something bothering him. Suddenly, he jumped up and went to a nearby table, grabbed a large map of the Nantahala Forest. He tacked it to the wall next to them, then selected the two photos of Fairweather and Ableman of the Long Hair and Panther clan respectively, and taped them over the locations of the first two crime scenes.

He pointed. "Look, the locations selected could mean something about their place in the tribe. Like the circle of the arbors in ceremony, they'll pick a place south and west of the last site. Here, somewhere between Briartown and Cowee, is where we should concentrate the search for the seven and Young Rabbit."

"How do we find them in two days?" Frankie asked. "Even with narrowing down the search, that's still like, what—one-hundred-thousand acres of forest—and most all of it is undeveloped and mountainous. Eric Rudolph, the Olympic Park Bomber, hid in these mountains for years before the FBI found him. They could be hiding anywhere. They've been raised in these mountains. They know every hill, valley, and stream."

Ben grinned. "Exactly. We let them close in on their own. Chief?"

The Chief gave Ben a nod, a sincere appreciation of his words. "Yes."

Ben turned and snapped his fingers at the sheriff's deputy, in charge of communication. "Notify everyone to refocus the search on these ridges. I know it's still a big area, but it's far more manageable than the entire forest."

"I will tell our people," the Chief said. He took Ben's hands in his own and spoke a Cherokee blessing, then did the same with Frankie before he departed.

After he left, Frankie felt a glimmer of hope. Maybe Ben was right. If anyone could find the seven, it would be their fellow Cherokee. They lived in these woods, knew these lands. In the same way those who lived on the urban streets knew how to navigate life there, these people had a street cred of a different kind, one of nature that could identify every tree, plant, stream, and cave within its boundaries.

She joined Ben in staring at the map. "I've not been a praying person for a long time, but I think if there was ever a time to start, now would be it."

It wasn't until 4p.m. the following day they received the news—a young Cherokee man named White Tail claimed he and his friend had discovered the location of the seven. They had heard the whacks of chopping axes and the spoken words of their native language high on a ridge, where they climbed and saw the men clearing a circle of land. But it was remote, nearly a four-hour hike in, and White Tail had to hike back out and leave his friend there in order to get word to them.

Chief Walker welcomed the young man, lanky with bad skin and some of the darkest eyes Frankie had ever seen, to their makeshift headquarters. Chief Walker spoke words Frankie couldn't understand but clearly communicated the Chief's sincere thanks and appreciation. His eyes were moist when he asked him if he'd seen his grandson.

White Tail shook his head. "But I am certain, it is the seven. I saw both Hiawasee and Wild Bear."

Ben took him over to the map and asked him to indicate the location of the men.

"I cannot say for certain, but we parked here in Cowee and hiked in. It is very remote, with dense woods and not much sunlight. We will need to leave by midday to get there before nightfall."

They spent the night huddling over various maps and studying the terrain of the area in question, George Riley and the U.S. Forest Service park rangers leading the charge. "We can follow White Tail in, then circle around the area once there."

"How many?" Ben asked.

"Fifteen should be enough," the FBI SWAT commander stated. "My six, plus Sheriff Cousins and his deputy, CI Riley, and six additional agents. I assume you and Agent Johnson want to go?"

"Damn straight," Frankie said.

"Should we bring some of our men to spread further out, in case one gets away?" Chief Walker asked. "The woods are dense. My people know the land."

Ben nodded his approval to the SWAT commander.

"Okay," he said. "As long as they stay back and don't interfere with the arrests."

Early the next morning, they geared up and headed south deep into the Nantahala Forest. Before they left, Ben rested a hand on Chief Walker's shoulder, promising him they would return with Young Rabbit. During the ride, Frankie glanced at the impending sunrise, the red sky, and thought of the Chief's words: the power of the east, the life-giver.

She hoped today it would prove true, be a life-saver.

Soon, the sunlight disappeared. They were deep into

the woods now, forest surrounding them on all sides. They parked, reviewed the plan again to ensure everyone knew their role, began to walk. The hike in was mostly quiet, but the nervous energy was apparent, the preparation before the hunt. Meals consisted of energy bars and orange juice. Four hours in, White Tail raised his hand, indicating for the party to stop. One by one the sign was given and everyone came to rest.

In the distance, Frankie could smell smoke, the sacred fire.

Her heart began to pound. *No, no, it couldn't be. Not yet.*

She checked her watch and shook her head at Ben. They needed to hurry.

White Tail signaled to his brethren that this is where they should scatter. The friend that had stayed behind joined them and the ten men of the Cherokee gathered, planned, then split up in many directions.

Night fell early deep in the woods. The agents relied on the SWAT members with their night vision to lead the way, the rest of the team assigned to stay at their backs. As soon as they approached the top of the ridge, they too split apart, into six groups, and went their separate ways.

Frankie was assigned to stay with one SWAT member along with another FBI agent. Together, the three climbed higher up the mountain, at times on hands and knees, until the sight of the fire came into view. In the center of the circle, a large fire was burning, the flames licking toward the night sky. Above that a bed, which was thankfully empty.

The seven members of the Keetoowah were dancing in a circle, reciting chants Frankie couldn't understand. Each was dressed in a different color and the fur of a different animal, the representative of their clan. She watched as each took various offerings and cast them into the fire.

She squinted, the urgency building, adrenaline coursing her veins.

Suddenly they stopped and the chanting ceased. They each took up point in their respective clan section and drank from the seven cups. In the center, the fire crackled, spitting embers high into the sky.

After the drink, they passed a pipe, each member taking seven puffs, just as Chief Walker described. When that was complete, Wild Bear came forward and recited a string of words that sounded much like the words of his manifesto.

Though the heat of the fire was intense, Frankie could sense the icy cold that gripped her body. Wild Bear was calling for the sacrifice. Calling for Young Rabbit.

Where the hell was the signal? What was taking so long?

Frankie gritted her teeth, glanced over at Ben at the next station, and shook her head. She didn't like this. She wanted to rush in with guns blazing, stop this right now. She started to move forward but the SWAT member held her back. He put a finger to his lips and mouthed, "Wait!"

The Wolf clan representative, Coateney, left the circle and walked to a nearby area that Frankie couldn't see from their vantage point. When he returned, he held Young Rabbit in his arms.

Frankie cursed.

The signal was given.

Chaos erupted as the six teams moved in. SWAT members yelled, screaming at the men to get down on the ground. Behind each SWAT member, two others fanned out, guns drawn, blocking their exit in every direction. Coateney dropped to his knees, still holding the boy. With the other agent covering her, Frankie raced to Young Rabbit, checked his pulse. To her immense relief, he was still alive.

Wild Bear, with his long raven hair and warpaint, screamed at his council, at the men in his midst. His brethren seemed uncertain whether to attempt an escape or not, when their own brothers came up as reinforcement behind the initial team. Harsh words were exchanged. Anger from his own people.

One by one they dropped to their stomachs, placed their hands behind their back. All except Wild Bear, who continued to chant and move in to the center, toward the fire, as they all closed in. When there was no place left to go, he grabbed the torch of the Fire Keeper and held it high, uttering the words later interpreted to Frankie.

Behold the sacred fire, the Creator, keeper of all life. Let it burn, the fire, offering blessings to all mankind. May my life be exchanged for the return of the Creator, and the blessing of our people. Then, along with the torch, he stepped into the fire, and the sound of his sacrifice was something Frankie would not forget. As the last remaining light went out of his eyes, Frankie swore for a moment she saw it, an image of the red, rising sun, reflecting there in his pupils.

Fire might be the keeper of all life, but that night the Sun, the life-giver, had emerged victorious, and it had extinguished the fire, at least for one man, for all the years to come.

THE END

ABOUT THE AUTHOR

Do you like FBI Agent Frankie Johnson, local profiler? Look for the first book in the Frankie Johnson Thriller series, *99 Truths*, to be released in March 2019 and the second, *The Art of Obsession*, in June 2019.

Lori Lacefield is a writer of suspense and thriller novels. Her first two suspense thrillers in the *Women of Redemption* series, *The Advocate* and *The Fifth Juror*, were released in May, 2018. To read more about Lori's novels, check out her latest giveaways and DOWNLOAD A FREE NOVELLA, *The Rumor*, go to https://www.lorilacefield.com.

Burning
by Simon Finnie

Professor Michele Agnello hobbles along the narrow side street, the shade of the tall buildings doing nothing to lower the oppressive heat. As always, the walk takes him past his local bakery; he nods at the owner pulling down its rusty corrugated shutters. As he turns the corner and looks up at his destination, the sweat starts on his brow. 'Not far now' he thinks, grunting as he leans on his stick to support his frail legs. He pushes away the familiar sad realization that his young, brilliant mind is not matched by this aging husk of a body.

Sometime later, he nears the summit and turns into a

short street ending abruptly with only a handful of doors on either side. The three walls facing him are a mix of cracked burnt orange and ageing brickwork, punctuated by wooden and iron shutters. Agnello heads towards the first set of doors, the only indication of what is to be found inside being a ripped burgundy canopy half extended over the entrance with faded gold lettering on its side: Café Fine.

Agnello reaches out a liver-spotted hand to the paint-flecked, half-open wooden doors and pushes through into the small café. The room is dark and bare, occupied by only a few tables pushed against one wall with a wooden bar facing them. Dust motes swirl and dance in front of him. With a knowing air, he ignores the room and walks across the dark, uneven floorboards to a doorway at its rear. He steps out onto a large patio with a handful of tables and an accompanying assortment of chairs. The area is as light as the room behind him was dark. Wires run above his head, decades of plant growth wrapped around them providing natural protection from the beating sun. But Agnello, like most others, does not see these. His attention is captured by the dramatic view of Rome and the red-tinged landmarks painted by the setting sun, and he feels a calm wash over him.

A man in black waistcoat and trousers folds the newspaper he is reading, remembers to smile, and gets up from his table to greet the Professor. The man silently but swiftly steps ahead of the shuffling old man and pulls out a seat at the edge of the terrace, bowing as he offers it to him. Agnello grunts as he deposits himself on the chair, resting his small briefcase and stick on the table beside him. The waiter moves inside and a few seconds later the reassuringly familiar clinking of glass signifies that Agnello's regular order is on its way.

The stifling heat of the early evening smothers Agnello as he grumpily considers the lack of breeze that usually makes this terrace his favorite place in the city. His thoughts are interrupted as the waiter places a large glass of Barolo and a small glass of iced water on the table. Agnello nods in appreciation and then turns back to the view as the waiter returns to his table and newspaper.

Agnello sips the wine and contemplates the city with its multitude of moving parts interacting with each other from second to second. For most of its inhabitants, this is the time of the day for a *passeggiata*; a stroll through the streets after work and an opportunity to catch-up with friends and family before the serious business of dinner is attended to.

As he nears the end of his glass there is a movement behind him and a young lady glides onto the terrace. Agnello can't help staring at her; she is classically beautiful. Golden blonde hair, angled features, tall and curvaceous, but it is her eyes that consume Agnello, for they are a striking shade of blue with near infinite depth. She is wearing a plain white summer dress that emphasizes her figure and emits an angelic, innocent air. She nods towards him and takes a seat at the other end of the terrace.

Agnello is smitten and unable to look away. His mind races through various unspeakable acts as his lust consumes him. The waiter walks over to her table, half-heartedly offering her a stained laminated menu, but she waves it away and asks for something that Agnello can't quite hear. As the waiter walks past Agnello's table, he arches an eyebrow and asks if there is anything else Agnello would like. Agnello orders the same again and, as the waiter leaves him, he tries to focus on the view and regain his previous stream of thoughts. But it is impossible, and he looks back again at the girl.

Taking a book out of her bag, she leans back and stretches her legs, holding the book high enough for Agnello to make out the cover. He pauses. He looks again but is not mistaken: it is his own book. She is reading *his* book.

The Invisible Cage: Why Free Will is an Illusion was written by Agnello over 30 years ago, but numerous editions and a continuous round of conference speeches have supported his career ever since. The book, whilst popular in its very specialized field, is otherwise relatively unknown. It has been many years since he has seen it outside of a lecture hall or seminar room.

She must be a student at the University, he thinks, and immediately discounts the thought. He only teaches a handful of classes these days, and he would remember such a beauty if she was studying in his department. As he watches her, wondering which sentence she is digesting, he can feel the sweat gather on his brow and lip. She, on the other hand, seems completely unaffected by the heat, her whole figure seeming to shimmer as though seen through a heat haze.

Agnello coughs and says loudly across the terrace, 'Interesting book.'

She looks up, shrugs and then stares back at the book in her hand as if she hadn't realized it was there. 'I'm not sure. Have you read it?' she asks.

'Read it? I wrote it!' he exclaims a little too keenly. She smiles, possibly unsure of how to respond. He stares at her, drawn in by her deep blue eyes and then motions towards an empty chair beside him, 'Why don't you join me and we can discuss it?'

The girl looks at him, pauses and then gathers her things and moves to his table. As she comes closer he unashamedly soaks up the images this offers. The paleness of her thigh as it breaks through her dress, the curves of her breasts as she leans over, the delicate unblemished skin of her face and neck. She is now sat so close to him that he can smell the faintest trace of her perfume.

'So, are you really Professor Agnello?' she asks, gesturing towards the book on the table between them.

'Yes, yes I am,' he replies. 'And what is your name, sweet one?'

'Oh, my name is unimportant compared to yours,' she says, shrugging, 'but I would be very interested in asking you about your book, if you would do me the honor?'

'Ah, trying to finish an essay, are we? Very well. Very well...' He mops his brow with a handkerchief and gestures to the waiter for a fan, or anything to reduce the sweltering heat, but the man, deep in his paper, does not look up.

'So it says here,' she taps the book cover, 'that you're a world-renowned professor in Ethics and Free Will. And your book, if I understand it correctly, seems to suggest that free will is an illusion. So, do you actually believe that none of us have the power to change our destinies? Wouldn't that mean that we are all just following a path that is already set?'

Agnello takes a deep sigh, picks up his glass and takes a sip before beginning a speech he has delivered many times.

'You understand, I presume, the physical laws that govern us from day to day?'

Before the girl can respond he holds up his index finger.

'Yes, yes. I refer to the Law of Gravity, the Four Laws of Thermodynamics and so on and so forth.' He waves his hand dismissively.

'Well, these reinforce our understanding of causality: that is, the relationship between cause and effect. That event A has a direct outcome that leads to situation B and this then leads to situation C and on and on.'

The girl nods.

'Well, over the centuries it has been confirmed over and over again that everything in the physical world is governed by the law of causality. That is to say that everything that happens has a physical cause to it. The wine in this glass, which is excellent by the way, has no real choice when I tip it, but to flow into my mouth.' Agnello pauses to drink the wine.

He continues with the detachment that normally accompanies his lectures, broadcasting his thoughts in the same manner regardless of the number of people listening. 'And so—and this is a critical point—as we human beings exist in the physical world, we too must be subject to these same laws. Our thoughts and our actions exist in this world and so must also be the product of a sequence of events: the causality I mentioned, not by some abstract notion of free will. Therefore, free will as most people understand it is…', he raises his voice and, with a flourish, says, '…an illusion!'

The girl wrinkles her nose as if encountering something unpleasant.

'I see you find this unpalatable,' he continues, 'but the causality I refer to does not diminish the greatness or otherwise that man is capable of.'

'But it must do. If humans don't make real decisions and only perform actions because of the sequence of events beforehand, then they are nothing more than actors following a script.'

Agnello chuckles at the girl's sincerity, wipes the sweat off his forehead with his handkerchief, and continues. 'When we talk of the factors leading up to even the smallest of actions, it is an equation of incomprehensible complexity. When I nudge this spoon off the table, Newton's law of gravity determines how fast it falls, its impact on the ground and so on, but it does not explain my motive. For that we must look at the natural laws and everything that has happened before this action—my genetic DNA, my upbringing, my education, my emotional state, this conversation with a beautiful woman.' He pauses to smile at her, but her face is frozen like a mask. Without encouragement, he continues, 'Only by knowing all of these factors would one be able to fully understand why that event happened. That is the theory of Determinism and the basis for my book'.

As he takes another gulp of wine, the girl shifts in her seat and timidly asks, 'But what about the soul?'

'Whether there is or isn't such a thing has no bearing on this discussion.'

'But I read that Descartes suggested that there was both a physical and a spiritual world? That our consciousness is essentially our soul and sits in the spiritual world?'

Agnello's mouth turns momentarily downwards, 'Yes… Yes, he did. He also postulated—that means to claim without evidence, by the way—he postulated that the soul controlled the body through an antenna in the brain: the pineal gland. Absolute nonsense that Neuroscience has since discredited.'

'But I read in another book that he was one of the first great founders of Libertarianism and that his theory showed that humans were free to make their own decisions.' The girl reaches over to her bag and pulls out a notebook. 'Didn't he write *"our will is so free in its nature that it cannot be constrained"*?'

Once again Agnello uses the increasingly sodden handkerchief to wipe his face. 'Look, Descartes was a great intellect, especially in mathematics, but his philosophy of mind does not bear scrutiny. He created Dualism—that is, the theory that we are individuals existing dually in both the physical and spiritual world—because he was trying to please the Church and in doing so had to come up with something that maintained the existence of a soul. There is no secret antenna in the brain. There is no soul. There is only this.' He gestures towards his own frail body and then slowly to hers, casting his eyes over her breasts as he does so.

The girl ignores this and looks out over the skyline, contemplating her response. Agnello seizes the break in conversation to finish his glass of water and once again try—and fail—to get the waiter's attention. He cannot understand why the evening heat is not abating.

The girl turns back to him with a fierceness in her expression and says, 'But it just doesn't make sense that one is not in control of their actions. If you want to drink this wine, then you would make the decision to drink it as so.' At this she lifts her glass and, staring at him over the rim, she takes a gulp of wine, swallows and then gently uses her tongue to wipe away the excess on her lips.

'Look,' he says, 'Determinism doesn't mean you cannot drink wine when you want to, or that you are simply an automaton. It is an explanation of what you do and why you do it, not a prediction of what you are going to do. Let's take a shark, for example. If I don't feed the shark and then put it in a glass tank with a particularly tasty fish, what do you think will happen?

The girl stares back at him, clearly unimpressed.

'Let me use a better example. Have you ever been in a café or a restaurant and, despite there being a range of attractive food on the menu, you end up going for the same dish you always do? Why?'

'Maybe it's simply because I like that dish.'

'Exactly. And your preferences, your tastes, your likes... You don't worry about them removing your freedom, do you? No, of course not. And Determinism is the same. It is simply saying that we are all the product of our past, our memories, our experiences, our environment, our DNA; and it is all of these factors and more that explains why we do what we do.'

The girl contemplates this and then says, 'But when I read Kant's *Critique of Pure Reason*, he seemed to be saying that humans are not just material creatures, but also rational beings of reason not subject to causality. As I understood it, Kant was challenging Determinism and suggesting that it only applied to material decisions such as whether to breathe or not. When it came to the type of decisions that I think of as being free, such as what to like and who to love, then humans are actually governed by what he called a *moral code*, which is in turn formed by individuals themselves. Therefore, man is completely free to make those decisions that genuinely define him.'

Agnello took a long, hard look into the girl's deep blue eyes. There was something troubling about this conversation; this girl had clearly read deeper into this subject then he had at first thought.

'Yes, you are broadly correct in your summary of Kant's position. But Kant was an avid protestant who spent 15 years trying to reconcile free will with his perception of God and other concepts that he considered beyond normal evaluation. I say this to indicate the stretch required to join up his theories. The world has moved on since Kant. Yes, there are still groups who follow the dogma of "Explanatory Incompatibilism" but...'

'...tell me about them.'

Agnello raises an eyebrow at her tone and considers commenting, but instead continues to answer.

'Well, these people divide actions into those that have mechanistic explanations and those that have what they call *teleological* or *purposive* explanations. The former is simple to define: like my pushing of the spoon, is the physical explanation as to why it fell. The latter, the teleological explanation is used for all those actions that are driven by the mind: intentions, desires, purpose. Yes?'

'Go on.'

Agnello, feeling the heat even more intensely, reaches for the glass of water, but it is empty. With a shrug, he takes another gulp of the wine and continues, 'Well, those who call themselves "Explanatory Incompatibilists" propose that all mechanistic events can be explained by our physical laws, but that not all teleological events can be explained. Why do we like to be scared? Why do we love some things that we hate and hate other things that we love? Because if there is no way of explaining all of our values, choices or purpose then Determinism is incompatible with the teleological aspect of being human and so should be rejected.'

'That sounds right.'

'No. It is a cop-out. A fudge!' He shouts and hits the table with his fist. 'It is the worst kind of philosophical argument. Philosophy is not a discipline for those who want to grab the nearest blanket for comfort. Just because something feels right, does not mean it is so. Otherwise, we would still believe the world is flat and that the sun moves round the earth.'

'But if you believe them wrong, Professor, then you are saying that even your feelings and desires are pre-determined and follow natural laws.'

Agnello sighs, looks out at the still burning sun hovering above the skyline and then nods, 'Yes. Yes, I am. But is that so terrible?'

The girl does not answer.

'There is a set of laws that only nature, or God if you like, has the freedom to create and amend, and which we must follow. And if we follow those laws then we do not have the free will that you describe. But look, as Spinoza says, this isn't that God is a puppeteer constantly pulling our strings. This is a world where God made the strings, how much they can hold, when they snap, how they move. God creates the framework, not every move we will ever make. As Hobbes once wrote, *"We are as free as an unimpeded river; Free to follow the rules set out for us"*.'

'Agnello, Agnello...' the girl's mouth curls into a gently mocking grin '....and what of Original Sin?'

Startled at her change in manner, Agnello turns to look at her again. Her deep blue eyes gaze back at him innocently and so he continues, unsure of what has just passed.

'There may be a God, but not of the form most people consider. For most, God is a convenient figure to help the weak rationalize the universe. The Bible offers no real insight into the philosophy of the mind. If there *was* an apple and a snake then the decision Eve made to take it was motivated by her psychological make-up, not by some existential willpower that sits outside the known universe.'

The girl laughs. When she stops, they both stare at each other with an undercurrent of confusion. Agnello feels conflicted. He is drawn deeply to this girl but is held back by the constant reminder that he is no longer the rakish, beautiful young man he once was as well as the feeling that this girl is not all she seems.

'And Professor, what of justice? What of punishment? If no-one is really free to commit a wrongdoing, then is anyone really guilty?'

'Of course they are!' The Professor pauses as he finds himself out of breath. After several mouthfuls of warm, humid air, he continues. 'It is wrong to think that without free will there can be no value in punishment. Indeed, punishment makes more sense when we can blame the crime on a motivation, predilection, or attitude that the perpetrator holds, rather than believing that they could have acted completely differently if they were in the same situation again. Punishment and deterrence rely on us rejecting free will and making fear of punishment the cause of good behavior.'

'But it does not hold the individual to account?'

'To account to whom? God? Does God hold the lion to account for killing the gazelle? Or the shark, the tuna? No. No, he does not.'

'These are beasts you speak of, Professor, not Adam nor Eve. Not the chosen ones carved in his holy image. Humans are capable of much good and evil and is God not the ultimate arbiter of which is which?'

Agnello chuckles. 'Ha. You are dragging this debate into the realms of spiritualism rather than free will. Look, I don't believe in right versus wrong; they are merely constructs we use to justify rewards or punishments that affect individuals and society. That is how an individual is held to account'

The girl pauses, takes a sip of wine, carefully places the glass down and then turns to face Agnello full-on. She sits up straight, her relaxed posture gone.

'And you, Agnello, does God hold you to account?'

Surprised, he pauses and then also turns towards her, 'What do you mean?'

With a smile that betrays a hint of cruelty she says, 'What I mean, Professor, is that there *is* a God and there *is* good and there *is* evil. And I know that despite your rhetoric you believe this, so I'll ask you again, does God hold you to account for your actions?'

Agnello feels his sweat increasing and finds himself short of breath. 'I... I don't understand' he stutters.

'Sofia Bianchi. Giulia Alfonsi. Francesca Romano. Need I go on?'

Agnello moves his mouth but cannot force the air out to make a sound. His body feels heavy, too heavy to move.

Finally, he blurts out, 'Girls. I mean, all girlfriends. Ex-lovers. Why? What? What business is it of yours?'

'All the souls you have damaged. All the abuse you have bestowed. Did you believe that the path you took was so ordained that the label of evil did not apply? Did you think that judgement of such evil would not occur?'

Whilst his mind whirls in confusion, Agnello suffocates with the lack of air and tries to grab his throat but cannot even move his hand in response.

The girl smiles in response, 'A reminder, perhaps?'

Agnello shivers and his whole body convulses in ecstasy. His eyes open. He is staring at the ceiling of his office, back in the university, its strip lighting, dappled ceiling panels and artificially cool air offering a welcome change from the suffocation and heat he just left. He barely has time to consider whether he is dreaming or just waking when he realizes he is not alone. He is lying back in his large reclining office chair and as he looks down a girl's head rises from between his spread legs. Her blonde hair parts to reveal a young, strikingly beautiful face looking up at him expectantly. 'Did I do well, Professor?' she asks of Agnello. Without waiting for an answer, she leans back on to her heels, turns her head and spits out his semen into a tissue that she then crumples and deposits in the nearby wastepaper bin. Looking back at him, she is suddenly struck with embarrassment. She covers her naked breasts with her arm and stands up, turning away from him as she does so. She picks up her bra and t-shirt from his desk and moves closer to the door to put them on.

He is gripping the arms of his chair tightly and he can feel the cracks in the leather that he knows so well. He can't be dreaming. This is too real. But his skin feels tight and the normal background hum of aching and pain that accompanies old age is gone.

Without willing it, he leans forward, stands up and buttons his trousers. Agnello realizes he is not in control of his actions; merely a passenger in his own younger body.

Then it hits him: he has been here before. It has been some years, but this is exactly what happened. Sofia Bianchi, of course. That's her name, this girl dressing in front of him. Is this what that crazy girl back at the café was referring to? He only vaguely recalls this scene, but he remembers all too well what follows.

Sofia reaches for her jacket and bag. She turns towards him, but keeps looking down at the floor as she says, 'Was I good enough, Professor?'

He reaches for the lit cigarette lying against his desk ashtray. It has almost burned to the filter, but he takes one last drag before stubbing it out.

'You were,' he says coolly. 'I'll see you the same time next week'.

She looks up. Her eyes are moist.

'But you said this was the last time. That this would be it and you would make sure my grades were okay and everything would be...' She breaks into quiet sobs and wipes her eyes with the backs of her hands.

'But Sofia, my angel, I love you. And I know you love me. How cruel it would be to keep us apart.'

Sofia swallows hard in an attempt to stem her sniffles and quietly says, 'Professor, I don't...' She pauses to gather her composure and an edge of anger creeps into her voice. 'Professor, I don't love you. I'm a good girl from a good family. I don't want to do this anymore. It isn't right.'

He moves towards her bringing his hand up towards her cheek gently wiping away her tears. 'Oh Sofia. You break my heart. How can you say these things?'

He moves his hand to stroke her hair and grabs a clump, aggressively pulling her head back and bringing his face close to hers.

He hisses into her face. 'Now listen, my *angel*. If you don't want me to report you to the university and have you kicked out and disgraced in front of all your friends and family then you will keep to our arrangement and keep quiet.'

Sofia is silent. Her tears, halted by the shock and pain, are replaced by a slight quiver of fear.

Letting go of her, Agnello says, 'Do you understand me?'

She nods, her eyes and pupils still wide.

Sitting back down at his desk, he adds, 'See you next week. Close the door behind you.'

Sofia stares downwards again and pulls a tissue out of her pocket which she uses to dry her eyes and nose. Eventually, with Agnello pretending to ignore her, she shuffles out of the door still sobbing.

He sits back in his chair and considers the encounter. His younger self is thinking what a stupid but beautiful girl she is and that he can't blame himself for his actions. After all, you wouldn't blame a lion for eating a gazelle...

The light in the office fades rapidly and as the room gets darker Agnello feels the heat rolling over him knocking him out.

He wakes to find himself walking along a busy street in central Rome at night. The headlights of the cars glare at him as they whip past. He looks down at the piece of paper in his hand. It reads: 'I need you. Come to mine at 10,' followed by the address of a flat. He lifts his other hand and his watch shows him that it is five minutes past ten.

He follows the building numbers as he walks past a series of closed shop fronts and doorways until he comes to the one matching the paper. It is a tall, dark door and is already open, filled with two elderly women talking excitedly. He steps into the communal hallway and walks past them towards a large stone stairway on the right.

He walks quickly up the stairs and knocks on the door. There is no answer, so he tries the handle. It is not locked and swings open. He calls her name but there is silence and so, closing the door behind him, he walks cautiously along the short hallway. He passes an open door to a small bathroom lit from the hall. At the end of the corridor there are two doors. He chooses one and walks into a neat, but depressingly small, room which is part lounge, part kitchen, part dining area. He imagines nothing but meals for one being cooked and consumed in the vacuum of this room. Hit by confusion as to what he is doing in this place, he watches as his body turns and goes back to the unopened door. He slowly opens it to another small room which the dim light from the hall fails to penetrate. He can make out a bed that takes up most of the room and a table, or maybe a dresser, against the wall under the solitary single-paned window. He runs his hand along the nearest wall searching for a light switch, which he finds and flicks. The light hanging from the ceiling is not strong and it takes Agnello a couple of seconds for his eyes to adjust and take in the scene. Sofia is lying on top of the bed fully clothed and asleep, the sudden light in the room making no difference to her state. As he takes in the scene, he sees a large piece of paper scrunched in her right hand.

He kneels on the bed to move close to her and becomes aware of her slow and deep breathing. He roughly shakes her by the shoulders, but she does not wake. He tries again but still nothing. Looking down at her, the paper catches his eye again. He carefully unclenches her fingers, unfurls the paper and reads it.

"*Dear Michele*

You have broken me. You have made me into something I never wanted to be. I hate you more than I can bear.

I give you the decision. When you find me, you can save me and show that I am worth something or leave me to die so that I may finally end this. The decision is yours.

I found out today that I am now pregnant and do not know what to do. All I know is that I cannot go on like this.

I only ever wanted to please my family, do good work and live a good life, but I have failed and for that I must pay.

If I do not live to see another day, then so be it.

Love

Sofia"

Agnello stares at her beautiful face. Once again, his mind and his body seem disconnected so without any direction, he gently moves a lock of hair from her face and sighs, 'Oh Sofia'.

He takes the note in both hands and carefully rips it in two, separating the first two paragraphs from the rest of the note and placing the top half in his jacket pocket whilst putting the remainder in the girl's hands which he clenches shut once more.

He then lifts a pillow and carefully places it over her face.

Once again the light fades completely and the heat hits him, fiercer than before. Slowly, as if he is waking, the familiar image of the café terrace swims into focus: the tables and chairs, the setting sun hanging in the distance, the waiter in the corner, and the girl. All just as they were.

The heat is unbearable. Every nerve ending in his skin is screaming alive, prickling with the burning sensation, but as he slowly looks down, all he sees is his pale, drooping hands poking out of his untouched cloth jacket. The pain mixed with the heat is clouding his thoughts and his movements are painfully slow. Every breath is difficult, the heat of the air thinning it and his attempts to breathe faster leave him feeling suffocated.

He looks across at the girl. Even in his distress he recognizes that something is different. She is leaning back with her long legs stretched out in front of her touching the railings of the terrace. She holds a glass of wine carelessly between her finger and thumb, holding it up to the setting sun and twisting it to see how the light diffracts through the liquid.

'Twilight, Agnello. So beautiful,' she says, not looking at him but staring directly at the sun. 'Oh *"stand still, you ever-moving spheres of heaven; That time may cease, and midnight never come"*. Oh, Marlowe...' She sighs loudly.

Agnello wonders if she has drugged him but, before he can react to this thought, his attention is drawn to the corner as the waiter coughs loudly, bringing his closed fist to his mouth. He momentarily looks up at the girl and then, lowering his gaze, returns to his paper.

The smile that had been dancing across the girl's lips vanishes to be replaced by a cruel sneer as she sits up and turns to face Agnello. Her eyes stare into his and he finds that he can look nowhere else. Despite the excruciating heat there is an empty coldness to her eyes that invokes a deep fear in him.

'Agnello, Agnello, Agnello' she says, her voice deeper than before with a mocking tone. 'What *are* we to do with you?'

She leans forward, maintaining her stare, and continues. 'You argued very eloquently this evening that man is not truly free but should still be held responsible for his actions. I even threw you some wholesome crumbs to see if you'd follow them out of the predicament you're now in, but alas your pride and ego failed you this time.'

He attempts to respond but he has nothing left. He is still struggling for breath and now, unable to move, he cannot manage even the simplest of sounds. Only his eyes can still move. He is trapped and afraid, especially of whoever this girl is.

Still staring straight into him, she says, 'You know what I find most disappointing about you, Agnello? You dedicated a lifetime to solving the question of free will and not once did you drag the existence of God and all his trappings into your work. I'm certainly not saying that doing so would have fixed everything but, and I'm not really meant to mention this—' the girl holds her hand to her mouth and pretends to whisper, '—but it would have got you closer.'

Despite the agonizing pain he is experiencing, he is still listening and taking in what she is saying. His eyes have now stopped their panicked rapid movements and instead are focused solely on hers.

'The question isn't whether there is a spiritual world influencing the material one. That ship sailed many moons ago. Why do you think every miserable group of humans on this planet ended up with some form of religion at the heart of their culture? Coincidence?' She stops and slightly cocks her head to one side in a parody of waiting for his response.

'No. It's not whether each being has a soul, it's how free that soul is to carve its own path through this world. Oh, and I know what you're thinking, Professor. You've been there. You've done that. I get it, but they got closer than you did. You see: God, and I'm sure *They* won't mind me pointing this out, doesn't predetermine who will be saved and who will burn. No, that's up to the individual and their free will. But that said, God does infallibly know what will happen because that is just one of those annoying things about eternal, almighty deities. But *Them* knowing everything that has happened and will happen doesn't mean that your decisions are not yours to make. Just that in *Their* eyes, time is not linear having seen all of the outcome before. Are you following?'

The girl stops and looks Agnello up and down to check that he is still conscious.

'You know, Professor, I thought this would be a lot more entertaining than it actually was. Truth be told, I'm actually a little bored. This is why I don't normally do these house calls; but when someone like you comes up... Well call me weak, but I couldn't resist. It's not just the supposed expertise and notoriety for understanding free will and the responsibilities of man, but the track record of sin was impressive for a boring academic like yourself. It was a heady mix if I do say so.'

Agnello's eyes start darting rapidly around again and he tries to scream but is unable to move at all.

'They say that every man plots his own course to Heaven or Hell, and if that's the case you did an excellent job of navigating to the latter. Small-scale theft all the way up to murder: what you lacked in quantity you certainly made up for in quality. Yes, you will fit in very well.'

Agnello tries to respond but still cannot move. The girl looks at his mouth and then shrugs, 'You may speak.'

Agnello immediately feels that he can move his mouth again and takes a large gulp of air, regardless of its warmth. He then stutters, 'But. But. I don't understand. Don't hurt me. I don't know what you've done. Whether you've drugged me, or...'

Agnello's words fail him as the girl slightly tilts her head. 'Oh dear. How insulting. Accusing *me* of parlor tricks and subterfuge? So disappointing.'

She sits up and moves her chair so that their faces are close. 'Tell me Agnello, can drugs do this?'

Abruptly he feels an intense pain sear through his brain. It is overwhelming but stops as suddenly as it started.

'Unfortunately for you, my dear Professor, I am no drug-induced hallucination. I am as real as your soul, which has been the focus of our discussion this evening.'

Still unable to move, Agnello's eyes moisten and a small tear rolls down his weathered cheek. The girl moves her seat back, still staring straight into him.

'Ah, now you understand. Good. Let me frame your situation for you, Agnello. You, rather patronizingly, tried to teach this young girl two lessons tonight. Firstly, that you humans are not trapped by causality, it is merely an explanation for their actions. You humans do what you do because of your DNA, as it were.'

Agnello finds his head is free enough to move slightly and so he nods.

'And secondly, humans *should* be punished for their actions as it both discourages them from future sins and serves as an example to others. And this is the interesting bit,' she smiles, 'this applies as equally to the after-life as the mortal coil.'

Agnello shakes his head violently and tries to scream. After a few moments, she indicates that he can speak.

'I don't want to go to Hell. I'll do anything you say...' His voice then leaves him again.

The girl smiles broadly, 'Thank you Professor Michele Agnello. Thank you so much. Your recognition of my home was the final piece of this mildly interesting jigsaw.' She places her hand on her heart.

'Oh, my dear, dear little man. The only restriction I have on welcoming individuals to my domain is that they have to believe in its existence. You can't go somewhere that doesn't exist. Annoying condition, but... unavoidable'

The girl stands up and picks up her bag. She walks over to the railings at the edge of the patio and faces this sunrise one final time. After a few moments of silence, she says quietly, 'Oh Rome. My country. City of the soul. Whose agonies are evils of a day...'

She sighs and then over her shoulder says loudly, 'Are we done here?'

The waiter looks up from his paper then slowly folds it and carefully places it on the table. He gets up and takes a few steps towards Agnello, looking at the immobile body and expression of terror.

'I said, *Are we done here*?' says the girl impatiently, facing the other two.

The waiter slowly turns to her and, in a gentle voice says, 'Yes. He's yours.'

'Excellent' she says and walks towards the door. As she nears the exit, she slows and turns to look back at Agnello. 'And I'll see you back at mine later, naughty boy.' She blows him a kiss and disappears through the door.

Agnello feels the heat intensifying and his vision blurring with a red tinge at the periphery. As the pain increases, he tries to scream but cannot. He is burning alive and the pain is horrific. Now he can see the flames and they are reaching higher and higher covering his entire body. Every one of his senses is overwhelmed and his mind is consumed with the pain.

He just wants the burning to stop.

THE END

ABOUT THE AUTHOR

Adventurer. Fighter. Lover. Simon is almost none of these, but has spent a lifetime talking, writing and talking some more. Emanating from the dreich banks of Loch Lomond, Simon has been described as a mash-up of Moore's Swamp Thing, The Crow Road's Prentice, and Gray's Kelvin Walker, but only by him. Just now.

A terrible writer, it has taken him until the second paragraph to mention that he is married with two children and an ageing goldfish in the outskirts of London. Any suggestions that Simon is only part of Burning Chair to make Pete look good will be dealt with most harshly and will involve the judicious use of the naughty step.

Find out more about Simon at: www.simonfinnie.com or www.burningchairpublishing.com

Burning Greed
by Peter Oxley

Burning.

The whole world was burning.

At least, that's how it seemed to Flynn Fergus as he staggered through the corridor of flames, struggling under the weight of two holdalls. He shrugged his shoulders hoping that it would lessen the ache of the straps. It didn't.

A distant part of his brain nagged at him, telling him to dump the bags and run as fast as he could. He pushed away the thought; on his back was the largest single score of his life, probably more money than he would ever see again. Bugger common-sense; it was worth risking a bit of heat for this.

He flinched at an explosion to his right, an intense blast accompanied by the distinctive smell of singed hair. He hurried forward, trying to ignore the distressing realization that the hair he could smell burning was probably his own.

The island through which he was running had, until just a few minutes before, been a paradise; a rich man's wet dream, far beyond most people's wildest imaginings. Arcadia, as it had been christened by some overpaid marketeer, was home to a scattering of luxurious villas which merged seamlessly into the lushest, greenest gardens looping around the clearest pools and glittering-est waterfalls. It was a place that insisted you create new superlatives just to be able to describe it.

It was through this paradise that Flynn now ran, dodging burning branches and choking on smoke.

A low wall appeared out of the smoke, offering him a brief chance to rest in relative safety without being burnt to death. He threw himself to the ground, grunting as the weight of the bags eased for a brief, joyous moment. He looked up, trying to catch his breath without coughing too hard and marveling at how the buildings around him still stood; for now, at least.

Through the billowing smoke Flynn could make out dark outlines of the luxurious mansions dotted around the island, buildings which were so sympathetically high-tech as to make them all but invisible amongst the elegantly tamed jungle. Heads of State had been entertained there, royalty had been overwhelmed by its sheer opulence, movie stars had fought over each other for the chance of an invite. The closest the common man or woman had been to any of it was through pictures in magazines. Unless they were servants, of course.

A far cry from where he had grown up, where the dirty slums had been a fraction of the size of these villas but housing ten or even twenty times as many people. His daily life had been one of struggle, with starvation a constant companion. It was almost impossible to imagine being one of the gilded guests, wandering along the pleasant tree-lined avenues on this island, their only concern being what time the next bottle of champagne would be served.

The image of his sister flashed across his mind, bringing with it the usual stab of guilt and longing. If only...

He shook his head, forcing the thoughts back down to the darkest depths. He needed to keep his focus on the job in hand; in the next few, crucial minutes any distractions could be fatal. Even the smallest chink of weakness could give the whole game away before it had a chance to play out. He forced his mind to the image of his parents, wondering what they would make of their runt of a son carrying the GDP of a small country on his back through one of the most expensively exclusive places in all the world.

Or at least, what *used* to be one of the most exclusive places in the world.

Now it was just burning. All of it.

"I know I wanted a distraction," Flynn muttered between coughs, "but this is frankly ridiculous." He rolled and squatted on one knee at the sound of a deafening crack just behind him. "Maybe we did go a bit too far this time..."

He looked up and squinted through the smoke, using his free hand to wipe away the tears streaming down his cheeks. He could make out a dark form not too far in front of him. At last. He allowed himself a satisfied half-smile. If his sense of direction still held true—admittedly quite a long shot given the present circumstances—then that should be the building which led to the landing strip: his ticket to safety.

He hefted the bags up for one last push through the corridor of flames. As he drew closer, he could see the fire licking at the building's walls. It appeared to be withstanding the assault for now, but Flynn wondered how long even the best-designed materials would be able to hold out against a battering of that intensity. It was, to be fair, the largest fire he had ever had the pleasure of running through the middle of.

The doors swept open as he approached, revealing a black rectangle mercifully bereft of flames. Flynn's eyes were blinded by the light of the fire, so he had no choice but to plunge in and hope for the best.

He skidded to a halt on the marble floor as the doors swept shut behind him, allowing himself to take a short breath while his eyes adjusted to the dimly lit lobby.

"Hello Flynn," said a deep, booming voice from somewhere in front of him. "How nice of you to join us."

Flynn squinted in the dimness, slowly making out half a dozen shapes in front of him, with at least the same number again to either side.

"Oh, shi—" he began, before the world exploded in a flash of red.

FIVE MONTHS EARLIER...

Tevlin Kraas slammed his fist on the table as the attendant backed away as quickly as he could without drawing too much attention to himself. "How," he said in a low, rumbling, almost strangulated voice, "did he get away with it. Again?"

The attendant's eyes darted around the room, desperate for some form of help or salvation. Instead he met the barely-disguised amusement of Titus Gardner, whose expression was a perfectly inappropriate counterpart to Kraas' rising rage.

"I..." stammered the attendant. "I do not know. I was just told to pass you the message. I did not... I cannot..."

"Get me the Head of Security, whatever his name is. And then get out of my building; I never want to see your face again."

"Sir? I..."

"You're fired, man! Get out of my sight!"

The attendant sprinted from the room as Gardner tutted, raising his champagne glass to his lips. "My dear

Tevlin, has no one ever told you the phrase: 'Do not shoot the messenger'?"

"Whoever said that was an idiot," snarled Kraas. "They clearly never understood how good it feels to shoot the messenger. Anyway, the man was weak. He should have refused to pass on the message, forced the one responsible to man up and tell me himself."

"And who would that be? Who is your Head of Security this week?"

Kraas glared at the other man. "I do not appreciate your tone," he said in a low voice. "Is my predicament that amusing?"

"I am sorry, dear chap," said Gardner, arranging his face into an expression of forced sympathy. "It does seem a bit odd, though, doesn't it? What's this, the fifth such robbery you have suffered in as many months?"

"Seventh," snapped Kraas.

"Do you not think that maybe if you didn't keep firing your Heads of Security...?"

"If they are not able to stop a little guttersnipe from taking my money, then they have no place in my employ."

"You could always go to the police?"

"You and I both know that that is not an option. The problem is that this... this common thief knows it too."

"And pretty embarrassing that you keep being bested by a common thief, no doubt," mused Gardner.

Kraas took a deep breath. "We know exactly who the thief is, and yet the idiots I employ seem to find it impossible to spot him when he wanders into my buildings." He frowned at Gardner. "You have no such problems. Why is that?"

"Because I, along with most of your other peers—who also do not suffer from your, ah, problems, by the by— choose to outsource our staffing to a reputable agency. They provide the very best, most reliable staff. Fully vetted and trained, and loyal to a fault. I am still more than willing to make an introduction, if you would like..."

"Maybe," grunted Kraas. "I seem to spend far too much

of my time hiring and firing.”

“Mainly firing, it seems to me.”

Kraas shrugged and picked up his glass. “Still leaves me with the problem of this damned thief. Unless your agency can solve that, too.”

“I’m sure they could help you catch the fiend. You’d just need to find a way to trap him.”

Kraas knocked back his drink. “And there’s the problem. Getting him *in* my buildings does not seem to be much of a challenge; keeping him there for long enough is the issue.”

They sat in silence for a moment.

“You know,” said Gardner. “I remember when I was a little child, we had a lake in our family estate. In the middle of that lake was an island. Nothing special, just big enough for a small farm, a store for some feed and the like. My brothers and I liked to row over there and play. One day we found a rat; huge thing, as big as your head. My father said that where there was one, there would be many.

“We tried setting a few cats loose on the island, but the rats were too cunning for them. The final straw was when we found a cat torn to pieces, floating face down in the lake, its stomach ripped open by a dozen rat claws. We were at risk of losing the island and everything on it to the vermin. So, what did we do? We sneaked out there one morning and built a big bonfire in the center of the island, right in the middle of the trees. We surrounded it with barrels of gasoline and plenty of kindling. Then we burned the island. All of it. After a while, there was nowhere for the rats to go but into the water, and there me and my brothers were, with our rifles, picking them all off, one by one.”

Kraas stared at Gardner, transfixed, licking his lips with a thick moist tongue as he imagined the rodents diving into the water, their helpless bodies peppered with bullets, the lake turning red with blood and the reflection of the dancing flames. “Did you get them all?” he whispered.

Gardner nodded. “Sometimes if you have a rat, the only way to get rid of them is to burn them out.”

PRESENT DAY...

Tevlin Kraas looked down at the prone form at his feet. "You know, I thought he would be bigger," he said. "I am almost offended. Roll him over; let's see his face."

The guard did so, and Kraas glared down at the youth, feeling the familiar anger rise up once more. Part of him could not believe that something so pathetic-looking could be the root of all his humiliations. It felt so... so *unreasonable*. Surely someone of his stature deserved a nemesis with a bit more gravity?

"So that's the one?" asked Gardner.

Kraas glared at his friend, not appreciating the tinge of amusement in his voice.

"Sir, what'll we do with him?" asked one of the guards standing over the young man's body. One of the new ones, from the agency company. Wilson, Kraas thought his name was. Or maybe Watson. Or Jones. It didn't matter.

"Take him out there," said Kraas, gesturing towards the doors at the far end of the lobby. "You," he said, pointing to another guard. "Bring the bags. I want them in my sight at all times."

"Sir." The guard snapped his heels together and then hoisted the bags over his shoulder. Kraas felt a small swelling of satisfaction. In this one thing, Gardner had been right; the agency which supplied these men was very, *very* good.

"Wait," said Kraas as the guard marched over to the doors. "I want to check inside the bags first."

The guard nodded and opened first one bag and then the other. Kraas bent over, giving a grunt of satisfaction when he caught the tell-tale sparkle of diamonds reflected in the flickering half-light. He gave a cursory glance at the papers in the other bag and then nodded. "Carry on. But not too far ahead; I want those by my side at all times."

Kraas returned his attention to Flynn, watching as

the young man's limp body was dragged over to the doors. Without thinking, he muttered, "He's just a boy," immediately regretting this betrayal of his true feelings as he heard Gardner's amused snort.

The large doors opened onto a long strip of tarmac which jutted out into space, high above the north side of the jungle canopy which, so far, was untouched by the flames spreading across the rest of the island.

Kraas took a moment to look out over what remained of his empire. Beaches and bushes. All he would have left, if the fire were allowed to complete its work, would be beaches and bushes. Mind you, they were the finest, whitest beaches in all the world, so that was another win right there.

It was impossible to ignore the crackling roar from just the other side of the building, though. The landing strip benefited from a headwind which pushed the smoke away and across the island behind them, but even so some remnants still reached them. There was no escaping the stench of money, wealth and enterprise being mercilessly destroyed by a force which cared little for aesthetics or hard work. All men were equal in the face of such destruction.

Well, almost all men.

He grinned at the thought of what his competitors would make of his current situation, how they would dance with glee as they imagined him ruined.

How little they knew.

"Wake him up," Kraas said when they were all outside and standing about a dozen yards from the hangar doors. He watched with amusement as the guard picked Flynn up by his collar and slapped him repeatedly about the face.

After half a dozen blows, the young man finally reacted, groaning and trying to flinch away. The guard—Williams? Wilkins?—dropped him to the ground and stepped aside.

"Ouch," said Flynn with not nearly enough pain and contrition for Kraas' liking. "That hurt." He pulled himself up to his knees and spat blood onto the floor. He tried to flinch away as a metal chair was dragged over with a screech, the guard picking him up like a large rag doll and forcing him to sit in it. He struggled vainly as he was secured to the chair with plastic ties to his wrists and ankles.

"Really?" asked Flynn. "Is this *really* necessary? Where exactly am I going to run off to? Everywhere's on fire!"

"I am taking no chances," said Kraas, "not after everything you have done to me. There are still ways off this island."

"Speaking of which," said Gardner, "I believe my transport awaits. It has been amusing to watch your plan come to fruition, Tevlin. Shall I take the package now?"

"Nice try," said Kraas. "I will keep it in my care until you show me that you have torn up the documentation and my debt to you is no more."

"The paperwork is back in my office safe, but I will give you an undertaking that it will be discharged and destroyed. I do not wish to see such a precious item just lying around here, that is all."

Kraas shook his head. "I will bring it to your office tomorrow and we will do the exchange then. Once I have dealt with our little rat here."

Gardner stood, fists clenched, staring at the other man. Then he seemed to deflate. "Very well," he said. "You win, as always. Until tomorrow." He glanced at Flynn, who had been watching the exchange with amusement. "I would wish you well, young man, but I would not waste my breath."

Kraas smiled and puffed out his chest as he watched Gardner walk round the side of the building to the other landing strip. A few minutes later they all winced as the sound of the helicopter taking off filled their ears.

Flynn craned his neck to watch the craft as it circled round and then sped off to the North-East. "You filled that chopper quickly," he said as the noise receded. "Kudos on the fire evacuation procedures: very efficient."

"It helps when the fire in question is expected," said Kraas. He turned to face Flynn, a smile spreading across his face. "What, you thought *you* were responsible for the fire?

That this was all *your* plan?"

"So... all of that," Flynn nodded at the flames which were now starting to spread around the base of the landing strip. "You did that? I did think it spread a bit too quickly; we only set a small amount, just enough to create a bit of panic."

Kraas nodded, enjoying watching his plan being unpicked by the so-called criminal 'mastermind' who had plagued him for far too long. "I gave your little blaze a helping hand; all the better to guarantee you'd come to us, rather than find another way off the island."

Flynn stared at him. "You burned down your whole island? What kind of madman does that?"

"The kind which finally ran out of patience." Kraas looked around, feeling a flash of alarm at how far the fire had spread. Inwardly he cursed himself; he had been too taken up with catching the boy that he had forgotten the one important part of the plan. Namely, not to allow the flames to spread so far that they did any lasting damage. "You," he barked to one of the guards, not even bothering to try and think of the man's name. "Get the fire crews working. It has served its purpose."

"You don't think this is a little bit of overkill?" asked Flynn as the man scurried off to do his master's bidding. "Doing all this just to catch me. I mean, don't think I'm not flattered, but even so..."

"I did not do this to massage your ego," snapped Kraas. "I could not allow your activities to continue. You were becoming a rather bothersome itch; one which it is now my pleasure to scratch out of existence."

THREE MONTHS EARLIER...

"Ah, Tevlin," said Gardner with a smile which did not quite stretch beyond his lips. "Such a pleasure to see you. You have been busy, I trust?"

Kraas shook the man's hand, nodding to the others in

the group gathered around their host. "Busy thinking and planning. May we speak in private?"

"Of course," said Gardner, turning to the others. "Please do forgive us. Important matters of business, as I am sure you understand. Please do feel free to mingle, admire my trinkets. I will make the grand unveiling very soon."

Gardner's smile faded as the people wandered off, muttering to each other. "Bunch of free-loaders," he muttered. "Only here to snoop and try to figure out whether I'm still worth as much as the newspapers say I am. This sort of thing tires me."

Kraas looked around the room, keeping his expression neutral so he did not betray his jealousy at the other man's conspicuous consumption. He ran his eye over the antique furniture, the Picassos and Rembrandts adorning the walls, the priceless Persian rug which the guests were invited to walk all over as though it were a common carpet. A famous musician played the piano in the corner—no doubt charging a million dollars an hour for the privilege of being studiously ignored by this gathering of the insanely wealthy.

There was a time when Kraas had been comfortably Gardner's superior in everything, especially money. But the thefts—and the distractions they caused him—had taken their toll. He had lost his focus, his anger making him charge into deals he would otherwise have steered clear of, or shy away from risks he would have previously thought well worth the punt. The last quarter had been humiliating, compounding the trading losses of the one before it. If this carried on, he might have to start selling assets.

He shook his head. That would never happen. He just needed to purge himself of that one particular distraction; a cleansing, which would set him back where he belonged— head and shoulders above arrivistes like Gardner.

"Do you like your new staff?" asked Gardner as he steered him through the crowd, occasionally nodding or smiling at those they passed.

"Yes. The owner is very accommodating. Although I hear

rumors he has been bought out. That disquiets me."

Gardner grunted. "It is just a transaction. You of all people know how these things are; the service will remain the same."

"Even so," said Kraas, "I would have liked the opportunity to make an offer."

"What? And wind up effectively employing your own staff again? My dear boy, have you learnt nothing?"

Kraas glared at him, recognizing the logic but not appreciating the way it was delivered. Gardner was getting far too familiar; he needed to be taken down a few pegs, and soon. He also couldn't help but notice the way that the guests around them were more interested in toadying up to their host than to Kraas himself, someone who had achieved more than Gardner could ever hope to do even if he lived two or three lifetimes.

Once the irritation of the thefts had been dealt with, he would focus his attention back on people like Gardner. They would bow down to him once again. That knowledge made the nature of what he had to do almost palatable.

Almost.

Gardner led him through a pair of large doors and into an office, at the center of which stood a large, ornate, mahogany desk.

Kraas tilted his head to examine the desk as Gardner perched on its edge. "The Resolute desk," he commented. "A fine replica."

"Not a replica," said Gardner. "The one in the White House is a replica. This," he rapped on it with his knuckles, "is the real deal. I made the President an offer he couldn't, in all conscience, refuse." He flashed a toothy grin which Kraas wanted so badly to break with his own knuckles. Instead, Kraas just nodded and grunted faintly but appreciatively.

"I have come to request a service," Kraas said.

"That is the Tevlin Kraas we all know and love so well!" said Gardner, jumping to his feet and marching over to the drinks cabinet. "Always straight down to business." He poured them each a glass of *1858 Cuvee Léonie*. "Shoot," he said, passing the other man his drink and then settling into a chair behind the desk, putting his feet up on the polished surface.

Kraas looked around for a seat, noting that all those around the desk were a good few inches shorter than Gardner's. Wherever he sat, he would be forced to look up to the other man.

He settled for the sofa, across the other side of the room.

"I have been thinking about what you said, when we last met. About the rats on your father's island. Burning them out."

"Ah yes." Gardner took a large swig of his drink. "He was a good man, you know. Just a little... pragmatic."

"I am not here to pass judgement on your parents. Your story... inspired me."

"I *inspired* you?" That grin again. That shit-eating grin.

"I believe you gave me the answer to my problems. A way that I can flush out my own particular rat."

"You are going to burn him out."

"I am. I will set a trap."

"Very good. What do you need me for?"

"I need something to bait my trap. Something big and eye-catching. Something he cannot help but notice and want."

Gardner grinned. "Something like my little trinket out there?"

"Not *like* your little trinket. I *want* your trinket."

Gardner choked into his drink.

PRESENT DAY...

Kraas gestured at the two bags at his feet. "So good of you to bring the contents of my safe all the way to me here," he said to Flynn. "You saved me the bother of sending one of my men to get it."

"I did think it was all a bit too easy," said Flynn. "And who keeps all their wealth in big-ass diamonds and bits of paper, anyway? Word to the wise: next time, choose gold. It holds its value and is a bitch to steal from a safe when you're escaping on foot through a burning island."

"Indeed," said Kraas. "But I needed to present you with a tempting enough target, did I not?"

"A lot of effort to get me here. Like I said, I'm flattered, but—"

"Again, I did not do all of this to flatter you. I did this to trap you. Your greed was your undoing, as I knew it would be."

Flynn swallowed hard, glancing around.

"Do not bother to try looking for some way to escape," said Kraas. "The only way you are getting off this strip is via a very long drop down to the jungle." He noticed Flynn's eyes flicker to the horizon and held up a hand. "And yes, I also know about your friends and their little plane. They won't be disturbing us."

Flynn's face reddened. "What did you do? Where are they?"

"I believe they are decorating a rather large area of the ocean, just off the coast over there." Kraas waved his hand vaguely over his shoulder. "That is correct, is it not, Wilson?"

There was a pause while each of the guards wondered which of them was expected to answer. Finally, one spoke up. "Yes, sir. We watched the contact disappear around two miles to the north east. I believe it will be reported as a fuel failure. Very sad."

"Very sad indeed," grinned Kraas, enjoying the impact the man's improvisation had on Flynn.

"You bastards!" Flynn shouted. "They did nothing to you! They were just..."

"Just another collection of thieves coming to steal from me?" finished Kraas. "It rather seems to me like I acted in self-defense, don't you think?"

"You... You killed them."

"Maybe," Kraas waved the accusation away. "But that's not what you should be worrying about right now. If I were you, I would be worrying about what I'm going to do to *you*."

Flynn struggled vainly against his bindings. "You've got the money. You've killed my friends. I don't care if you hand me over to the police; I've got nothing left."

Kraas laughed. "The police? Ha! Highly amusing. Why would I hand you over to the police? At least, not yet. First you are going to tell me where the rest of it is."

"The rest of what?"

"My money. My paintings. My jewelry. All of the things you have stolen from me over all this time. You are going to tell me where it all is, and then you are going to help me get it back."

Flynn stared at him. "Or?"

Kraas stepped back to allow a large guard to fill Flynn's sight. One swing of a large meaty fist and Flynn was doubled up, gasping for breath.

Kraas cleared his throat. "As entertaining as it would be for you to stubbornly refuse to answer our questions, it would be in your best interests to tell me what I want without all of the heroics." He glanced around, noticing that the flames and smoke were showing no signs of abating. "What is going on?" he muttered. "The flames should be out by now. Someone go and hurry the fire crews up."

Flynn coughed, managing to croak, "Having some staffing troubles?"

Kraas glared at him. "Never mind about that. All you need to concern yourself with is answering my questions. Where is my money?"

"Gone," shrugged Flynn.

"Gone? Gone where?"

"I spent it."

Kraas' eyes narrowed. "All of it? Impossible." He gestured to the guard and then watched with barely disguised amusement as the man swung fist after fist into

Flynn's body and face. "Not too much with the face," he said after a few minutes. "We still want him to be able to speak."

After a few more minutes of punishment, Kraas barked, "Enough," gesturing for the guards to stop the beatings and offering a mock wince as Flynn bent double, straining against the bindings in a mess of coughing and blood. Kraas lowered himself down on one knee, leaning in so that he could whisper to the other man. But not so close as to risk getting covered in spittle.

"We can finish this now, you know. Just tell me where you have hidden everything you stole from me, and I will let you go. We both know that you still have it squirrelled away, or at least most of it; there is no way that you would be able to spend as much as you have taken without it being noticed."

"What if I've given it away?" Flynn managed in between coughs.

Kraas shook his head. "I know you like to spread that reputation, of being a modern-day Robin Hood. But I also know that is bullshit. You see, I know you, Flynn Fergus. Probably better than you know yourself."

Flynn glared up at him. "You know nothing about me."

Kraas chuckled. "You poor, naive child."

"I'm not a child."

"What are you: nineteen if you're a day?"

"Twenty-one," Flynn pouted. "Not a child."

Kraas waved this away as an irrelevant detail. "When you have lived as long as I have, you learn a few things. My particular talent is the ability to read other people, to know their innermost thoughts before they even know them themselves. That is how I built my fortune; how I became the dealmaker of my generation. No. Of *all* time."

Flynn squinted at him. "Bit big-headed, isn't it?"

"It is a fact. For example, I know that you came from one of those slums which litter so much of our cities. To your credit you choose not to wallow in self-pity and squalor like most of your compatriots, instead trying to claw your way out. However, rather than doing so by using your skills to build something of your own, you instead chose to steal from those better than you."

"I object to that," said Flynn. "It takes a lot of skill to do what I do. And anyway, I've not seen anything to prove you're better than me."

Kraas barked an outraged laugh. "Look around you, boy."

Flynn glanced around, wincing as his injuries caught up with him. "I see a lot of stuff burning?"

"All this I built," growled Kraas, "and will do so again. I am creating a legacy which will long outlast my death. What will you leave behind?"

"What's the use of a legacy if you're not around to enjoy it?"

"Spoken like a true sewer rat. You're not able to see beyond your next meal. Whereas men like me are true visionaries. We plan for the long term."

"Doesn't really change the fact that you're burning down your home," said Flynn. "All because of me."

"Makes you proud, does it?" said Kraas. "The thought that you're costing me untold millions, just so I can catch you."

Flynn shrugged and then winced as his body protested against the sudden movement.

Kraas leered at him. "I am sorry to disappoint you, but all of this was planned way in advance. I have had the finest engineers working on this project for months, calculating exactly how we could create the most impressive fires whilst inflicting the least amount of damage. It is all down to the timings, you see. As long as the blaze is put out before it reaches a certain point, all I lose is some landscaped gardens and a handful of unused buildings. Nothing which can't be replaced." He grinned. "Did you not at any point think it strange that the flames and smoke created a corridor which led you directly here to me?"

Flynn frowned. "But I planned it all myself. We could see from the plans, from the layout of your estate, that if we started the fire in just the right place…"

"Because we created the conditions for it to do so," grinned Kraas. "And then gave the fires a bit of a helping hand. I worried that by doing so we might tip you off, but I clearly overestimated you."

Flynn shook his head. "You were ahead of us all along."

"I was. And now you are going to tell me where the rest of my money is."

"Why?"

"Because, my little sewer rat, if you do not then my men here are going to pummel you into the concrete and then throw you off the edge." Kraas looked down to the jungle, frowning again at the flames which still showed no sign of abating.

"Seems to me that you're going to do that anyway," said Flynn. "There's no way you're going to let me leave here alive, even if I give you what you want. So where's the incentive for me to tell you?"

Kraas ground his teeth together. The child had a point; that was why he had always used physical violence as the last resort. It was much more effective to play on people's worst fears, to find the lever which would leave them begging to give him what he wanted, almost voluntarily. So much easier and quicker than extracting information through force.

That was the problem with torture; once someone's body had started to be ripped apart there was a disconnection, a realization by the victim that there was nowhere to go but death, and then to yearn for that release. Unless, of course, they were weak enough to say anything to save their skins. That situation was even less optimal, as it had been proven time and again that people would just say what they thought their torturer wanted to hear. Which was often a far cry from the truth.

His instincts had told him that Flynn would be the type

to fold under the slightest bit of roughing up, the merest hint of torture. After all, he was a common criminal, a thief; someone who had always shied away from any form of physical confrontation. Everything Kraas knew about that type of rogue told him that he would buckle as soon as he was shown a fist.

Yet here he was, having borne his punishment like a man and showing no sign of being fazed by the threat of more.

Therefore, greed could only have been a part of it. There must have been a deeper motive for everything Flynn had done, after all. Something or somebody he had done it all for, someone he was protecting. That was Kraas' way in.

He lent in closer to Flynn, a small part of him impressed with the boy's stubborn gall in refusing to cringe away from him.

"You have family," he breathed, watching closely for a reaction.

"You tell me," said Flynn. "You're the one who knows everything about me."

Kraas allowed himself a brief tinge of satisfaction. The boy had hidden it well, but there had been a tiny flinch at the mention of the word: *family*.

"Your parents," said Kraas. "They are sick." He frowned and shook his head. "A bit of a cliché though, isn't it? No. There's a sibling: a brother or sister you're trying to protect."

"What makes you think it's that? I could be trying to protect a friend; I have lots of friends."

Kraas peered at him. "No. You are trying to distract me. Family is at the core of all this. I would bet that if I found your sibling, I would find the money."

"But I thought you knew everything about me," said Flynn. "Could it be that your research isn't as complete as you thought?"

"The problem with guttersnipes like you is that you don't leave the same sort of digital trail as other, normal, law-abiding people," snapped Kraas.

"Law-abiding people like you?" Flynn chuckled.

"What are you implying?"

"Not implying. Stating. Did you not wonder why, out of all your fellow rich bastards, it was you who I chose to target, over and over again?"

"Just me?"

Flynn nodded. "That's why none of your fellow rich bastards were much interested in joining your little crusade against me, and why you felt paranoid about being targeted; it's because you *were* targeted. Not just because of your wealth but because of who you are. What you've done. To me."

TWO MONTHS EARLIER...

"You're making a big mistake," said the man in the big chair.

Flynn grinned. "Not the way it looks from where I'm sitting."

"You're literally the only person here who thinks that. And please will you stop throwing that thing around: you'll break it."

Flynn caught the large glass paperweight with a flourish. "OK. Humor me. Why is this such a bad idea?"

"You're already ahead. We've stolen enough from him over the years... We never need to work again. And you decide to throw it all away on..."

Flynn tossed the paperweight in the air again, wincing as he caught it one-handed. "Ah!" he hissed.

"And there we have it," the other man said. "A perfect metaphor for what you're planning. You could have played it safe, avoided the pain. But instead you just had to risk it, just so that you could show off."

"Showing off does not come into this," Flynn said, then shrugged. "All right, so maybe there's a little bit of showing off. But this is about so much more than that."

"Greed, then. You've done more than enough. Remember what I taught you, all those years ago. When you get too greedy, that's when you're most vulnerable."

"Correct." Flynn pointed the paperweight for emphasis, twisting it so that it caught the light and reflected it straight into the other man's eyes. "Greed is always the undoing. But it won't be mine."

The man sighed. "If it works, you'll find yourself the prisoner of a man crazy enough to burn down his whole island just to get at you. If, on the other hand, it all goes wrong..." He shook his head.

"It won't go wrong," said Flynn.

PRESENT DAY...

Kraas shrugged. "One does not rise to the top without stepping on a few heads. Making enemies is a professional hazard in my line of work." He frowned at Flynn. "But I cannot think of any situation where I would have come across you, let alone any family of yours. Unless it was one of my clearance projects..." He stared at Flynn with a renewed intensity. "Is that it? Is all of this revenge for you being made homeless?"

Flynn shrugged. "I doubt you ever gave much thought to all the people you turfed out so you could build your glittering palaces. But homes can be rebuilt. I've taken enough from you over the years to build a thousand houses. I'd have stopped years ago if that was all I wanted to do."

"It *is* personal, then," breathed Kraas.

"Very," said Flynn.

"Then let me make this even more personal for you. Tell me where the rest of my money is, or I will kill you and then make it my life's mission to hunt down and destroy everything that counts for a family in that miserable little life of yours. I have the connections and the resources to achieve that: you know I do."

Flynn smirked and shrugged. "You're too late."

"What do you mean?"

"Aren't you wondering, as the world's self-proclaimed expert at reading people's motivations, why I pursued you, and only you, with such single-minded focus? I could have stopped at any time if I was just after money, or if I wanted to prove that I was better than the most sophisticated security you could ever dream up. No: I kept on going no matter how much I earned."

"Stole," corrected Kraas.

Flynn shrugged again. "Potato; pot-ah-to." He grinned at the look of fury which flashed across the other man's face. "You rich people are so easy to wind up."

"Get to the point," growled Kraas. "Before I have you killed: here and now."

"The point is," said Flynn, "that you of all people should know that the most dangerous enemy is one with nothing to lose."

"You lost your parents because of me?"

"They died a long time ago. As much as I'd like to blame you for that, I can't. After they were gone, it was just me and my sister, until you took her from me as well."

"Your sister?"

"Niamh." Flynn stared at him intensely.

Kraas turned and took a few paces away, tapping his lip with his finger as he thought. "Niamh..." he muttered. "Young kid. Dark hair, not too tall. Just like..." He twisted his head to look back at Flynn. "Yes. There is a strong family resemblance."

Kraas noted with satisfaction the tears moistening the corner of Flynn's eyes. *Good,* he thought. *I have you now. There is always a trigger.*

"When she went to work for you, she was so proud. Thought she'd finally found a way to escape the streets, build a new life for herself. And then she was gone."

Kraas tilted his head, soaking in the young man's weakness. "Do you want to know what happened?"

"No," said Flynn, clamping his eyes shut and turning his head as far away as he could.

"She was a bright girl. Loyal to a fault. I trusted her maybe a bit too much. But not totally; I'm not stupid. One day she stumbled upon some information she should never have been party to. Some dealings which never saw the light of day; rather illicit. Highly profitable, but not the sort of thing the authorities would approve of."

"Townsend," whispered Flynn.

"So she did tell you," said Kraas. "She swore she told no one. Yes... Townsend. My biggest triumph. Looks like I was right to kill her after all." He smiled down at the wreck in the chair before him. "I should thank you. You have salved my conscience, young Mr. Fergus. I had feared I had killed a blameless girl, that she had told me the truth as I cut her open. Once you tell me where my money is, I will consider this a very profitable evening. I will even raise a glass in a toast to your corpse."

"Profitable!" spat Flynn. "What about all your guests? What if they had been killed in these fires?"

Kraas barked a staccato laugh. "You really think I care one jot for them? They got away safe, although I am sure they would have loved to stay and watch my island burn to the ground." He frowned, noticing once again that the flames were showing no sign of dying out; if anything, they were even more widespread. "You," he pointed to a guard. "Where are the fire crews? What are they up to?"

"I suspect they're waiting for the order from their boss," said Flynn.

"Their boss?" asked Kraas. "What on Earth are you—?"

"What do you think, Gardner?" asked Flynn. "I think that's enough, don't you?"

Kraas spun round, open-mouthed, as Titus Gardner strolled round the corner, a phone in his hand.

"Gardner?" asked Kraas. "What are you doing here? I thought you left on the transport. Wait... Are you filming me?"

"It's called evidence, dear boy," Gardner said, before nodding to Flynn. "And yes, I think that's more than enough."

"You live-streamed it all, as we agreed?" Flynn asked. "Straight to the police?"

"Pretty much all of it. May have accidentally got a bit muffled for a few bits at the beginning. You know, when you talked about stealing from our friend here. Didn't want you to incriminate yourself, young Flynn, now did we?" He waved his phone at Kraas. "Outstanding Wi-Fi signal, by the way. I was worried we'd struggle to get a signal all the way out here, but then I could always rely on you to look after *every* detail."

"Mickey," Flynn said to the nearest guard. "You couldn't untie me, could you?"

"Wait," snapped Kraas, his head spinning. "No, don't listen to him. I'm in charge here."

The guard ignored him. "Hope I didn't hurt you too much," he said to Flynn as he cut him free from the bindings. "You know, with the punches and the like?"

Flynn rubbed his wrists. "We'll have words later. I know I said to make it look realistic, but there's looking realistic and then there's trying to separate my head from my body."

"Knock any sense into you?" Gardner asked.

"Very funny." Flynn stood and took a couple of uncertain steps, putting a hand to his head. "And who was behind the door at the start? That whack on the back of my head really hurt."

"Had to look realistic," grumbled another guard, looking slightly sheepish. "You said so yourself."

Flynn opened his mouth to respond but was cut off by Kraas.

"What is going on here?"

"Don't you get it?" Flynn asked. "In a few moments the police will be here, armed with the confession you kindly gave us."

"Confession!" spat Kraas. "That's worthless. I have the best lawyers money can buy; they will easily extract me from this tiny inconvenience."

"Not sure that's quite the case," said Gardner. When Kraas turned to glare at him, he shrugged and continued, "Lawyers, especially the ones you'll need, cost money. Money you don't have. After all, burning down your own luxury island was a rather costly mistake, don't you think?"

"I never intended... The fire crews should have... Why have they still not done as I ordered?"

"Because," said Flynn, "they were waiting on confirmation from their boss." He stretched his arms out wide. "You wanted to know what I did with the money I stole from you? I decided to embark on a little diversification. That's what you business types say, isn't it?"

"More or less," said Gardner.

"Point is," continued Flynn, "I decided to branch out into the services industry. I bought the company that supplies your staff."

"The one you recommended to me," Kraas said slowly, staring at Gardner.

"Indeed," smiled Gardner. "It appears that the penny has dropped. Which brings me to the next order of business, and the main reason I stayed here rather than escaping with the other rats on that helicopter. There is the small matter of the debt you owe me."

Kraas picked up the bag which Flynn had used to carry the contents of his safe. "There's the diamond. You can have it. Take it back; our debt is settled."

Gardner opened the bag and looked inside, tutting. "Oh, no. No, no, no. That will not do at all. I lent you a priceless diamond. Not..." He pulled a glittering object out of the bag. "A worthless paperweight."

Kraas stared at him open-mouthed. "But the real diamond... I saw it... You... You planned this all along. You made such a show of not wanting to give me the diamond, forcing me to pay a high price so I could have it as bait."

"The highest," said Gardner. "A mortgage over everything you own. Or rather owned. Under the terms of our agreement, given that you are not able to fulfil your side of the bargain and return my property to me, all that was yours is now mine." He sighed. "It is amazing how a desperate man, blinded by his own desires, will clutch at even the most preposterous deal."

"You took the diamond, surely!" raged Kraas. "You have it! Our agreement is null and void. You—"

"There is the little matter of proof, dear chap," said Gardner. "Whereas I do have the strength of a legally binding agreement behind me."

Kraas seemed to fold into himself. "You played me," he spat.

Gardner smiled, tossing the paperweight to Flynn. "I cannot claim all of the credit. After all, I had a very keen and able apprentice."

A gun appeared in Kraas' hands, the barrel wavering as it pointed at the two men. "I won't let you do this. You can't..."

Flynn and Gardner stared at him. "Why didn't you tell me he'd have a gun?" asked Flynn.

"I didn't know he'd have a gun," snapped back Gardner. "Does he *look* like the sort of person who would have a gun?"

"Without wanting to state the obvious," said Flynn, "right now he does very much look like the sort of person who would have a gun, yes."

"Shut up, both of you!" bellowed Kraas, walking round slowly so there was nothing but the edge of the runway behind him, the burning jungle casting a long shadow before him.

"Now listen up, old chap," said Gardner. "You've got a dozen guns all pointing at you. Do the math: there's no way this is going to end well for you."

"I can still take you two with me!"

"You can't get us both. You'll be dead as soon as you've fired once," said Gardner. He pointed at Flynn. "He's the one who robbed you. Shoot him first!"

"Hey!" protested Flynn. "It was your idea all along. You were the one who played him for a fool to his face. If anyone should be shot first, it should be you!"

"I told you to quit while you were ahead!"

"Shut up!" screamed Kraas. He pointed the gun at Gardner. "You might have tricked me and taken the diamond, but I still have my papers, my promissory notes. There's enough value there for me to rebuild." He gestured at the other holdall. "Throw it to me."

"If you insist," said Gardner. He scooped up the bag and threw it underarm in the general direction of Kraas, who stretched out to catch it. Distracted and off-balance, he did not see the paperweight flying toward his head until it was too late.

Kraas was so focused on his bag full of paper money that it was only after he had caught it that his brain registered the blow to his forehead. He staggered, his body given momentum by the twin projectiles of bag and paperweight. Inevitably, inexorably, he swayed and stumbled toward and then over the edge of the runway.

"Looks like you were right after all," said Flynn as they approached the edge. "Greed really can be your undoing."

They watched as Kraas' body disappeared into the flames. "Niamh sends her regards," Flynn said softly.

THE END

ABOUT THE AUTHOR

Peter Oxley is a writer and publisher who lives in the English Home Counties.

Born around 200 years too late, Pete is unusually comfortable in Regency clothing. He fell into a career as a writer and publisher after dalliances with the law, accountancy and washing dishes left him with calloused hands and an allergy to spreadsheets and long words.

A sucker for a good story, Pete enjoys reading pretty much anything which has interesting characters, shocking twists, gripping action and talking mice. Particular influences and guilty pleasures include Clive Barker, Bernard Cornwell, Scott Lynch, Isaac Asimov, Douglas Adams and Joss Whedon. And yes he knows one of those isn't an author, but that's the way Pete rolls.

He is the author of the gothic fantasy *Infernal Aether* series, and the nonfiction book: *The Wedding Speech Manual: The Complete Guide to Preparing, Writing and Performing Your Wedding Speech*. Check out peteroxleyauthor.com to see all his current books and sign up to receive updates on future works.

When he's not reading or writing, Pete enjoys binge-watching box sets, mangling perfectly good tunes on his guitar, and writing about himself in the third person.

That's not all! You can get the prequel series to *The Infernal Aether*—*The Old Lady of the Skies*—delivered direct to your inbox for FREE!

To get this exclusive series now—as well as advance notice of all new releases and offers, simply go to: peteroxleyauthor.com/stories

This is the bit where we put on our 'macs and our best Columbo impressions, and say...

...Ah, Just One More Thing...

Did you enjoy this book?

If so, you can make a HUGE difference.

Each and every one of the authors in this book are independent authors. And we at Burning Chair are an independent publishing house, pulling together this book to give those independent authors some extra exposure and give you, the reader, a chance to discover some awesome new authors.

For us indies, reviews are the most powerful tools in our arsenals when it comes to getting attention for our books. Much as we'd all like to, we don't have the financial muscle of a New York publisher. We can't take out full page ads in the newspaper or put posters on the subway.

(...not yet, anyway...!)

But we do have something much more powerful and

effective than that, and it's something that those big publishers would kill to get their hands on.

A committed and loyal bunch of readers.

Honest reviews of our books help bring them to the attention of other readers.

If you've enjoyed this book we would all be so, so grateful if you could spend just a couple of minutes leaving a review (it can be as short as you like) on the book's page.

You can find it at: hyperurl.co/BurningBook

Thank you so much—you're awesome, each and every one of you!

Warm regards

Carla, Fiona, Dana, Tom, Michael, Craig, Will, Marcus, Pat, Peter, Simon, Lori, the other Pete and the other Simon.

ABOUT THE BURNING CHAIR

Burning Chair is an independent publishing company based in the UK, but covering readers and authors across the globe. We are passionate about both writing and reading books and, at our core, we just want to get great books out to the world.

Our aim is to offer something exciting; something innovative; something that puts the author and their book first. From first class editing to cutting edge marketing and promotion, we provide the care and attention that makes sure that every book fulfils its potential.

We are:
- Different
- Passionate
- Nimble and cutting edge
- Invested in our authors' success

If you're an author and would like to know more, visit www.burningchairpublishing.com for our submissions requirements and our free guide to book publishing.

If you're a reader and are interested in becoming a beta reader for us, helping us to create awesome books (and getting free reads in the process!), please visit www.burningchairpublishing.com/beta-readers

OTHER BOOKS BY BURNING CHAIR PUBLISHING

The Infernal Aether Series, by Peter Oxley
    The Infernal Aether
    A Christmas Aether
    The Demon Inside
    Beyond the Aether

The Wedding Speech Manual: The Complete Guide to Preparing, Writing and Performing Your Wedding Speech, by Peter Oxley

www.burningchairpublishing.com